High praise for
NIRVANA IS HERE
by Aaron Hamburger

A TENDER SELF-RECKONING, *Nirvana Is Here* brings the past full circle. Hamburger deftly reveals how incidents recede—even if they leave their mark—to bring new hopes into focus.
FOREWORD REVIEWS

A BEAUTIFUL, SAD, coming-of-age story that is a heartily welcome addition to the LGBTQ literature pantheon.
I LIKE TO READ

QUITE SIMPLY, THIS is a coming of age story but it is also so much more; it is a story of recovery and dealing with both past and present as set against the band Nirvana. . . . Hamburger beautifully captures the decade of the 90s and his characters who come of age then.
REVIEWS BY AMOS LASSEN

IF YOUR IDEA of Heaven is sitting down with a beautifully written book full of complex, compelling characters, then get ready. . . *Nirvana Is Here*! This is a drop-everything, stay-up-way-too-late, unputdownable novel written by an amazingly talented author. Funny, sexy, wise, and thought-provoking, *Nirvana Is Here* is a book that has it all, speaks to our times, and is an absolutely necessary read.
LESLÉA NEWMAN, author, *October Mourning: A Song for Matthew Shepard*

A WONDER OF a book, often funny, sometimes heartbreaking, and always enormously honest about what it means to be young and in love. As a Jewish Gen-Xer, the novel reminded me exactly of who I once was—and all that I still want to be. *Nirvana Is Here* is a brilliant accomplishment.
LAUREN GRODSTEIN, author, *Our Short History*

A YEARNING, GENEROUS, coming-of-age journey. Captures both a decade, and those scary, vital moments we reveal who we are, inside. Aaron Hamburger's prose is alive: what's here is funny, painful, heartbreaking. If you miss (or missed) the 1990s, read this book.
BRANDO SKYHORSE, author, *The Madonnas of Echo Park*

LIKE EVERYTHING HAMBURGER writes, *Nirvana Is Here* is compulsively readable, charming, and suffused with deep humanity. The title is truth in advertising, folks: this novel is nirvana indeed.

ELISA ALBERT, author, *After Birth*

WITH RICH, REAL characters and an evocative sense of time and place, Aaron Hamburger movingly explores the ways our pasts accompany us into our future lives. *Nirvana Is Here* is tender, wise and deeply affecting.

TOVA MIRVIS, author, *The Book of Separation*

A TOUCHING, FINELY wrought portrait of secrets lying like buried ordinance beneath ordinary lives. The delicacy and observational wit of Aaron Hamburger's prose are a marvel.

LOUIS BAYARD, author, *Courting Mr. Lincoln*

NIRVANA
IS HERE

NIRVANA
IS HERE

a novel

Aaron Hamburger

THREE ROOMS PRESS
New York, NY

Nirvana Is Here
BY Aaron Hamburger

ACKNOWLEDGEMENTS:
Portions of this novel appeared in a different form in the following anthologies, journals, and magazines: *Promised Lands: New Jewish American Fiction, Zeek, Law and Disorder: Stories of Conflict and Crime, Sudden Flash Youth, Attitude, Carolina Quarterly, Michigan Quarterly Review, Zone 3, ImageOutWrite,* and *Jewish Education News*

This is a work of fiction. Names, characters, businesses, places, events, and incidents are either the products of the author's imaginations or used in a fictitious manner. Any resemblance to actual persons, living or dead, or actual events is purely coincidental.

ISBN 978-1-941110-77-5 (trade paperback original)
ISBN 978-1-941110-78-2 (Epub)
Library of Congress Control Number: 2018962450

TRP-075

Publication Date: May 14, 2019

BISAC category code
FIC011000 Fiction / LGBT / Gay
FIC043000 Fiction / Coming of Age
FIC072000 Fiction / LGBT / Bisexual
FIC019000 Fiction / Literary

First edition

COVER DESIGN AND ILLUSTRATION:
Victoria Black: www.thevictoriablack.com

BOOK DESIGN:
KG Design International: www.katgeorges.com

DISTRIBUTED BY:
PGW/Ingram: www.pgw.com

Three Rooms Press
New York, NY
www.threeroomspress.com
info@threeroomspress.com

This book
is dedicated
to my friend
Avi Landes

NIRVANA
IS HERE

ONE

IT'S BEEN A COUPLE OF DECADES since Ari last held one of these chocolate bars, and the gold plastic wrapper crinkles in his jittery fingers. The red Hebrew letters on the label spell out the name of the candy: Pesek Zman, which means Free Time.

Free time, he thinks. Sometimes I'm sick to death of being free.

As a teenager, Ari used to keep a stash of those candies in his closet, on the shelf above his prep school uniform. Every morning, he buttoned up his dress shirt, yanked the knot of his necktie up to the collar of his button-down shirt as dictated by school dress code, and then deposited a piece of Pesek Zman in the inside pocket of his sport jacket.

And now, this Valentine's Day, as a forty-one-year-old Medieval history professor residing in University Park, Maryland, he'll repeat this ritual once more, at least the candy part of it.

He rips one of the wrapper—Ari requires three tries to tear it open—and bites into a cube of the milk chocolate, filled with a crispy wafer and hazelnut cream. According to the company's website, he is tasting the king of chocolate bars, a moment of pure indulgence. Everyone needs a little time out from life, to stop and enjoy a beautiful moment.

To Ari the chocolate tastes cloyingly, stunningly sweet, makes his tongue curl. He mashes the candy into a grainy chocolate paste that sticks to his teeth and the roof of his mouth, struggles to get it down his gullet. He didn't like the candy then and he doesn't now. But liking Pesek Zman was never the point. He'd doled it out as a gift, piece by piece, day after day all throughout high school, to a boy he used to know.

He'd forgotten all about the candy until he'd been reminded of it by his husband—now ex-husband—a poet on suspension for screwing a student. The ex-husband's name is M. Not an initial, just the letter, to express solidarity with the transgendered.

On their first evening together, after a few mojitos, the poet confessed his birth name: Michael.

They'd met the old-fashioned way, in a bar. Ari had been dragged there by a colleague, who'd expressed disbelief that Ari had never hitherto visited the one gay bar on campus. And there, holding court among a coterie of gay faculty, just over six feet tall, was M, wearing his oversized dark-framed glasses (prescription strength of zero, a fashion accessory), a purple checked shirt, and white pants that seemed to glow in the darkness of the bar, hugging his hips and thighs. "You're a quiet one," M told Ari at the end of the evening, when the rest of the crowd, recognizing the charge between these two, had filtered away. "What's going on in that cute brain of yours?"

"How can you see it, I mean, my brain, to know that it's, well, cute." Ari hated that last word, one of those nauseating contemporary locutions.

M put his hand on the small of Ari's back, a few fingers drifting playfully down, just inside the back of Ari's belt. "If it's anything like the rest of you," he whispered, his breath tickling Ari's ear, "then, well, that's how I know."

Two years later, they were investing in real estate. Or, rather Ari was investing and M was coming along for the ride. M would have preferred to live closer to downtown, to the "action," but it was Ari who was supplying the down payment.

"I'm a man against action," said Ari.

"You were born old," said M.

It's strange that they became a couple. Ari hates bawdy humor or raunchy talk, ironic considering that he teaches and writes about the Middle Ages, a time when nothing could be funnier than listening at the door as a groom deflowered his bride after a wedding, or raping a dozen nuns at a local convent. By contrast, the naughty M relishes dirty jokes, crass innuendo, stories involving the rudest of body parts. He writes odes to gay sex with rough men at rest stops in the small Kentucky town where he grew up. He regularly accuses colleagues of "slut-shaming."

And in the final months of their marriage, M regularly bemoaned their "vanilla" sex life, comparing their bedroom to that old Woody Allen joke about a restaurant where the food is terrible—and such small portions!

Last August, several months before the suspension for sexual harassment, M and Ari had been unpacking boxes in their new home, a ten-minute drive from the University where he recently received tenure in reward for occasionally interrupting his students' drinking, drugging, and texting to inform them about equivalent bad behavior centuries before they were born.

M was making a show of straining to lift a heavy cardboard box which, oddly, the movers had marked in all capital letters "CATHOUSE." Finally, he gave up and pushed the box across the floor into one of the bedrooms, putting his whole body into it, so that his low-cut jeans rode even further down his hips. In another context, it could have been a strip tease, which Ari wouldn't have enjoyed. Frankness about all matters sexual turned him off. Ari required romance to be served with a good helping of subtlety and shadows. He'd once stopped an encounter cold when M turned on the lights midway through, so they could see themselves performing in the bedroom mirror.

Ari was in the kitchen, carefully unwrapping a coffee mug that said, "In Dog Years, I'm Dead." A present from M, who used to give more thoughtful gifts like books of poetry, and once a heavy Latin dictionary Ari had been craving. Ari didn't care for the mug, but couldn't throw it away.

M came in holding a heavy blue book in his hand, a high school yearbook. "Who's Justin?"

Ari backed himself against the sink, pressing the mug against his chest. "What?" he said.

M opened the book to the inside of the back cover, pointed to a few scribbled lines, and held out the book for Ari to read. "Justin," he said.

The way he said the name felt dirty, or maybe like an accusation. "I already know what it says," said Ari, finally setting down the mug on the chipped countertop. They were hoping to replace it someday with some tasteful quartz. "I just was surprised to hear you mention his name."

"He wrote, 'Thanks for the candy, you're so sweet,'" M recited.

"Yes, he did write that," said Ari, turning to face the sink. "He's just, well, that's his sense of humor."

"You're so sweet? That doesn't sound like a joke. Was he cute?"

"I don't know," said Ari, digging around in a cardboard box marked "FRAGILE." "I never realized we had so many damned coffee mugs."

"This is the most romantic thing I've ever heard about you," said M. "What does he mean, thanks for the candy? Is that code for something nasty? He must have been cute."

"Very well. Give me that book. You can judge for yourself." Ari takes it and flips to the relevant page with Justin's picture, Justin's eyes staring off into space, into a distant, better future. Ari's reluctant to let the book go, but he does. "Satisfied?"

"He's black," said M.

"And?"

"So you like black guys? Ari, you should have told me. I know lots of cute black guys. We could finally have a threesome."

"You misunderstand me," said Ari. Not for the first time, he thinks, but does not say aloud. "It's not that I'm attracted to black guys per se. Or that I'm not attracted to them. I just liked him. Not his race. Him."

"Where is he now?"

"I don't know. We lost touch. He was just a boy I once liked in high school. That was centuries ago."

"Ari, I love this. I'm seeing you in this whole new light. Haven't you thought of Googling him?"

"No, I have not. That would be a violation of his privacy."

"Oh, stop it. Don't you ever Google yourself?"

"Whatever for? I know myself."

"Well, I'm going to." M whips out his smartphone.

"Please don't. I really don't like to do things like that. I'm not a fan of this brave new world that you're so fond of."

But M's fingers are too nimble for Ari to stop him. "Uh-oh," says M.

"What?" Ari catches his breath, feels something sink inside his chest. "He's dead, isn't he?"

"No, worse. He's straight."

Ari wants to throw one of his mugs at M's head. Instead he gives a good tug at his husband's carefully sculpted, dark wavy hair tamed with something called "product." "Darling, please shut up."

"Don't you want to hear more?" asks M, using the reverse camera in his phone to pat his hair back into place.

"No."

"You know, I found his wife. Hang on." Tap, tap, tap on his phone. "Look, here she is. She's cute."

"I'm not interested."

"She's white. Maybe there's hope for you, after all."

"Okay, okay. You've had your little joke. Can we get back to these boxes now?"

But M would not be deterred. As Ari resumed the work of unpacking, M settled on a footrest and sporadically shouted out bits of news. For instance, after living in Michigan, North Carolina, and Boston, only a few years ago Justin and his wife settled in northern Virginia. Justin recently assumed the position of CEO of Shut Up and Kiss Me, a popular online dating app with over a million registered users. (Why this company was headquartered in non-romantic Washington of all places, Ari had no idea.)

Later, as they went to pick up pizza, M teased Ari, "Shut Up and Kiss Me, Justin!"

"Aren't you the soul of wit," said Ari, whose nerves were frayed from both the tedium of unpacking and the tedium of M's teasing. His hands felt rough against the steering wheel, his skin dry from handling all that paper and those boxes. The house had been built in the late 1920s and was in dire need of a remodel, especially the kitchen and bathrooms. It was small, meant as a starter home for lovey-dovey newlyweds, rather than a bickering gay couple.

"You could send him some candy, at his office, you know? Like anonymously," said M later at the restaurant. "Then see if he can guess that it was you."

Ari was working on a meat lover's supreme while M had ordered a cheese-less pizza, gluten-free. He was watching his waistline, part of his master plan to defeat the aging process. In anyone else, Ari would have written off these machinations as vanity, yet in M's assiduous efforts to keep up with the young people, their bodies, fashions, music, slang, and above all their phones, Ari saw something like nobility, a touch of Don Quixote.

"Alright, you've had your joke. Can we just eat our pizza in peace?" Ari pleaded.

THROUGHOUT THE FALL, THE TEASING CONTINUED. Ari gritted his teeth, waiting for his husband to tire of the joke. Anyway, he was busy with his teaching, plus a new journal article on the shift in the language of reproductive health in the early Middle Ages. High school seemed tucked away even further back in time than the Middle Ages in his consciousness. His therapist had taught him a mantra: "I'm not a teenager anymore. I'm a grown man, and I'm safe."

But sometimes, particularly while stuck on a knotty sentence or marking up a particularly turgid student essay mistaking *Braveheart* for a documentary on Medieval battle dress or battle tactics, he looked for Justin online and found him there, on the cover of *Black Enterprise*, or in the pages of *Crain's*, *Wall Street Journal*, *Digital Commerce*, *Market Watch*, so many publications and websites with which Ari was unfamiliar, publications whose authors lacked PhDs and whose works did not conform to the Chicago Manual of Style. Some of the articles were accompanied by pictures of Justin, looking energetic and confident, but also, most painfully, like a full-grown man, a forty-year-old man. That other time, the one they'd shared, that was ancient history.

Finally, overwhelmed with shame at his own curiosity, Ari swatted down his laptop with a vicious click.

We were better off in a different age when we weren't able to see these things, he thought, then vowed never to look at these things again. And he did not look at them again, until he did.

IN DECEMBER, JUST BEFORE FINALS, M stopped by Ari's office on campus, sat on the edge of his desk, and handed him an envelope. "An early Christmas present," he explained. Inside the envelope were two tickets to a University basketball game, on Valentine's Day.

Because of the date, Shut Up and Kiss Me was sponsoring the game. Free hats with the website logo would be given to all in attendance and a "kiss-cam" would be installed above their heads, with a cash prize for the best kiss caught on camera, as voted upon on social media.

"Sounds gruesome," said Ari.

"Don't you get it?" M said. "He'll be there. He'll have to be. He's the goddamn C.E.O. It's the perfect excuse to run into him again."

"No, no, I won't do it."

"But you have to, I already got the tickets." M slid off the desk, kneeled beside Ari's chair, ran his hands over Ari's knees. Ari finds it odd to look down at his tall husband for a change. "Come on, have some fun for once. We need more fun in our relationship."

"Is our present romantic life really so dreary that you have to involve yourself in my romantic past?" asked Ari, eyeing M's hands on his body and absorbing this touch that had arrived without invitation. Its spontaneity, occurring as it did after they'd been together for two years, still caused an instinctual shriveling inside, which Ari tried to overcome. That was the whole point of being with a man like M, so comfortable with touching, feeling, grabbing, so contemptuous of personal boundaries.

Sometimes, Ari liked M's blunt passion. It was a relief never having to make the first move, to let M take the lead when it came to sex. M brought a certain energy to his quiet existence, broke up its pleasant monotony just enough to make him feel alive.

At other times, it all became too much. Ari fantasized about telling M to fuck off—fuck, a nice old English word dating back to the *Canterbury Tales* and beyond. Just fuck off and leave me alone, leave me in peace, calm, safety.

ARI STILL INSISTED THAT HE WASN'T going, but M continued to badger him right through the holiday break while they were in Florida visiting Ari's parents, who thought M was a real hoot, a charming, sparkling glass of gay champagne. The badgering continued into the New Year, and up to Martin Luther King Day when Ari relented, for reasons he still did not understand. Prurient curiosity? Nostalgia? Sexual frustration? Peer pressure? All of these and none of them. Why was he going back in time like this?

Ari considered backing out of the whole plan as M helped him craft a carefully worded, jaunty Facebook message:

"Hey, what a coincidence, we're both in the area now. I'm heading

to your big hoops game next month—I teach at the University—
and was wondering if you were going too. It'd be fun to say hi. Let
me know."

ARI HESITATED TO PRESS SEND. "I don't want to stalk the guy."

"How can such a subtle, careful thinker as you be so dense about
affairs of the heart?" said M, a bit of a gossip like most poets. "It's as
if there are only two choices, to be a stalker or a monk, and nothing
in between."

"It's not that," said Ari. "There are things you don't know. I'm
not ready."

But M reached over Ari's frozen fingers, went ahead and sent
off the message. "You needed a little boost," he said, kissing Ari on
the cheek.

Ari stared at his words, now lit up in irrevocable blue. "Get
out," he said. M seemed to think he was joking, so Ari said, "I
didn't mean it as a request, M. I'm ordering you to get out of my
fucking study."

"Touchy," said M in a small, cowed voice and obeyed. Ari buried
his head in his hands, sat alone in his dark study. He felt like crying,
but no tears came. Even with his eyes covered, he could feel the
faint blue light of the laptop screen on his face. How did I end up
with this, this person? We don't belong together, like a mismatched
pair of socks that happened to fall behind the dryer while doing the
laundry. For too long, I've been lying to myself and to the world,
boasting about our complimentary differences, his ying to my yang.

When he removed his hands, Ari discovered, to his surprise, that
Justin had written him back almost immediately. Wow, yes, that is a
coincidence. Yes, saying hi sounds great. Yes, here, this is my phone
number. Go ahead and send me a text that Sunday. We'll definitely
meet up. Yes, yes, and yes.

That word, "definitely." It was so startling. It sounded so definite.

Now that Valentine's Day has finally arrived, a few things have changed. For one, M is on suspension for making unwanted overtures toward a student and Ari's been assigned to his review committee.

Ari had complained to his department chair, who wears thick socks with hiking sandals and has an enviable mop of thick gray on white hair. He's an expert on the history of American dissent. "He's my husband. How can I be impartial?"

"You weren't actually married, not legally," was the reply, which was true. They'd never undergone the formal procedure at City Hall, had never seen the need for it. Rather, they had had a ceremony in the gay synagogue, conducted by a real rabbi, just without benefit of a real civil license. M was against the idea of a civil marriage because it smacked too much of heteronormativity, and yet because he'd been born into a family of evangelical Christians, he loved the idea of being married by a rabbi. As for Ari, he was worried about the messy ramifications of legal marriage if he and M ever separated—all too prescient—though he wanted to mark their sense of commitment, no, not commitment, but achievement, with something tangible, like a high school diploma.

"Even so," says Ari. "This is a very delicate matter."

"It isn't a judicial proceeding," said his chair. "It's a university committee, and we've got to appoint someone to serve on it. You're the new guy, so it's your turn." He faux-punches Ari in the arm. "Just review the facts, and then make a recommendation."

"To end my ex's professional career? Oh, it's that easy?"

The chair offers a helpless shrug. He knows the answer as well as Ari: of course not. Nothing in life that means anything is easy.

"There's got to be some university policy about conflict of interest," Ari continues.

"No, none," he says cheerfully.

There's an awkward pause as they stand in the chair's office, which strangely is smaller than Ari's office, though it has the better view. The chair wants to head out, to go home for the night to kick off his hiking sandals, maybe to watch the *Woodstock* documentary on Netflix for the umpteenth time while smoking pot and eating vegan brownies or something, and Ari's blocking the door. Before stepping aside, Ari can utter his get-out-of-jail-free excuse, the iron-clad one that will exempt him from this hellish duty of judging his friend, of hearing the nasty particulars of the story.

The thought is tempting for a few seconds. But invoking that excuse would be the coward's way out, positively ungentlemanly. It's the kind of crap his students would pull to get out of a reading assignment. "I'm triggered! I'm triggered!" No, he must not sink so low. He's not triggered. He's just fine. All that mess was over two decades ago.

Isn't that why Ari steps aside, allows the chair to leave his own office?

So now he's going to this fucking basketball game all by himself without M at his side to coach him on what he must say, how he must behave. For instance, what would M have thought about bringing along this piece of Pesek Zman candy?

When Ari was in high school, he used to find Pesek Zman at a Jewish bookstore near home. Thanks to Amazon, there's no need to trek out to a Jewish bookstore—a good thing, since he has no clue where there are Jewish bookstores in the DC area, and he has no desire to set foot inside one.

It really is a stupid idea, getting this candy, and now giving it to Justin, in public, no less. Like some dewy-eyed high school kid. Clearly Justin has moved on, onwards and upwards. How will it look if Ari appears not to have moved on?

But there's no backing out. He'd promised to meet Justin, and if he doesn't show up, they'll never meet again. Until now, he hadn't been aware he'd been hoping they might again.

Ari has stashed the bag of Pesek Zman on the bookshelves in his study, where in addition to the texts of his trade, he keeps multiple copies of his own two books, plus the journals in which he's published his articles—his small paper castle that eventually will turn to yellow and then to dust and blow away.

Somewhere behind these books, there lurks another story, as yet unprinted, yet fully written, a story Ari carries with him everywhere, though he's shared it with no one. Or at least, not the full version. During his first visit to a local therapist, he'd given her the short and sweet abstract of it, followed by "But I'm over all that now."

She'd spent a couple of years showing him that wasn't true.

Another story, another time, another Ari.

Self-Defense

Dad didn't approve of surprises. Even the Soviet Union's recent collapse bothered him because it had happened without warning. A year later, he still grumbled that the whole thing was likely a plot to catch the Free World off our guard.

So when my father came home early from his dental clinic to take me for a drive, saying, "Come on, Ari, I've got a surprise for you," I didn't believe him. I figured it was another trick to get me out of my room with the blinds drawn and the lights low.

We headed down Northwestern Highway, toward rather than away from Detroit. Though we rarely went to the city, I'd heard all the Detroit stories on the news and repeated over dinner, stories of gangs and drugs, rap music and sawed-off shotguns, welfare queens and gold teeth. I wanted to scream, stop, stop! But Dad would have driven further, faster, to prove I didn't have to be afraid, that past was not prologue, and from now on, I could trust him to keep me safe.

As the Mile Roads nudged closer to the Eight Mile border—Twelve, Eleven, even Ten—I gripped my seat cushion and bit the inside of my sweatshirt, impractical for a hot, humid Michigan summer afternoon, but for the past few months that was my uniform: puffy sweatshirts over extra-large T-shirts and track pants that ballooned around my legs, anything that swallowed the contours of my body.

Shortly before we reached Eight Mile, Dad steered our blue Chevy into a tired-looking strip mall. My father, a pediatric dentist, wasn't quite successful enough to afford a Mercedes or a Beamer like the ones many of our neighbors drove. Even if he could have afforded a pricy import, my father would have bought American, just to be contrary.

"Let's stop here, Ari," he said, as if it had been a spontaneous decision. "Here" meant the United Studios of Self Defense, squeezed between a grimy Coney Island style diner and a video store that hadn't yet been taken over by Blockbuster. We parked next to a rusty Toyota with a commemorative Operation Desert Storm bumper sticker on it.

The front door of the United Studios of Self Defense was decorated with a cardboard cutout of Uncle Sam in a white uniform, performing a karate kick. Inside, I inhaled the smell of dried sweat and dust. A handwritten sign said, "A Black Belt is a White Belt that NEVER Quit."

Never? I thought, a wave of nausea rising in my throat.

We were greeted by Brad, the owner and "sensei," a friend of one of Dad's racquetball partners and Vietnam vet who'd opened the studio a few years ago in hopes of capitalizing on the success of *The Karate Kid*. So far, not much luck.

As a Bruce Springsteen song played in the background, Brad scratched his spiky grey mustache and inspected my delicate frame. I folded my arms over my chest so he couldn't get a good look, then scanned the walls of his office: framed martial arts prizes, a free calendar from a tire company dangling at a crooked angle beside a print of a fire-breathing dragon, and a photo of a younger, blonder, handsome Brad in full karate regalia.

"Ari or airy?" he said, trying to pronounce my name in a flat Downriver twang.

"Ari," I said, wishing my name weren't so foreign, so Jewish. In my fantasies, I was called James or Sebastian, and I'd been born in a castle.

"Airy," he said. "You like sports?"

"I like to draw," I said in a small voice.

"Your dad told me you wanted to learn to defend yourself."

He had? My cheeks flushed as I imagined the conversation:

Can you teach my son to fight off bullies?

Oh, yes, we have a bullying special. Even a wimp like your son can learn to take on the biggest brute on the block or your money back. Satisfaction guaranteed.

But Brad didn't guarantee anything.

"Listen," said Dad, "they're playing the Boss."

"'Born in the U.S.A.,'" said Brad. Thankfully, he did not attempt to sing it.

Dad asked me, "Isn't that who your friends listen to?" Before I could say yes, no, or that I could no longer afford the risk of friends, my father bought us two white uniforms wrapped in plastic and two yearlong memberships. It all happened so fast, I wanted to scream, but I knew even if I opened my mouth that no words would come out.

"Hey, Doc Silverman," said Brad, "you know the six scariest words in the English language? 'The dentist will see you now.'"

"Good one," said Dad, though he hated dentist jokes.

What the hell was happening? I could barely catch a softball. Now they expected me to learn to chop a wooden board in half with my bare hands or kick some musclebound jerk into a pit of quicksand?

"We've got a class starting in T-minus five minutes," said Brad, taking a swig of peppery Vernors ginger ale, which I hated, but which most people I knew drank proudly because it was made in Michigan. I preferred the chocolate sodas my Mom brought back from her "mental sanity" vacations in New York.

"Remember," Brad called after us, as we headed to the locker room to change into our new uniforms, "the aim of karate is not victory or defeat, but perfection of character."

"Sounds like a Jewish proverb," my father whispered.

I wrinkled my nose. To hell with Jews and their useless proverbs.

The locker room also functioned as a storage space for brooms, mops, and boxes of paper. As I fumbled with my stiff white jacket and pants, I kept an eye on the other boys, who looked at least five years younger than I, flinging their karate belts at each other like whips, calling each other pussy, lady-boy, faggot, just for fun. It felt strange being in their company after staying out of school for months. My parents had worked out a plan with my principal for me to finish my freshman year of high school by working independently at home, as if I'd contracted a contagious illness.

I folded and re-folded my navy blue Michigan sweatshirt, which my older brother David bought for me when we visited his dorm last fall. If my body wasn't the puniest in the room, it was still shameful. My arms were pale and thin, my shoulders soft and rounded. Anyone who wanted to could have snapped me in half like a twig— and someone wanted to. That's why Dad had dragged me here.

I gave up waiting and retreated into the bathroom stall to finish the job. Maybe I could just stay here, I thought, fingers trembling as I jumped into my starchy white karate pants. Maybe I could lock myself in this stall and wait out the whole lesson.

But finally, I took several deep, hot breaths and forced myself out into the studio.

Brad had us stand in a single line on the mat, or the "dojo," which reeked of Windex. The other boys kept breaking their ready stance to cheerfully punch each other in the ribs. Dad loomed over them. His white uniform, just a bit too tight, kept opening across his chest, showing off the hair that he kept threatening would one day sprout on my own chest. I slouched at the end of the line, my bare feet gripping the cool, waxy mat, my sweaty fingers clutching my jacket lapels closed. I felt naked.

People said I resembled my father, but I didn't see it. Dad's pink cheeks were dusted generously with freckles, and his hair was a tight wreath of red curls, now fading to auburn. Meanwhile, my complexion was pale, my hair brown, straight, and boring.

As MC Hammer's "U Can't Touch This" squealed in the background, Brad taught us to bow, and then step forward while simultaneously punching out our fists. "A punch should stay like a treasure in the sleeve," he said. "We do not attack or defend. We reflect our enemy's negative energy back at his unworthy face."

Dad and the boys learned quickly Brad's moves. I planted my feet, thrust out my fists. Step, punch. Step, and then punch. I believed that I too was getting the hang of it, that eventually I might learn how to really hurt someone. But then Brad came over to show me what I was doing wrong. He rolled back my shoulders, raised my chin, pushed on my spine. "You're real jumpy," he said. "Stand up tall, Ari. Like a man."

Dad offered to help, but Brad had me practice alone for the remainder of the hour, insisting, "He's got to figure this out for himself." So I struggled to make my arms and legs shoot forward in stiff energetic bursts while on the stereo, "U Can't Touch This" changed to "Blaze of Glory," "Cradle of Love," "Ice, Ice, Baby," and other manly anthems, perhaps meant to inspire fighting. Usually, when it came to learning, I did well without trying. But here, the harder I worked, the less I learned.

"No, no," Brad said, twisting my arms around. His fingers tickled like twitchy spiders. "Buddy, don't you want to be able to take care of yourself?"

"I . . . I don't know," I said, feeling lightheaded from all these questions.

Now watch me. I'll do it for you in slo-mo, so you can get it."

He planted his feet, balled up his fists, and punched. Right, left, then right again.

"Oh, now I see," I lied. "Thanks. That was helpful."

Brad gave me a sorrowful look, then patted my shoulder and left me alone.

Before we left, Brad confessed to my father that he hadn't been to the dentist in a while. "Makes me uncomfortable, sitting all helpless in that chair," Brad said. Then he asked, "It's not true, is it, that you can get AIDS from your dentist?"

"We wear gloves now," said Dad, though I knew he didn't always. He hated the slippery latex, said he couldn't get a firm grip on his scaler, which ironically made him more likely, not less, to draw blood, and wasn't that what they were trying to avoid?

During the drive home, Dad said in a shaky voice, "Well, that was a good start. A few more months of this, and—"

Before he could finish any more of his false promises about my body or spirit, I switched the radio on. I'd had enough trumped-up optimism for one afternoon.

"I'll tell you one thing," he said. "I really like Bruce Springsteen."

You're a Funny One

I WOULDN'T HAVE NEEDED TO LEARN karate if Mark Taborsky had kept his promise last fall to teach me to fight in good old American style, with fists. He said a kid my age should know how to pound someone.

But then Mark decided that I was the one who needed the pounding.

For years, the narrow patch of pine forest across the street from our house had remained vacant, a refuge for birds, black squirrels, and kids sneaking cigarettes. The lot was too small, and my parents worried that the wrong kind of people might buy it and lower our property value. People who cut their own lawn in summer or shoveled their own driveway in winter. People who parked RVs in their driveway.

So my parents were relieved when the land went to Rabbi Taborsky and his family, poor by our standards but respectable. The Rabbi served a small congregation who'd stayed on Nine Mile Road, though most of the other Jewish families around them had fled to suburbs several miles further from Detroit. After a local news feature about how his synagogue was bucking the white flight trend, Rabbi Taborsky became a minor celebrity, called into service when a rabbi was needed to hold hands with a black minister or Iraqi imam during an "interfaith" dialogue, or to light Hanukkah candles and have his picture taken with Governor Blanchard or Mayor Young.

While the Taborskys were visiting the house during its construction, Mom dashed across the street to introduce herself. She discovered their two sons would be transferring to my school, the Lev Stern Hebrew Academy, where half the day we studied in Hebrew, and the other half we solved algebraic equations or read *Catcher in the Rye* like normal kids. Mark was the older son and would be in my grade, though I was a year younger than he was. I'd been promoted—my punishment for being freakishly smart.

"You two might become friends," said Mom, who liked the idea of matched sets, coordinated colors, pairs of shoes lined up heel against heel in a closet. She ran her own business designing intricate *ketubahs*, or Jewish marriage contracts, carefully inscribing creamy archival paper with Hebrew calligraphy, and then embellishing the words with delicate flowers and Biblical animals in thin shades of gouache or watercolors. When she wasn't home, I'd peek in her studio, the tubes of paint clipped to a pegboard on the wall, shelves piled with colorful patterned fabric swatches, and her pens and pencils standing stiffly at attention at the back of the broad glass table where she worked.

"I worry about you spending so much time alone," Mom said.

"I'm fine on my own," I said. Actually, I was so desperate to find a friend, you could smell it on me, like bad breath.

When I was younger, I used to ride tricycles in packs of boys and girls at the park and draw funny pictures that made my friends laugh at school or birthday parties. But then my voice dropped, hair sprouted under my arms and between my nipples, and the rules of fitting in became mysterious and complicated. As other kids peeled off into private twos and threes and fours, I'd watch from behind my sketchpad and draw cartoons of hairy, sharp-toothed animals chasing my classmates into a deep lake.

In late August, the Taborskys finally moved in. Their builders had demolished the pine forest, except for a thin line of trees at the edge of their backyard, preserved for privacy. All they had left to do was to finish the front lawn, a bumpy patch of plowed earth and a pile of bluegrass rolled up like a carpet.

I was sitting on our front step, trying to draw a rhododendron when I first noticed Mark Taborsky, dressed only in a pair of jeans and stretched out on a newly hung porch swing. Either sleeping or sunbathing—I couldn't quite tell as I peeked at him through waxy rhododendron leaves. He wore dark aviator style sunglasses, and his bangs fell in soft waves over the lenses. An open book rested on his bare chest, and his rosy feet dangled off the edge of his swing, which swayed slowly in the breeze.

I liked his hair and his sunglasses; both had a sense of style. He was a rabbi's son, so maybe he had a kind heart. He was reading a book in summer, another hopeful sign.

I tossed my sketchbook on our front steps, then wiped the sweat off my forehead, combed through my hair with my fingers, and crossed the street.

Mark barely stirred in his swinging as I walked up the Taborskys' newly paved driveway, still tacky from the freshly laid asphalt. I could have stepped away and he probably wouldn't have noticed, but I kept coming, the way you do in bad dreams. When I stepped onto the porch, he bolted upright, catching the book as it slid down his tanned chest. As he gave my hand a rough shake, I noticed his thick gold ring with his initials, "MT," and a tiny diamond studded inside the "M."

"Great book," I said, nodding at his paperback, *To Kill a Mockingbird*.

"Yeah, great for putting you to sleep," he said. "My mom's making me read it."

Mark gave me a tour of his house, which smelled dizzyingly of fresh paint. A large neon-colored abstract painting of floating triangles and circles hung above their cream-colored leather couch. Mom could have made them something way better than that.

His bedroom faced mine, and I thought of Anne Shirley and her bosom friend Diana in the book *Anne of Green Gables*, flashing each other messages using their window shades like telegraph signals.

Mark put on a T-shirt, then fed a cassette into his stereo, something called Bel Biv Devoe. His parents were transferring him to Lev Stern Hebrew because it was closer to their new house than his old school, also Jewish, but more conservative than Stern, the kind of place where boys dressed only in black and white and girls wore denim skirts down to their ankles. At Stern, only tank tops were off limits, for both sexes.

Strangely, Mark didn't sound the least bit nervous about going to a new school. Already he was going to a party hosted by one of my classmates, a party I hadn't heard of.

"So the girls at Stern, are they easy?" he asked, flopping down on his bed. His jeans weren't regular old Levi's, but Guess, an expensive brand I'd never seen displayed on the crowded racks at Boesky's Discount Shop for Boys, where my mother bought all my clothes. Next to his bed were a pair of Reebok high tops, fastened with both Velcro and laces, a thing I had not thought possible.

I looked for somewhere to sit, then settled on the carpet, which felt rough on my palms and smelled like wool. "I guess they're as easy as anywhere."

Mark grabbed a blue rubber ball off his nightstand, pretended to whip it at me, then snickered when I flinched. "What base have you gotten to with girls?" he asked.

"Not to any base in particular, I don't think," I said above the Bel Biv Devoe music, a pack of shrill-voiced guys who kept yelling "Poison!"

"You're a funny one," Mark said.

He'd sized me up quickly. The few times I'd politely ask a girl to dance at a bar mitzvah party or school mixer my parents forced me to attend, she'd bite her bottom lip in sorrow and claim that her ankle hurt, or she was saving her dance for someone else. So while my classmates rocked back and forth in each other's arms, I sipped a Coke at the edge of the dance floor and warbled along faintly to whatever syrupy pop ballad was playing, as if to say, I can be one of you, give me a chance! But the notes rang false. It was like reciting a prayer for a religion that wasn't mine.

"You guys get in a lot of fights in your school?" Mark asked.

"Fights? Not really."

Mark made a fist and held it up to my face, very close. "I got this ring for my bar mitzvah. It's pure gold. See how heavy it is."

"I see," I said. The air in that room felt very hot and close.

"If I punched some kid in the face with this ring on, he'd be wearing my initials for a week." He snorted, then noticed me fanning myself with my hand. "You can take your shirt off if you're hot."

"It's not that bad," I said, quickly whipping my hand away. "I'm okay."

"Me and my brother used to live in a rough hood," he said. "The kids there called us 'honky' and 'cracker.' It was cool."

"I bet." I offered him a tight-lipped smile. I was in way over my head.

"The black kids there used to pound on Jewish wussies like you for fun," Mark said. "This one kid I knew, they stripped him naked, to see if he was cut." I shook my head, not understanding. "You know, circumcised." I said I didn't believe in lumping people together like that based on skin color, but Mark replied, "Try saying that when they strip you naked. Anyway, they never touched me, or my brother." I asked Mark why not, and he widened his eyes. "Because they knew if they bothered either one of us, I'd go Medieval on their asses. Want to see? Try to hit me."

"No thank you."

"Come on, hit me." He leaped out of bed and put up his fists.

"I'm really not in the mood . . . " I was racking my brain for an excuse to leave but coming up empty. Meanwhile, he was moving his fists in tight circles, bouncing on his toes. I backed up toward the wall. "Please, stop."

Mark broke out laughing. "Hey, dude, you don't have to do everything I say," he said when he'd recovered. "If I told you to strip naked right now, would you do it?"

"No," I said.

"I think you would." His eyes darkened. "Amazing."

"No, I wouldn't," I said, but he didn't believe me.

THE ACCIDENT

A YEAR AFTER MEETING MARK, MY life had changed entirely.

Mostly I stayed at home, going out only for karate classes and my Monday, Wednesday, Thursday appointments with Dr. Don, who came from Virginia and spoke with a slight Southern drawl that his time at N.Y.U. hadn't quite erased. When I laughed at the way he talked, Don said that I and everyone else I knew spoke in a Midwestern accent that came out in words like "car" or "apple." Horrified, I practiced my speech at home. I wanted to sound as if I'd been born on a coast.

"What do you feel like working with today?" asked Dr. Don after I'd been taking karate for a week. There wasn't much improvement in sight.

"Oh, I don't know," I said. "Maybe just pen and paper."

"Suit yourself," he said, settling back in his chair as I took out my sketchpad.

Dr. Don worked out of his back porch, which he'd converted into an office. In the waiting room, Mom chose the one seat that wasn't broken or stained and sat there with her legs tightly crossed and her elbows pinned to her sides so they wouldn't come into contact with the arms of the chair while she read about Princess Diana's marital troubles, General Schwarzkopf's private life, or Mike Tyson's latest arrest, for rape. At the end of my appointments, I found her in the same place, sitting that same way.

Don's office, with children's drawings taped to the wood-paneled walls, looked nothing like Mom's tidy studio. At the end of each day, she wiped her desk with glass cleaner and a soft rag, and checked the linoleum floors and the walls for stray flecks of paint. Don's floors were a mess of splotches and streaks and in certain spots stuck to the soles of your shoes. His bookshelves were crammed with plastic bins of markers, pens, pencils, paints and brushes. His carpet was marked with dried blobs of Play-Doh and clay.

"Can I see what you're working on?" Dr. Don asked me after a few minutes.

"It's not ready yet." In fact, it was just doodling. I marked my page with three heavy penstrokes, then flipped my sketchpad shut.

I disliked the idea of making pictures for him to analyze. You know, that blob's really a vagina, and this one here's a penis. I knew all about Freud and his tricks. But Don wasn't as obvious as that. He preferred more open-ended questions like what's that shape about? What's going on in this picture? Can you tell me more?

Finally, I just straight up asked, "Don't you want to hear about the accident?"

"Accident?" said Dr. Don.

"What?" I asked.

"You asked if I wanted to hear about the accident."

"I didn't say accident."

"You did say it," said Don. "It's okay. We sometimes transpose words."

"Well, I meant incident," I said, but maybe I did mean accident. In my mind, that's how I thought of it, like the car crash that had killed an older classmate of mine. His school picture, with its modest saintly smile, had been printed in the *Jewish News*. We paid for trees to be planted in his honor in the Negev desert. We congregated in the school parking lot to release blue and white balloons printed with his name.

But if the story of my "accident" had gotten out at Stern, I would not have earned balloons in the sky. Mine was the kind of misfortune you kept hidden, like an ugly rash, or the fact that I felt horny at times and did something about it at night.

No one noticed my absence from school except for Benji Pearlberg, who sat next to me in art and drew dwarves and aliens. He called once, but I wouldn't come to the phone, so Mom said I wasn't feeling well enough yet, wasn't up to "full strength."

That's what I needed, strength. Full, half, even a quarter would have helped.

"Tell me more about karate," Dr. Don said. "The teacher, and the other boys?"

I shivered. I didn't like the word "boys." "It's fine," I said.

"Last time, you said it made you uncomfortable."

"No worse than coming here," I shot back before I could stop myself. "I'm sorry," I added. "I didn't mean that."

"Maybe you did mean it," Don said. "You feel uncomfortable here at times."

"Sometimes," I admitted, squirming a bit in my chair.

"Especially when we talk about feeling horny."

Dr. Don's favorite topic: "feeling horny." He kept pestering me about what I wanted and how I wanted it.

"These days, how often do you . . . " Here he paused, searching for just the right term, both direct in its meaning, yet not too unsettling in its rudeness. We'd begun with "masturbate"—too clinical. Moved on to "jerk off"—too violent. "Touch yourself" sounded mushy. So the search continued.

"Oh," I said airily. "You know, the normal amount."

And then he asked me, as he had two or maybe three times before, or maybe more, "When it happened, where was your head in that moment? What did you notice?"

"What do you mean?" I snapped. "I was trying not to get hurt. I was terrified."

"Sure, of course," said Don, "but was there any part of you that was curious?"

I wanted to please Dr. Don, to be the best patient in the history of therapy. And I wanted to get the hell out of that chair. Or maybe I wanted him to see me as a virtuous cherub-cheeked young man, still too young to shave, the type of boy who said please and thank you. Sex was the act of a bully, committed out of a forceful, driving need requiring a victim, who did not participate, but just lay there. A witness, not an accomplice.

"I don't think so," I said. "I'll think about it, but I don't think so."

"You want to think about it now?" he asked.

"No," I said. "I want to think about it later."

We Just Had to Hear You Say That

THAT FIRST NIGHT AFTER IT HAPPENED, I was too terrified to sleep in our home, so we all stayed at a hotel: me, my parents, and my brother David, who'd just come back from finishing his first year of college.

The next morning, I asked why we had to go back. Couldn't we move?

"Let them move," Mom said. "We did nothing wrong."

The house was suspiciously quiet. I waited for my parents to go inside before I would. Inside, everything was in its place except for the clothes I'd worn, and a towel Mark had used to wipe himself. The police had those. Otherwise, it was nothing like a crime scene, no lamps on the floor or chairs knocked on their side like in an episode of *Murder She Wrote*. I felt almost insulted.

After we dropped off our bags, we had to go out again, to the police station to file formal charges. Though we'd driven countless times past the building, an old schoolhouse that dated back to the early 1900s, I'd never realized it was a police station. Behind the stone facade, they'd built an ugly modern addition with padded gray cubicles. The sole decoration of our cubicle was a yellowing spider plant languishing in the corner.

There weren't enough chairs, so I shared one with my mom, who patted my back as if I were a baby needing burping. My father occupied his own chair, sitting forward in his seat, chin raised. David slouched behind him. Maybe he was ashamed to be here. "Why does he have to come?" I wanted to ask, but I had trouble finding my voice. Better to let it all happen, play out, burn out, naturally shed its energy.

The detective asked how Mark had gotten into the house—or rather, how I'd let him into the house. I explained that Mark had given me two choices: either he'd kill me, or if I let him in, he'd think about killing me. I went with the second option. The detective recorded me on a handheld cassette player, and he also took notes with a pen that said "Lose Weight Now, Ask Me How."

The cassette ran out, and as the detective had to get another, it hit me, that this was really happening. This was no dream. I felt woozy with the weight of this knowledge. Focus, I told myself. Or maybe pretend you're somewhere else. That's what Mark told me, before the worst of it. Relax, and it'll be over sooner.

The detective returned, and had me continue the story. When I got to the part when Mark had dragged me into the kitchen, the detective said, "He made you pull down your pants?" I said nothing, pretended it wasn't a question that demanded a yes-or-no answer. My vision went a bit bleary. "Did he pull down his pants?" the detective repeated.

"I wasn't really able to see."

"Why not?"

I cleared my throat, which felt red and raw. "Because I was on the floor." I couldn't look at my parents, so I looked at their shoes, my father's shiny brogues catching the glare of the ceiling light. My mother's feet sliding inside her high heels.

I heard Dad say, "David," and my brother left the room.

"Facing him or facing the floor?" the detective asked.

I closed my eyes and saw pink streaks of light running across the insides of my eyelids. Don't throw up, I thought. "I don't remember. Maybe the floor?"

"Was he on top of you?"

My mother gripped my shoulder. And then the answer slipped out: "I guess."

The detective looked down at his notepad. I could hear the pen scratching across the paper, and I sensed the permanence of those ink marks. Mark had threatened to kill me if I told. So now I could expect death.

We were then informed of Mark's statement. He'd claimed he'd fought me in self-defense. He said the sex was consensual. His evidence? In school, everyone knew I was a fag, and as logic would dictate, like all fags, I must have wanted it. Fags wanted it constantly. I hadn't managed to fight him off, so I must have wanted it, right?

The detective watched me from behind his desk. I was expected to talk.

"But that's a lie! I told him no, no," I said firmly. "I didn't want it."

"We know." The detective let out a deep breath. "We just had to hear you say that. We know you weren't like that."

Like that, I thought, my heart pounding. Like what?

The detective added, "He's not going to be bothering you anymore, alright?"

"How?" I asked. "What if he comes back?"

"We won't let him get anywhere near you. We're making that very clear."

Now I understood. Because I'd said no, it was their job to keep me safe. I could cling to my no like a life preserver. Nothing could be allowed to muddy that no.

Preparatory

SCHOOL WOULD RESUME IN THE FALL as if nothing had happened. Back to Stern Academy, which Mark could no longer attend. Still, his shadow would linger.

I begged my parents to send me anywhere else, somewhere far from our district, somewhere I had no history. Somewhere with strict rules to keep me safe.

Our local public school was too close by, too Jewish. The Taborsky family was known there.

There was Rockingham Private Preparatory Day School, but a few years ago, a scandalous article in the *Jewish News* had alleged that Rockingham's admissions department was marking the applications of Jewish students with hand-drawn bagels.

Another possibility was the Eaton School for the Arts, which Mom ruled out. "You need somewhere that will prepare you for a real career," she said.

"What about your career?" I asked. "You're an artist."

"That's different," she said. "I don't have to support a family."

So if I didn't have to support a family, would it be alright then to make art?

The winner by default was the Dalton College Preparatory School for Boys and Girls of Detroit, which despite its name, was not in Detroit, but in a suburb known for tasteful Protestant churches and private lakes. Mom canceled an appointment with Dr. Don so we could meet the assistant headmaster to discuss my prospects there.

The Dalton campus was a twenty-minute drive from where we lived. The entrance was next to a once "restricted" golf club that had banned Jews entirely and blacks outside of the kitchen and gardens. We drove past an unmanned gatehouse and up a severely sloped hill that hid the school from the road. Was it the elevation that made my stomach churn? The day was disgustingly humid—we were the Great Lake State, after all—and a pack of football players in full pads jogged uphill alongside our car. They carried their helmets, and their damp faces, in shades of black, brown, yellow, and white, glistened with sweat. "Let's pick it up, ladies!" yelled their coach, trotting behind them.

Watching them, I realized we'd made a mistake.

Dad was watching them too. "Do any Jewish kids go to this school?" he asked.

After swerving around a flag plaza, we were confronted by the school itself: a sprawling brick palace with glass skylights poking out of the roof, reflecting the heavens. The front door was framed by Doric columns and an arch, like a Greek temple.

Inside, a group of moms in pleated slacks and glossy penny loafers were decorating the lobby with gold and blue signs to welcome students back from vacation. A sign-up sheet to volunteer at a food bank was filled with signatures. I took this evidence of the Dalton students' kind hearts until I read the note at the bottom: "Fulfills your community service requirement!"

A few students dressed in soccer uniforms—shiny jerseys, shorts, kneepads covered in socks—roamed the halls. One girl gave us a strange look, then dissolved into a fit of giggling. Why? What had I done? But she immediately went quiet when an adult with a whistle around her neck appeared from around a corner.

"A place like this, you could learn some stuff," Dad said, admiring a schedule of football games tacked to a bulletin board like a dead moth. "Dee, why didn't we send David here?"

Because David wasn't the kind of kid who needed to be "sent" anywhere.

My mother touched his elbow. "Max, let's focus." She peered at a row of student artwork hung behind glass: a watercolor of a race car; an awkward black and white ink drawing of Cindy Crawford; and a close-up color photograph of a flower that had won a prize. I was jealous. I too wanted to win a prize.

Two kids carrying tennis rackets, one of them white and the other black, stopped us. "You lost?" asked the black kid in a gentle, relaxed voice, so clear it startled me.

"We were hoping to find the office," my mother said.

He pointed us down the hall. "You won't miss it," he said, though at first I thought he'd said, "You won't miss me." He had deep brown eyes, the color of warm mud, and his face, like his body, was long and lean. I liked the way his collared Dalton polo shirt fell naturally and easily over his shoulders.

I watched him over my shoulder as we walked to the office. He waved back at me, then held up two fingers, the peace sign. Peace sounds nice, I thought.

Dean Stephen Demuth was a lean man with big teeth, a bushy mustache, and tortoise-shell framed glasses. He offered his bony hand for us to shake across his thick-footed mahogany desk. We sat in wooden chairs painted navy blue and printed with the school logo, a Medieval shield with a laurel wreath surrounding a Ford Model T. The Dean's secretary brought out Danish butter cookies and hot tea with thin slices of lemon. Mom held a cookie up to the light, bit into it, then nodded her approval.

Hanging over the Dean's head were several photos: portraits of white football players in black and white; portraits of black basketball players in full color; and a sepia-toned shot of the Dean posing stony-faced in a Civil War uniform and carrying a musket.

"Before I went into admin, I used to teach history. Once a year, I still lead a tour of the Civil War Battlefields for the seniors, mostly boys." He smiled my way.

I set my teacup a little too firmly on its saucer, almost knocking it over. "Sorry," I said, still absorbing the idea of sharing a motel room with a mob of strange boys.

Demuth scored points with my father by calling him "Dr. Silverman." Oddly, my father always insisted on his title, despite the fact that he never seemed very proud of being a dentist and referred to his education as trade school. "Fill and drill," he called it.

The Dean then listened patiently while Mom explained slowly and at length, as she always had to for non-Jews, about her *ketubah* business. "People think Jewish art is all landscapes of Jerusalem, bearded rabbis and Stars of David. But that was just a trend that started twenty years ago and got stuck until it became so obvious and overplayed," she explained. "I do incorporate traditional, biblical symbolic images in my work but in a fresh and modern artistic way. I find inspiration from all kinds of sources, textile patterns, architecture, nature. Gustav Klimt. I like bold colors."

"Ke-TOO-ba," Demuth said carefully, and I blushed. I hated trotting out our Judaism in front of Gentiles. "I'd love to see your work."

Mom immediately handed him a brochure from the pack she kept in her purse. "Just in case you have any Jewish friends. Or even non-Jewish friends. You don't have to be Jewish to want to memorialize your marriage vows in a work of art."

The Dean turned my way and so did my parents, and I felt the stiff wooden back of my chair digging into my spine. Was it time now to confess my story? How much was required? But luckily, the Dean seemed more interested in telling Dalton's story. "Our mission is to prepare young people for college by providing a well-rounded education, nurturing minds as well as healthy bodies," he said. "A Dalton student is equally at ease discussing history, serving a tennis ball, or analyzing a European painting."

The current crop of Dalton students included children of the top brass at GM, Ford, Chrysler, as well as the auto unions. There were two sons of a State Supreme Court Judge, grandchildren of three Governors, and the niece of a local broadcaster who'd challenged Mayor Young to a boxing match for charity.

Demuth handed us wallet-sized cards printed with the school's address, phone number, and two-sentence honor code, like an article of faith:

"As a member of the Dalton community, I stand for what is good and right. I resolve to act with respect, honor, and compassion."

In other words, if I put my head down, did my work, and spoke to no one for four years, I could survive high school. Maybe I'd develop a healthy body, a football player's body. I'd bang lunch tables with my powerful fists. I'd throw, catch, and carry things without tripping over my own legs. Pounding down school hallways, I'd draw the attention of students and teachers. I'd turn myself on by looking in the mirror.

"And he could start this fall?" Mom asked. "He'd fit in?"

"I know he would," said Dean Demuth.

"Do you attract many students from the city?" Dad said, eyeing the pictures of the basketball players behind the Dean's chair.

"A few, on scholarship," Demuth admitted. "However, at Dalton, we keep our students too busy to get into the kind of trouble so common in other schools." He gave me a long, sad look when he said "other schools," and I dug the toe of my shoe into the carpet, dark green like a forest where I might lose myself—if I were lucky.

"Busy doing what exactly?" my dad asked.

Busy with the "Three A's," academics, athletics, and the arts. Busy adhering to a dress code (jackets, ties, slacks, dark socks and shoes for boys, blouses with skirts or dresses for girls). Busy earning red points (for clubs), white points (for community service), and most dauntingly, blue points (for doing sports after school).

But I didn't "do" any sports.

"Not even skiing?" asked Dean Demuth.

No, not even that. Dad had seen too many teeth knocked loose in ski accidents.

"Ari has some experience in the martial arts," my mother said.

"Mom, please," I said.

"There's always track," Demuth suggested, his voice dripping with pity. "All Dalton students do a sport. Our motto is *mens sana in corpore sano.*"

Dad approved. He liked Latin, almost as much as he liked Hebrew, though he didn't know that particular phrase.

"Healthy mind in a healthy body," I said, translating for him.

"Did you hear that?" Demuth said. "He'll fit right in."

Promises, promises, I thought, as my mother uncrossed her legs and picked up her purse. Were we leaving? Yes, it seemed we were leaving. I sprang to my feet.

Mom shook the Dean's hand, promising to donate a print to their next fundraiser auction. "I have ones that aren't too religious, that anyone would like," she said.

Demuth glanced my way, then added, "We take care of our students."

He must know, I thought. For sure, he knows. My skin prickled with shame.

After our meeting, I hurried past my parents toward the car. This had been a mistake. Maybe if we never came back, the school would forget all about us. Didn't the Constitution protect my right to be homeschooled?

Driving out of the parking lot, Dad said over his shoulder, "Hey, Ari, maybe you could try the baseball team. You'd make a natural shortstop."

"Shut up!" I burst out. "Stop trying to make this all so . . . different from what it is."

"What?" said Dad. "What is it? What am I trying to do?"

"Please, Max, don't push him," said Mom.

For the rest of the quiet ride home, I thought of the tall, thin boy with the warm brown eyes, the one who'd directed us to Demuth's office and promised peace. I could still hear him saying: "You won't miss me." Wasn't that what he said? I was almost sure of it.

Shirts and Skins

Last summer, not long after we'd first met, Mark knocked on my door and dragged me back to his house to play "hoops."

The Taborskys had nailed a basketball hoop above their garage door. The rim seemed impossibly high and narrow. Could it really swallow the plump orange ball Mark had chucked at my waist?

"Shirts and skins!" Mark announced.

"Careful, he trips people," warned his little brother, watching from the porch.

I refused to take off my shirt, so he took off his Detroit Pistons "Bad Boys" T-shirt, black with a skull and crossbones printed over a basketball.

Though I was supposed to look at the basketball, my eyes drifted down to Mark's brick red nipples, his navel, his hips, and his legs, thick, toned, and laced with dark hair. Girls my age were starting to shave their legs, and their smooth creamy skin reminded me of spoiled milk. Maybe I'd have liked girls more if they had hairy legs.

Pausing mid-dribble, Mark said, "Here's a tip. Watch the guy's hips, not his chest. The hips tell you where he's going to go."

He'd noticed me noticing his body, yet he didn't seem to care.

"Did your dad teach you that?" I asked.

"My dad can't even dribble the ball. I learned it at basketball camp." I hadn't realized there was such a thing as basketball camp. "All the coaches were black. Don't let them send you to one of those crappy camps with Jewish coaches."

We played to 21, and Mark beat me 21-0. "You shoot like a girl," he said, not unkindly, more like a scientist making an empirical observation. "What sports are you good at?"

"I'm the same at all of them." True enough. I stood in left field during softball, warmed the bench for basketball, or ran along the sidelines for football or soccer. The other boys charitably avoided aiming any balls in my direction. In return, I occasionally helped them out in art class or with history homework.

"Any faggot can be good at sports." Mark stretched his shirt back over his head.

"You just need practice. Use our net. I'll be waiting for you."

He'd be waiting for me, I thought, with his bared nipples, his scaly-skinned basketball, and crude talk about "faggots," or as he called them, "faggies." Mark claimed that a faggie had offered to blow him in the bathroom at Hudson's department store.

"Never let a faggie walk behind you," Mark advised before I trudged home in defeat. "They're always trying to stick stuff up your ass, trying to give you AIDS."

An Old Soul

THAT FRIDAY, BOTH MY PARENTS WERE too busy to pick me up from karate class, so they sent my brother David in Dad's old Buick. He'd clawed off the "Bush Quayle 88" bumper sticker and replaced it with one that said, "Nice Planet, Don't Blow It."

"Hey, you're sweaty," he said, mussing my hair as I ducked into the passenger seat. The floor mats were crusted with dirt and dead leaves, and the glove compartment kept falling open. He wiped his hand on my shoulder. "Don't they have a shower?"

"I don't like to parade around naked in public," I said. "I'm not Dad."

David giggled. "You're funny, dude. You're an old soul."

"Have you been smoking one of your pot cigarettes?" I wanted to sound haughty and indignant, but David just giggled again. He had an unexpectedly unexpectedly high-pitched laugh.

David didn't need karate class to learn to defend himself or a therapist to teach him to like girls. In high school, girls sought him out, mistaking his natural shyness around them for sensitivity. He was tall with hazel eyes with a kind of shine to them that caught your attention, and he had curly hair, a relaxed smile, broad shoulders. His high school jacket, pinned with varsity letters in skiing and track, now gathered dust in his bedroom. I went in there sometimes, traced the outlines of the letters, inhaled David's distinct masculine smell, a mix of talcum, musk, and, oddly, decaying plant matter.

Now that he was in college, David had given up sports and cheerleaders to do things like build houses in Detroit that summer for Habitat for Humanity, which as my father pointed out, was a Christian organization. He'd stumble into the house late, sweaty, unshaven, and stinking of body odor since he'd stopped using deodorant. At breakfast, he drank wheatgrass juice, and at dinner, he avoided red meat. He replaced the Billy Joel posters in his bedroom with spiraling psychedelic prints and or posters of Neil Young and The Who. Because of David's long hair, Dad started calling him "the ladyboy," a name that on me would have left a bruise, but somehow made David seem more masculine.

When we got home, David invited me to hang out in his room, which faced the back of the house instead of the Taborskys' place. I challenged him to a round of my favorite board game, called *Masterpiece.* Mom had bought it when I was younger to turn me on to art, though I bet now she was wishing she'd bought me a football helmet instead.

In *Masterpiece,* you had to bid on classic paintings from museums in New York, Paris, or Amsterdam, cities big enough to get lost in, and sophisticated enough so that no one as crude as Mark would want to visit them.

I drew a Renoir, prompting David to say, "I don't get why you're still into these kid games. You think much about girls?"

"I think about them," I said. Recently, my family had become preoccupied with the subject of girls. Dad pointed out the lips, hips, asses, even boobs of girls on TV, as if teaching me to recognize the markings of a rare species of butterfly. David taught me to pronounce "Paulina Porizkova" and promised to buy me a poster of her for Hannukah. Mom prompted me to open doors and pull out chairs for any female nearby.

"Yeah?" David said. "So what do you think about when you have wet dreams?"

I'd bent my wrinkled Renoir card in half without realizing it. "I don't have them."

"Why not? You jerk off too much?" Expressions like "jerk off" rolled easily off David's tongue, in the same natural way he flung baseballs or stained his jeans with mud and grass. My words, like my clothes, were always spotless.

I knew what he really wanted to ask, a question too horrible to state plainly.

We had a gay cousin who had an awful habit of squeezing your elbow or wrist when he talked to you and leaning too far forward into your face as if he wanted to eat it. His breath smelled of violets. My parents greeted him politely at family dinners and afterward shook their heads and said, "That's a lonely kind of life."

In seventh grade, we used to imitate the way our effeminate drama teacher would flare his hands around his mouth and urge us to "Sing out!" Occasionally he sprayed saliva when he talked, and we stayed far out of his spitting range in case he had AIDS. Not that we really thought we'd get AIDS, but AIDS jokes were popular that year.

Eventually we learned it wasn't nice to tell AIDS jokes, though we still told them, just not when any adults could hear. In health class, our teacher told us how to stay safe and whispered the word "condoms." You couldn't get it from sharing a cup with someone, or kissing or toilet seats, at least they didn't think so. On the news, I'd seen bony men in hospital gowns, their skin marked with lesions, their cheeks hollowed out like the pictures of Holocaust survivors they used to show us in Jewish History.

What if I had AIDS, from Mark? Shouldn't I be tested? The detective had suggested it, but my parents refused to give their permission. Later I asked my mom why, and she said, "That's for practicing homosexuals in New York. He couldn't have been . . . He's healthy. You're healthy. You're fine."

But I worried that inside I was all messed up, as bad as those New Yorkers.

"Let's keep playing," I told David and drew another card, a Miro. He said, "That one looks like a vagina."

"Gross," I said on instinct, then wished I could take it back.

"Not to me." He traced the offending outlines with his finger. "You won't think so either, when you're older. You know, all girls have them."

"I know that," I said indignantly. "I've seen Renoir's late paintings."

Uniform

DALTON STUDENTS WERE REQUIRED TO WEAR a uniform, available only at Stewart's, a department store in tony, WASPy Birmingham, where the streets were lined with expensive German cars or Jaguars, and shops selling imported British tea and jams.

In Stewart's, the staff dressed in tailored knit suits and stood off to the side, speaking in tasteful, quiet tones only when spoken to. The air was perfumed with wood varnish and the walls were decorated with black and white photos of classic roadsters. Here you could buy such exotic articles of clothing as wool coats with wooden toggles, cable knit sweaters, plaid ties, or "boat shoes" whose wearers might wear them on actual boats.

Like poor relations, the Dalton uniforms were hidden in a special section at the back. "He's in high school?" the saleswoman asked in a doubtful voice. "He might do better in one of our junior sizes." We found a tight polyester blue blazer that fit like a straitjacket and stiff grey wool slacks that scratched my legs.

"Cute," Mom said, but didn't sound very convincing.

Watching my unending reflection in a three-sided mirror, I felt like a victim of multiple personality disorder, with all my various selves staring back at me.

Sensitive

DR. DON WANTED ME TO PRACTICE standing on our front porch, for one minute, then two, then three. He loaned me an egg timer shaped like an angry tomato for this purpose. So I took it out there and stood with my eyes closed.

Faintly in the distance, I heard the angry buzz of a lawn mower, or maybe a hedge trimmer sawing away stray branches. I recalled Dr. Don's promises that I'd be safe standing here, but he didn't know Mark, who might appear on his porch and wound me with a frown, or raised eyebrow, or a blank look in my direction.

This exercise was supposed to get easier with time.

Back inside, Mom was explaining on the phone why I was suddenly switching schools: "It isn't a snob thing. He's just sensitive. At his old school, he attracted bullies."

Sensitive, I thought. It sounded like code for something much worse.

The Storage Room

The trouble began when our Torah teacher chose Mark and me to travel to the gym storage room, to return a stack of prayer books she'd borrowed for class that day.

A single naked bulb on a string lit the dark and dusty storage room. The dull metal shelves were filled with deflated dodgeballs, bruised field hockey sticks, and stacks of prayer books, both the new versions we'd started using this fall as well as the outdated ones, without those stickers that covered up the prayer "Thank you God for not making me a woman" with "Thank you God who made me in His image." Some of the kids, though, still said, "Thank you for not making me a woman."

Mark shoved the books onto a shelf above a sack of field hockey sticks, then flexed his arm. "I've been working out." He slapped his bicep. "Rock hard. Feel that."

"No thank you," I said, and my yarmulke slipped off. Before I could retrieve it, Mark grabbed my hand and placed it on the bicep, which was rock hard as advertised. My fingers probed his warm skin, red and frighteningly firm.

"Let's see yours," he said, so I let go and flexed as hard as I could. "Soft," he said. "Soft as the inside of a girl's thigh." He flexed his arm again, and this time I squeezed his bicep without any invitation. Would I have one like that next year, when I was his age?

"Touch it as long as you want," he said generously, and I quickly let go, prayed I wouldn't get an erection. The books were successfully put away, but Mark stood in front of the door to the storage room. "Be honest. Have you ever done anything with girls?"

I said that I had.

"With who?"

"Whom, not who," I said on instinct, then offered a name: "Adrienne Cohen." Adrienne had been my babysitter when I had needed the services of a babysitter.

"Never heard of her. How do you know this Adrienne?"

I thought fast. "I saw her standing on her lawn. I thought she was cute. So I asked if she wanted to go record shopping at Harmony House sometime."

Mark seemed pleased. "You're lying," he said.

"Honestly," I said, which I knew sounded desperate.

"No one says, 'honestly.'" He edged closer to me. "Unless they're lying."

"I told her to meet me at Harmony House."

"No one meets anyone at Harmony House except faggies." He bumped his hip against my hand, so I jerked it back and a squeak escaped my throat. "Tell me the truth. I'll have so much more respect for you if you say, 'Mark, I was lying. I don't know anyone named Adrienne Cohen.'"

"I really do know her," I said. Unfortunately, my voice cracked.

"So what did you do with this Adrienne?"

"We frenched," I said.

"What does that mean?" He giggled a little. "We frenched."

"Aren't we done here?" I reached for the door, and he grabbed my hand, put it on the front of his pants, then rubbed it there. "Did she do this to you?"

His jeans felt rough and, where I was rubbing, very full.

"Don't," I whispered, anxious to get away yet curious to know what exactly he wanted me to do. "Please." But my hand went on moving as if separate from my arm, my brain. Mark crowded me against the wall. His body blocked the light, and the door.

"Don't let go until I say so," he told my ear, his hips grinding rhythmically into my right hand. "Or I'll tell everyone you're a fag."

I felt lightheaded, as if I were disappearing from that room. The outlines of my body were dissolving, and what was left of me floated above the two of us, free and weightless as a ghost, so I could slip through a crack or pass through a wall.

Mark let out a painful moan. Oh, no, I thought, I'm screwed. I was afraid I'd hurt him somehow and he'd hit me. But then I saw the mess on the floor.

"You're disgusting, you know that?" He jerked himself out of my reach and ordered me to clean myself off as he yanked up his pants. Then he ran back to class. My hands still throbbing with the feel of him, I followed his orders, wiping my hands on an unwashed wrinkled jersey. But his smell, a strange mix of sea salt and spoiled milk, remained on my skin.

This is not me, I wanted to scream. I didn't ask for this. I screwed my eyes shut and tried to focus, prayed that I might like what he liked, not the healthy resistance of the hard bodies of men, but girls and their soft slippery skin and slimy insides, whose briny scent Mark had described for me in nauseating detail.

I made myself imagine fingering various girls from my grade as Mark had boasted of doing, but my fingers kept getting lost in the weeds. I tried mimicking Mark's talk, "I felt her up. I squeezed her tits." I recited those words like the blessings we recited each morning in services, hoping with practice they might sound firm and convincing. *Thank you God for not making me a woman.*

At least for the rest of that day and the next one, Mark did me the courtesy of not even looking my way, let alone talking to me. Maybe, hopefully, he was so disgusted by what he'd done, he'd never speak to me again.

But then two days later, I opened my locker, and a slip of white paper with Mark's handwriting fell out. He wanted me to meet him once more in the storage room.

"You get my note?" he whispered when I passed his desk in class later. "Be there unless you want me to kill you after school."

"Why are you doing this?" I said. "Why me?" And then Elise Fein, who in elementary school had taught me how to tie my shoes, looked over at us.

"You shut the fuck up," said Mark. The debate was closed.

For the next few weeks, when the mood struck him, Mark summoned me to that cramped, stuffy storage room, leaving me a note in my locker or buzzing a command in my ear when we passed in the hall. Mark Taborsky—red, throbbing, stinking, sour—became as inevitable in my life as weather.

I got very quiet in school. Kids who'd never noticed me stopped me in the hall to ask if I was okay. Even Benji Pearlberg and his crowd of socially awkward boys who let me sit with them at lunch noticed I wasn't grinning stupidly as they discussed movies I hadn't seen or role-playing games in which I had no role. In art class, I was staring at my empty sketchpad when Benji came up next to me and asked, "What are you drawing?"

I shrugged.

"You mind if I sit here with you?"

I shook my head to say I didn't mind, and he sat next to me quietly for the rest of the class and painted a green-scaled dragon. How could I burden Benji with my story? He still believed in dwarves and magic swords. I wasn't even sure he'd hit puberty.

Every morning, as I dialed the combination on my blue pad-lock, I held my breath. When there was no note from Mark inside, I felt relieved, yet also weirdly disappointed, like a death row pris-oner whose execution had been delayed. Mark and I shared a secret, something dangerous, shocking, and grown-up. For once, I was the insider.

RESEARCH

AT TIGHT-LACED, BUTTONED-UP DALTON, I COULD disappear into my new blue sport coat, school tie, and wool pants. I'd brush my hair in a new way and say "cool" in a low, rumbling voice when I meant yes. The Dalton Handbook mandated "soft conversation" between classes, so if I could just think of a few witty things to say in the hallways or during lunch, maybe I'd never be popular, but I could blend in with the walls.

So I did research.

I bought a copy of *Sports Illustrated* and skimmed the articles about Michael Jordan or Mike Tyson, then compared the taut bodies of underwear models to mine. I wanted to linger longer over those ads, but finally I forced myself to put down the magazine, feeling both turned on and engulfed by despair.

I borrowed Dad's mini cassette player, recorded my voice, and played it back. Horrified by what I heard, I attempted to speak in lower tones, like a bullfrog.

And in karate, I squared my shoulders in front of the mirror, threw out my non-existent chest. I practiced walking as if I were a gunslinger in a Western, like Sensei Brad. Between exercises, I did modified bent-knee push-ups and dreamed of doing real ones.

I listened to hits by Paula Abdul, New Kids, Vanilla Ice, and Janet Jackson. I tried to like their songs, but the words and the musical notes were tiresome and repetitive, as if glued together by machines for the listening pleasure of other machines. The messages of the songs were always the same. I'm so cool. You're so hot. I get laid a lot.

Mark could have breezed through my self-imposed training regimen without breaking a sweat. He knew all the right movies to see and sports to watch and songs to listen to and video games to play as well as the right things to say about them (like "Sweet!" with the "s" pronounced as an "sh," ergo "Shweet!"). He was fluent in the language of boys. Of course, he had the advantage of being spectacularly unkind, taking relish in crude insults that on first hearing seemed startlingly original, though they always amounted to the same thing: girls were sluts, and boys were girls.

The Sunday before my Dalton debut, my father told me to grab my karate uniform and get in the car. Brad was opening the school early, just for us two, a private lesson.

Dad didn't put his new Springsteen tape on the stereo as usual. He was strangely quiet as our car crunched down our snowy driveway onto Maggie Lane.

Most of the subdivisions in Bloomfield had streets with distinguished-sounding names like Haverford or Maplewood, with pleasant pretensions of being British. However, as a lame joke, the builders in our sub had named the streets after their all-American daughters: Jenny Drive, Stacy Court, and our own Maggie Lane.

Turning onto Jenny Drive, Dad said, "I heard from Detective Marten."

"Oh?" I said, digging my thumbs into the seat cushion.

"They went before a judge." My father, like me, never said Mark's name aloud. "They talked about, you know, juvenile hall, but there was the problem of kosher food. You know, the dad's a big rabbi. So they're sending him to a strict Jewish boarding school in Toronto. He can only come home for closely supervised visits."

But the Rabbi was never home, and I'd seen Mrs. Taborsky in her red ski jacket struggling to walk their yappy terrier, pulling at its rhinestone-studded leash. If she couldn't handle some dumb dog, how could she restrain her son?

My father concluded our conversation with some advice: "If that monster ever manages to get into our house again, you lock yourself in the bathroom. It'd take a sledgehammer to bring down that door."

That's when I understood: Dad was afraid too.

At our special karate practice, Brad blasted Guns 'n' Roses while demonstrating how to hit someone's nose with my open palm. "The nose is vulnerable on anyone. Even if you're as big as Hulk Hogan, you can't build any more muscle on your nose."

"Thanks," I said.

"I taught this to all my girls. Even a girl can throw a grown man to the ground that way. No man's going to mess with them in some dark alley, I can promise you." My ears flushed a deep crimson. Was that how he saw me, a girl who'd been messed with?

For an hour, we practiced the same three moves, block, block, and pow, right to the face. I followed Brad's instructions, feeling the anger surge under my forearms. I imagined what it would be like to make real, powerful contact with someone's smirking face, soft warm skin masking a hard, solid jawbone.

At the end of class, Brad drew a stripe in black marker on the tip of my white belt. "Keep it up," he said, "and you'll get to yellow belt." As Brad clapped my shoulder, I caught a whiff of his aftershave, a mix of pine needles and car wax.

Both Brad's and Dad's eyes grew misty, and then mine did too, just a bit.

First Day

THAT NIGHT, I CRAWLED OUT OF bed, opened my window, and breathed in the night air, so cool it almost felt wet.

Mark's bedroom windows were dark. He'd been shipped off to serve his sentence at that Canadian yeshiva. Yes, let the Canadians handle him.

What if he genuinely believed that cover story he'd told the cops, that I wanted it? Maybe I'd been the one who was wrong—for being too weak to resist both Mark's advances and the police's pressure to break my promise to Mark to keep my mouth shut. If this was my fault, then I'd have to be punished. Perhaps Mark would recruit a gang of his Detroit friends to rake my windows with bullets. Or they'd be waiting at Dalton to choke me with my new tie and string me up the school flagpole, so I'd dangle in the wind.

Whichever punishment they chose, I wished they'd get it over with. The suspense was too terrible. I already felt that first prickle of skin touching skin, the kiss of knuckle pounding cheek, the tingle of shiny blade sparking blood.

* * *

MY FIRST MORNING AS A DALTON boy, I woke to a thrashing thunderstorm that pelted our lawn and clogged drainpipes with grass trimmings and fallen leaves. Worried about traffic, Mom rushed me through my morning bagel. She'd skipped her usual breakfast, a microwaved frozen egg white omelet. According to her daily morning weigh-in, she'd gained a couple of ounces, and so she was glaring at a mug of raspberry-flavored coffee.

"Mom, please eat something," I begged her. "Or drink some juice."

She said, "I don't believe in juice. I don't believe in drinking my calories."

Before leaving, I did a quick spot-check in the hall mirror. No messy hairs to tamp down, no zits to pick. Then I noticed something missing behind me.

"Where's the de Chirico?" I asked. A few years ago, Mom had bought a tiny sketch of a faceless man strumming a guitar, which had cost more than she liked to admit. The image had always unnerved me, but she proudly pointed it out to guests. When they complimented the de Chirico, she blushed as if they were complimenting her.

Mom's shoulders fell. "Dalton's expensive," she said, then cleared her throat. "Don't think about it. I don't. I've put the de Chirico right out of my mind." I gave her a hug, and she said, "What was that for?"

"Sorry for being so expensive," I said, shrinking into my stiff new blazer.

"Don't say that. What else is money for?" she said. "Never think about money, okay?"

Even if it was money we didn't have? "Okay," I said.

The rain pounded our car on the way to school. Mom played the soundtrack to *Les Miz*, which she'd seen on her last mental sanity vacation in New York. The singers' voices sounded cruel and shrill, as if sneering at us for listening.

How would my mother keep up with her New York theater and art galleries now that we had Dalton tuition to pay every year?

When we pulled up to the front entrance, the sight of all those uniforms streaming into school deflated me. Mom put the car in park. "Their grounds always look so neat, so trim." She gave me a long, sad look. "Enjoy your day, honey."

Outfitted in my own tight, new uniform, I entered the front doors alone, my feet damp inside slippery dress shoes. No one returned the anxious smile I'd plastered to my face. Where was that boy with the warm brown eyes from my first Dalton visit, the one who'd flashed me the peace sign? Maybe I'd dreamed him up.

Dean Demuth had stationed himself beside a glass trophy case filled with news clippings trumpeting our school's success on courts, ski slopes and ice rinks. Hoping to make a good start, I greeted him with a hearty, "Good morning, sir!"

"Your tie," he replied.

I looked down. My polyester tie had slipped a half-inch from the top button of my collar. I yanked it back up, made sure it was choking my neck.

At Lev Stern Hebrew, we used to start the morning with a religious service. Here the day began with our homeroom teacher checking our uniforms, then reading the headmaster's daily brief, followed by Dalton's equivalent of school prayer: "Fly, Eagles, Fly!" Then she released us to dash to our lockers, which were lined with wood-veneer and had faux brass handles. We were supposed to call them "cabinets," but we all called them lockers, and even the faculty occasionally slipped up and called them lockers too.

Between classes, I wandered the halls feeling lost, often getting lost while trying to find the Commons Room, The Quad, The Levee, The Chapel, and the ominous-sounding Dixon House. When I sought out help, I stammered like an idiot.

"Are you an exchange student?" one girl asked me.

Some of the guys I passed in the halls were almost twice my size. I took care to stay out of their sight lines, walking close to walls, peeking around corners. In class I always chose a seat with a view of the door.

At lunchtime, we filed into the cafeteria, a.k.a the "Dining Hall," and sat at one of several long tables with place settings where all meals were eaten with a fork and knife, even burgers and tacos. I chose the end of a table occupied by African-American girls whose families drove them to school from Detroit.

I'd expected my Dalton classmates to be mostly Aryan, blue eyes, snub noses, with names like Biffy or Tiffy. In fact, our hallways resembled Jesse Jackson's "Rainbow Coalition." There were Christians of all stripes (I didn't know there were different stripes of Christians before), as well as Jews, Muslims, Hindus, Buddhists, even a Zoroastrian. Native tongues included Spanish, Arabic, Thai, Korean, and working class slang.

Today for lunch, we were served decidedly non-kosher cheeseburgers.

I'd never tasted a cheeseburger, though I'd always been curious about them. For a second, I considered peeling the melted cheese off my meat. Finally, I just bit into it. It was delicious, the gooey cheese melting over the seared brown patty, and the juices running into the bun. I finished the whole thing in a minute.

Why would God make something so wonderful and then forbid us to eat it?

Out of Proportion

IN ART CLASS, WE COULD TAKE off our jackets and cover our shirts and ties with pale blue smocks. After outfitting myself in a smock, I opened the metal supply cabinets, filled with an impressive array of pens, brushes, paint tubes, and expensive paper. I thought of asking Mom if she wanted me to steal some for her.

I chose a piece of good paper and sat at one of the tables. The other kids dirtied their hands with ink or paint, or snacked on granola bars in plain view of our teacher, Ms. Hunter. One kid fed an Ice-T tape into Ms. Hunter's old stereo, which she'd brought from home to inspire us, and another guy said, "Hey, faggot, turn off that rap crap."

"Who you calling faggot, faggot?"

"You, faggot."

I fixed my eyes on my drawing. My pen had torn a small hole in the paper.

"Hey, hey, hey . . . " Ms. Hunter came scooting over, stopped the stereo. "Watch the language, guys. And no more stereo privileges for today."

"Aw, come on, please . . . " both boys begged, almost in chorus.

"Alright, but don't let me catch you talking that way again."

Ms. Hunter, the only female teacher in school who wore pants, didn't give much in the way of instruction beyond how to work the projector, so we could trace images directly onto paper or canvas. "No one draws freehand anymore," she said, winding her long hair into a bun that inevitably came loose. "You think Andy Warhol drew freehand?"

Despite Andy Warhol, I stuck to the old-fashioned way, drawing a multi-panel cartoon of Dean Demuth choking several students lining up for uniform check. "Cool beans," said Ms. Hunter, peering over my shoulder.

Cool beans? I thought. Was that something people said?

"Your faces are good," she added. "But the bodies are out of proportion. You might want to spend a little time looking at your-self naked."

How Are You Liking It?

"So, how are you liking it?" Dad wanted to know when he picked me up for karate class, at the end of my first week at Dalton.

I'd practiced my answer to this question. "Oh, you know." I unbuttoned my collar and loosened my tie. "Fine." Nothing out of the ordinary. Nothing to stare at here.

In school, I kept my Dalton tie neatly knotted, my shoes and socks regulation black, and my hair cut several inches above the collar of my starched white dress shirt. I ate cheeseburgers and ham sandwiches without thinking twice. I pledged my undying support for the Dalton Eagles at pep rallies and attempted to live by the guiding principles in the Headmaster's Message of the Day. I learned how to move between the library, the "new" gym, and the Dining Hall without passing the Commons Room, where the burliest, angriest football players rammed into each other for fun, or the photo lab, where burnouts and bohemian types played with X-Acto knives and toxic chemicals.

Before driving out of the Dalton parking lot, Dad looked at me for a few seconds, then patted my seat belt. "All strapped in?"

Mark's father used to pick him up from Stern every afternoon, kissing him noisily on both cheeks, like a dog slurping up a fallen ice cream cone off the sidewalk. I used to watch the whole process, mesmerized by every gruesome detail. My father wasn't a kisser. Sometimes I wished that he were, but never in his actual presence, thank God.

Lion

In French, Justin Jackson sat on the edge of my desk. "Hey, what's your name?"

Justin was that kid with the deep brown eyes who during my first visit to Dalton had claimed, "You won't miss me." Though I'd seen him a few times, he hadn't seem to recognize me, so I ignored him right back. I overheard him laughing with his friends, "Everyone thinks I'm on scholarship for basketball." In fact, he played tennis, and his scholarship was academic, not athletic. He'd won some kind of trophy in math. Socially, he wasn't a jock or a nerd, but belonged to another, mysterious crowd of ironic, smirking kids whose circle I couldn't place because it hadn't existed at my old school.

"What kind of name's Ari?" he asked, setting his briefcase on my desk like an explorer planting a flag to claim some undiscovered country. Justin carried a slender black leather briefcase and a silver pen, and no one mocked him. It was part of his image. "Is it French? Is that why you're so good at French?"

I loved speaking French. It made me feel more sophisticated, all-knowing, confident, and less Jewish. Also, in French class I didn't have to invent interesting things to say to people. The lines of dialogue were already printed for me to simply memorize.

"No, it's Hebrew for lion," I explained. Under my desk, I flattened my palm as Brad had taught me, in case I needed to smack him in the nose.

Justin stared at me. "Lion, huh? You seem more like a dove. Well, I'll just call you Brain. Did you do that workbook assignment last night? Mind if I take a look?"

I took this as a command, not a request. "Okay." I dug through my bag for it.

"Hurry, if you don't mind, before Monsieur Gilbert gets here."

While copying my answers, Justin asked why I'd transferred to Dalton. I recited my standard excuse: My parents felt my old school didn't offer enough "enrichment."

"I love the suburbs. The land of enrichment." He resumed copying my work in swift lacy writing, with the bored efficiency of a British lord signing a check. "Thanks, Brain," Justin said in his slow, careful baritone, handing me back my workbook when he was done. He got up to sit with another black kid in the back of the room. "You're cool."

I was so startled to hear it that I almost dropped the workbook on the floor.

Was I really? Why did he think so? I wanted to know more.

The Quitter

"Who died?"

Not understanding the question, I looked up blankly at Justin from my seat on the bench by the school entrance. A brass plaque indicated it had been donated by a local car dealership in honor of Dalton's girls' softball championship team, 1982.

"Why do you look so down in the mouth?" he asked, swinging his briefcase.

I said I was waiting for my mother to take me to karate, and then, maybe because I'd been suppressing the thought for so long, I admitted, "I hate it."

"Then don't go."

"But my mom is coming to take me."

Justin cocked his head to the side. "Follow me," he said.

Flattered by the invitation, I went with him to the art room, shut up for the evening. Justin calmly unlocked the door. How did he have the key? "Ms. Hunter likes football players. My buddy Marlin made us all copies."

Inside, we sat there with the lights out, swiveling on the metal stools and staring at the paint-speckled floor, like a Jackson Pollock painting. "Just hide out here until your karate class is over," said Justin.

"Don't you have to be somewhere?" I asked, but I didn't want him to go.

"It can wait." He had a lean, hungry look that I liked. I felt uncomfortable on my hard stool, but I didn't dare move, or do anything that might disturb the moment.

"Want to listen to something?" he asked and pulled out a tape out of his briefcase. The tape was marked on the front: MIX. "This is Nirvana," he said.

The band's name, Nirvana, made me think the music would be soothing, New Agey, like Enya. But the song announced itself with a brief guitar snarl, followed by a fury of driving drumbeats and metal. I didn't usually like loud metal music—it sounded too much like violence—but this song didn't seem to qualify exactly as heavy metal, with all the sounds fitting together in a pattern. It was more like separate noises, each with its own direction, like the paint splatters on the art room floor.

Just as I got used to it, the noisy part died down, and Kurt Cobain began to sing.

What first caught my attention was the ache in his voice. First he'd mumble, even growl for an unintelligible line or two, then he'd fling out the next few words in a trembling, cracked yelp edged with a nervous resentment, or draw out words with a strange sarcasm. He held a sarcastic yowl for several strained seconds that felt more like ages, giving them a mysterious, eerie emphasis. His voice sounded both tired and anxious, as if he'd been ignored all his life and was finally sick of it. Why will no one listen?

Justin drummed his silver pen against one of the tables along with the song. I wanted to tell him to stop so I could hear everything. I didn't want to miss a note of it.

The chorus was a storm of guitars, drums, and Kurt Cobain's ragged yowl. I made out a few words in flashes, like "contagious" and "stupid." But I didn't need the words to know what Kurt was feeling, an emotion I too had felt, though I couldn't name it just then. Yes, I too have been as desperate as you. I was thinking of how I felt right after Mark, when my mother found out and she folded me in her arms, and I grabbed her tightly, rubbed my cheek against her warm sweater, yet it didn't help.

When Justin shut off the tape, I was perched on the edge of my chair, my brain tingling. I'd never heard a pop song like this, complex like a work of art, with a deep emotional pull like a novel or a movie. By comparison, everything else on the radio sounded candy-coated and fake.

I realized what that feeling was, the one Kurt was singing about. It was anger.

Justin was staring at me, waiting for me to speak. He must have felt as I did about the song, and I wanted so desperately to say something meaningful, important.

"Uh, are they British?" I asked.

"No, they're American. But not commercial." He said the word "commercial" with a pained look on his face.

All I could think of was, "Neat."

"Neat?" he said.

My stomach sank. I'd messed this up. "Why? Was that wrong?"

"No. You never get anything wrong. You're an intelligent young man." He ejected the tape from the stereo.

"Why?" I asked. "Wait, what did I do?"

"That's all I got. I didn't bring any Julie Andrews to play you," he said, and left.

I sat alone and replayed the conversation. What else could I have said? Cool. Cool beans? No, just cool. And "cool" was supposed to be my new word! Why couldn't I have remembered it? I could even have said nice, good, great, anything but neat.

Maybe I could run after him, or find him tomorrow and say I'd been taking some kind of medication that had messed with my head. "Neat," I'd say. "Can you believe I said that?" And then we'd laugh together about it. Yes, that might work.

I got off the stool and went to the parking lot to find my mother, who was livid.

My punishment and reward were the same: I was grounded for a week, which wasn't much of a punishment since I never went anywhere anyway. But first, I had to go to the United Studios of Self-Defense and apologize to Brad for dropping out. While my mother waited in the car, Brad stood in front of his dojo, dressed in his black uniform. "I never pegged you for a quitter," he said, arms folded. The other boys were laughing on the mat behind him, tumbling all over each other, digging elbows and knees into ribs.

"I guess you're right, that's what I am," I said.

"They still picking on you in school?" he said.

"No," I said, then added, "I have a friend there."

"Sorry I couldn't help you more." As he shook my hand goodbye, he said, "You've got nice soft hands. A real gentleman. Anyone can see that."

On the way home, Mom said that Brad was disappointed to lose me.

"He probably didn't want to lose a paying customer," I said.

"That's a terrible thing to say," she said. "He really liked you. Didn't you know?"

What she was saying didn't seem possible. I hadn't even made yellow belt. Still, now that I thought about it, Brad had been nice about my leaving. Maybe there was more to the guy than I'd given him credit for. Maybe I'd dropped out of karate too soon.

Oh, well. I was free now, and I wasn't going back.

TWO

A COUPLE OF HOURS BEFORE THE basketball game, Ari goes for an extra run. He hates running, but he tells himself that if he runs for half an hour four times a week before trooping off to campus to teach *Special Topics in Medieval History* or *Women of the Middle Ages: Feminism's First Wave?*, then he's allowed the occasional doughnut for breakfast. As a result, he has knee trouble and a small potbelly.

What the hell is he going to do about M? He has to make some kind of decision, the right one, the ethical one. But how can he ruin the man he once believed he'd be spending the rest of his life with? E. M. Forster used to say if forced to choose between betraying my friend or my country, I hope I have the guts to betray my country. Yet this doesn't seem to be the same kind of situation. So what is he going to do? For the time being, he keeps on running.

Ari's neighborhood, called "the Park," is a pleasant enough area northeast of DC that was once working class but is now the kind of place where residents recycle and buy raw water at Whole Foods. The sidewalks are marked with children's chalk drawings of hearts, moons, and stars that wash out with the rain. Sometimes Ari stops to look at these drawings, scanning them for traces of talent, though he himself hasn't picked up a paintbrush or drawing instrument in years.

These days, Ari takes pleasure in art by looking rather than producing, a shift of mind dating back to sophomore year of college, and a required survey class, *Art of the Western World Part I: The Ancient World to the Late Middle Ages*. While cramming for finals, he'd stare at textbook images of stained glass windows and manuscript illuminations, with their broad panes of flat colors. He wanted to know about the people who made these. What were their lives like?

He felt especially drawn to the concept of courtly love. In the early days of Ari's relationship with M, M would quote bits he'd memorized from love poems by Audre Lorde or Thom Gunn while Ari read from Andreas Capellanus's twelfth-century treatise *The Book of the Art of Loving Nobly and the Reproving of Dishonourable Love*:

> *He who is not jealous is not in love.*
> *The lover regularly turns pale before his beloved. His heart pulses.*
> *He rarely eats, sleeps little.*
> *A love easily won is of little value; difficulty makes it valuable.*
> *A true lover thinks of nothing but that which will please the beloved.*
> *When attained, love disappears, like a piece of ice in the fist.*
> *When made public, love fails to endure.*

He's taught these verses so often he knows them by heart. Sadly, they seem especially quaint and amusing in the age of social media, in particular the idea that "When made public, love fails to endure."

Is that why any exchange of genuine emotion seems so rare now, so hard won? Because so much of our lives are lived in public?

Ari's convinced that Orwell was right about Big Brother, but wrong about how such an arrangement would be achieved. No one forces us to live our lives under constant surveillance; we happily give away our privacy without coercion or reward. He used to warn

M about this. "Every time you stream something, you're giving up your information to Big Data, to be tracked."

"Oh, Pooh-bear,"—that was one of M's favorite ironic nicknames for Ari—"you're as addicted to paranoia as I am to online amateur porn."

His neighbor, a single mother with two teenage girls, is tying pink balloons to her porch. She's hosting a Valentine's Day party. Her windows are decorated with cardboard hearts printed with messages like "Be Mine," "Real Love," and the odd "Not Tonite." She waves to Ari, asks when M is coming home. Ari's been spreading the story that M has taken an artist's fellowship at a colony in upstate in New York for the semester.

"Hard to say," Ari pants, pretending he's too out of breath from jogging to talk for long. "He's having a great time up there. Later!"

It's an especially chilly morning for February in suburban DC, and the weather makes Ari lonely. Had he accepted his parents' invitation to visit them this weekend in Florida, he could be running in shorts and a T-shirt. Afterward he'd have to fight for bathroom time with his brother and his wife and their gaggle of chatty children. And at meals, he'd be the odd "plus one," stuck in wherever there was an extra chair. Maybe his parents had only invited him in the faint hope that M might come too.

Also, if he were in Florida, he'd miss the basketball game.

Still puffing his way down the sidewalk, Ari decides to rouse himself from his usual amiably melancholy state of mind. Today isn't a day for doldrums. Today he's going to a basketball game, so rahrah. And today, at this basketball game, he'll see Justin for the first time in twenty years. Rah-rah indeed.

He'd taken up running in college, when he needed to do something for exercise, and the business of trying to find a partner to play tennis was too tedious. He didn't particularly like running, but it had its advantages. No racquet strings to snap on you without warning, no balls to chase, no club memberships or court time to pay for, no partners to let you down by failing to show up, just you against the pavement, running as fast and as hard as you could, as if your life depended on it.

One time, while in grad school at Columbia, he'd been running in Riverside Park, and it had seemed to him his life really had depended on it. He'd stopped to catch his breath, near Grant's Tomb, and caught eyes with a man standing in the trees. A white man in a black denim jacket. Not moving, not even seeming to breathe, staring fiercely at Ari as if he wanted something.

Ari began running again and the man followed, staying in the cover of the trees, but following. So Ari ran faster, and the man ran faster too, weaving in and out of the trees, his sneakers crunching leaves.

What do you want? What the hell do you want from me?

His breath short, his throat closing up, his chest tight, his fingers clenched, Ari cut across an open lawn and under a bridge toward the river. The man still followed. All around them were parents pushing strollers, other joggers, bicyclists, but no one could help Ari, none of them could stop this man from taking what he wanted, if he were bold enough to reach out and take it.

Ari continued running, panicking, unsure of where to go, what to do. He turned haphazardly, zigzagging in different directions, tripped up by a divot in his path, his legs scarred by errant thorny branches, his lungs filling up with the humid air that came off the Hudson River, bearing a strangely cool, metallic scent.

And then he turned around and the man was gone.

He told this story to M, who said, "He was probably just cruising you."

"Or trying to beat me up and grab my wallet," said Ari.

M sighed. "There are men out there who just want to get laid, not to hurt you. They're horny, not criminals. Do you get the difference?"

"Of course," Ari lied. He has never told M about what happened with Mark. So why does M seem to know about it anyway?

ARI TURNS DOWN HIS FAVORITE STREET, a sheltered cul-de-sac of identical homes, all built in the 1920s from a Sears Roebuck kit. There's been talk of landmarking them, but the owners are against the move, which would make the renovation process a pain in the neck.

Does Justin still play tennis? He used to have such a graceful forehand.

Some people run listening to music or podcasts, but Ari prefers his ears naked as it were, to be alone with his own thoughts. And to be alert, in case someone's sneaking up on him. Their area is safe, but he's read reports of crimes on the neighborhood list-serve, and in that free local newspaper that most people throw away but he reads every Thursday, always turning first to the "crime blotter," to learn of the odd burglary, a good many instances of car theft, and the occasional gun sighting. One young woman living alone had witnessed a young man bang her front door open holding a gun. The man, stunned, asked, "What are you doing here?" Then he smacked her across the face. She fell down, blacked out. He took a laptop and some cheap jewelry.

Now, when Ari leaves his house, he turns on the burglar alarm, a few lights, and the television. He bought several signs and nailed them up on the fence around his backyard: "Beware of Dog" and "Warning: this area under video surveillance." But he has no dog. He has no cameras.

HE'D LOOKED UP MARK ONLINE. THE trail has mostly gone cold, but Ari has learned that for many years, Mark lived in New York City, though far from where Ari went to school, in an area of Brooklyn where street signs are printed in Yiddish. He'd written advice columns for parents, for a religious newspaper. Once, he'd talked about the struggles of bringing up adolescent boys, "that age when your body is like a ship at sea, tossed around violently by raging hormones and all you want to do is reach out and touch someone . . . "

SO TODAY IS FINALLY THE DAY of the game, the reunion with Justin, his high school first crush—though maybe crush is too faint a word for what Justin was. Is? No, was. Definitely was. Not crush, but love. That he can freely admit. Love.

And then tomorrow there's another meeting of M's review committee.

The first meeting had been torture. They'd met in one of the older classrooms on campus, which still had a chalkboard and overlooked a barn where agricultural students were looking after cows, pigs, and chickens. Not a place where you'd want to open the windows in nicer weather.

They were a committee of five, four faculty members, one administrator. There was also a student observer with no voting rights, but she had texted the head of the committee five minutes after the start of the meeting with an excuse for why she couldn't make it. She had to meet her mother at the airport. "Have fun without me!"

The proceedings were not too dissimilar from Medieval notions of justice, when the accused might have to hold a hot iron bar and walk several paces, or retrieve a stone from a vat of boiling water. They began with a brief review of the sordid details of the story. A party off-campus, in a house rented by four English majors. In addition to underage drinking and a joint passed around, there'd been a hot tub, and students in varying states of undress getting in and out of the tub, until somehow, as in a game of musical chairs, only M and the student were left, dressed only in their underwear.

The words "hot tub" were articulated with disgust, as if they were the smoking gun.

Ari recalled the story all too clearly, beginning with the confusion of the young man, who at first enjoyed the attentions of his charismatic mentor, the mildly flirty compliments, the excitement of being treated as an intellectual equal by a real working poet who wore purple sneakers to class and was equally at ease making jokes about William Wordsworth or Kim Kardashian. And when the other students disappeared, the poet moved closer, his arm resting on the ledge of the tub, not a long distance from the bare shoulders of the young man, now feeling dizzy from the alcohol, the hot bubbling water, the excitement of being away from home and doing adult things. And now the arm was slipping off the ledge, resting on bare skin, with a gentle presence that felt friendly, familiar, so why not go along with it? Where was the poet's other arm? Under the water, traveling, exploring like Magellan, trying to get to the other side of the world, or at least to crawl up the student's thigh. "You're very sweet," said the poet in a soft voice. "You should have more confidence in yourself. You have so much to offer someone." It almost might have been alright had it stopped there. It was a nice thing to say, right? But then those fingers kept moving. "You're very sweet," the poet said once more. "You said that already," said the student, wishing not to feel that familiar tingle in the groin, the involuntary stiffening. "I don't think we should . . . " "No?" said the poet. "No," said the student. "No?" said the poet again, grabbing hold, now stroking. "Or yes?" "No," said the student. "Just a little longer," said the poet. "See how good it feels, how good I can make you feel. You'll like it."

Who the hell is this treacherous predator, Ari thought. Is he really my husband? Have I helped him in some way, by listening to his stories?

Because in M's retellings of the various romantic exploits of his past, all his partners had been willing, complicit, fun-loving worshippers of Priapus. Listening to him, Ari had always felt like a sex-shaming prude for feeling both uncomfortable yet curious, sometimes even experiencing a vicarious thrill or two. He was convinced that he in fact needed to work on himself, perhaps force himself to initiate sex more often to catch up—or at least subscribe to more porn online. Now he wasn't sure of what he thought. How many of M's stories were in need of some historical revisionism?

"At first, I wasn't even sure what was happening," wrote the complainant. "But later when I got home, it sank in. This was wrong."

How did you figure it out? Ari thought. Even now, years later, I still have to remind myself that what happened to me, the accident or incident, that it wasn't my fault.

One of the members of the committee, an art history professor in a baggy neon wool knit sweater that smelled as if it needed washing, raised her hand to say she was already prepared to render judgment. Her first name was Aimee, and Ari resented its unorthodox spelling.

"But we haven't interviewed the respondent yet," said Ari.

"I don't agree with you. As a woman, particularly a woman of color, I don't believe in being soft on sexual harassment." Aimee, whose skin was paler than Ari's, identified as a woman of color because her equally fair-skinned mother had been born in South Africa to white parents. She also made it known that though she was married to a cis man, she identified as bisexual and disabled. In case there was any mistaking the latter, she carried a cane, which she'd covered in shiny silver duct tape, and made a point of loudly dropping on the floor several times during the meeting. Occasionally she used it while walking, or at least, she tapped the ground with it every so often.

"I bought it at Bed, Bath and Beyond," Aimee told the head of the committee at the beginning of the meeting. "Bed, Bath and Beyond sells the best canes."

"Excuse me, when did I say I was soft on sexual harassment?" Ari asked.

"Well, I just thought, I mean, when you said . . . " she said. "These are real lives at stake. We have to protect our students."

"Yes, but when did I say I was soft on sexual harassment?"

"When you disagreed with me, I thought . . . "

"No, you didn't think," Ari said. "You assumed."

Aimee turned to the head of the committee. "I'd like to finish what I was saying without interruption, without being man-splained."

Ari kept his mouth shut for the rest of the meeting. There had been a time when his queerness had made him an object of fascination, but now queerness was waning out of fashion in academe, having been trumped by disability studies. Anyway, he was glad. He'd never enjoyed being looked at for too long.

In the end, the committee voted three to two to keep the inquiry open until they could hear direct testimony from the claimant and the respondent. The decision surprised Ari since no one said anything openly to indicate that they agreed with him—perhaps they didn't dare. The art history professor often called people out on Twitter. However, he noticed the two that had voted with Ari gave him sympathetic looks while Aimee was preoccupied with dropping her cane on the floor before getting out of her chair.

The battle-lines were becoming clear: Aimee and another committee member leaning toward lowering the boom, Ari and the other two disposed toward leniency. Though Ari could tip the balance the other way with his vote if he so chose.

A mistake of judgment made on a drunken night. A few fateful minutes. Bad enough to end their marriage. Should it also wreck a man's life? Ari feared that he already knew the answer, yet could he trust himself to be impartial? Not just because of his relationship with M, but also that other reason, that horrible history Ari carries with him everywhere.

ARI'S ALMOST AT THE END OF his run, and his cheeks are hot pink, burning from the cold air. There's no one chasing him, though whenever he passes a boy or worse a pack of boys, about the age of fourteen, he feels a deep sense of panic. Sometimes they show up at his front door, carrying boxes of candy to raise money for their high school, or offering to shovel the snow out of his driveway for a few bucks. Every time they ring the bell or pound his door, he freezes, closes his eyes, and waits for them to go away.

And while he's waiting, he reminds himself that he's not a teenager anymore. He's safe.

He recites his mantra over and over, hoping that if he repeats the words enough times, he'll believe them.

The Difference Between Wishing and Wanting

I sat across from Dr. Don, watching the sinking sun burn orange lines through his drawn wood-slat blinds. I heard voices of mothers and fathers from the neighboring homes calling their children inside because it was getting late.

Don asked: "Do you ever think about Mark in any other way?"

Did he have to say that name aloud? "What other way?" I said.

Dr. Don rolled his chair an inch forward. "Do you ever fantasize about him?"

I got where he was going. So he too thought I was guilty, a criminal.

"You're saying he was right?" I asked. "That I wanted it?"

"There's a difference between wishing and wanting," he said, rubbing the arm of his chair. "Things we wish for in fantasy, we don't necessarily hope to become real."

But in my case, I had both wanted and wished for something similar to what had happened with Mark, only different. On a few lonely nights I thought I missed him.

Right before the worst of it, while I was lying on that kitchen floor, my pants down, and his too, Mark knelt beside me, smoothed my hair, whispered into my ear, "Shh, shh, just relax, think of something nice." When he wasn't angry or horny, he could sound very sincere. "Think of something that makes you feel happy," he said in a soft voice, his fingers trailing down my neck, kneading my shoulders. He said it was important for me to relax, asked me to think of a nice trip I'd taken. Had I ever taken a nice trip?

"Once when I was little, we went to Jerusalem," I said.

"Okay," he said, "you're in Jerusalem now. Imagine you're in Jerusalem."

I still thought of that part of the story sometimes, his fingers smoothing my skin. His voice whispering in my ear that I was going to be just fine. Next year in Jerusalem.

College Rock

I surprised and delighted my mother by asking her to take me to the mall. Boys my age didn't generally go to malls clinging to their mothers, but I had no other choice. I wanted that Nirvana record, and I couldn't go alone to a mall. I needed protection.

If Mark was there and had a gun, we were done for. But if he had a knife, then I could ward him off with Mom's purse, just long enough for mall security to tackle him to the ground. Or maybe I could punch him in the nose, the way Sensei Brad had shown me in karate. I imagined the satisfying crunch of his chin hitting the dusty floor tiles.

Our trip was entirely peaceful. The only person at the mall who accosted us was a woman who approached Mom to say, "I love your hair. I just had to tell you."

"Oh!" said Mom, acting startled, as if she didn't get these compliments from strangers all the time. "Thank you. That's very sweet." I should have been proud to walk by her side. My mother was sophisticated. She'd grown up "out East" and wore higher heels than any other woman her age. At home, she kicked off the heels and complained about standards of beauty while chewing a Weight Watchers ice cream bar. Her *ketubahs*, with their supple yet precise Hebrew letters curled around peacocks or the prophetess Deborah strumming a harp, were displayed in synagogue hallways and Jewish gift shops. She visited galleries and drank white wine out of thin glasses. Even her first name, Deanna, sounded exotic and beautiful.

She wanted to know if I was looking for anything in particular. I said I was just browsing, no, nothing in particular. More and more, I took comfort in secrets.

We passed a chain music store, and I asked casually, "Can we stop in here?"

"Sure, sure!" Mom said, sounding too excited.

Inside, she rifled through the cassettes, occasionally pulling one out at random and saying, "Maybe this has some good songs."

I ignored her and approached the cashier. "Hi, there!" I shouted, trying to sound friendly, and the teenage girl behind the register tapped her neon pink nails on the counter. "I was wondering . . . I'm looking for whatever you have by this band . . . Nirvana."

"Who?" The girl wore a green silk button-down shirt and a faux diamond brooch at the collar. Her hair was teased up above her forehead like the pop singer Tiffany, who'd famously launched her career by singing peppy dance tunes in malls like this one.

"Nirvana," I repeated in a small voice.

"Oh Nirvana. Yeah, college rock," she said and pointed me in the right direction.

"What kind of music is this?" Mom asked, frowning at the cover: a baby in a pool swimming toward a fishhook with a dollar bill as bait. The title was *Nevermind*, one word.

"Oh, you know," I said airily. "It's rock."

She handed me back the tape. It was a quiet ride home. I ducked my chin into my scarf and listened to the rush of hot air coming from the car heater on full blast.

In my room, I opened the plastic case, removed the tape and the cover packaging, and unfolded the glossy paper liner to read song titles and fragments of song lyrics printed in black and white. I studied blurry photos of baby-faced drummer Dave Grohl, lanky bass player Krist Novoselic, and then Kurt giving the camera his middle finger.

After "Teen Spirit," the other songs on the album seemed a bit of a letdown on first listen. Some of them seemed merely noise and anger, occasionally punctuated by an eardrum-rupturing guitar riff. Nothing as catchy as that song Justin had played for me. I wondered: was it the song I loved so much or the fact that Justin had played it for me? The slower, quieter songs caught me by surprise, Kurt Cobain's quivering voice a hair above a whisper, as if it were too painful for him to speak. As if he'd survived something worse than I had. As if he needed my sympathy, not the other way around.

There were no liner notes with the words to the songs, so you had to listen carefully to the album to try to pick them out. When the words came through, in bursts, they didn't fit together neatly like a story. Still, they belonged together, a kind of sound collage of resentment. Pick me, please pick me. I'm ugly, but that's okay. No, stay away. A little group of self-assured pricks. A dream, a horny dream. I know it's wrong, but there's nothing I can do. Just stay away. Something's in the way.

As the final slow, somber notes of the last song faded, I leaned back on my bedroom carpet and stared at the ceiling. A worn-out teddy bear from my younger days, slumping on top of a set of bookshelves, stared down at me with its one good eye. The other had fallen out years ago. From his study, my dad was yelling at my mom that she had a phone call. I picked at a hangnail on my thumb, and accidentally drew blood. And then I felt it, the full weight of that album. The moodiness, the exhausted anger.

I flipped the tape over, back to Side 1, and played it again.

The Lumberjack

I watched the video for "Smells Like Teen Spirit" on MTV with rapt attention, trying to match a face to the voice I'd heard in the art room. It was almost as hard to make out Kurt's face as it was to figure out what he was saying. For one thing, the video had been shot in a room filled with a yellow fog, like mustard gas. Also Kurt kept leering sullenly over his guitar, so his stringy, greasy blond hair kept crowding his cheeks, while behind him, cheerleaders in black uniforms performed for a crowd of punk rock kids slamming their bodies into each other and occasionally Kurt himself.

One night I showed up to dinner in a T-shirt over a long-sleeved thermal that I'd dug out of the back of a drawer. Mom had bought it a couple of years ago, hoping that I might try ice-skating. "What are you, a lumberjack?" Dad said.

But I wanted to do worse than shock my parents with my new fashion choices. I wanted to cause real trouble: thrash my head back and forth, jump into a mosh pit, smash a guitar—or perhaps just a kitchen chair.

Later that night, I was leaning against the frame of my bedroom window, staring across the street. Dad paused in my doorway, an empty bowl of ice cream in his hand. He asked what I was looking at.

"Nothing," I lied.

For a brief while, he stood there with the empty bowl balanced on his open palm. "I'm sorry," he said finally. "When I was your age, things like this didn't happen."

"How do you know?" I shot back.

"Maybe you're right," he sighed. "Maybe they did."

Psych 101

David came in from Ann Arbor, wearing a ponytail and threatening to become a vegetarian. He'd decided to major in environmental science.

"What's environmental science?" Dad asked Mom, who was plucking apart David's laundry, separating stinky dirt-streaked whites and stinky dirt-streaked colors with her fingertips. Finally, she just threw it all into the machine at once, with extra soap.

"Max, stop with the curmudgeon act," Mom said, slamming down the washer lid.

But he didn't stop. "No, really. I want to know what someone does with a degree in environmental science. Can't I ask a question?"

"No," said Mom. "Go change your shirt. We're leaving in twenty minutes."

David was here not only so that Mom could do his laundry, but also to join our visit to the brand-new Detroit Holocaust Memorial and Center for Jewish Life, my parents' idea of a family outing.

I pointed out that for the past fifty years, Detroit had been without a Holocaust Memorial. All of a sudden we needed one now. Why?

"Go find your brother," Mom replied. "He's probably still sleeping."

David was stretched out my bedroom floor, not sleeping, but because he said it was healthier than sitting in chairs. His ponytail had come untied, and his long, wavy brown hair framed his head like an electric halo. Also, he wasn't wearing socks and the soles of his feet looked cracked and dirty. *Nevermind* was playing on my stereo. He sat up and turned it off. "I like the single," he said, "but the rest of the album's just okay."

I was angry that he'd played it without my permission, but I said nothing.

"I hear you're taking tennis lessons now," he said.

Now that I wasn't doing karate, I needed another sport to fulfill my Dalton "blue point" requirement, so I'd filled out a form requesting "off-campus sports credit" for taking a tennis clinic at Mom's racquet club. Tennis seemed neither too macho nor too delicate. Also, I liked that tennis players thoughtfully substituted the term "love" for "zero," as if to comfort you when you had nothing.

"Yeah," I said. "And yes, I suck at it."

"Stop doing that to yourself." He pointed at me with a dirty toe. "You making friends at that Dalton?"

"Yeah, sure," I mumbled.

"Seriously. You're my kid brother. I worry about you."

I wished I weren't the kind of kid brother that needed worrying about.

"If that fucker bothers you again, I'll kick his ass," he said. "I should have done it before."

"I'm fine," I said. "I've moved on."

"Wait a second." He closed the door, then lifted a hank of hair above his forehead to show me a divot in his skin with his pinky. "I got this when I was really stoned one night and I hit my head. I told Mom and Dad I tripped on a rug."

"Nice," I said, but I wasn't interested in his story, his typical teenage hijinks, the life I should have had but was missing out on. I'd been robbed of it.

David tilted his head. "You ever tried pot? It's better for you than getting drunk."

"Wow, really deep," I said. "Where did you learn that? In Psych 101?"

"Does being a wiseass all the time make you feel superior?" he said and got up from the floor to find some shoes. "Not a good way to win friends and influence people."

MEMORIAL

THE HOLOCAUST MEMORIAL WAS THE HOTTEST show in town. Tours had been sold out for months. We'd gotten our tickets for free because Mom volunteered for a group that bused Detroit kids out to the Memorial, the way they used to bus students back and forth across Eight Mile to integrate the schools. "Many of them have never met a Jew before," she said, as if to know us were to love us.

The outside of the building, which had been converted from a defunct movie theater, looked like a real concentration camp. They'd even laced decorative barbed wire around the red brick walls. As we entered the exhibit hall, the doors swung shut behind us with a loud slam, and all the lights abruptly went off.

I spun around in the dark, trying to remember how we'd come in. Someone's elbow jabbed my side. I caught a whiff or someone's perfume, a sweet yet prickly scent that reminded me of Mark's favorite cologne. He'd spray it on liberally like mosquito repellent, then jam his wrist into my nose. "Drives the bitches wild," he told me.

Then I started crying. It was so stupid. I didn't even know what triggered it. I felt the darkness pressing my skin like a heavy blanket, muffling my breathing, closing in.

After a few shaky strains of a violin, a string of tiny spotlights flickered to life above the showcases. The few of us already in the know about this special effect—sudden darkness, then fade back to the light—smiled in recognition.

"Was that necessary?" Mom muttered, touching her heart. I wiped my eyes. If anyone noticed they were damp, I could pretend it was the Holocaust that had upset me.

We inspected grainy black and white pictures of Dachau and Auschwitz, and rumpled yellow stars that had been worn by real German Jews, a generous gift of Farmer Jack supermarket. I paused by a row of paintings done by children at Treblinka. Who'd given them paper, watercolors? I felt dizzy, selfish, with no right to my private pain.

Mom, Dad, David, and I followed the exhibit trail until its end in the media room, where a video of five survivor interviews played on a loop. One of them we recognized because his daughter had hired Mom to paint a *ketubah* embellished with flower vines sprouting out of snarls of barbed wire.

Before leaving, we signed our names on the Tree of Life guest-book and dropped a few bucks in the donation box by the exit. Then we drove to Sanders Chocolate and Ice Cream, just as we did after visiting our dead relatives at the cemetery.

"Can't we just go home?" I asked. "Who wants ice cream in winter?"

"It's always a good time for ice cream!" Dad said.

Later, while licking a thread of hot fudge off his spoon, he warned us: "That hatred of Jews is always there, just under the surface." Oddly, he sounded happy to tell us this. Maybe he just liked having all three of us reunited, the usual audience for his performances. "They suck it up in their mothers' milk."

"Mom, tell him to shut up," said David. He untied his ponytail, combed through his long, wavy hair, then tied it up again. A couple of girls watched him and giggled—not because they thought he was weird but because they thought he was cute.

"Really, Max, we're in public," said Mom, scanning the faces in Sanders as she stirred her plain iced coffee. She was on a new diet consisting of "simple" foods. Like the first few weeks of every new diet she tried, it was absolute genius, a new religion—and ice cream wasn't on it. Neither was coffee, but for that, she made an exception.

"In high school, some of the black kids they bused in from the city, they'd never met a Jew before, and they used to toss pennies at our feet to see if we'd pick them up," Dad went on, all revved up now. "If we did, they laughed, and if we didn't, they beat us up. That's how they ruin schools, and then neighborhoods. That's the story of Detroit."

"The black kids?" David repeated, shifting uncomfortably in his tiny black metal chair, too small for his long body. He was even taller than Dad now. "Dad, do you even hear yourself? Detroit has some very nice neighborhoods."

"Oh, yeah?" said Dad. "You want to move there?"

"Why not? My friends who go to Wayne State say it's nice."

Dad snorted. "So Ann Arbor has turned you pinko."

"Because I'm a Democrat? Democrats are not Communists," said David.

"No," Dad replied. "A Democrat is a Republican who hasn't grown up."

They started arguing about Bill Clinton, who was on *60 Minutes* to explain the pain he'd caused in his marriage. Dad said he was tired of hearing about sex on the news. David said we were all Puritans and prudes. Mom said she was for Ross Perot.

The little bell over the door rang and a crowd of boys my age came in, stomping their Timberland boots. They were arguing about a girl, or about several girls, in loud, heated voices. No, they were arguing about dicks. "Yours is so small, it's going to dry up and shrivel off," one of them said. I was eyeing another boy. He had Mark's same hair, those same shoulders, the way of walking. But it couldn't be. Mark was in Canada, right? Or had he slipped back across the border? I leaned back in my chair and stretched my neck to see.

"Ari, be careful!" Mom said, too late. The chair legs gave way from under me and I was on the floor. "Are you alright?" She bent down next to me, held my elbow. Everyone was staring. Those boys too. They probably thought my dick was small.

"I'm fine," I said as a spike of soreness shot up my left hip. "Can we go? Now."

* * *

AT HOME, I RETREATED TO MY room, put on the cheerfully melancholy song "Like the Weather" by 10,000 Maniacs, and tried to imagine the goyim I knew from Dalton sucking up Jew-hatred in their mother's milk. None of them seemed like the type. Certainly not Justin, who commuted to Dalton from somewhere below Eight Mile. Or sweet Old Mr. Hoffman, our Headmaster Emeritus, who in his retirement still wandered the halls wearing a bowtie and an amused smile.

In my experience, it had been Jews who were dangerous. I preferred to take my chances with the *goyim*, the anti-Semites.

Someone knocked at the door, and I jumped. "I'm going back to Ann Arbor," David called out. "Aren't you going to see me off?"

So I grabbed a jacket and followed him to the front door, then stopped there as he went to his car. Rabbi Taborsky's empty convertible was parked in front of their house. The top had been left down even though it was winter.

"Come on," said David.

"I'm fine where I am," I said.

"Just get out here," said David.

My knees went wobbly as I stepped down from our front porch, and I felt a rush of cool air between my temples. I picked my way across the driveway as if the asphalt were covered in ice, though it hadn't snowed in a week, and it was almost fifty out. The gutters of our house and the tips of the trees were dripping with melting ice and snow.

David threw his laundry in the trunk, then slammed it closed. "You should come visit me in Ann Arbor sometime. I've got an extra bed in my room."

"Sure." What if Mark was at home right now? He might see me and come outside, just to show me that he could. Please keep him in, I prayed. I was too nervous to look beyond our property lines. Instead I focused on the worn tips of David's boots.

"You know," David said, "my roommate is gay. He's got all these posters of guys everywhere in my room. He said he'd take them down, if it bothers me, but I don't care. Actually, my girlfriend thinks they're hot."

"Why are you telling me this?" Finally, I couldn't stand the suspense. I sneaked a glance across the street, saw no one. David saw me looking, and then he looked too.

"Because this neighborhood where we live, it's so stiff, so monocultural. Fuck, we might as well live in the Warsaw Ghetto. But in college, all the shit that matters so much here doesn't matter there. You won't be stuck here forever."

"Don't forget your new socks," Mom said, running outside with a plastic shopping bag, then she saw me and froze. "Well," she said, "you're out here too."

At that moment I hated her, for noticing.

David grabbed the socks, which he promised to wear himself, rather than give to the first homeless person in his path. He looked across the street again. "You let me know if that kid even thinks of bothering you again," he told me. Mom turned her head, searching in vain for a stray piece of lint on her perfectly clean sweater.

"Thanks," I muttered.

"I can get you a pair of brass knuckles." David made a fist and slammed it into his left hand. "Hit him just once with those. Bam!"

I shuddered at the impact of fist to palm.

David hit his own hand once more. "Bam!" he said. "He'll leave you alone."

LOLLAPALOOZA

AFTER OUR VISIT TO THE HOLOCAUST Memorial, Mom began describing Jewish youth group activities I could join: skating and kosher pizza, an evening of Israeli dancing, and the "March of the Living." If I worked hard enough, I might get to visit Auschwitz.

"No, no, and no," I said to all of them.

The dangers of Jewish geography: someone in those groups had to know Mark. Anyway, I didn't want to go to Auschwitz. I wanted to see the Lollapalooza tour, which stopped in Detroit every summer and would be coming here again in July.

From the clips I'd seen on MTV, I'd gleaned that Lollapalooza was something special, more than just a group concert or a touring music festival. It was a carnival populated by friendly, untroubled non-Jewish kids who waved to the camera with sunny smiles or twirled in sack-like dresses or hopped up and down in black Converse sneakers like They Might Be Giants in the video for "Birdhouse in Your Soul." At Lollapalooza, you could hear the bands whose music videos I watched on *120 Minutes* on MTV, not just Nirvana, but also R. E. M., They Might Be Giants, Simple Minds, Luscious Jackson, and Michael Stipe's girlfriend Nathalie Merchant and her 10,000 Maniacs. Men with over-sized dark-framed glasses, women with short greasy hair. Musicians of both sexes who dressed in thrift store clothes and danced in jerky, unpredictable steps.

At Lollapalooza, you could blow bubbles or dye your hair fluorescent blue or weave dream catchers or get a tattoo. You could eat Thai food.

But how would I make it all the way out to Pine Knob Music Theatre and Fairgrounds? Getting a ride from Mom would have been too shameful. David wouldn't be interested. He only liked music made by guitar-playing white guys between 1960 and 1975. And buses didn't go out there. One afternoon while my parents were out, I called a taxi company to check the price for a round trip. The dispatcher called me "ma'am" and told me the ride would cost two hundred bucks, an impossible sum.

I bet Justin would be going. His alternative friends would give him a ride, no problem. If only I could get there too, just so he'd see me strolling the grounds of Lollapalooza. Then he might finally recognize we were on the same team.

But this was all a fantasy. I'd never make it to Lollapalooza. I could barely make it past our front porch.

Finally, Mom decided she'd had enough of my excuses and signed me up to join a Sunday afternoon teen trip to *Lazer Zone!*. Apparently, the God of Abraham, Isaac, and Jacob wanted Jewish teens to play laser tag, noisy arcade games, and contests of strength and skill where guys could win stuffed animals to give to some girl they liked, though if I'd been good enough at games to win a plush stuffed animal, I'd have kept it for myself.

I wore an old army jacket I'd found in our basement, a striped shirt two sizes too big for me, my dirtiest pair of jeans, and a pair of black Converse sneakers, my best imitation of Kurt's outfit in the "Teen Spirit" video. Still, my look seemed off. I didn't appear wounded or defiant. More like a kid in a hand-me-down Halloween costume.

Mom squinted at me. "Are the other boys dressing this way? Is that the style now?"

"I don't know." I was still unsure whether this outfit really fit this new style I was trying to cultivate. It was so easy to make mistakes. "I just like it."

As we pulled up to the Jewish Community Center, I kept hoping that by some miracle she might turn the car around, say it was all a joke. "You promise you'll be back right at four?" I asked. "You won't be late?"

Lazer Zone! was just inside the Detroit city limits, and while lining up for the bus, we were instructed not to open the windows. The boys dared each other to do it anyway, said anyone who wouldn't was a pussy and a homo. Gripping a small sketchpad, I shuffled back and forth beside them in my new black Converse, their soles as flat and hard as boards. They looked cool, but they killed my feet and smelled of burnt rubber.

The few of my former Stern classmates in attendance were kind enough to ignore me until Elise Fein stepped in my way to ask, "Where have you been?"

I recited my enrichment excuse, but she cocked her head and crossed her arms. "I heard you called the cops on Mark Taborsky."

My brain went black. I dropped my sketchbook on the sidewalk.

I wanted to explain that I didn't mean to call the cops. I didn't mean anything, didn't think anything while balled up on the kitchen floor, my back against the cupboards, my jeans bunched around my ankles, the inside and outside of my body feeling scraped and sore. Mark stood over my waist in triumph, his belt buckle jangling.

That's when I saw the panic button by the back door. We had two of those buttons, one here and one in the front hall. Dad warned me never to press either because if you called in a false alert, the alarm company charged a hundred dollars.

I pressed it anyway. I'll pay the hundred dollars, I thought, even a thousand dollars. I'd earn the money by doing chores for the rest of my life, whatever it cost. It didn't occur to me that I had genuine cause for panic.

A loud, angry noise cut through my ears, a chorus of chainsaws buzzing in rhythm.

"Turn that off, you fucking faggot!" said Mark.

"There's no way to turn it off," I told him, which thank God was the truth.

"Jesus," he said, which I remember thinking was an odd thing for a rabbi's son to say. He crammed his feet into his shoes—somehow they'd come off—then took off.

Elise Fein was still there, arms folded, face sullen and drawn. She wanted an answer. She heard that I'd called the cops. Apparently, I'd violated some unwritten eleventh commandment: Thou shalt not snitch on thy fellow kid. She had this dark look in her eyes, this feeling of contempt, and I wondered if the others innocently milling around, waiting to board the bus, felt it too. They all hated me. They all knew.

And I hated them too. So much that I could no longer see or think straight. I told Elise, "Oh, yeah? You know what I heard? I heard you give blow jobs for five bucks."

Her face crumpled. "Fuck you," she said.

"I heard you would, for ten bucks," I said. Where had those words come from? They seemed to just slide through me, as if from a ventriloquist.

Elise fell out of line and ran away. "What's with her?" someone asked. I stood my ground, held my place in line, felt the blood rush into my cheeks and the universe get very quiet as I studied a tiny weed trying to push through a crack in the sidewalk. When it was my turn to board the bus, I heard two girls debating whether they should check on her. I got on and took my seat alone, up front near the driver.

The door closed. The engine started. Elise hadn't made it. Too late for me to apologize. And anyway, why should I? We rolled slowly, softly, away from the Jewish Community Center, toward Detroit. A pack of boys behind me were trading the secrets of skee ball. I took out my Walkman, put on "Smells Like Teen Spirit," and tried to sketch the contours of my painful new Converse shoes, but my feet wouldn't stop shaking.

* * *

"I'm still not understanding what you did wrong," said Dr. Don in that infuriatingly calm voice of his at our next appointment, the day after my trip to *Lazer Zone!*. Was he just pretending to be a dunce?

How had we even gotten on to this topic? I'd started off the session telling him what Ms. Hunter had said about my drawings of bodies, how they were out of proportion. She said every body was seven heads tall. I wanted to know if Don agreed.

But then in that weird way of his, Dr. Don led us skipping like frogs from conversational lily pad to lily pad, from Ms. Hunter and bodies to my body and then by some weird path, to Elise Fein, who'd sensed somehow that I had caused the accident.

"How did you cause it?" Don asked.

"I called him a fag," I said. "That's what set him off. I shouldn't have said that."

The morning before the incident or accident or whatever you wanted to call it, Benji Pearlberg had witnessed Mark talking to me, and Benji said something, I couldn't remember the exact words, but something like you two are hanging out a lot lately. What are you, friends? Alarmed that he'd guessed what we were doing in that storage room, I said no, no, a thousand times no. "Mark hates me," I'd said, and desperate to prove it, I added, "He calls me a fag." And then Benji asked me snidely if I was one. He probably meant it as a stupid joke. "No way," I'd told him, panicking. "If anyone's a fag, he is."

"And did you think it was possible he was a homosexual?" said Dr. Don.

"Of course not!" I said. "He has girlfriends. He does things with them."

"And he did those things with you too. Maybe he's confused."

"That's the last thing he is," I said. "He's very sure."

"You merely voiced an opinion," said Dr. Don. "Those were just words."

"I wasn't careful enough to see who might be around, who might be listening," I said, annoyed at Dr. Don for being so dense.

In fact, I forgot about our conversation until the end of the day, when I took the bus home from school. Climbing down the steps of that bus, I heard, "Hey, fag!" The bus drove off and there was Mark, pacing at the edge of his lawn.

"Where were your parents?" Dr. Don asked.

Dad was taking care of strangers' teeth and Mom was volunteering at a mixed school just inside Eight Mile, where she showed prints of famous paintings to "darling black children, very nice manners, so quiet."

"I said, hey, fag!" Mark sprinted across the road and up our lawn, his checkerboard-print Vans spraying stones all over our lawn. Later, I'd have to collect the stones or they'd kill the grass.

No time to escape, no place to run. No neighbors in front of their big houses with their sprawling lawns. Our subdivision had no sidewalks, and the mothers didn't like pushing strollers in the street. "Too ghetto," one of them told my mom, who nodded in sympathy. People complained there was no community feeling here.

"I heard you said I was a faggie," said Mark, so close behind me he could have stepped on my heels. He wore his glasses, which I took as a bad sign. Usually he was too vain to wear them in public. "I ought to slice off your balls."

"No, no," I said. "I never." I turned and walked calmly toward my empty house, like a child who believes that what he can't see doesn't exist. My head was throbbing. My foot slipped on a stray twig, but I caught my balance.

Mark put up his fists, dug one of them into my shoulder. "Oh, yeah you did. Let's see who's the real faggie here. Let's duke this out, once and for all." He stuck out his shoulder. "Just tap me here. Unless you're too much of a faggot to hit me."

The magic words. I couldn't let them stand. I closed my eyes, made an awkward fist, and jabbed his shoulder.

"Oh, you want to fight, faggot? Okay, let's fight." His fist flew into my stomach. I'd never been hit before, not seriously, and the shock hurt almost as much as the pain. As I strained to catch my breath, he hit me again, then again, hard and fast, backing me up against a flowering eucalyptus. I bit my tongue so hard, I drew blood. I buried my face behind my hands as his fists sought out the soft spots on my body, his arms moving so fast and with such fury that his glasses rolled down his nose and hit the ground.

"Fuck!" he said, picking them up. A loose earpiece swung foolishly from the frame. "You broke my glasses."

I ran to the porch, but he followed behind me. As I fumbled with my key, he asked, "You aren't inviting me in? That's the least you could do after breaking my fucking glasses."

"I'm not allowed to have guests when my parents aren't home," I said. The key slipped through my fingers into a potted begonia. Mark grabbed it, snapping off one of the blossoms. "Give it back," I said, reaching awkwardly as he held it over my head. Why was there no one out on the street? No witnesses at all . . .

"Now are you going to let me in?"

I was crying now. "I told you . . . " I tried to say.

"You have two choices. If you don't let me in, I'll kill you right now. If you let me in, I'll think about it."

I couldn't think. I didn't think. I chose to let him in.

After I closed the door behind us, he punched me in the stomach, and I crumpled backwards onto the carpet. "I thought about it," he said. "I decided to kill you."

Embarrassed, I looked up at Dr. Don to see his reaction. Now he knew what a simpering weakling I was, how much I was to blame.

"Have you ever considered the possibility that you did the right thing," he said. "You thought you were going to die. You protected yourself. You're still alive."

"Alive, but look what he did to me. What I let him do . . . "

"You did what you had to," he said. "You survived. I think you're very brave."

And you're supposed to be a psychologist? I wanted to say. You're crazy. "I don't know how I'm supposed to answer that."

"Let's not say anything," said Dr. Don. "Let's just sit here a while, think it over."

For the remainder of the session, we sat in our chairs as the paints and inks and clay on his shelves dried, and shaggy piles of paper on his desk fluttered occasionally in the breeze of the vents. I stared at some little kid's drawing of a crude angry-looking sun in red crayon. Dr. Don chewed at one of his nails, then stopped. Don's getting off easy, I thought, getting paid just to sit there and say nothing, but I knew that wasn't my true feeling. Just a passing thought, like so much of what ran through my head these days. Thoughts, feelings, it was hard to tell the difference anymore.

Study Buddies

In school, I mouthed my version of the lyrics to "Smells Like Teen Spirit" over and over as I walked the halls. Since I couldn't quite make out the real words, I'd invented my own: "When the lights are out, it'll change us! Here we are now, imitate us! Acting stupid is contagious! Here we are now, imitate us!"

Maybe I was imagining it, but Dalton really seemed different now that winter was almost over. There was a frisky undercurrent of rebellion in the air. Boys wore orange, red, and yellow socks with their dress shoes. Girls hiked their tube skirts just above the knee. Gum-chewing was rampant. Coaches said we weren't giving enough effort at practice. Ms. Hunter complained that we weren't putting the caps back on her paint tubes.

Students strolled into classes a full minute after the second bell, and then two minutes. A pep assembly was canceled after a few stoners drowned out the standard school cheer with a rowdy rendition of "How I Could Just Kill a Man" by Cypress Hill.

Whenever they passed a male faculty member, the seniors on our championship basketball team would pretend to cough and then say, "Homo!" just under their breath, and then a few seconds later burst into hysterical laughing. Finally their coach called a special meeting and ordered them to stop. Apparently he said, "Magic Johnson has AIDS. You want to call Magic Johnson a homo?"

And then suddenly, Demuth and his minions were everywhere. There were spot checks for gum, white socks, and short skirts. Our football coach threatened to disband the entire team if they didn't lose an average of five pounds per player. In art, Ms. Hunter no longer allowed us to listen to music, and there was no more paint, just oil crayons and colored pencils. The detention room was flooded with petty criminals, condemned for snickering during the fall choral concert, dawdling during a tornado drill, or changing the words of the school cheer "Fear the Eagle Claw" to "Eat My Wiener Raw."

In the midst of this crackdown, I received a terrifying note in homeroom: Dean Demuth wanted to see me.

While trudging to the office, I touched the knot of my tie to ensure it was in place, and checked my socks, which were regulation black. Nothing wrong there. My fantasies of delinquency seemed so much more glamorous as long as they remained fantasies.

"Hello, Ari," Demuth said, adjusting the green shade of his banker's lamp so it shone in my face. "You're growing into quite a young man."

"Thanks," I mumbled, embarrassed and flattered that he'd noticed. I sat and waited while he scribbled on a notepad. What had I done wrong? Why the mystery?

After a dramatic pause that felt planned, the Dean said, "They say when a bone breaks, it's stronger in the place that heals than before it was broken."

I shriveled in my chair. He meant well, but what had happened with Mark was nothing like breaking a bone. A real man broke a bone while going out for a long pass on a football field or nailing up a roof. Dad liked to say that Jews didn't break bones, and in my case, he was right: my bones were the same ones I'd been born with.

Demuth went on. "We're hoping you might be part of a new peer tutoring program, called Study Buddies. The idea is that maybe you're strong in one area, while another student is strong in another, so you each can support the other."

"Happy to help, sir," I yelped, so relieved to be back in his protective good graces that when Demuth told me the name of my Study Buddy, it took me a few seconds to realize he'd said "Justin Jackson." I'd tutor him in history, while he'd help me with math.

"Oh!" I said, as if I'd sat on a tack. I saw the two of us sitting side by side, his head bent over a book. I'd try to look too, try to concentrate on the lesson, but then an evil spirit would take possession of my body. I'd pull his head close, kiss his cheek, and then he'd shove me to the ground, stomp on my face until it was flattened.

"Justin's a good kid," Demuth said. "A bit of a wisecracker, but nothing you can't handle."

That's right, I thought. I'm tough. Tough as a broken bone.

* * *

"What if you invited Justin to hang out sometime?"

I supposed nothing Dr. Don should have startled me anymore. Still, my pen skidded across my sketchbook, running right off the page.

It was an unexpectedly warm day, and we were sitting on lawn chairs in his backyard—it was like having class outside. I was sketching the daffodils, which were just starting to bloom, silly, frilly things, nothing like the hardy geraniums and begonias my mother preferred. In the middle of his flowerbed, Don had stuck a Pope John Paul II lawn sprinkler, with an image of the pontiff, hands outstretched, and the words, "Let us spray."

"Justin's just a kid I talk to sometimes in school," I said. "We're study partners."

"Does that mean you couldn't be friends?"

"We're not in the same circle."

"Did he say that to you?"

"I just can't," I said. "No matter what you say."

"Are you afraid he'd hurt you?"

"No, no, he'd never do that. He's not like that at all. He's nice."

"So then why couldn't he be your friend?"

Don had it all wrong. I wasn't afraid of what he would do, but of what I might do or say in some unguarded moment.

Finally I told him: "If you don't understand, then I can't explain it to you."

Chocolate from Israel

Because we all dressed alike, one way that guys at Dalton stood out was by grooming their hair, usually with lots of gel. You could spike it on top or let it grow long in back, the ends flirting with the collars of our blazers. No longer, or a Dean would send you for a haircut. The basketball team favored the "hi-top fade," like Will Smith in *Fresh Prince of Bel-Air*, while our swim team shaved their heads. When I first saw them, for a second I worried that Dalton had been invaded by those neo-Nazi skinheads they warned about in the *Jewish News*.

Before my first tutoring session with Justin, I searched for a tube of gel at the drugstore, but they had too many hair products and I was afraid of accidentally buying a brand for girls. Instead I sprinkled my hair with warm water and tugged it toward the ceiling. The result was such a mess that I finally just pushed it flat again.

We'd been scheduled to meet in the Dining Hall, an hour before lunch. Walking in with my boring hair, I smelled something greasy and breaded being warmed in the kitchen. Not a good smell, but it made me hungry. Hopefully it wasn't pork.

Justin was by the salad bar, his smooth head nestled on one arm, eyes screwed shut, a small black button pinned to his lapel. No more briefcase—he'd given up that affectation. Now he carried his books in an army surplus duffel bag, big enough to conceal a rifle and painted in Wite-Out with names of bands I didn't know. He snored softly and his cheeks looked very full. I wondered what was in his dreams.

Finally Justin yawned, stretched his long, thin arms, and said, "Hey, Brain." His wrists were so delicate, I could have circled my index finger and thumb around them like a bracelet. "I know you're good at French. How's your history?"

I wanted to show Justin my new apathetic persona, inspired by several listens to *Nevermind*. "Not bad or whatever, I guess," I said.

My history grade was 105 out of 100. The other five points were for extra credit.

He said, "I asked for you," and the back of my neck felt very hot. "Can you get me a A?"

Though we tutors were supposed to always reward effort and never promise results, I blurted out the wrong answer, "Yeah, sure. Whatever."

"I can't lose my scholarship." As he leaned back in his chair, his dress shirt came untucked from his pants, but he didn't tuck it back in. "I got A's in math, science, even English. But history . . . what's the point? All those dead people."

That was just what I liked about it. Dead people were harmless. Hitler himself wasn't half as scary as Justin now, waiting for me to get him an A in history.

"Not everyone can be good at every subject," I said, immediately aware that I sounded like Barney the purple dinosaur. "I mean, I totally suck at math." Not exactly true, but math wasn't my best subject. "It's like, boring."

"Boring!" he said. "Without math, this table, this room, this school, this whole universe wouldn't even exist."

"Anyway, I suck at it."

"It's nothing to be good or bad at. Just follow the rules. I'll show you."

I held out a piece of candy, like a peace offering. "Here," I said. "This is for you. It's chocolate, from Israel. It's called Pesek Zman. That means Free Time."

Justin's sleepy eyes widened, and he traced the unfamiliar Hebrew letters on the wrapper with his slender finger. "I never saw anything from Israel."

"No big deal," I said. "My mom buys tons of them for this dumb fundraiser for our synagogue. Like God's going to give her brownie points for buying candy." I hoped I sounded genuinely apathetic, not just like I was doing a good job of faking it.

"Brain, you're the best," he said and my chest flooded with pleasure. He eyed the kitchen ladies struggling with their foil-wrapped bins. At Dalton, there was a rule against consuming any food outside of lunch. "I'm starving. I wish I could eat this right now."

"This school has too many dumb rules," I said, which was a lie. I was grateful for the rules because they made me feel safe and gave us students a common enemy in our administration. "Go ahead. I'll make sure no one's watching."

Justin slowly unfolded the wrapper, taking care not to tear the Hebrew lettering. As I held open the wings of my blazer to block the view, he wolfed down his candy and explained through chocolate-stained teeth that he often fell asleep in his first period history class because it took him an hour to get to school. He woke up at half-past five every morning and ate breakfast at six.

"I wish I had something else for you," I said, forgetting my apathy again. Maybe I could tie a black thread around my finger to remember.

"Nah, this is good." He licked the chocolate that had melted on the inside of the foil wrapper. Why couldn't his alternative friends ever try to sneak him food? They didn't deserve his company.

I lowered my voice and flattened out the tone, trying to sound bored, emotionless, like Kurt Cobain in his MTV interviews. "So, I guess we're supposed to study or something. Who goes first? Math or history?"

"History. Might as well get this over with." He handed me his textbook.

"Hey, you're doing the Julio-Claudian emperors!" I said. "I mean, they're almost interesting, in a dumb sort of way."

Justin rewarded me with a theatrical yawn.

To prove my point, I told him about Tiberius, destroyer of Jerusalem and number one enemy of the Jews before the Nazis. I described the depravity of the dying emperor's court in Capri before moving on to his successor, the flamboyant Caligula, the orgies, bestiality, and incest. It was one of the longest conversations I'd had since I'd been at Dalton, and I enjoyed the sound of my own voice, as well as Justin's rapt attention. "The Romans would, you know, screw anything," I said, hoping to shock him.

"Cool," said Justin.

"Yeah, cool except if you were a slave and you were forced to have sex, like with some old woman, or a dog." I swallowed. "Or another man."

"I'd tell them to fuck off."

"What if they forced you?" I asked, my voice rising like a girl's. Cringing, I cleared my throat, then added in a flat baritone, "If they forced you, what would you do?"

"Depends on how attractive the dog was." No, I thought. I meant what if they forced you with a man, then what would you do? I must have made a weird face, because he snickered and said, "Relax, Brain. I was just making a funny."

"Oh, yeah. I knew that," I said, my tightened stomach muscles relaxing.

"You sure are nervous," he said.

"No, I'm not."

"Is it some Jewish thing? Because they cut off your wiener after you're born?"

I slammed my book shut. "Whatever."

Justin shook his head. "Seriously, Brain, you need to lighten the fuck up."

Lighten up, lighten up. I had to practice at lightening up, like practicing a forehand for tennis. Maybe they had drills for that.

* * *

I TOLD DON I THOUGHT I needed to lighten up and he laughed. I must have looked hurt because he said, "I'm sorry, I was just surprised, that's all."

"That's exactly what I mean," I said. "I want to laugh more, especially when other people laugh, like you just did, not be so sensitive all the time."

"We all want that for you too, Ari," he said. "Would it help if you knew that?"

Just a Religion

THREE TIMES A WEEK, JUSTIN AND I met by the salad bar, studying equations and Romans while kitchen ladies brought out clanking metal vats of pale iceberg lettuce, flabby cucumber slices, and shredded carrots. I drew him a cartoon of a Dalton student writhing in agony from food poisoning in the cafeteria. Once, Justin sneaked over to the bar and arranged the vegetables into the shape of a giant question mark. Another time, he stole two cucumber slices and put them on his eyes. "So beneficial for the complexion," he said in a British accent that made me giggle. By then, I'd given up my apathy act.

The outside wall of the Dining Hall was taken up entirely by windows facing the baseball and lacrosse fields, and beyond those, a grove of oaks and maples whose tiny leaves were tinted sour apple green leaves. It was my first spring at Dalton, when the campus was at its most picturesque, with the dogwood trees blooming pale pink and rows of red and purple tulips shooting up around the school walls. Justin pointed out a team of photographers on the grass, taking beauty shots of the building for promotional material. Several of our best-looking students posed casually with their books on the lawn.

As we huddled over our homework, I imagined the two of us going for long walks and discussing Nirvana, the sunlight spilling over his shoulders, our dress shoes crunching through dried leaves and twigs, our hair dusted with pollen. Between quadratic equations or the sack of Rome, occasionally our wrists bumped or our feet touched. When Justin had a cold, I heard his labored breathing like a tiny saw in my ear. When he bent over the map in the book to trace the routes of various barbarian tribes, I dreamed of resting my chin on his shoulder. Some guys in school smelled of cologne or sweat or cocoa butter, but Justin's body smelled like mine, which was to say, it seemed to have no particular smell, which was what I liked.

A few times, I left my *Nevermind* cassette on the table. Then I hummed a few bars from "Smells Like Teen Spirit." He didn't seem to catch on. Finally, while Justin was prepping me for a math quiz, I burst out with: "You know, you introduced me to Nirvana."

"What?" he said.

"When you played that song in the art room, I never heard their music before."

"Okay," he said in a slow, slightly impatient voice, the way he sounded when I couldn't follow one of his algebra explanations. "Why are you telling me this?"

"Because," I faltered. Because this conversation was supposed to have been a moment of connection and instead it had only brought awkwardness. "I was wondering what you thought of the new stuff."

He leaned back in his chair, stretched out his long legs, like a pair of field hockey sticks. "That song was okay the first million times I heard it. I like the first album better, the one that didn't sell. Now they're just ripping off The Pixies. Even Cobain admits it."

"Ripping them off, how exactly?" I asked, embarrassed that I didn't know who The Pixies were or how one might rip them off.

"You know, the whole loud, soft, then loud again."

"And The Pixies have a copyright on that?"

Justin laughed. He laughed at a lot at things that I said, which I liked, even if it was at my expense. "You know, it's okay to like who you like."

But I wanted to like who he liked.

"Okay, back to work. Let me see your last homework," he said.

I gave it to him. I'd earned a B–. "Sloppy." He shook his head.

"I mostly got the right answers."

"Yeah, but in math, it's about how you got the answer. First rule of math, you got to be neat." He showed me some of his homework, neat as a work of art.

I followed Justin's directions and soon my math grades shot up, though Justin's history grades remained stagnant. His problem was when a subject didn't interest him, he'd try to distract me with wise-cracks. To hold his attention, I tried gladiators, Roman orgies, and candy, emperors wearing gold coronets or fragrant laurels, but what really fascinated him was the fish-and-onion-stinking culture I'd grown up with.

"Tell me the real dope about being Jewish," he said.

"No, I don't have horns," I said wearily.

"Duh. I ain't that dumb."

"Okay, I'll make you a deal. For every lesson you learn about the Romans, I'll tell you something about Judaism."

"You're on, Brain," he said.

And so, after an explanation of Nero and the burning of Rome, I asked, "What do you want to know first?"

He paused. "What is Jewish exactly? A race or just a religion?"

I chose "Just a religion," which seemed like an evasion.

As we moved from the Julio-Claudian dynasty to Constantine, Justin asked about the Jewish New Year, which he called "Rash Hashashashnash." Yom Kippur became "Yam Keeper" and "Hanukkah" was "chuh-NEW-ka." I loved that.

Once, I brought him a Kit Kat instead of the Israeli candy. "Thanks," he said, chewing with his mouth open. "But tomorrow, just bring the Jewish one."

Another time, he brought in a mezuzah wrapped tightly in crinkled tin foil. "I found it at our church. I never showed it to anyone, not even my dad."

"Why was it in your church?" I asked.

"It used to be a temple, or a what did you call it? A school?"

"A *shul*."

"Yeah, a *shul*. Before the '67 rebellion." I realized he meant the riots, which in my house were the original source of all evil. "I ask you all the time about where you come from," said Justin. "How come you don't want to know about where I'm from?"

"But I do want to know," I lied. Detroit represented all our differences, and I wanted as few of those as possible. To me, Justin was from Lollapalooza, not Detroit.

Justin seemed pleased by my answer. He pushed his chair back so the front legs floated in air, the way teachers warned against doing. "Ask me anything."

"Well," I said, stalling, "what's your opinion . . . about the rebellion?"

"My dad says it didn't work because it turned into something else. Rebellion against racism is one thing, but when you steal radios or shoes, that completely negates the whole concept. And then white people were looting too. Nobody talks about that."

"My grandparents used to live in the city," I admitted. "Now we're all out here. They think it's safer." Safer, I thought. Directly across the street from my enemy, that was safe. Yet far away, lost in the violent and dangerous wilderness of Detroit where Justin lived, Mark would never dare come look for me.

"You guys need to stop isolating yourselves in one area like Bloomfield," said Justin. "Spread yourselves around so people can get to know you. People talk all kinds of shit about Jews where I live."

I thought of Dad's theory of anti-Semitism and mother's milk. What if Justin had sucked up just a drop or two of hatred?

"Isn't that racist?" I asked Justin.

I worried that I'd offended him, but he seemed more surprised than offended, maybe even sad. His face looked long and doleful, like a saint in a stained glass window of a cathedral, and I almost changed my mind. He didn't know that I sketched him when he wasn't looking, from the side or the back of his head. I liked his kind of handsomeness, the kind that only I recognized, and could keep all to myself.

"Black people can't be racist. Racism is about power. When a white person calls a black racist, I know the basis they're thinking on. Blacks can be prejudiced or bigoted, but not racist because the power isn't there."

"What power do I have?" I asked.

"The power to walk into any store and not be afraid," he shot back.

"You're wrong," I said, and for a moment it was as if I were stepping outside of myself and watching myself speak. "I feel afraid all the time. Even here at this school."

"Why, what are you afraid of?" he asked.

He had this soft, understanding look on his face, and for a second or two, I wanted badly to tell him the truth. But then the moment passed, and my soul returned to the prison of my body. "Maybe I'm just the nervous type."

"You should ask yourself if it's worth it, being afraid so much."

"Why? Because it's a waste of my white privilege?"

Justin laughed so hard that he started coughing. I patted his back and asked if he wanted some water. "Nah, I'm fine," he said.

"Alright, so what do you think about Jews?" I asked.

He stopped laughing, and I saw a hurt look in those sad, funny eyes of his. "Come on, Brain," he said. "Don't you know me?"

No, I didn't. How could I? At the end of our tutoring session, we got up from our table separately as usual, allegedly to put our books back in our lockers or go to the bathroom. But our real purpose was to re-enter the Dining Hall at different times and sit far apart, at our respective tables.

Justin sat with hipsters who sneaked in thermoses of espresso and argued about bands with mysterious names like Sonic Youth or Husker Du. One of them had dyed his hair a ghostly shade of blond that almost faded into his pale skin. He'd told the deans that it was his natural hair color, and until now he'd been dyeing it brown. Justin and his crowd laughed a lot. They knew the secrets of conversation.

I occupied the end of a table of stoners who bantered endlessly about the Grateful Dead, Cheech & Chong, bong water, and their favorite time of day, 4:20. Perhaps by sitting with them, I prevented a bigger social misfit from taking my place. I'd smile, laugh, wrinkle my nose on cue, usually not knowing why. Each day before school, I prayed for the health of my seatmates because if one was sick, I had to move closer to the center of the table and maybe say something funny.

Once, I impressed them by mentioning an Alice in Chains song that Justin had played for me. But then someone said, "Kurt Cobain's a whiny heroin-addicted homosexual fag who ruined rock," and I cried out, "No, he's not!" which set them all to snickering. "Well, he's not," I said, lowering my voice. "He's a serious artist."

"You're too funny," said Jeremy Michaelson, their ringleader, and a Jew, so he might have taken my side. "Go sit somewhere else, okay?"

I had nowhere else to go, so I slid my chair over a little and put on my Walkman. I was listening to a Pixies album called *Doolittle*, which I'd special ordered at Harmony House. The screaming hurt my ears, but I listened anyway, like it was homework. Jeremy and the other stoners moved on to some other topic, and I said a silent prayer of thanks that they hadn't called me a homosexual fag too.

At the end of lunch, as I stashed my Walkman in my bag, I found Justin's textbook at the bottom of it. He was sitting with his friends, the group of them all leaning forward, speaking intently together. Don't do it, I thought while crossing the room. Wait until tomorrow's study session. But what if he needed the book to study?

I ended up behind his chair and tapped his shoulder, too hard. I felt the bone through his jacket. He turned around, and this awful confused expression crossed his face.

"I have your book," I tried to say, but my voice caught on a nonexistent bone in my throat. The book slipped through my hands, onto the carpet. "I, I, I," I stammered as I picked it up. "I'm sorry." Then I shoved it onto his lap.

"You know that guy?" one of them asked. But I was already rushing away, to avoid the humiliation of hearing Justin's answer.

* * *

"WHY ARE YOU ALL QUIET TODAY?" Justin asked me the next day.

"It's just the way I am," I said, then repeated something he'd said to me: "Don't you know me?"

"Yeah, but today you're really quiet. Even more than usual."

"Why should you care? You only talk to me when you want something," I said. My throat seized up. I couldn't look at his face.

"Whoa, where's this coming from?"

"Yesterday, when I talked to you, in public, you couldn't even say anything."

"Hey, don't cry."

"What? I'm not," I yelped, then lowered my voice. "It's the lights. The reflection from the lights. This school's too cheap to install decent incandescent lighting."

"Okay. Have it your way." Justin opened his history book. "Let's just get some work done, alright?"

"Yeah, whatever."

We got quiet for a while, just working. And then out of nowhere Justin piped up with, "Let me ask you something. So how does a brain like you get blue points?"

"I play tennis," I muttered. "Off-campus."

He paused to think over my answer. "You any good?"

I almost said no, but then I risked a: "Not yet." Who knew? Someday I might be good enough to help Justin out with his backhand or his serve in addition to his homework. "How about you?" I asked. "When did you start playing tennis?"

"How'd you know I played tennis?" asked Justin.

I panicked. We hadn't discussed it, so there was no reason I should have known that he played tennis. But there were lots of things about him I knew because I observed him at a distance, collecting clues to savor later in private, like a private detective. His father was a minister. His black friends teased him for liking white boy music and being good at math. He had only one pair of dress shoes, well-worn brown topsiders. And five pairs of dress socks, black with what looked like white dots but were really tiny skulls, plain black, brown with an argyle pattern, navy blue with green zigzags, and dark gray. Each color reserved for a different day of the week. You could use them as a calendar.

"I-I-I think I heard you talking about it," I stammered. "With a girl."

I thought he'd accuse me of lying, but instead Justin said, "My dad taught me to play when I was a kid. He thought I was going to be the black Pete Sampras." He snorted. "One out of several disappointments."

This was news to me: Justin disappointing anyone.

"Some of us like to hit on the courts after school," he said. "You should stop by."

"You hit? After school?"

"Yeah. When else? We're playing tomorrow." He pointed his silver Cross pen at me. "You should come."

It was impossible. The second that last bell rang, I flew out to the parking lot and my mother's comfortable gray four-door sedan. Teachers suddenly became powerless to keep order. Ties came loose and collars unbuttoned. Dress shoes were kicked off in exchange for sneakers. Hushed voices rose into shrieks and howls.

There was also another reason: I had to see Dr. Don, whose existence was yet one more of my secrets. I'd instructed my parents to refer to him as "an appointment."

"I'll ask my mom," I said.

"Oh, I see how it is," he said. "You have to ask your mommy."

"No, no. I mean she drives me."

Justin didn't seem convinced. "If I see you, I see you. Let's leave it at that."

THE SHOW

My mother was delighted when I told her about Justin's invitation to play tennis. I said I'd understand if she said no, especially since I had "an appointment" that afternoon.

"I'm sure he wouldn't mind rescheduling," she said. "I'm sure he'd love it. I know I'd love it. I'd love to meet your Dalton friends. You never invite them over."

"Okay, okay. Maybe someday," I said too quickly, but I'd never allow that to happen. Our home was a crime scene.

The next afternoon, I entered the boys' locker room at Dalton for the first time. I pushed my duffel bag against the heavy metal door to open it, and immediately inhaled a sharp grassy stink. The walls were decorated with old wooden tennis racquets and sepia-toned pictures of boys in leather helmets, clutching pudgy footballs. Dodging baseball, lacrosse, and basketball players in various states of undress, I tripped over a bench.

"Good Vibrations" by Marky Mark and the Funky Bunch thumped out of a boom box, while a baseball player with massive shoulders and thighs danced in his jockstrap for his hooting teammates. He swung his jersey in the air, turned his ball cap sideways, thrust his pelvis, drummed on his chest, beat up an invisible enemy with his fists.

"'Good vibra-sha-hans!'" he squealed in a fey falsetto. "'Sweet sensation!'"

Sheltered by my open locker door, I watched, wishing I didn't want to. If I were a year older, like the other guys in my grade, would I have shared their interest in girls?

Brandon Jenkins opened the locker next to mine and belched in my face.

"Sorry, was I in your way?" I asked, pulling my duffel bag to my chest.

"Seems like I'm in your way," he said. "You enjoying the show?"

I dropped my eyes. "What do you mean?" Keep your head down and you won't get hurt, I thought. You have a right to change your clothes just like anyone else.

Brandon grabbed his crotch. "Suck, suck, suck," he said and whipped a lacrosse stick at the back of my legs. I caught the end of the stick and threw it on the floor. Brandon looked shocked. Maybe he said something, but I couldn't hear it because I grabbed my bag and ran out of the locker room, then out of the building and across the beautiful school lawns, past the beds of tulip shoots piercing through mud, the brick-paved walking paths which only weeks earlier had been buried under snow. I finally ducked for cover between a waist-high bush and the cement wall of the "old" gym.

There I crouched for fifteen, then twenty minutes, then more, catching my breath and rubbing my legs, still stinging from the lacrosse stick. I had to keep shifting my weight so that I wouldn't dirty the knees or seat of my dress pants. Maybe I could hide until Mom came to pick me up, or until college.

Brandon knew what I was looking at. How? Did everyone know? There seemed no way to keep that particular secret anymore. Maybe it was time to take up karate again. Maybe instead of hiding who I was, I simply needed to learn to defend myself.

Finally, tired of kneeling, I crept over to the tennis courts. I leaned on the fence as Justin and a few other boys hit around, their racquets swirling freely across their bodies like joy. If he asked, I could say I'd forgotten to bring my tennis clothes, but Justin didn't notice that I was or was not there. He wore all black: sweatpants, socks, tennis shoes, even a black T-shirt with an "A" in the center and a line through it.

Then the girls' team came on. The boys left, but Justin stayed behind to assist the coach. I sat in the stands and watched. Our school was playing some team from the city with mismatched uniforms and scuffed, loosely strung racquets. Between matches, they spread out on our manicured lawns or smoothly paved asphalt and soaked up the sun.

The coach sent Justin to get some water, and from my seat at the top of the bleachers, I watched him dash behind the fence. I imagined him running up the steps to rescue me, take me somewhere far away, maybe as far as Detroit.

Who's Trent Reznor?

Our next study session, Justin sauntered in late to the Dining Hall. Would he mention that I'd failed to meet him on the tennis court? I decided to keep it casual, distract him with a joke.

"Well, if it isn't the Emperor Augustus deigning to make an appearance," I said.

He slid into his chair. "Jesus, you act like a girl who got stood up for a hot date." Justin had this sexy way of slumping back against the plastic seat, legs spread wide, crotch exposed. Why? There were no girls around.

"Sorry," I said, though I wasn't. Apologies were simply a reflex, like gagging.

He pulled out a wadded up sheet of paper from his pocket: a quiz with a D circled on top. The only questions he'd gotten right were about Caligula and gladiators.

After all that Israeli candy, all my tasty tidbits about Judaism . . .

"Did you even study?" I asked.

The left corner of his mouth curled up. "I'm not going to lie. Last night Trent Reznor was on *120 Minutes*, and I stayed up to watch. And yes, *120 Minutes* is corporate cheese, but it was Trent Reznor."

"Who's Trent Reznor?" I asked.

"You know, Nine Inch Nails?"

"Oh, is he the lead singer of Nine Inch Nails?" I asked.

"No, he *is* Nine Inch Nails." He held out his hand. "You got any candy?"

"I don't think you deserve candy," I said in a quiet voice.

"Now you sound like Dean Demuth."

No, actually, I sounded like my mother.

Three kitchen ladies in white came out of the kitchen in a line, bearing foil-wrapped steaming bins that smelled meaty and yet strangely sweet.

"Why is *120 Minutes* cheesy?" I asked. "They play cool music, right?"

Justin made a pitiful looking face and put his hands together as if in prayer—a gesture he'd picked up in church? "Please can I have my candy now?"

I slid the chocolate across the table. "What's the point of us meeting if you're getting D's?"

"So I got one D," he said with his mouth full. "I'll do better. It's no big thing."

"It is to me," I said.

"Why?" he asked. "It's my D, not yours."

"You're wrong. When you take a test, I feel like I'm taking it too. Like it's me and you in there together. So I take it personally when you get a D."

Justin stopped chewing. Maybe I'd said too much, but I went on.

"You could do better, if you worked harder."

"Time for that old lecture?" He cocked his head. "Just pick yourself up by your bootstraps, boy. Or, are you too lazy, or too dumb?"

"You're not dumb, Justin."

"Nah, just lazy. Right?"

"Why are you angry at me?"

"I ain't angry at you specifically."

"Well, I am. I'm angry at you, very specifically."

He narrowed his eyes. "I'm confused."

"One time, couldn't you try? As a favor to me. Just to see if all this work we've been doing might pay off."

He thought for a minute. Then he asked with a sly smile, "And for the candy?"

"Yes. And the candy."

Justin studied his fingers, stained with melted chocolate. I wanted to lick them clean. "Brain, it's not personal. I didn't think of it as letting you down."

"Well, you did."

"There's another quiz next week. I'll study for that one."

"I'm going to make sure." I took out a pencil. "What's your phone number? I'm going to check up on you."

That night, I unplugged the phone in our guest room, took it into my room, shut the door, and then opened it again to make sure my parents weren't listening. My fingers shook as I dialed Justin's number. He lived in a different, unfamiliar area code, and I kept pressing the wrong digits.

A strange man answered. "Yeah?" He sounded surly, though I couldn't pinpoint what specifically gave me that impression.

"Good evening." I don't know why I said that. "Is Justin home?"

"You're one of his Dalton friends, right?" said the man. "Are you that Brandon?"

This must be Justin's father, the one who apparently did not approve of Justin's musical and stylistic tastes. Maybe he blamed me for them. Maybe he could tell through the phone that I was a Jewish idol worshipper, guilty of carving those Hebrew letters onto the roofline of his church.

"Uh-uh. It's Ari."

"Ari," he repeated slowly. "Is that short for something?"

"No," I said, losing my confidence. But it was too late to hang up, like a prank call. I'd given my real name.

"Well, he's around here somewhere."

The man put the phone down without asking me to hold. I pressed my ear to the receiver, trying to make out a few sounds. This was Justin's private house I was calling. Were they eating slices of honey-baked ham on plastic TV trays? Were there iron bars over the windows? Was there a snarling pit bull in the backyard?

"Hey, Brain," Justin purred into the phone. "Didn't think you'd really call."

"I told you I would." After a pause, I said, "If you study for the quiz this week, I'll get something really nice for you. Better than candy."

"Like what, a blow job?"

I almost dropped the phone.

"Relax, Brain. I was just messing with you. Obviously, that ain't going to happen unless you know some girl who owes you a real big favor."

"I don't know," I said. "Maybe she'd want to." Then I dared to add, "I guess you're good-looking enough."

"Yeah, you think so?"

I quickly changed the subject. "I'll buy you a can of tennis balls," I said.

"Why do you care so much what I do? Do you get extra brownie points from Demuth or something if I get an A?"

It hurt when he talked this way. "Just shut up and get your book out and I'll quiz you on Diocletian and the lions eating all the Christians."

"I bet that's your favorite part. Lions eating all the *goys*?"

"Yeah, that's it. I'm prejudiced against *goyim*."

"*Goyim*," he repeated. "So I'm a *goyim*. Love that. Well, listen to this, Brain. Constantine the Great, first Roman emperor to convert to Christianity, after seeing a cross in the sky, issued the Edict of Milan in 313."

"You're reading that from the book."

"Nuh-uh. Swear to God. And I mean your God. The Jewish one."

"Tell me more, then."

"What else you want to know?"

"Anything at all," I said. "Just keep talking."

* * *

I DECIDED TO STOP SEEING DR. DON.

"I feel better now," I told my parents. "I'm running out of things to talk about."

The truth was I wanted to make myself available in case Justin ever invited me to play tennis after school again, or maybe a run to 7-Eleven for a soda. A walk in the woods. It didn't matter what it was. I needed my freedom.

Mom kept asking if I was sure, but Dad was on my side. A lifelong Republican, he had an ingrained suspicion of therapists, counselors, and psychologists. They met with Dr. Don without me to discuss it, and then I talked with him too. He surprised me by saying, "You're ready. You've been ready for a while now."

I'd worried that he'd see right through my plan. Did he really think I was ready?

In our final session, I studied his sunroom-office, memorizing it in detail: the ink and paint splotches crusting the carpet, which Don kept saying he wanted to remove and replace with linoleum; the chipped, rickety side table, always on the verge of tipping over though it never did; the collection of arty clocks ticking away our minutes together.

In the last few minutes, I asked for a kind of unified theory of Ari, what essentially was wrong with me and how to fix it, but Dr. Don didn't have one. "Because there's nothing wrong with you," he said.

"Then why does everything seem so hard?" I asked.

"It's because you haven't realized yet that there's nothing wrong with you." He nodded at one of his clocks. "Well, it's time." And then he stood.

I stood too.

"If you ever need or want to, you can always come back, even for one session."

"I know," I said.

"Do you want to take all your artwork with you?"

I did, but I said he could keep it, as if I were too cool to care.

Then he asked if I wanted a hug. "I wouldn't really do it, because I think it would embarrass you. But it's okay to admit you want one."

"I'm fine," I said, though I did want one, for a full minute, with my tear-stained face pressed to his chest. "I'm fine with a handshake."

His hand felt plump yet dry as it enveloped mine.

Alternative

A noisy storm rolled in, and Justin and I watched the wind and the rain from the Dining Hall, where a mere sheet of glass separated us from the chaos outside. I dreamed of a sudden gust cracking those windows and sucking us out there to dance through the mud, the fat droplets of rain drenching our clothes to the skin.

Justin got a B+ on his next quiz, and I wanted to squeeze him. Instead, I squeezed the edge of our table.

Justin was helping me do much better in math, while his grades in history went up and then down, but on the whole they improved. Whenever he backslid into the C-range, he'd say to me, "You gonna call me tonight, Brain?" I never did, yet I almost looked forward to his C's, just to hear him ask if I'd call again.

Every morning, I'd put the Israeli chocolate in the pocket of my Dalton blazer. Then in our tutoring sessions, he'd say, "You got that candy?" I'd hand it over, the chocolate slightly warm and soft from the heat of my chest. And he'd say, "Thanks, Brain," in a husky, deep-throated voice that made my ears tingle.

I ran out of candy and bought another bag at the Jewish bookstore. Justin never questioned how my supply lasted all those months. He promised to bring me something from Detroit, but none of his suggestions were very practical. Ribs or peach cobbler were too messy. As for pork rinds . . .

"Oh, yeah, the kosher thing," he said, remembering.

He never brought me anything, but every so often he'd say, "One day, Brain, I'm going to surprise you. You'll see."

"There is one thing you can do for me," I said. "How do you know about the Pixies and all that?"

So Justin explained the difference between *Spin* and *Rolling Stone.* He gave me the address of Other Music in Royal Oak. He said a pair of Doc Martens would last your entire life. He brought me a copy of a free alternative weekly called *Metro Times.* At home, I looked at the provocative ads in back, the ones with friendly-looking and unfortunate guys who lacked shirts and were begging to be called. I wondered what had brought them so low, and what I might do to help.

He told me about a club downtown called The Shelter, which had an all-ages night. There seemed no limit to his experience.

"And it's . . . alternative?" I asked.

He laughed. "Brain, let me explain you something," he said. "Alternative doesn't exist anymore. Maybe it did once, before it was co-opted by all these idiots who are now running to the mall to buy some new Pearl Jam record or a plaid shirt. These are the same kids who used to spend all their time worrying about what Whitney Houston song was cool or how to beat up some kid who thought a little differently or wanted to dress differently. They didn't care that the Earth was going to shit, or that our army was spilling blood for oil in Iraq every day in the name of democracy. But anyone smart enough to feel alienated by this mainstream hegemony was called 'alternative.'"

"But why alternative? Alternative to what?" I asked.

"Alternative to listening to what the radio stations were jamming down our throats," he said. "Alternative to participating in our mindless MTV no-brainer beer-guzzling culture. But then MTV and the greedy record companies realized they could make money by turning a good idea into a neat little marketing label for our generation, like a dark flipside to the hippies. So all the followers started listening to so-called alternative bands and wearing plaid and thinking, wow, aren't we cool, without realizing the whole point of wearing a plaid shirt was to differentiate yourself from mainstream assholes however you could. Now the situation has deteriorated so any music by a white artist that sells gets labeled 'alternative.'"

"Then what's really alternative?" I asked.

"Basically, nothing anymore. A few people like to think they're alternative, but they aren't really. The mainstream has poisoned it by taking it over. Now, even though I listen to bands like the Breeders, it bothers me that some mainstream asshole out there is listening to them too."

"And you think I'm like that? A follower? Mainstream?"

He looked at me as if to think about it. I held my breath. "No," he said. "You're your own category."

I didn't get it. Wasn't that alternative?

Another time, Justin asked me about Hannukah. "Is that when you can't eat bread for a week?"

"You're thinking of Passover," I said. "You know, when we murder Christian babies and use their blood to bake matzo."

One of the kitchen ladies gave me a funny look, and I leered back at her.

Justin had taught me so much, most importantly how to develop a saucy sense of humor, which had helped infinitely with the stoners at lunch. My mistake, I now realized, had been in trying to be "nice." Boys were not interested in "nice." They wanted to hear something so disgusting it would make them laugh.

"I'll keep an eye on my little brother next Passover," he said.

"You have a brother?" I felt betrayed that he hadn't mentioned it, especially since I was a little brother. Didn't he notice the coincidence? "Why doesn't he go here?"

"My parents can only afford to send one of us, even on scholarship. They picked me because I'm smarter. Plus, he's a douche. So if you want to eat him for Passover, go ahead. What else you guys eat for Passover?"

And then I had to ruin everything between us by saying, "Come see for yourself."

"What?" Justin asked, his voice cracking.

The words were out, and I couldn't take them back. Swallowing hard, I said, "Come for dinner, on Passover."

"You mean like a real invitation?" he asked.

"Why not?" I said, high on the intimacy of our conversation.

"Maybe there's some Jewish state secrets you wouldn't want me to know."

"I have no secrets from you." On a certain level that was true. In addition to the state secrets of Judaism, I'd confessed to him how it felt to be an outsider at Dalton, my fear of the stoners I ate lunch with, my dreams of escaping Michigan. The only secret I hadn't confessed was the biggest, most dangerous one.

"So what do you say?" I asked.

"Free dinner? You're on."

YES TO BE NICE

THE REST OF THAT DAY, I recalled my rash invitation with shame. Justin, at our house for Passover? I pictured him reciting one of the prayers in our *hagada*, a stiff yarmulke perched on top of his hair at an awkward angle. A lone black face in a crowd of white, and me, pretending blithely to my aunts and uncles that it made no difference.

Maybe I could say he was one of those Ethiopian Jews.

I was so worried about how to break the news to my parents that when I wandered out to the parking lot after the final bell, I didn't hear Justin calling me. Finally, he fake-punched me in the stomach and said my real name. "Ari." It almost sounded like a cool person's name the way he said it. "No sloppy math homework tonight, okay?"

"Okay," I said.

"I'm going to check tomorrow, to make sure," he said, pretending to hit me again before ambling away. I lost track of where to because out of nowhere, Mom came to my side.

"Was he bothering you?" she asked, grabbing my shoulders.

"Oh my God, Mom, no," I said. Had Justin heard? Thankfully, he wasn't nearby.

"You're sure you're not hurt? I saw him hit you."

"He was playing. He barely touched me." It hurt more to admit that he'd barely touched me, that he'd never want to do it for real. "Can we go, please?"

We were pulling out of the parking lot when I worked up the nerve to say that I'd invited him over for Passover.

The last time I'd seen my mom so upset was when I'd expressed an interest in studying German, which I'd said only to get a rise out of her. "Why would he want to celebrate Passover with us?" she said. "He's not Jewish and he's not our family."

At least she didn't point out that he wasn't white.

"Justin is very interested in Judaism," I said. "He might convert someday."

We rolled to a stop at the traffic light at the end of the Dalton driveway, where a sign read, "You are now leaving the Dalton campus, but you take our spirit with you, wherever you go. Fear the claw!" Mom waved to the security guard, then turned left on Fourteen Mile Road. To go to where Justin lived, you turned right.

Mom asked, "Why are you so bent on your friend coming?"

It felt thrillingly naked hearing her call Justin my "friend," though the label wasn't accurate. Then what was he? My associate? Accomplice? Tender comrade?

"Because I already told him he could come."

Also because he calls me Brain, and I want to enter his brain.

"Couldn't he come over another time? You know your father. He'd make some dumb joke, thinking he's being funny."

"Then tell him not to," I said.

The light changed, but my mom didn't move until the car behind us honked. "Maybe your friend doesn't really want to come. He might have just said yes to be nice."

"No!" I barked. "That's not what it was."

At the next red light, Mom reached over and smoothed down a lock of my hair. "I'm sorry, but this is a celebration for Jews, and he's not Jewish. You should have asked us first. You'll just have to explain it to him."

I refused to dignify her conclusion with a response.

"You want to put your music on the tape deck?" That's what she called Nirvana: "your music," something strange and distasteful, like a taste for horsemeat.

I burst into tears. "You've completely wrecked my life!"

An Honorary Jew

WOULD HE THINK I WAS DISINVITING him because he wasn't Jewish—Justin said that Jews only helped their own—or because of the other reason? My only hope was that he might forget the invitation altogether. But at our next tutoring session, Justin said, "Can't wait for that free dinner you promised. Just don't expect me to eat that matzo. That shit tastes like cardboard. I'll bring my own crackers."

What if I said nothing, and Justin just showed up? My parents couldn't close the door in his face, not after he'd have driven all the way from Detroit to Maggie Lane. Mom would prepare an extra place setting next to mine, Dad would make his usual bombastic pronouncements, and Justin and I would exchange secret smiles or bump knees under the table. Then we'd disappear in my room and bang our heads to Nirvana, or to whatever music Justin liked. "Thanks for a wonderful dinner, Mrs. Silverman," he'd say and shake my mother's hand. "I feel like an honorary Jew."

No, he'd never say that. Why had I even thought it?

Finally, the week before Passover, it was time to face the truth: I was putting off the unavoidable.

This time when I called, his mom answered, the one in whose milk Justin might have sucked up anti-Semitism. She had a honeyed voice and when I asked if I could speak to Justin, she replied, "Why, surely!"

Justin came on the line, and before we could even get to chatting, he said, "Listen, brain, I don't think that dinner of yours is my thing."

"Why?" I asked, so hurt by this news that I forgot to feel relieved.

He paused. "We're in different crowds, you and me."

My throat tightened. Was this the anti-Semitism Dad warned me about?

"I mean, we've never hung out after school or anything, and now I'm going to go all the way from where I live to where you live for dinner with your whole family?"

So that was how he saw me. He wouldn't dine at my house because I wasn't alternative enough. Why couldn't he just have been an anti-Semite? And I had thought the whole point of being alternative, Nirvana and Lollapalooza and the Feelies, was that you accepted everyone, that you didn't think this way.

I still wasn't speaking, so he said, "You there?"

"Yeah, I'm there," I said. "It's fine. Don't worry. I'm totally fine."

"Why are you being so dramatic?" he asked.

My inner faggot was popping out again: dramatic, sensitive, needy. Maybe I should just go ahead and become what everyone seemed to think I was already.

"See you in school," I said. After hanging up, I went to the kitchen to get something to eat, something rich and sweet and soft.

Mom hummed her favorite song as she set the table for Passover, when all diets went out the window. Wedding season tended to die down in winter, so she often took a break from painting then, channeled her creative talents into cooking. In addition to her famous potato kugel, she'd make brisket, crispy roasted potatoes, sponge cake topped with a creamy lemon curd she'd carefully stir on the stove with a wooden spoon. This year, she'd bought a new seder plate at the Holocaust Memorial gift shop. A replica of an original from pre-Holocaust Poland, it came in a box marked "A Precious Legacy."

"What's wrong, honey?" she asked. "You look as though someone had died."

I claimed that nothing was wrong.

"Okay," she went on. "If it means that much to you, your friend can join us."

"Forget it," I said. "He can't come anymore."

"Oh, too bad. Maybe next time." She resumed setting the table, lining up silver and folding napkins into birds.

Back in my room, I put on *Nevermind* for the hundredth, no maybe, the billionth time. If I had gone to school with him, would Kurt have treated me this way? No, I decided. Kurt could never have been this cruel.

But maybe Justin hadn't meant to be cruel. Maybe he wanted to come over, but something had stopped him. Maybe he felt as lonely as I did, only his loneliness was the kind you experienced in a group, surrounded by people who didn't see you—or not really, not the way you really were.

However, I saw him. And maybe that was what had scared him into chickening out of dinner—yes, chickening out. Justin could be afraid, just as I felt sometimes.

I absorbed the weight of this thought as I rewound *Nevermind* to its beginning and turned up the volume, so the chorus to "Teen Spirit" echoed against the four walls of my room. Thrashing my head and screaming out the real lyrics, which I'd finally figured out and memorized, I decided that Justin was dead wrong. Nirvana wasn't ripping off The Pixies or anyone else. They were simply great.

THREE

After his run, Ari cuts his hair, what there is of it, checks his stomach and his arms in the mirror. Everything looks flabby. Not that Justin is going to see him naked, yet the added puffiness in his cheeks makes evident that he's gained weight everywhere else. Since when has his belt gotten so tight at the waist? Why has M never warned him that he was getting so out of shape?

By chance, Ari discovers that when he cocks his head, just so, the slight suggestion of a jowl under his chin tightens up. He must remember to cock his head.

Ari puts on his faded sweatshirt and a worn University ball cap, just to see what he'll look like when Justin sees him. Answer: like a plump elf. His problem is he holds onto his clothes for too long, long past their expiration date. But he's sentimental that way, thinks of old clothes as old friends. He still has the T-shirt they'd given away at his high school graduation party, a T-shirt that he sometimes sleeps in.

He should buy himself a nice new ball cap, like the ones his students wear in class, to shade their eyes while texting and clicking things on their laptops while he lectures to them, alone at the head of the room. Occasionally they peer over the edges of their screens to see if he's doing anything interesting. No, just the usual passionate fulminating about fallacious stereotypes of life in the Middle Ages, like that Medieval people thought the world was flat, or that they belched their way through roasted turkey legs at dinner, then tossed the bones on the floor. Or that a lord had the right to sleep with a peasant woman on the first night of her marriage to some lowly serf.

If only he could put every goddamn Medieval Times Dinner Theater permanently out of business. And choke the owners by ramming one of those buttered cobs of corn they serve with those goddamned turkey legs down their throats.

None of this concerns his students, who go back to their screens. Probably they feel sorry for him, to feel this intensely for something as pointless as the subjects he teaches. But he inflates their grades and in return they give him nice enough ratings on RateMyProfessor. They call him enthusiastic, caring. They say he "understands the plight of the student."

By the way, M's RMP ratings were through the roof. One of his students gushed, "He's just like one of us!"

Too late now to buy a new cap, so Ari gives the old one a sponge bath. Thankfully, the night before he'd washed his zip-up hooded sweatshirt and his jeans, so those are clean. Anyway, he doesn't want to look too fancy. Can't betray the meaningfulness of this occasion with nicer clothes. Too bad M's so much taller than he is. Otherwise Ari could try wearing one of the shirts he'd left behind.

Ari checks Justin's phone number again. Yes, miracle of miracles, he'd copied it correctly into his phone. He's not good with numbers, that is unless they correspond to dates of battles, royal successions and the like. In his nightmares, he's back in high school pre-calculus class, there's a quiz, and he hasn't touched his textbook in months. He doesn't even know where his textbook is.

Justin, however, is the kind of guy who makes the business page when he exercises his stock options. Of course, he's always been good at numbers.

HOPING TO SOLVE HIS PROBLEM LIKE a math equation, Ari has spent several evenings reviewing his university's policy on sexual misconduct. Maybe he can use it like a litmus test, comparing the rules with M's story, to determine an appropriate verdict.

The relevant categories seem to be "sexual intimidation" (defined as indecent exposure), and "sexual assault, category B" (unwanted touching of intimate body parts). "Sexual assault, category A" means that penetration has occurred, "however slight."

The categories feel lacking to Ari. For example, why is there no Category C, for sexual activity accompanied by threats or acts of violence? He answers his own question: because rape itself is a violent act.

In my own case, Ari thinks, I could have done with a little less of the violence. He succeeded in fucking me. He didn't need to beat me too, to leave bruises, to cause pain to the other parts of my body that he didn't need to get himself off. Why shouldn't that count as an additional injury?

As required by the university, Ari recently completed his annual sexual harassment training, in the form of an online video followed by a quiz to prove he hadn't just hit play and turned off the sound while watching Netflix in another window. The video featured overly expressive actors, with make-up glistening in cheap lighting. The women wore their hair pulled severely away from their faces and dressed in dark, severe suits. A man with puffy black hair and a shiny silk shirt earnestly protested his innocence in a way that made it clear he was a self-deluded villain.

The quiz was a cinch. Real life proved more vexing.

Last fall, before this whole mess, M told Ari what at the time seemed like the funniest story. M had been in his office, killing time between classes, and though he never did this on campus (at least that's what

M said), he opened his Grindr app, the one he said he only looked at for a laugh. Indeed, Ari and M used to sit on their living room couch together at night, and instead of watching TV, they'd look at the profiles together, and often conduct insightful dissections of the language in the profiles, the lighting in the photos, the various outfits and lack thereof. In any case, M was looking through this app when one of his male students popped up. After a quick, friendly chat, the student asked if M would like to go out for dinner sometime.

"I never date students," M wrote back.

That's your reason? Ari thought. How about that other inconvenient little detail: that you're supposedly already taken?

"Ok," replied the student, "then do you just want to fuck?"

"What did you say?" asked Ari, aghast.

"I declined as politely as possible and then logged out," said M.

Ari has not shared this story with the review committee. He's not sure whether it hurts or helps M's cause. Either way, that story has bothered him for a long time.

BESIDE ARI'S BED-TABLE HANGS A SMALL framed print of a painting titled *The Old King*, by the twentieth century French expressionist Georges Rouault, another modern man whose mindset is stuck in the Middle Ages. Ari's owned this print for more than a decade, and takes it with him everywhere he's lived. The image shows a bearded, somber monarch in profile, eyes cast down, fist clasping a white flower. It took the painter twenty years to complete the work, with its rough planes of color bordered by thick black lines like a stained glass window. Ari wasn't surprised to read that Rouault was inspired by the windows of medieval churches. However, he has never been able to explain why he loves this painting so much, or why the face reminds him so much of Justin's face.

"WHY DID YOU DO IT?" ARI asked M during their last conversation, over coffees at a Belgian café in Dupont Circle—several miles from campus. It was one of those places that charged seven bucks for a latte because the barista poured the foam on top in the shape of a heart, though the coffee underneath tasted surprisingly bitter.

As Ari walked in, M half-rose from his table to greet him, as if for a hug, but Ari kept at a distance. Even when times were good, Ari had never been much for public displays of affection. So why now did he feel this strong urge to lean across the table and kiss his ex-husband passionately on the lips, despite the presence of all these strangers?

"Setting aside the moral questions here," said Ari, "just on a practical level, why? If you wanted to cheat, I'm sure you had lots of other opportunities with more age-appropriate partners. So why go after a student? In this day and age?"

Ari wanted to believe somehow that the student was guilty, that he was the one who'd preyed on M in some way and that the whole thing was a misunderstanding.

"All I did was touch his dick, and he said no," said M, who was wearing purple sneakers and a Taylor Swift T-shirt. He could have easily passed for a student. Was that why he wanted to have an affair with one? "Then I stopped."

"It was a bit more than that, and it took you a while to stop," said Ari. He noticed that M's black wavy hair, usually carefully brushed and set in place, looked a bit wiry. A few curls stuck out in odd places.

"It was one of those parties," said M. "Everyone was making out everywhere with everyone. If you'd been there, even you would have been doing it."

Had these types of parties taken place when Ari was in college? He wouldn't have known. His friends were mostly nerds who ate microwaved popcorn in front of movies played on someone's dorm room VCR. It wasn't until junior year that he went on his first date, with a guy from rural Pennsylvania who kept marveling at Ari's smooth hands. At the end of their night, he said, "Deep down, under that nice boy façade, I bet you're a dirty Jew boy, am I right?"

Ari, confused, took a second to reply, "Er, no."

Is there something wrong with me, Ari thought. Why don't I want sex the way other men seem to want it, need it, so badly they lose all self-control?

"But I wasn't at that party, that's the point," Ari told M. "I don't put myself in these situations. You know, with hot tubs."

"Show me the rule."

"What are you talking about?"

"Show me the rule against getting in a hot tub. Show me the rules for how two people who are checking each other out should treat each other. And where do they shift? At exactly what point does maybe become definitely not? And what happens if you're a second too early or late?"

Looking at M in that café, Ari saw a shade of vulnerability cross his ex's face, a rare sight. M had worn that same expression on the evening of their marriage ceremony. Maybe it wasn't an actual wedding, registered with the state. Still, at the crucial moment, when the rabbi invited them to look into each other's eyes, each other's souls, they both felt the gravity of it. What they were doing mattered.

"You're being disingenuous now," says Ari. "You've put me, all of us on this committee in a terrible position with your recklessness. We have to decide what to do."

M was tearing his paper napkin into confetti. "I'm not a monster. The . . . person in question wasn't a child. Whatever happened to personal agency? You try some things, you don't like them, then you say no and you fucking move on. Regardless of how this has affected our relationship, you don't ruin someone's entire professional life for a bit of groping in the dark."

"Listen to you," said Ari. "Jesus, I'm on your review committee, we shouldn't even be meeting like this." He pushes his bitter coffee aside. "You were his teacher. It was a betrayal, not just of me, but of your integrity. Can't you be honest about this, at least with yourself?"

M folded his arms and said in a clear voice, so anyone at the neighboring tables could hear, "And when have you ever been honest with yourself?"

"Me?" said Ari. "What am I supposed to be honest about?"

"How about the fact that you're only ever drawn to men who are unattainable, straight guys, dead kings, a hopeless high school crush." He looked Ari in the eye. "And incorrigible sluts like me."

"Wait a minute," said Ari. "Looking up Justin was all your idea."

"And you were all too happy to go along with it, right?

Ari said nothing.

"You're still going to that basketball game, aren't you? To see your lost love, the boy you always wished you could have had but never did."

"Shut up," said Ari. "You know nothing about that."

"Basically any guy you can't have, any guy who can't commit to a serious relationship, that's enough to win your tender heart. And then you congratulate yourself for being alone, make yourself out to be this romantic. But the truth is you're afraid, only you call it something else."

"Thanks a lot, Dr. Freud," Ari said. "I should go."

As he got up, M grabbed him by the wrist.

"Are you trying to hurt me?" Ari said, staring at M's tight pink fingers. "Ow, you're hurting me. You're hurting me!"

"Jesus, I'm sorry," he said and let him go. "Ari, are okay? Jesus, what just happened there?"

Ari felt the blood drain from his cheeks. Everything was going wrong. "Oh, nothing," he said and hurried away.

SKIP BOLTON

THE SUMMER BEFORE JUNIOR YEAR, I attended a tennis camp at Mom's tennis club. Our pro was Skip Bolton, captain of Dalton's tennis team. He bounded onto the court, tucking his flowing blond locks under a turquoise-colored backwards baseball cap.

Skip was being recruited by tennis teams from three different colleges and had been voted Homecoming King two years running. His gold-framed picture was destined to appear on the Dalton Hallway of Fame next to the boys' locker room. Because of his WASPy nickname, sharp nose, and easy popularity, I'd assumed that Skip came from old money. The truth was he commuted from Wyandotte or Waterford or one of those W-suburbs to Dalton, which he attended on scholarship.

Eye on the ball until point of contact. Hit out in front. At the end of your swing, let your racquet arm wrap around your neck like a scarf. All summer, I repeated Skip's advice in my head, on the tennis court, in the shower and the car and bed, at the lunch table at school and the dinner table at home. And though I couldn't hit the ball as hard as some of the other students, I could move them around the court until they ran out of breath. I could chase down every ball they hit. I could be a human backboard.

"Don't let your mind run away on you," Skip told us, feeding us dusty balls from an orange hopper. "Focus, one movement at a time. You've got all day, nice and easy."

Once, just before class, I was dawdling, waiting for the handicapped stall to be empty so I could change into my tennis uniform when Skip barged into the locker room, grabbed the bench next to mine, and took off all his clothes.

His body was as smooth as an illustration from a biology textbook, and his skin radiated light. Ms. Hunter was still criticizing the proportions of the bodies in my work. Maybe Skip would let me study his body if I said it was a homework assignment.

By some miracle, Skip didn't notice me staring at his penis, which was pink like the rest of his skin and hung lazily above his jockstrap until he snapped it into place. After dusting himself with clouds of medicated talcum powder, he stepped into his socks. Our bodies were so close, I inhaled his scent: a stiff blend of starch and iron.

He pulled up his shorts and asked me, "You go to Dalton too, right?"

I nodded vigorously. What if he'd caught me staring? But then, he was so beautiful, he had to know that he earned the admiration of men, women, animals . . .

"But you're new, right?"

I admitted I was new. Would he snap a towel at my legs or belch in my face?

"I've been going there since seventh grade. That's when they noticed my forehand." He held a pair of tube socks, squeezing them as he talked, as if he were the one who was nervous. "You seem like a smart kid," he said.

That old slur: smart. Not handsome, strong, fun, or even funny. "I guess," I said.

"They like that more at Dalton, you know, smart kids. They keep kids like me around, but if I got injured, I'd be out of there so fast.

They think I'm like a prize racehorse. When they look at me, all they see is a body, not a brain."

"Wow," I said, only half-listening because my eyes kept returning to the flat space between his nipples.

"Anyway, now I'm graduating, so they can't touch me."

Hearing him say "touch," I blushed. "Are you going to be a pro tennis player?"

"Yeah, right," he said. "I want to study veterinary science. I love animals."

He sounded serious. I looked him in the eye, and maybe it should have been obvious, but to me this was a revelation: Skip was a human being who got scared, and even felt pain, just as I did. His looks were perfect, but his life was not. No one's was.

Skip shook his head, as if waking from a daydream. "Now go out there and kick some ass." He mussed my hair. "Kick some ass!"

"I'll try," I said, an immense warmth spreading inside my stomach. I was asking for trouble. And yet that faint blond fuzz on Skip's chest and the feeling of his fingers in my hair made me want trouble. Though the handicapped stall was open now, I changed into my tennis clothes out in the open, in front of anyone who might be watching.

The Visit

A LAZY SUMMER AFTERNOON. I SAT on my bed, drawing pictures of Justin, using his stubbornly silent school yearbook photo for inspiration. A terrible likeness, but all I had.

All summer, I'd filled my sketchbook with dark ink drawings of Justin slouching at a school desk, Justin clutching a tennis racquet, Justin goofing off with his friends. Now I was running out of blank pages. I worried what Mom would think if she saw these drawings, but then she never seemed interested in my art.

Our doorbell rang. I couldn't see who it was because I always kept my blinds closed. Probably one of those volunteers drumming up votes for Clinton, Bush, or Perot, or the little old rabbi who collected the blue metal charity boxes where Mom deposited spare change.

Whoever it was, Mom seemed to be talking to him for a long time. I put down my sketchbook and tried to hear. Their voices sounded muffled through my bedroom wall, so I went out into the hall to see who it was, but before I rounded the corner, I knew.

"This has been a very painful year for us as well," said Rabbi Taborsky. "I hesitated a great deal before coming here. But I hoped I might express . . . "

My head was swimming. My stomach sank.

"Don't bother," Mom said. "We don't want to hear what you have to say."

"He was a boy experimenting with a man's body, a man's feelings. We're sending him to get help. He's confused. And from confusion can come a great deal of sorrow."

"I'm shutting the door," Mom said. "Then I'm calling the police. You're trespassing."

"All of us, we're so terribly sorry. We only wanted you to know."

When Mom got angry, she'd speak in a slow thin voice, brittle as her prized china. "What your son did to mine, we will never forgive you for. Don't come here again."

The door slammed shut with such force, I felt it in my chest. I tiptoed back to my room, turned on the stereo to some random radio station, pretended I hadn't heard what happened, though with "Smells Like Teen Spirit" blasting at the highest volume, I'd have heard. Mom didn't mention it, then or later at dinner, or ever.

I punched my pillow three times, as hard as I could, then buried my face in it, closed my eyes. I can beat this, I told myself. I can beat this and him right out of my mind.

CARNATION DAY

THAT FALL, I WENT BACK TO school with a new sense of purpose and a killer forehand. I wondered how long it might take for Justin to notice either. We were no longer Study Buddies, but we were in French again, and Pre-Calculus. We sat together sometimes and made fun of our school's prized traditions, like Carnation Day.

Every autumn, the Friends of Dalton (our school's P.T.A.) sold buckets of dyed blue carnations tied with yellow ribbons. Guys bought them for girls, who twirled their dopey carnations in each other's faces. A few brazen girls bought carnations for guys, who engaged in flower duels in the hallways, littering the green carpets with blue petals.

Justin never bought anyone a carnation. "Waste of money," he said. No one bought him one either. I kept an eye out, just in case.

This year on Carnation Day, I was standing by my locker when a slender boy named Rory Fox sprinted past me. Behind him, two beefy lacrosse players struggled against the bulk of their bodies to catch up, yelling, "Get the faggot!"

Out of instinct, I flattened my body against the wall, willed my skin to dissolve into the wood veneer of my locker door. I squeezed my eyes shut, prepared for a beating.

The lacrosse players were chasing Rory because he'd bought one of them a flower. It shouldn't have come as a surprise. Rory's name was a punchline for any number of gay jokes. What's Rory Fox's favorite planet? Uranus. What's the difference between a loser and Rory Fox? A loser has no friends but Rory has friends up the ass. If Rory Fox got murdered, the police would charge the murderer with homo-cide.

Rory outran his tormentors all the way to the main road. Ultimately, the lacrosse players were caught and suspended, causing some grumbling, since by leaving school property without permission, Rory had also violated the Dalton Handbook. Didn't he deserve some punishment?

And maybe I deserved punishment too, for wishing to buy Justin a flower, though I'd had the good sense—or at least the survival instinct—not to actually do it.

Life Drawing

I was still thinking about Rory the following Saturday, when I should have been focusing on the naked women sitting in front of me. I was attending my first life drawing class at the Royal Oak Art Association, and all morning, my mind had wandered, here, there, and everywhere but where I was, perched on a cold metal stool just feet away from a plump middle-aged and buck naked woman sprawled on an old armchair covered in a sheet. I had only my easel and pad of newsprint to protect me.

Ms. Hunter had been bugging me to learn figure drawing for the longest while. Finally, that fall, I'd convinced Mom to register me and sign the permission slip I needed because I was under eighteen. Strangely, she seemed less bothered by the nudity than the art part of the class. "If your grades go down because of all this time you're spending on art," she said, scribbling her signature with a sigh, "then the art has to go."

"Can't stand the competition, huh?" I said, trying to make a joke.

"You're right," she said. "You'd have me beat any day of the week."

But now that I was in class, I felt incredibly awkward staring at all that lumpy flesh for so long. I'd never seen breasts in real life, and they reminded me of cow udders.

"You're holding your pencil wrong," said Ian, our teacher, who'd lived in New York and roamed the room clutching a paper cup of coffee that he called a latte. His hairline was receding in front, and grown out long in back. He only wore black: black t-shirts, black jeans, black sweaters. I'd never known people like him existed outside of the movies. "It's not a chopstick, it's an extension of your arm. And quit going over your lines. Drawing isn't a multiple-choice activity. Stick to one line and get it right."

I went back to work, wondering how the model felt, on display like that, with all of our eyes free to roam over her body, wherever we wanted, and no way to tell us to stop.

The Safe Word

ONE AFTERNOON, ON MY WAY TO the gym for a special assembly, I was approached by Candy Greenberg, who said: "I hear you're on the inside track for the Carleton Award."

I shook my head, not understanding.

"You know, for history."

Candy knew a lot about winning. She'd won several awards for her writing, including the Expository Essay Contest for Young People, which landed her an internship at *Inside Detroit*. People said that Candy was being groomed to become editor-in-chief of the *Dalton Lion*, our student newspaper. They also said, "She has a pretty face."

"Where did you hear that?" I asked.

"Rory Fox's mom works in the office," she said. "She says you're smart."

"You should see how bad I am at math," I said.

"Hey, I'm all honors except for German. I can't get that Genitive case, you know? And you should see the kids in regular track German." She formed her thumb and index finger into an "L" for loser and touched her forehead.

My parents would have disowned me for studying German. They wouldn't even order Black Forest cake in a restaurant. In their book,

Jews who bought Mercedes were self-hating traitors. During Oscar season, they were first in line for Holocaust movies.

"Want to sit with our crowd at the assembly?" she asked. By "our crowd," she meant the types who won the year-end achievement awards or competed in Quiz Bowl or Chess Club. Between classes, they waltzed down the halls in jolly clumps of twos, threes, and fours, always laughing at jokes with punchlines featuring Pythagoras, the Emperor Hadrian, or Oscar Wilde. And at school dances, the boys and girls paired off and attended as couples—all except Rory Fox.

Over her shoulder, I saw Justin, laughing with one of his alternative friends.

"Okay, sure," I told Candy. "Let's do it."

Candy's friends sat in front, beneath a line of navy blue felt championship banners dangling from the ceiling, reminding those of us without varsity letters that we would never add to their number. For some reason, Candy deposited me in an empty space next to Rory.

Up close, his eyelashes were frighteningly dark and thick. He'd grown out his hair in the front and gelled it into a blond wave across his forehead. I moved over to keep my blazer from brushing against his.

"Hello," Rory said with a sidelong smile. "Are you joining our Circle of Friends?"

"Maybe." I quickly looked down at my dress shoes before he could offer me a carnation or something. What a strange, almost magical way to refer to your group of friends, as a "Circle." Just enter our "Circle" and all will be well.

Behind us, Justin jostled for space at the top of the bleachers with the alternative kids, the ones who twisted up the backs of their collars, wore blazers a size too small so their shirt cuffs stuck out, and rolled up the cuffs of their pants, which were a size too large and hitched up by black belts with sharp-pointed metal studs. In math, they complained the batteries in their graphing calculators had died. In French, they spoke Spanish. In biology, they could have learned the differences between meiosis and mitosis if they'd wanted to, but they didn't want to. If you got too close, they'd spit tiny wads of paper in your hair or yank your tie into a noose. Still, I craved their friendship, maybe because their gleeful rudeness reminded me of Kurt Cobain.

Sol Kahn, King of Quiz Bowl, reached across Rory's lap, squeezed my hand like he was trying to juice it, and invited me to try out for the wrestling team. "I can show you a few moves I learned from *The Principles of Shuai Jiao*." He flipped his tie over his shoulder and spread his arms like wings.

"I'm not great at sports," I said.

"No worries. We always need new guys. We take everyone."

Candy giggled so widely you could see her braces, which spoiled the effect of her pretty face. "Watch out for Sol. He thinks he's Beowulf."

Leethi Adiga, who had a 4.0 average and one ear that wasn't fully formed, invited me to accompany her on a field trip to hear the Detroit Symphony. "So far," she said, "I'm the only person signed up from our Circle of Friends. Come on. It's Mahler!"

"Is that neighborhood safe at night?" Rory asked.

"Of course. I go to Detroit all the time for work," said Candy, who apparently thought of her *Inside Detroit* internship as "work."

"I just went there to see Morrissey at the Shelter," said Sol. "It was no problem."

"What was the Shelter like?" I asked, forgetting to disguise the awe in my voice.

"Mostly college kids," said Sol. "It's a more mature crowd, very refreshing."

Who'd driven him there? Could he take me? I wanted to know

more, but Candy interrupted, "What's this assembly for? Did someone die?"

"I haven't a clue," said Rory. He touched my arm. "Ari, what's your opinion?"

Did he speak that way, nasal and high-pitched, on purpose? And did I sound like him? Mark used to think so. He made me repeat my words in my "man voice." "You're talking in your woman voice," he'd say. "Use your man voice." So I'd practice in my room again and again, talking in a slow rumble, pretending I had pebbles in my mouth.

"I don't know," I said, shrugging off Rory's hand.

Demuth announced that we were here to learn to resist the temptations of underage drinking. In theory, Dalton students never drank—it was against the honor code. But in fact, every weekend there were keg parties in the refurbished barns, carriage houses, and swim cottages of some of the metro area's most expensive McMansions.

Our first speaker, a Dalton alum from a decade ago, rolled up to the microphone in a wheelchair. His freshman year of college, he'd gotten in a car accident while driving drunk and now he was paralyzed for life. We all gave him a hearty round of applause.

Next Demuth said we would hear a police officer explain the toll that drugs and alcohol took on the body. I sank down a bit where I was sitting, as if to duck out of the rain. The policeman was older than the one who'd interviewed me in his office last year. He was white, clean-shaven, and he wore a blue uniform. As he spoke, he kept his free hand in his pants pocket. Had he ever arrested a kid like Mark? Had Demuth warned him about my story before the assembly? I tried not to look at his eyes.

Rory whispered something to me and I hissed back, "Not now!"

The police officer told us what to do in a situation where "substances" might be present. "We like to call this strategy RACE. The R stands for Remove yourself from the vicinity of the alcohol or controlled substances. Say you have to go to the bathroom or check something outside. Next is A for Ask yourself, is this a decision I want to make, knowing it could ruin the rest of my life, or am I being peer pressured into it? Now comes C, Call your parents or a trusted loved one for advice. You may be in a situation in which you feel uncomfortable explaining what's going on, so we suggest you and your parents come up with a "safe word," some agreed upon term that indicates, 'Hey, loved one, I want to be picked up now, no questions asked.' Finally, we get E for Evacuate, which I believe is self-explanatory."

The officer turned to Demuth and held out the mike. "What do I do with this?"

Dean Demuth took the microphone and told us, "That's your homework. I want everyone in this room to choose your safe word."

* * *

THE REST OF THAT DAY, PEOPLE joked about their safe words: "Budweiser," "I'm wasted," and "cocksucker." Did cocksucker count as one word or two?

Hoping to make him laugh, I asked Justin what his safe word was. The Dining Hall had been locked by mistake, and the study hall monitor was looking for a janitor. We stood outside the room, basking in a few minutes of unscheduled freedom.

"Safe word, my ass," said Justin, who wore his socks with the skulls though it wasn't a Tuesday. "If I was at some party and I wanted to go home, I'd just say it."

I'd once heard a rumor Justin was biracial, which my mind kept wanting to confuse with bisexual.

"Oh, yeah," I said. "That's what Sol Kahn and Candy Greenberg were saying." Maybe he'd see that I had my own friends.

Justin wrinkled his nose. "Why are you hanging out with the Nerd Herd?"

Because being a part of a group, any group, made me feel safer in public. And because being a part of Justin's group was too much to hope for. "They're not all nerds. Candy has a pretty face." We were standing close, virtually toe-to-toe.

"Okay, but look at the rest of her."

"And Sol Kahn listens to the Smiths. I know Rory's a little weird, but . . . "

"He's the only one of them with balls," Justin interrupted. "The second that kid steps outside his house, he's up against it. That ain't easy."

"I guess," I said, resenting Rory's compliment. I wanted one too.

Justin lowered his voice as if to utter some sage words of wisdom. "Just watch out for their crowd. They try to trap new kids."

So save me from their trap, I thought. Bring me into your circle, if only to keep me out of theirs.

"At least they're friendly," I said. "More than other people."

"What does that mean?" he asked.

I cleared my throat. "What would your friends say if I sat with you at lunch?"

Justin didn't answer. Then the study hall monitor returned with keys. "Please don't mention this to anyone," he said, though it wasn't his fault. Time was up. We were heading in. There were so many words I wanted to say to Justin, but none that were safe.

"I like," I said, then swallowed, "your socks."

Justin asked, "Why?"

"I can't tell you why," I said. "I just do."

* * *

IN MY NEXT LIFE DRAWING CLASS, the safe word became a funny story to tell my fellow students, adults with college educations, jobs, houses with gutters that always seemed to be leaking. I'd become our class's Generation X mascot. While Ian went outside for a cigarette, grumbling about Midwesterners and their intolerance of smoking, I entertained everyone with stories about high school, grunge, and Kurt Cobain. They laughed at my imitation of the police officer explaining to us about RACE and volunteered suggestions for my safe word, like "I didn't inhale." They wanted to know what I thought of Sinead O'Connor ripping the Pope's picture on *Saturday Night Live*. Were any kids my age Democrats? Or had Reagan destroyed youth counterculture permanently, turning us all into preppy money-grubbing clones like Alex P. Keaton from *Family Ties*? And was it true Kurt Cobain was doing heroin, making it cool again?

No, those are just rumors, I assured them, as if I knew what I was talking about.

Someone said, "Bullshit. I know a horse junkie when I see one, and that guy's a horse junkie."

It was our model, wearing only a worn terrycloth bathrobe and standing in our circle as if she belonged there, even though a minute earlier, she'd displayed herself for us. Now just a flimsy piece of material protected her from prying eyes.

When our break was over, she said to me, "You sure you're an artist? You don't look like an artist."

"Why?" I said, worried she'd seen through me. "What does an artist look like?"

She dropped her robe and stepped up to her platform. "You act like an old person, but you're young. Try dyeing your hair or something."

* * *

I HAD NO NEED OF A "safe word" because I didn't go to parties and was not likely to any time soon. Still, Dean Demuth had given us an assignment, and I'd learned to take Demuth seriously. So I consulted my parents.

Mom had been trying new recipes from the Dalton Family Cookbook, an annual compilation of parents' recipes to raise money for school. Back in the day, a Dalton Family Cookbook was filled with cream cheese-based canapés or deviled eggs. Now it featured stir fries flavored with fresh ginger root, bright red curries, and collard greens.

Tonight, Mom had cooked the cover: *channa masala*. She sprinkled our plates with minced cilantro. "How about 'Van Gogh'?" Mom said, pronouncing the second "g" in "Gogh."

"How about Barry Sanders?" Dad said.

"How would Ari work Barry Sanders into a casual phone conversation?" Mom asked. "He doesn't even like football."

"He would if he watched more of it with me," said Dad, idly stirring his chickpeas.

No way, I thought. Nirvana fans did not watch football.

"Your channa masala is getting cold," she warned, then sniffed at her fork. "I wish this recipe had more flavor."

"He could say 'This is really a terrific party. By the way, did you see that amazing run by Barry Sanders last night?'"

"I'd never say that," I said. Listening to the two of them bickering like normal parents on a TV sitcom, the Cosbys or something, I felt all the more keenly aware of how not normal I was, how unsafe I felt so much of the time, and how hard we were pretending that none of this had ever happened.

"Why are you Michiganders so obsessed with football?" Mom said.

"They don't watch football in Philadelphia?" Dad asked. "The Philly Eagles?"

"I could say 'How are you?'" I interjected. "Normally, I'd have no reason to ask how you are."

"It's his word, not yours," said Mom. "Stop pushing him."

Dad pushed back his chair. "This isn't dinner. It's baby food."

"Where are you going?" Mom asked.

"I'm not hungry," he said and left the room.

* * *

I FOUND MY FATHER IN HIS den, sitting in his easy chair with the Detroit Tigers logo sewn in the headrest. A baseball game played on TV, the volume at full blast. The walls were crowded with diplomas, a form letter from President Reagan in response to a letter my father had written the White House outlining his suggestions for reforming the tax code, and a finger painting I'd done in kindergarten. Mom wanted him to replace it with a nice modern print, but he'd stuck with my painting.

My mother's wedding picture sat on the TV, the size of a large suitcase. She and Dad had an old black and white *ketubah* stuffed inside their wedding album. Mom wanted to make a new, pretty one to hang, but Dad thought it was silly at this point, so instead, when she had time, she liked to whip up different designs for David and for me. His would be red and navy blue, accented with sharp-edged Jewish stars, while mine would be in soft pastel vines and flowers. The obvious difference annoyed me.

"Are you still mad?" I asked him.

Dad muted his TV. "I wasn't mad." Though he loved baseball, he never went to the actual games, even during the day when the area was flooded with suburbanites. Dad said Tiger Stadium was a low class facility, where people went only to get drunk.

I shrugged. "Do you mind if I sit here with you and watch the game?"

"Of course not. Don't I always say, my door is always open?"

I sat in the empty seat next to his. Mom sometimes sat there and read while he watched his games. Dad turned up the volume again and I looked up at Mom's wedding picture; she was prettier than Michelle Pfeiffer. Then I studied the players, trying to guess what secrets they were confiding to each other in the bullpen.

David once told me that Mom and Dad had hoped I'd be a girl, to balance out the family. But I'd had the audacity to be a boy, and not even a real boy like my brother.

Last year, I'd sat in this same chair next to my father and worked on my police statement, which he critiqued for grammar as well as content, reminding me of details I'd skipped: a knife, the punching, the things Mark had grunted in my ear. Dad made me delete the word 'threateningly'—too melodramatic. "Adverbs often are," he said.

Mark was the guilty one, yet I'd been punished with the home-work of recreating those scenes with just the right language, the most visceral turns of phrase.

I wrote a new draft, which my father corrected again. "You've got to be precise," he said. "This is a legal document. Let's do one more draft. You need to put in the part about where he found that knife. Where he threatened to cut off your genitals."

"I can't," I said, going rigid in my chair.

Dad tried to argue some more, but I interrupted him with a piercing, girlish, high-pitched scream that brought my mother run-ning into the room. "I thought you'd been hurt," she said. In the end, we compromised. I made an asterisk in the appropriate place, drew a line from there to the bottom of the page, made another asterisk, and wrote, "He searched all the drawers in the kitchen, found a bread knife, and threatened me with it."

The baseball game on TV was almost over, and Mom brought us a plate of homemade apricot rugelach. She even ate one. "I'm not making that Indian meal again," she promised as Dad squeezed her hand. Once more, we were a united front, the three of us against the evil forces lurking just beyond our property lines.

Mom screwed up her eyes at the television. "Is it halftime yet?"

The Circle of Friends

The Circle of Friends. A.K.A. The Nerd Herd, the Geek Clique, or simply, Those Freaks. They shared my tastes for They Might Be Giants and 10,000 Maniacs, but not Nirvana—too rough. Sometimes when we sat together in the school library, I got tired of listening to them discuss what colleges they were applying to in two years, so I'd look up Nirvana articles in the green *Reader's Guide to Periodical Literature*.

"Why don't you take that thing home?" joked Mr. Wentworth, our junior librarian, who also coached girls' field hockey and boys' soccer.

At our study table, Candy asked, "What did Wentworth say to you? He's cute."

"He looks like Tom Cruise," Rory agreed. I was getting more used to being seen in his company, as long as it wasn't the two of us alone.

"Is that cute?" I said, and they laughed. But Tom Cruise was the wrong kind of handsome. His hair, personality, and films, they were all too well scrubbed. His cheeks, like Rory's cheeks, were as smooth and soulless as those of a porcelain doll.

The Male Models of New York City

A WOMAN IN MY DRAWING CLASS asked Ian why all our models so far were female. I pretended not to care about the answer as I closed up my pad of newsprint at the end of class, my fingers black with vine charcoal. Now that I was over the initial shock of nudity, I liked drawing bodies, the subtle lines of ankles, shoulder blades, cheekbones. And I was good at it. I had a feel for proportions, or how other people's body parts fit together.

"That's because we're in the Midwest," Ian said.

"Really?" I asked. "Why? You mean there are more male models in New York?"

"Sure," he said. "Most of them are gay. They don't mind being naked in public. They work as go-go dancers at night, you know, in the clubs."

"That makes sense," I said. I had no idea what he was talking about.

Ian asked me if I'd ever thought about going to art school in New York. "I sometimes evaluate portfolios for Parsons," he said. "You should think about it."

"New York," I said. "Is it safe there?"

He smirked. "You're asking me that and you live in Detroit?"

How Are You

That weekend, I went to a Halloween party at Candy Greenberg's house. It was taking place on a tame Sunday afternoon rather than a rocking Saturday night, and we'd be decorating pumpkins with Candy's mom instead of playing beer pong or something, so I doubted I'd need my safe word. Still, it counted as my first high school party.

The Greenbergs lived surprisingly close by, in a wood-frame farmhouse that dated back to the days when our township was mostly farmland. This was before Jewish families like ours invaded, fleeing a wave of middle class black families who in turn were fleeing Detroit for safer streets and schools in the suburbs.

"Lovely to meet you," said Mrs. Greenberg when Mom dropped me off. "I had no idea you had such a beautiful mother."

"Thank you," Mom said. Did she ever tire of these tributes?

"Come on, Ari. We're just starting on the pumpkins." Mrs. Greenberg resembled a Dutch schoolboy with her bobbed blond hair, a pale blue button down shirt tucked into salmon-colored chinos, and polished penny loafers. While my mother was striking-looking, Mrs. Greenberg was a more muted kind of pretty, giving off the calm, serene competence of lemon curd. I wanted to be in her universe for a while.

Mrs. Greenberg had decorated her front lawn with scarecrows, cardboard ghosts on stakes, and a blue placard declaring her support for Clinton/Gore. The election was a couple weeks away, and everyone seemed to think they were sure to win.

Inside, the hallways were decked out in chains of orange, purple, and black crepe paper. Every horizontal surface was covered with haunted houses, cotton spider webs, witches on broomsticks, and wicker baskets of bite-sized candies.

I took a handful to give Justin later.

I'd changed my outfit three times, then settled on black jeans and an olive-colored shirt that Mom said made me look like an army deserter. But when I walked in, everyone cried out my name as if they were happy to see me anyway, drab shirt and all. They surrounded the dining room table and handed around baby pumpkins and magic markers, foam stickers and popsicle sticks. I drew goofy faces on the pumpkins and we named them after teachers we didn't like: the ones who sucked up to star athletes; the ones who gave out A's too liberally, weakening the impact of our overachievements; and the ones who gave easy homework, leaving us unprepared for our future competition at the Ivies.

"Have some candy corn," said Candy, waving a bag of it under my nose.

"Candy corn is made from horse hooves!" Leethi said. "You're all eating dead horses!"

"Isn't this fun?" said Candy, waving off Leethi's comment. "I feel like a kid again. I don't even remember what the letters S. A. T. stand for."

"Warm cookies, oven fresh," Mrs. Greenberg sang out, setting a plate next to a tray of cupcakes topped with thick clouds of frosting and a crater-sized bowl of red-speckled nacho chips. The cookies were from a tube bought at the supermarket, but I didn't care. We grabbed cookies and cupcakes, our shoulders bumping, our mouths muddy with chocolate, our fingertips stained from the magic markers, our brains buzzing on sugar. I was pulling this off. I was having fun like everyone else.

All was well until someone turned up the music: Weird Al Yankovic's new parody album, featuring "Smells Like Nirvana." Everyone cheered and giggled while I dug my hands deep in my pockets to keep myself from smashing all their pumpkins. Apparently Weird Al was the soul of wit for singing that he couldn't understand Kurt Cobain's singing in "Smells Like Teen Spirit." No one saw what a fraud he was, a tool used by the mainstream corporate music world to push back against a band like Nirvana, more interested in making art than in making butt-loads of cash to impress shareholders.

Calm down, I told myself. So they have bad taste in music. There are worse crimes. They're nice to you. You're safe running in this pack.

"Ari, where do you live?" Candy asked, chewing a handful of candy corn.

"Maggie Lane? Across Fourteen Mile from you."

"Oh yeah? My friend Amy Finkelstein lives on Maggie Lane. We took a summer German class together. Have you ever met Amy? She used to have this annoying boyfriend who lived down the block, Mark Taborsky."

A terrible lightness bloomed between my ears. Say nothing, I thought. Act normal. But as I shook my head to indicate, *no, I did not know anyone by the name of Mark Taborsky*, a wave of nausea rushed up my throat, my vision clouded, and then I saw him clearly in my mind, teeth bared, fists clenched, belt loosened and clanking.

Candy went on, "They broke up when his parents sent him to a religious school, what do they call it, a yeshiva, right?" I told her she'd gotten the word right. "I haven't thought of Amy in months. We lost touch. I should call her."

Of course she wouldn't really call her. This was just idle party chitchat. But what if she did? What if right now, Candy excused herself from the party to call Amy, who'd then call Mark, who'd run over to get his long overdue revenge? Was there a side door I could use to get away, or a window large enough for me to crawl through? Some other escape route I hadn't noticed?

Then Candy whispered, "Rory's coming, but he's going to be late. I didn't want you to think he wasn't coming."

Was she mocking me? Candy wore a friendly, even encouraging smile, as if she believed Rory was the real reason I'd come to her party, and she was a-okay with it. Maybe she really felt that way. Or maybe she was playing dumb. Maybe she was friends with Mark, and her whole purpose in hosting this party had been to expose my past.

"I'm sorry," I said in a high voice. "I need the bathroom."

"Upstairs," she said in a cheerful voice. Too cheerful. She knew something.

I locked the door, then dropped to the ground and curled up on the fuzzy pink rug. Above my head, on the water tank of the toilet, sat a Barbie doll with a sinister smile. Her crocheted skirt hid a spare roll of toilet paper. Dad said it would take a sledgehammer to open a locked bathroom door.

I'm safe, I'm safe, I repeated to myself. Even if Candy did call her old gal pal Amy, Amy definitely wouldn't call Mark, and if she did, Mark was in school in Toronto, guarded by rabbis, and let's say he caught the next plane to Detroit, I'd have time . . .

So why did she make a special point of telling me Rory was coming? Had she heard a rumor about me from Amy?

I walked in front of the mirror. Not even a hint of a swish. Yet something had given Candy the idea that I wanted to know if Rory was definitely coming, and I had to figure out what that was soon, because Rory was coming, Rory was coming—to do what? To pull down his pants for my entertainment? To pull down mine? Rory the professional homosexual, hooking his pinky around one of my belt loops and reeling me close, digging his tongue into the cavity beneath my jawline, trailing his fingers down my back.

I rolled up some toilet paper, which I wrapped over my left hand like a baseball mitt. My pants slipped to my ankles, and I got on my knees, sat back on my heels. Rory was slightly taller than I was, but weaker. I could use my old karate moves beat him up, tug down his pants, push him to the ground. Then again, being gay, he'd probably do whatever I asked him to without force. A happy ending for everyone.

I finished in a minute, even with that evil Barbie doll watching me, and the usual after-shame flooded in, only worse, as if a pipe had burst somewhere. I dumped the wad of damp paper into the toilet bowl and waited for my heart to slow to its usual pace. Mrs. Greenberg had decorated her bathroom so nicely, had even thought to hide the spare toilet paper—and look what I'd done here.

I didn't belong with these people, this crowd of Weird Al Yankovic fans. Rory's friends. I washed my hands in scalding water, as if to sterilize them. Then I sneaked into the living room and grabbed the phone. When Mom answered, I said, "Hi, how are you?"

She said, "I'll be right there."

* * *

"Please accept my condolences about your uncle and come back again soon," said Mrs. Greenberg as she escorted me out, clutching my trembling elbow. She'd packed me a plastic container of desserts and one of the sandwiches she was serving later for dinner: two slices of white bread licked with mayonnaise, filled with iceberg lettuce and a thick glistening slab of ham. I didn't tell my mom about the ham. Later, in private, I tore off a soft pink shred of meat and touched it to my tongue. All I tasted was salt.

"Oh, I will," I promised. As usual I was too chicken-shit to say no to any direct order. The other kids hollered out their goodbyes, then went back to candy and cupcakes.

My mother remained seated in her white Cadillac, ignoring Mrs. Greenberg's frantic waving. As soon as I'd shut the passenger door, we zoomed down the driveway and into the street, where several rough-faced men, about to fix a pothole, were setting out traffic cones. These men were what I wanted: to have as well as to be. But the universe had gotten it all wrong, trapping me with this soft body that failed to perform on command, this overactive mind that vexed me with strange and worrying cravings, and this crooked heart that resisted being molded into its proper shape.

"What happened in there?" Mom demanded.

"When I say the safe word I'm supposed to be picked up, no questions asked."

"Never mind. What was going on?"

"Nothing," I said, furious that she'd violated our agreement. What exactly had she imagined going on in that cheery white house with wooden bunnies on the lawn? "I just," I fiddled with the plastic containers on my lap. "I got scared."

Mom stopped the car in the middle of the street. Thankfully we were still safely in the subdivision, with no traffic in sight. "Look at me. Are you telling the truth?"

"What, you think I'm a liar? On top of everything else?"

She seemed sad to hear it. "I don't understand. What scared you?"

"One of the kids there . . . he might be gay." I hated moving my lips and teeth and tongue to form that word. "I don't want people to get the wrong idea about me."

"Oh," said Mom, relaxing her grip on the steering wheel. "But why would anyone think you were gay?"

My God, I thought, do you really have to ask? But then, what if she thought so too? Had she always thought so? Long before Mark, high school, this whole mess?

"Someone there knew," I said, then took a breath, "about Mark."

There. I'd said his name aloud in front of her.

Mom continued driving. "Ari, he can't hurt you. You know that, right?"

No, I didn't know that. Here's what I knew: for now I was safe because I was known to be straight, Mark's unwilling victim. But what if I had offered a subtle, squishy answer to that police officer who'd asked if I wanted it. What if I'd said something like, not with him, but maybe some other guy? Or if I explained that I had these urges mixed up in my own head for reasons that didn't make sense to me?

Mom pulled over to the curb and put the car in park. "You could go back."

"I don't know if they believed my excuse, about my uncle."

I imagined Candy spreading my story all over Dalton, or calling Amy and asking if she knew this kid Ari, who'd acted so strange at this party?

"Just say you found out he's better now." Mom backed into a driveway and turned around. "If you can go back there now, then you can face the next challenge. But if you run away, it'll just take longer and make it harder to work up your confidence."

I argued with her, insisted no one would talk to me, but in two minutes we were back with the scarecrows and grinning ghosts on stakes. Before pushing me out of her car, Mom explained that the secret to making conversation at parties was asking lots of questions. "People love to talk about themselves. And next time, try wearing something more cheerful-looking. You're going to a party, not off to war."

"Why can't we sell our house?" I interrupted her. "Why can't we move somewhere no one knows me, like Troy or Novi. Or Detroit?"

"Detroit!" she said.

I sounded pretty dumb. Too fearful and feminine.

Pumpkins

Mrs. Greenberg looked confused when I rang the doorbell again.

In the dining room, I made my excuse as instructed, though no one seemed to buy it. I guessed I wouldn't be welcome to sit with the Circle at lunch on Monday, which maybe wasn't so terrible. Kurt Cobain would never have sat with these people.

Dinner was being served outside, so I followed the others onto the patio. As the crowd broke off into twos and threes, I sat alone on a plastic lawn chair and worked on a pile of soggy cole slaw until Rory appeared. He wore a mint green shirt that looked new and set off his blue eyes. Gay guys would probably have liked him.

"Can I join you?" he asked. "Unless you're embarrassed to be seen with me."

"Of course I'm not embarrassed." I hated myself for lying.

"I want to decorate some pumpkins," he said. "Join me?"

"Lead the way," I said.

Back inside, Rory showed me how to use a coin to rub off plastic decals of googly eyes, crooked noses, and devilish grins onto the pumpkins. He drew elaborate designs with the glitter wand, then passed it to me, but my glitter clumped up in awkward piles.

"It comes out better if you do it this way." Rory took the wand and showed me how once more. His fingers moved carefully over mine, but never touched them.

"What was it like?" I asked, studying his face, smooth as a baby's cheek. He pretended not to understand. "You know, when those boys chased you."

"I was petrified," Rory said, but he sounded more resentful than petrified. "I thought they'd kill me."

"So why did you do it, I mean, with the carnation? Why not stay out of their way?"

He shrugged, offered a feeble smile. "I couldn't help it. He's just so beautiful," he said in a small voice, and then I understood everything. My eyes drifted down to his fingers, so long and white, the nails filed down to beautiful curves that shimmered in the dark, as if they'd been painted. I stared at them more closely, feeling curious, nauseated, horrified. They *had* been painted, with a thin layer of sparkling nail polish.

Jesus, I thought. What are you, asking to get killed?

But that afternoon, Rory seemed perfectly at ease, more worried about the glitter on his pumpkin drying evenly than someone punching him in the face.

As the sun disappeared behind the roofs of the colonials at the end of the cul-de-sac, we decorated pumpkins together in the fading light of the late afternoon. I forgot the existence of the Greenbergs, their guests, the men fixing the street, the whole world. Rory and I let the room get very dark, and then we looked up from our work.

"That's very nice," he said, admiring my pumpkin.

"How do you know, without the lights on?" I asked.

"I can just tell." He looked right at me, the whites of his eyes glowing through the shadows. "Can't you?"

I paused. "Yeah," I admitted.

We sat there a while, our eyes straining to make out the beauty of all these pumpkins laid out before us like a feast, but they were not to eat.

"It'll be our secret," Rory said, then turned the lights on.

FOUR

SHUT UP AND KISS ME DATING SITE'S NEW LEADER—WHY HE MATTERS

By T. A. Severin
Washington Post

Justin Jackson, who helped hot new dating site Shut Up and Kiss Me extend its reach to over a million subscribers, has been named the company's new Chief Executive Officer.

On Tuesday the DC-based site announced that Jackson will replace Steven O'Connell, who will stay on at the company in an advisory role.

Jackson, who joined the company two years ago as Chief Digital Strategist, managed the successful launch of a shopping app, harvesting the data from Shut Up and Kiss Me's users to connect them with retail sites, restaurants, movie chains, as well as weight loss companies, medical practices, and other sites tailored to their interests.

"At Shut Up and Kiss Me, we respect the privacy of our subscribers and we take that commitment very seriously," said Jackson in an interview last summer. "What we're doing is empowering our subscribers to achieve their personal goals by providing them with choices that they might otherwise not have been aware of. The data they've shared with us gives us a unique window into their lives, creating perhaps the fullest picture out there of who they are and what they value, their hopes and dreams, and we believe what makes us stand out from other dating sites is that we want to bring them closer to making those fantasies into a tangible reality for them."

Shut Up and Kiss Me's investment in digital has not come cheap. And yet that investment has recently paid off, resulting in a 44% growth in e-related commerce in the final quarter of last year.

"As the newest member of our leadership team, Justin has been a shining star," says company founder and board chair, George Locker. "And now in this new position, with Steve at his side, I'm confident he'll continue to thrive, as he tells our story to our American consumer base as well as our increasing share of the international market."

During the transition, Jackson, the company's first African-American CEO, will continue his duties as Chief Digital Strategist and manage the search for his successor in that role. ■

BOOK REVIEW:
Passion Rationalized: a History of Medieval Manners, Romance, and Courtly Love by Ari Silverman

Review by Rafael Gutierrez

The Review of Medieval Studies (formerly the New York History Quarterly)

Ari Silverman, an emerging expert on Medieval manners, begins his new book *Passion Rationalized* by asserting that although contemporary Western notions of love and romance are commonly traced to the Roman poet Catallus, they are actually more firmly rooted in conventions that developed during the Middle Ages.

"For the common person, life in late Medieval Europe may have been, as was once famously described 'nasty, brutish, and short,' but for those who were buffeted from the vicissitudes of their contemporary age by the stout walls of a castle, monastery, convent, or institution of higher learning, the Middle Ages were a stimulating time of intellectual and artistic innovation."

Arguing that the in-aptly named Renaissance was not a time of rebirth but the flowering of a blossom that began to open several centuries earlier, Silverman details how the codifying and dissemination of codes of social behavior formed a new social order and laid the foundation for democratic movements that occurred centuries later. "When the rules are known only to a select few, social advancement is impossible."

Some may quibble at the grander contentions of this deftly written and often witty volume, but few can argue with Silverman's acumen as a scholar. Highly recommended. ∎

"Finding Your Way to Yes"

(excerpts from guest lecturer Justin Jackson, CEO of Shut Up and Kiss Me, to business students at Howard University)

" . . . because the thing you've absolutely got to know about the past is that it's over. And the thing you've also got to know about the future is that it's unknowable. I mean, if you'd asked me ten years ago, where would I be now, what would I be doing now, I'd have been dead wrong. That's one hundred percent sure. I wish you guys could have met me in high school. You know what I wanted more than anything else in high school? I wanted to pierce my nose. Yeah, I'm not kidding. Thank God my wife talked me out of that bullshit. Can I say bullshit here? Yeah? No? Okay, well, I'm just going to go with it.

Anyway, what you can do, and this is always true no matter where you are or what you're doing, is embrace the present moment. Say yes to now, that's a little saying of mine. Do the best job you possibly can at what you're doing right now. Love it. Even if you're, I don't know, cleaning toilets or something. Because first, whatever you're doing, it's not like you have a choice. You don't choose the hand you're dealt, just how you play it. And second, that energy, that's attractive to people. That makes them want you to be around. That makes them want to give you stuff to do, more opportunities.

So I quit worrying about the past, the present, a long time ago. I just focus on what I'm doing now. I say yes to now. And I'm a lot happier that way. And a lot more successful. People want to keep giving me stuff to do, you know, like managing brands and all that. So it's worked out, and it's kind of cool . . . " ∎

WE'RE SO PROUD OF YOU!

(a card Ari received from his parents after he earned his Ph.D)

Printed on the front of the card:

WE'RE SO PROUD OF YOU!

(pink background, white lettering)

Printed on the inside of the card, right flap:

SON, You are
Loved for the BOY you were,
Honored for the special MAN you have become,
Treasured for the wonderful SON you'll always be.

(white background, pink lettering)

Hand-written on the inside of the card, left flap:

Dear Ari,

Your dad and I are so proud of your many accomplishments. You've made a full life for yourself, with friends, and now a new position at a fine university, and someday you'll find someone else, someone worthy of you to share it with. I know you joke about being alone, an "old maid", but I just want to tell you don't believe it's your destiny. You have too much to offer someone. We just want you to be happy. If it took us a little time to realize it, please know that we're sorry. Maybe it took us a while, but we've caught up now to where you are.

We love you.

Mom

(black pen, in fluid, lacy handwriting)

Yes or No

THE LONG HARD WINTER WAS ENDING. We could play tennis outdoors.

If we raced out to the courts the very second the last bell rang, my friends from the Junior Varsity tennis squad and I would manage to squeeze in a set before the girls' team practice. To save time, we'd wear our athletic gear under our Dalton uniforms, which we'd quickly peel off on court as if doing a strip tease on fast forward.

While practicing, we'd yak about school, cars, or music, which I now spoke about with authority. I explained the differences between Nirvana and Pearl Jam, the Stone Roses and Stone Temple Pilots, the Happy Mondays and the Sundays. I handed out mix tapes or zines like *Kill Your Offspring*, which I'd picked up at a Royal Oak coffeehouse.

One afternoon, we were fooling around, hitting hotshot overheads and wicked, razor-fast serves a mile wide—we called them Scud missiles—when Elaine Rosen came over and challenged me to a set.

Elaine was the top player on girls' varsity. Her name had appeared in the *Detroit Free Press*. Why would she want to play me? I found out why after Elaine kicked my ass 6-1, in a mere twenty minutes. As we shook hands at the net, she asked me to take her to Spring Cotillion.

I stood there, mute. Was this a joke? Then Elaine snapped her fingers in my face and said, "You know, Spring Cotillion? The dance? Or don't you want to go with me?"

In front of my new tennis friends, I liked to mock Dalton traditions like cotillions, the White Gifts Pageant, the Junior Ring Prize, the Passage of Leadership Assembly. "Imagine how much the music must suck at a Cotillion," I'd say. "And who wants to wear a fucking tie on a night off?"

But it was easier to claim I was boycotting our school dances when it seemed impossible that I might attend one.

"It's not you personally," I told Elaine. "It's just, I don't normally do stuff like," I waved my hands in the air, "cotillions. Rah-rah-rah, all that mainstream consumerist bullshit. You know?"

"No, I don't," she said. "Are you saying yes or no?"

Why me? I guessed because there weren't many Jewish boys my age at Dalton, and Elaine came from a family—like mine—that considered these things important.

It just didn't seem right, going to a dance, with a girl, after, well, everything. And strangely, I didn't remember telling Elaine "yes," but the word must have slipped out. I had trouble sticking to my principles when cornered. Plus, the invitation was flattering. Elaine was one of the most popular girls in school, a "lifer" who'd attended Dalton since kindergarten, and she strode through the halls with the easy confidence of an empress surveying her empire. She had a long, leggy body, thick, dark hair with auburn highlights, and a tiny feline nose. Her clear skin was as smooth as notebook paper. Her full lips were often parted just slightly, as if she were about to say something significant.

My parents were thrilled to hear the news. I had a 3.8 grade point average. I was playing a team sport. I was attending a dance with a Jewish girl. Now if I could just lose my smart mouth, and my taste for art and for what Dad called "that awful music of his . . . "

In other words, maybe I'd finally gotten over this whole mess.

Elaine said we'd be attending the dance with her best friend, Heather Gordon, runner-up for Autumn Cotillion Queen. Oh, and Heather's date was Justin Jackson.

* * *

"SO, BRAIN, I GUESS WE'RE DOUBLE dating."

Just when I'd thought I'd finally caught up with him, Justin had grown another couple inches over spring break. His eyes seemed an even richer shade of brown, more sensual than ever, and underneath his Dalton letter jacket, his shoulders were firm, deeply defined. He'd gotten a part-time job rolling out dough at a bakery down the road from school, and he smelled faintly of cinnamon and sugar.

We were talking about the Cotillion during Pre-Calc, taught by a rookie math teacher named Sarabeth Laker. You could always identify the new teachers, the ones who still seemed impressed by the whole Dalton aura, the well-mannered students in uniforms, the parents waiting in Beamers and Mercedes for their kids after school. Later they'd learn to make wisecracks about their low salaries, or complain about what they would have earned teaching bored public school brats.

Justin liked to test Miss Laker by mouthing off in class like some slacker—"How do you spell 'the'?"—though he was our class star. He'd told me his dream was to invent a mathematical theory that would bear his name.

"So you like Heather?" I asked, idly massaging the buttons on my graphing calculator. What was he doing with someone like Heather, blond and sometimes bubbly? She wore frosted lipstick. She liked chirpy songs by Wilson Phillips.

"She's ok," he said, stretching across the aisle. If he'd leaned over any further, his head would have been in my lap, where I could stroke his hair, pinch his nose and ears, trace the ridges of his lips with my finger. "You got any tips on dating Jewish girls?"

"Yeah," I said. "If you meet her parents, tell them your last name's Levy."

He laughed. "Good one." His voice sounded deeper this year. It made my stomach rumble as if I were starving.

* * *

I'D WANTED HIM SO LONG, I ached with it.

At night, I rubbed my face into my pillow and fantasized about asking him to pose with his shirt off so I could draw his torso, strictly in the name of art. I'd pull him into some corner of school and suck on his face, plunging my hands into his pants, hearing his breath get hot and tight in my ear—the kind of tricks Mark would have played.

I kept trying not to think about Mark, but he and his little stratagems had gotten stuck in my fantasies. He was all I knew about sex, the first person to prove that the things I'd only heard or read or wondered about could happen in life.

In that school they'd sent him off to, in Canada, had he found another weakling to prey on? Some mama's boy whose parents couldn't figure out why every vacation their darling kept begging to stay at home? Did Mark slip into his bed at night, slowly loosen the drawstrings of their pajamas, his cool fingers tickling strange skin?

I'd wake up before dawn feeling sick to my stomach, with a crick in my neck.

Whatever You Prefer

I'd brought Justin candy from Israel, bagels and cookies from a cousin's Jewish bakery. Sometimes he watched me work on my drawings in the art room or walked me to my locker after class. Still, we weren't what you'd call friends. I'd learned to play the role of trusty subordinate, the affable sidekick, always offering homework help, candy, and worshipful obedience.

Now thanks to Elaine, I had a chance to be Justin's equal, or at least almost equal. Thanks to Elaine, I could play the part of the ardent, devoted lover, the suave boyfriend, desired and therefore desirable.

I was so determined that Justin would see me being a good date to Elaine that I'd have gladly laid myself down over a puddle for her to step on if she'd asked me to. Fortunately, Elaine expected very little of me. Unlike other couples in our grade, giggling, teasing, bumping bodies, we behaved ourselves, our comportment conforming strictly to the guidelines in the Dalton Handbook. Elaine was surprisingly easy to talk to, and with the Cotillion coming up, we had a lot to talk about.

What would she wear, and what would I wear to match?

Could we go somewhere nice for dinner before the dance?

Oh, yes, of course. My father was a dentist—we could eat as nicely as Elaine wanted. And I would pick her up.

Should we pick up Heather and Justin or meet them at the restaurant?

Either way is fine. Whatever you prefer.

Elaine decided that I needed a new look, so we drove to the mall on Saturday. I skipped art class for the trip.

She picked me up in her zippy red Honda, with TLC blaring on her car stereo. I'd never heard a TLC song all the way through, but it wasn't bad. At Hudson's, I wriggled out of my flannel shirt and into an oatmeal-colored wool cardigan that hugged my body. Gone were my ripped jeans in favor of a crisp navy polo shirt and khakis.

"Stop hiding your body in those baggy plaid shirts," she said. "You're in good shape. Show it off a little."

We shared a pink frozen yogurt, studded with gummy bears. The yogurt shop was filled with couples our age, attractive, noisy girls and bored young men. I kept studying the guys, their hair, their postures, to see what I should do. One of them caught my eye and we exchanged helpless smiles, as if to say, the things we men did for our women!

Next, Elaine introduced me to a "stylist" who finally solved the problem of my hair, teaching me how to mess it up on purpose in a technique known as "feathering." As the hair stylist's hands fluttered over my ears, Elaine read a tennis magazine in the waiting area. Next to me, a good-looking man was getting the back of his neck shaved, and the stylist whispered into my ear, "Are you nervous about something?"

"What?" I asked.

"You keep looking at that guy in the next chair."

I felt something drop in my chest, down to the pit of my stomach. "It's just . . . I don't . . . " I tried to say. I should have known. All hair stylists were gay. He could tell that I could tell when a man was good-looking.

"I just need you to keep your head still so I don't mess up your cut," said the stylist.

"Yeah, of course. I'm sorry."

As he went back to work, I closed my eyes and thought about how I needed to be more careful in the future. Then I thought of something I'd read about Kurt Cobain, that he used to wonder if he was gay because he wanted a male friend he could talk to intimately, and "be as affectionate with that person as I would be with a girl." Ultimately, he realized he was only "gay in spirit" and hooked up with Courtney Love, whom he called the most attractive person he'd ever met. I didn't see it. With her plump, red-velvet painted lips, ragged bleached blonde hair, and low-cut "kinder-whore" baby doll dresses with lacy collars, Courtney looked like a sloppy drag queen.

Maybe my girl problems weren't with all girls but just the ones I knew. Maybe I wasn't homosexual but Kurt-sexual, gay only in spirit, in need of a Courtney Love.

Maybe Elaine was my Courtney Love.

Your Hair Looks Good

When I showed up to school on Monday, I feared that Justin would mock me for going mainstream, but he said, "Your hair looks *goooood*."

This new hairdo of mine was a responsibility. I cut out of AP American History to study my reflection in the bathroom mirror. Justin was right: it did look *goooood*.

A toilet flushed and Rory Fox popped out of one of the stalls.

I considered giving him with a grunt, a nod, or a tight-lipped smile, but before I could choose, Rory turned on a faucet and said, "Moving up in the world, I hear."

"What?"

"You and Elaine Rosen, Spring Cotillion."

He was right. With my new hair and wardrobe, and Elaine as my guide, I could pass for normal, listening to albums by Billboard chart-toppers and eating frozen yogurt. Elaine would introduce me to popular boys, so that one day, when she and I broke up, my new good-looking friends would clap me on the back, and utter manly words of wisdom like, "Plenty more fish in the sea," or a simple, knowing, "Women!"

Rory stood there watching me as if he saw through my act.

"Elaine asked me to go with her," I mumbled, "so . . . "

"I'm going too." He scrubbed his hands, finger by delicate white finger, under the water. "I don't want to, but it means a lot to my mom."

I stepped toward the door, but he blocked the way with his arm, reaching for a paper towel. His nose was inches from my face. He smelled of lilacs.

"You're taking a girl to Cotillion?" I asked.

"Actually, I'm taking a boy to Cotillion."

"What?" I said. "Does anyone know? I mean, does the school know?"

Rory shook his head.

"But what if . . . They'd never let you!"

Rory put his finger to his lips. "Our little secret," he said.

But how? Of course, I knew how. You showed up, walked into the room with a boy next to you. Exactly as I'd walk in with Justin, plus our dates, of course. I pictured Rory and this boy clinking glasses of punch by a buffet table, before getting punched by some football player. And this time Rory would get punished by the school. I was pretty sure taking a same-sex date to a school dance did not conform to the Dalton Code.

Is Everyone Here High?

DAVID CAME IN FROM ANN ARBOR with his new girlfriend, a messy-haired Jewish girl who lived in Detroit, where she'd started a sustainable pickling business. "Yeah, just what the city needs," my father said. "Pickles."

They made us a stir-fry with vegetables from the garden of David's co-op, plus guacamole, which Dad refused to taste. "Looks like something out of your nose," he said.

David's girlfriend described the revitalization of the city, all these young entrepreneurs like herself moving in and making the most delicious beer and beautiful art, or maybe it was delicious art and beautiful beer. And the pickles! Had we ever tried a pickled radish? "Like candy!" she gushed. "Naturally healthy candy."

"Have some guacamole," Mom said, passing the bowl to Dad.

"I don't eat green stuff," Dad said.

"Come on, Dad," said David. "Cut the Archie Bunker act for once, okay?"

"But I would try one of those pickled radishes," Dad said. "Did you bring any?"

They had not.

"Oh, too bad. Next time, I expect you to bring some pickled radishes," Dad said.

After dinner, David and his girlfriend drove me to an event called "Community Concert Series," a kind of hippie fair held in the basement of an organic food store in Royal Oak. No leather or meat products were allowed, so I left my belt in the car. Luckily I was wearing my cool-kid Converse sneakers, still as uncomfortable as ever.

Inside, guys and girls in dreadlocks waved their arms like snakes over their heads while a band played guitar, drums and a flute in the corner. There were little tables of people selling tie-dye shirts, candles, and honey.

"You should sell your drawings here," David said.

"I don't believe in doing art for money," I said.

David's girlfriend, who'd placed a ring in her nose, joined the dancing, bouncing up and down like a beach ball. I'd once overheard Justin debating with some friends which type of piercing was cooler: eyebrow, nose, or ear, and if ear, which ear? One of them said the right ear was the gay one, and Justin said, "Please, that's so 1985."

Maybe it was better to pierce both ears, just to be safe.

David's girlfriend tried to drag me onto the floor, but I planted my feet. "I'm no hippie," I said. "Where's the mosh pit?"

She laughed, then went back to dancing.

As we sipped paper cups of organic juice, I bragged to my brother about my date. David told me that to please a girl, you should talk about things she liked.

"Elaine likes tennis," I said.

"Tennis is such a white sport," said David, licking a honey sample off a popsicle stick. "'I play tennis at Dalton,'" he added in a British accent.

"My friend Justin plays tennis," I said. "And he's black."

"Good for him," David said. "Come on, dance with me." He dragged me by the hand to where the others were jumping around. But weirdly, when we got there, he didn't let go of my hand, just twirled it around, as if two guys dancing together were a normal thing. I hadn't held David's hand since I was a kid, and it felt kind of nice. I thought about saying something then, like, "I've had thoughts about guys." Or "I might be bisexual." But no, that was a cop-out. Just tell the truth.

"Can I ask you something," I panted when we finished dancing, both of us out of breath and sweaty. He nodded. I closed my eyes, then opened them. *What would you think if I was gay?* "So, uh, is everyone here high?" I asked.

"No way," he said. "This place is strictly straight edge."

A Gentleman

On the evening of the Cotillion, my mother straightened the tie Elaine had picked for me to wear, a subtle navy blue plaid. Dad gawked at me as if some alien had inhabited his son's body. Mom dusted off the shoulder pads of my sport coat, and asked three times if I needed money, then told Dad to offer me some man-to-man advice.

He thought for a minute. "Be a gentleman," he said. "We brought you up to know what that means."

Before leaving, I studied my outfit in the mirror. Kurt Cobain could wear a pinstripe suit and tie on the cover of *Rolling Stone* and appear subversive. But in my suit, I looked more like a nice Jewish boy getting ready for his bar mitzvah. I needed something to mess up my facade: a funny pair of glasses or a spangled green bowtie. Finally, I stuffed a yellow paisley handkerchief into my lapel pocket.

Elaine Rosen lived in a gated community of townhouses with her mother and aunt, both divorced. I rolled down my window to tell the guard my name, and he nodded as if he'd expected me, then let me pass.

The Rosens owned an end unit framed by stiff, silver-needled pine bushes and a few daffodils that had popped up between their roots. A rayon flag with two cuddling kittens fluttered beside the garage. Gross, I thought. To buck myself up, I listened to "Mandinka" by Sinead O'Connor, all the way through. Twice. Yes, I could do this.

Elaine's aunt opened the front door. Her hair, bleached platinum blonde, looked as if it had been blown up and backwards by a sudden gale. "Well, Ari, I hear you're a real *mensch*. And nice that Elaine's seeing a Dalton boy who knows the word *mensch*." She pulled me into her soft, round body, kissed my cheek, then wiped away the lipstick mark with a tissue from inside her sleeve. "Let's not make her jealous," she said.

Their living room was crowded with sharp-edged furniture in metal and Lucite. The TV was showing footage from the raid at Waco, switching back and forth between orange flames and plumes of black smoke and then tall, stern, mannish Janet Reno in her over-sized glasses. Did no one think she was a lesbian?

In the kitchen, Elaine's mom was telling someone off on the phone while taking deep puffs on a long, thin brown cigarette. She had short dark hair and a hard face with lines around her eyes, and her nails were painted a shade of red so deep they might have been black. Elaine said she was a lawyer at a firm downtown and she carried a gun, in case she got stuck at the office late. I wondered what it felt like, to carry a gun.

Elaine's aunt muted the television and invited me to sit beside her on the overstuffed couch, which was covered in a shimmery pearl-like fabric. The spongy cushions sank alarmingly beneath my weight; I feared I might drown in them.

Perhaps they were a family of three witches, trying to trap me. And where exactly was Elaine's Dad? Why had she never mentioned him?

"Elaine says you two play tennis on weekends," the aunt said. "In this cool weather, you could hurt your back. Promise me you'll be careful."

Although we'd only played just that once and Elaine had never said a word about doing it again, her aunt sounded so worried that I made the promise.

"We all love tennis," she continued. "Next summer we're going to Wimbledon."

"Really? I didn't know just anyone could go to Wimbledon," I said.

She looked at me with pity, as if I'd said something bizarre. "Well, you can."

Elaine came downstairs in a sparkling copper-colored dress, pausing before the bottom step. Her cheeks were dusted in a faint layer of blush and her lips were painted dark red like her mother's nails. "Hey," she said.

I knew she looked beautiful, that I should do or say something.

"I'd hug you," I said, "but I don't want to crush your dress."

"That's okay." She reached out her right arm. I leaned over the bannister and patted her shoulders, taking care not to touch her body with mine.

"What's that?" she asked, pointing to my yellow hankie.

"My outfit's too boring," I complained, but she pulled out the hankie. "Hide this somewhere," she said, so I stuffed it in my pocket.

"Sorry, kids," said Ms. Rosen, coming from the kitchen, and we jumped back, away from each other. "Nice to meet you, Ari."

"Oh, he's very, very nice," said Elaine's aunt.

For our pre-Cotillion dinner, Heather and Elaine had chosen Cobra, a trendy restaurant in Royal Oak that served exotic fare like mesclun salad with breaded wheels of goat cheese on square white plates. The centerpieces were crayons and bubble wands in bottles of soapy water, and throughout our meal, bubbles floated over our heads. The tables were covered with sheets of butcher paper, and you were expected to draw funny pictures in crayon. When you left, your busboy crumpled up the paper and threw it away.

Elaine wrote, "Bubbles blow!"

Heather, blonder than ever that night, scribbled a stick figure portrait of one of the deans scolding Elaine about her short skirt. In fact, Elaine and Heather were model Dalton students, varsity athletes with summa cum laude grade point averages. Heather won our class citizenship award last year, while Elaine had won it the year before.

It was my turn to draw something. My broken red crayon hovered over the butcher paper for several seconds. I only knew how to draw for real, not to amuse friends at dinner. Finally, I drew a daisy shedding a single petal. I felt like a sell-out.

"You can do better than that," said Justin.

Shut up, I wanted to say. Didn't he appreciate how hard I was working to erase myself, to be worthy of being his friend?

"Okay, your turn," I said. What would Justin draw? A skull? An anarchy symbol?

"No thanks, Brain," he said. "Coloring's for kids."

"Do you see any kids here?" I said. "This is an expensive place."

"Wait, what did you call him?" Elaine asked. "Brain?"

Justin seemed caught off-guard. "That's his name."

"His name is Ari."

"So? I call him Brain."

I was going to say I didn't mind, but Elaine asked, "Why don't I call you some other body part? Like Dick?"

"Because." He scratched one of his lovely ears. "That ain't my name."

Justin had worn the wrong thing: an old-fashioned tweed jacket that was too large and swallowed up his body, and the same worn topsiders he wore to school, which would be awkward for dancing. A polyester blend pale blue button-down shirt open at the neck, a gap just wide enough for me to slip my hand inside, to touch one of his nipples.

"What are you looking at?" Elaine asked me.

Fuck, I thought, trying to blink away the image I'd just conjured. She'd caught me. "Nothing," I said, but she frowned as if she didn't believe my answer.

Our waiter brought an *amuse bouche* of whipped chickpeas and toast points.

"Hey, we didn't order that," said Justin.

"It's complimentary," said the waiter.

"Oh, alright then." Justin promptly scooped up a heaping dollop of chickpeas with a piece of toast. "Not bad," he said, gulping it down, "but they could give you enough for the whole table." For once he seemed out of his element, more nervous than I was. Nodding at the waiter, he said, "Did you catch his attitude? He thinks he's the boss, but we're the ones paying."

"He's just doing his job," said Heather, who like Elaine had eaten here and at other restaurants like it many times. They exchanged ironic smiles.

"Well, his job is to serve us, so he better do it if he wants his tip."

"Okay, Mr. Testosterone," said Heather.

"Let's see what's for dinner," I interrupted.

Heather and Elaine glanced casually at their menus, but Justin looked panicked. I understood why when I saw the prices. "My treat," I said, claiming my dad had given me his credit card (true), and insisted that I pay the bill (false).

"Oh, no," said Heather. "We'll pay our share."

"My dad said specifically that he wanted to take us all out. He'd be upset if I didn't pay," I said.

"Thanks, Brain," said Justin.

"Anytime, Mr. Testosterone," I said.

His face darkened. "You call me that again, I'm going to hurt you."

"What a bully you are," said Heather.

I was surprised to hear them arguing. I'd thought that she and Justin were a good match. I pictured the two of them perched on the bleachers during tennis, making wisecracks about Dalton students below. Did Heather know how beautiful he was? And what did Justin think of how I looked? I was at least as good-looking as Heather. Not that I'd been in the running, but if I had been, how would I have fared?

"You punch my date and I'll punch you," said Elaine.

"Really, I didn't mind," I said. "Let's just enjoy our dinner."

"He thinks he knows what comedy is," Heather sneered.

No More Wild Orchids

SYLVIA FOX, MOTHER OF THE FAMOUS Rory, had been the assistant to Dean Demuth's executive assistant for sixteen years, as long as her son had attended Dalton. That was how they got the tuition remission.

The highlight of Ms. Fox's year was decorating the Dining Hall—recently renamed the Chrysler Dining Hall after a gift from the puniest of Detroit's Big Three auto companies—for the Autumn Cotillion. And since this year Rory was going to the dance, Ms. Fox had outdone herself. The fiberglass ceiling tiles were completely covered by helium balloons in blue and gold, the school colors. Folding tables, disguised in crisp blue linen cloths, were set out with bowls of blue raspberry punch with floating pineapple rings, and trays of mini tarts (blueberry and lemon, another nod to our school colors).

As we walked in, we passed a box to donate money for care packages to the troops still stuck in the Persian Gulf. A pair of photographers stopped Heather and Justin to take their pictures for the alumni newsletter. They couldn't have been the more perfect Dalton couple: two clean-cut kids, one white and blond, the other black without facial hair or visible tattoos. As they were posing, a couple of Detroit guys brushed by Justin and touched two fingers to their eyebrows. Justin repeated the gesture.

"What was that?" I asked.

"You wouldn't get it," he said. "You're not from the city."

Rory arrived with Leethi Adiga. Had he chickened out with the boyfriend? But then some nerdy looking guy I didn't recognize shuffled in just behind them. His hands were stuck in the pockets of his corduroy sport coat and he kept swiveling his head, as if he'd been caught stealing something. Did anyone notice, make the connection between him and Rory? It was something awful, like out of a nightmare.

"Nice tie," Justin buzzed in my ear.

His breath reeked of alcohol. "Elaine picked it," I said.

"I'm glad for you two," he said. "Yeah, Elaine . . . " His voice trailed off. Where'd he gotten the alcohol?

"Ice, Ice Baby" came on, and everyone rushed to dance, including Miss Laker, who was chaperoning along with our school librarian Mr. Wentworth, the one Rory had compared to Tom Cruise. He'd recently gotten divorced, and we all ooh'ed and ahh'ed over their pairing except Heather. She thought Wentworth could do much better.

I'd expected Justin to sneer at white rap, but he was out there with everyone else, moving in stiff jerking motions until it was time for the slow dance, when he tripped over his own shoe, its rubbery sole sticking to the dance floor. Heather laughed, and he abandoned her, mid-song. She shrugged, then went to find some friends.

Meanwhile, Elaine and I floated across the floor and gossiped about our favorite tennis stars. When we sat down again, I pulled out Elaine's chair for her without asking. This impressed Justin, who was sulking at our table and sipping at a plastic cup of punch that I guessed had been spiked.

"Jealous?" I said. "I could pull out your chair too." I wished he'd say yes. We could pretend it was all for laughs, but Justin ignored me. "Seriously, are you still upset?" I whispered. "About dinner?"

"Brain," he said in a slurred, sleepy voice, "just go have a good time."

Not long after that, Justin left early, dragged outside by Brandon and some kid from Detroit who apparently was driving him home. Heather, incensed at being stranded, promptly caught her own ride home with some friends. I offered to take her, but she said, "Just because my night's ruined doesn't mean you two kids can't stay and have fun."

I looked at Elaine. "What do you think?"

Elaine wanted to stay, so I thought, why not? Justin had told me to have a good time. We did our own versions of the Swim, the Hustle, the Cha-Cha-Cha, and even Walked like Egyptians, laughing at ourselves the whole time. Then we slow danced to some stupid love song by Toni Braxton that neither of us liked, but we danced to it anyway. Elaine rested her hands lightly on my shoulders, while I laced my hands around the small of her back, the two of us maintaining a thin sheet of air between our waists, unlike the other couples, packed tightly together like pickles in a jar of brine.

"My parents love you," Elaine said. I'd figured out that whenever she said "parents," she meant her mother and aunt.

"Because I'm Jewish and I have a healthy grade point average?" I said.

"Oy vey!" she said. "Our little Elaine found a nice Jewish boy in that WASPy school. Such a miracle, thanks be to God!"

This was working. Maybe it could go on working. Not only for tonight, but also next week, and another, and then the rest of my life.

"Why did your folks send you to Dalton?" Elaine asked.

"Oh, you know." Mark's angry face blazed through my mind, and I blinked him away. "The education."

Later in the car, I said, "Let's not go home yet."

"Yeah?" she said. "What do you want to do?"

I suggested a movie. It was late, but wasn't that what you did when you were out on a date? See a movie?

The box office at the Showcase 17 was mobbed with noisy kids in jeans. I felt freakish in my sport jacket, next to Elaine in her party dress. When we reached the head of the line, everything was sold out except for a special late night showing of a NC-17 film. This week it was *Wild Orchid*, which was supposed to be sexy. Elaine raised her eyebrows. I shrugged, then bought two tickets.

I'd mistrusted movie theaters for years. All those seats in the darkness, no way to know if any of them were occupied by Mark or some other bully. But that night, walking in with Elaine, I felt like a normal patron. Even if Mark sat next to us now, what could he do, hit me? I'd smash his car windows with my tennis racquet.

The lights went down. I thought of putting my arm around Elaine or holding her hand, but I kept my body in my own seat. The movie itself was badly acted and boring. There wasn't much actual sex, though once, I saw a swollen orange breast with a huge nipple like a sunny-side-up egg. Look, I told myself. Get excited. But I couldn't. Maybe I'd gotten too used to seeing breasts in my life drawing class, which I'd skipped for three weeks in a row. Also, women's breasts seemed so fat and absurd. The male form made much more sense, the clean square lines of a flat, firm chest, solid like a Greek column.

After about half an hour, Elaine leaned over. To lick my ear? No, thankfully. She whispered. "You want to go?"

"Yeah, let's," I whispered back. Giggling, we squeezed out of our row.

The ride home was so quiet, I could hear the wheels on the road. I tuned the radio to 89X, which was playing Alice in Chains, but Elaine said, "Ugh, not that noise," and snapped it off. Hey, this is my car, I was going to say, but then she asked: "So, you and Justin are friends? What do you like about him?"

I could have replied, "Everything. The way he lives, talks, breathes." But I said, "He knows a lot about music."

We didn't talk after that. At Elaine's subdivision, she waved to the man in the booth, who let us through. I parked by her townhouse and walked her to the door.

"No more *Wild Orchids*," she said and we laughed.

"No more *Wild Orchids*."

Without warning, we lunged for each other's lips. Apparently this was a real date. I tasted her muddy brown lipstick, and then we stepped apart and laughed softly. I felt a strange fluttering in my stomach, like that fruity punch from the Cotillion had gotten mixed with the popcorn at the movies, and they were spinning around inside me, threatening to bubble up my throat and explode out of my mouth.

We Can Change It

My parents were pretending to watch a movie on TV, as if they weren't waiting for me to get home.

"Did you have fun?" Mom asked, straining to sound casual. My father stared at the television, but I knew he was waiting for my answer. All night I'd been looking forward to declaring proudly that I'd had fun, that I'd successfully dated a Jewish girl. But now, at the big moment, the truth felt like a lie.

"Yeah," I said.

Satisfied, they relaxed against the sofa.

I sat down to watch with them. "What's on?" I asked.

"We can change it," Mom said quickly, picking up the remote.

"Hey, it's almost at the end," Dad objected.

It was *The Accused*, heavily edited for television. Dr. Don and I used to talk about watching it. I never wanted to.

"Let's change the channel," said Mom. "It's right in the middle. You don't want to watch something right in the middle."

"Don't bother," I said. "I'm fine, really."

But I was not fine. I sank lower into the cushions, rubbed my sweaty fingers against the fabric, and as Jodie Foster wriggled beneath her attackers, I wanted to reach through the screen, wake those idiot bystanders doing nothing. Help her, dammit! I told myself this was art, and the filmmakers were rooting for me, against rape. But did they have to show us this ugliness? And did we have to witness it?

I said my stomach hurt and went to my room. For a while I lay fully clothed on my bed and stared at the ceiling. Would this ever stop? I wanted to feel normal.

With Tongue

The next day, I called David to report that Elaine and I had kissed.

"With tongue?" he asked.

Shit, I thought. No one had told me I was expected to use my tongue.

You're Not Playing Tennis

JUSTIN HAD SAVED A FEW BOTTLES of soapy water from the restaurant and invited me to blow bubbles with him in the parking lot. Lately, he did a lot of things like that, writing messages in sidewalk chalk, scattering birdseed over the bushes outside the headmaster's office so the birds would poop all over his windows, ordering a pizza to be delivered to his English class. He wanted to come up with as many ways as possible to break Dalton rules that hadn't been invented yet.

While we blew bubbles at an ugly abstract statue in cement, ringed by newly planted red and white geraniums, Justin asked how things were going with Elaine. I told him we'd kissed and waited for his reaction.

"With tongue?" he asked. Even he knew.

"How are things with Heather?" I asked.

He shrugged. "I only went with her to the dance because, well, it was a kind of experiment. A failed one."

"She's not right for you," I said.

"No?" he asked, suddenly interested. "So who is?"

I wanted to scream out my reply. Those sharply cut lips of his, slightly chapped from the cold, I bet they'd taste like two strawberries. Or better, like nothing at all, just plain, like lips were supposed to taste.

"I don't know," I said. "Just not her. She doesn't deserve you."

"At least one of us has a girlfriend. Give me the gory details."

Is that what I had, a girlfriend?

I steeled myself to kiss with tongue at the next opportunity, but the next few days, when I stopped to say hi to Elaine in the halls, she said hi back and went on walking. I dropped by tennis practice and asked if she wanted to play. "Maybe," she said. "Let's talk tomorrow." But we never did talk tomorrow or the day after. I thought about that moment at dinner, when she caught me looking at Justin. What else could she guess about me?

I called her at home. Her aunt answered.

"Elaine's not with you?" she said. "You're not playing tennis?"

"No." I realized too late I'd given the wrong answer.

Those Who Stay Will Be Champions

Like Kurt Cobain, I now had a public image to maintain, an eager fan base consisting of my parents, my brother, and Justin, all hungry for news of my new romance. I couldn't go on forever rehashing details of our evening at the Cotillion, or our afternoon in Birmingham, plastic spoons knocking through a soup of melting frozen yogurt. I desperately needed new material, but Elaine refused to cooperate.

I waited after school for her by the entrance to the girls' locker room, next to a sign declaring: "Those Who Stay Will Be Champions!" I wanted to know: how long did you have to stay before becoming a champion?

A humid blast washed over my face as girls went in with sweaty foreheads or came out with damp hair, fresh from the showers. Standing there, I felt a bit like a stalker. Finally, Elaine emerged with Heather, the two of them looking crisp and fresh in their pleated navy skirts and white polo shirts with crossed racquets over their hearts.

"Oh, hey, Ari," she said. "We're just heading out to the courts."

"I need a minute," I said. "Heather, please excuse us."

They looked at each other and then Elaine said she'd be out there soon.

When Heather had left the building, I asked Elaine what I'd done wrong. "Am I not cool enough for you? Not good-looking enough?"

"That's not it," said Elaine, looking over my shoulder down the hallway. "Can you keep a secret?"

"Sure," I said.

"You have to swear to keep it a secret. If you tell even one person, I'll destroy your reputation at this school forever, and you know I can. I know how this place works."

She was small but severe. "I swear," I said in a small, awed voice.

So Elaine took me to an empty office which was shared by the few coaches who didn't also teach regular classes at Dalton. Somehow, she had the key. We went in but didn't sit down. A "Just Say No to Cheating" poster hung over the window in the door, blocking out the light.

"I've been going to this group in Ferndale," Elaine said. "It's for teenagers dealing with some issues, issues of confusion."

"Like therapy?"

She twirled her racquet. "Kind of, but there's nothing wrong with me."

"Then what are you confused about?"

"It has to do with sex."

She's having sex, I thought. Of course, I'd heard stories of people doing it, but no one I knew had admitted it to me directly.

I said, "I get that. I'm confused about it too. It's confusing."

"I'm confused about it in a more specific way. I have feelings for women."

My first thought: Now I wouldn't have to kiss her with tongue.

But what I just heard? Elaine Rosen, queen of the eleventh grade, gay? It didn't seem possible. Maybe I'd misheard. Sometimes lots of words sounded to me like "gay." But then she hadn't said gay. She'd said she had feelings for women.

"So," she said, strumming her racquet strings. "What do you think?"

Once while playing doubles, I'd been smacked in the back of the head with my partner's serve. I just sat there, stunned, in the middle of the court. Physically I was fine. It was just the shock of it, not the actual pain.

"What do I think?" I said finally. But what I wanted to know was, what did *she* think? Could she tell what I thought? Who else could tell? "What about the Cotillion?"

Elaine blushed. "I needed a date, and I thought you might need one too."

She didn't need to explain. In this, we'd been equally guilty. And yet, what must it be like for a popular Dalton girl to keep this secret? It was easier to keep your mouth shut when it rarely opened.

"Remember," she said, "you can't tell anyone."

"Of course not. I'd never do something like that." I felt exhilarated, talking this openly, this nakedly. I didn't want it to end. "Does your mom know you're going to this group?" I asked, hungry for more information. "Or your aunt?"

She shook her head. "They think I'm out with you. Playing tennis."

I understood it all now. If my life had been an Oscar-nominated movie, I'd have been nominated for Best Supporting Actor. I was Hana Mandlikova to Elaine's Martina Navratilova, who happened to be Elaine's favorite tennis player. Of course.

"So is Heather your girlfriend?" I asked.

"Heather? No, no. She's not gay. Just I am."

Elaine had the answers to so many questions I'd wanted to ask, and yet standing there, I couldn't think of what they were.

"I should get to practice," she said.

"No, wait," I said, but I had nothing to say. "This group, what's it like?"

"We talk about different stuff. I found them in the phonebook. Can you believe it? They list things like that in the phonebook?"

"Yeah, that's funny," I said.

She tapped her racquet on the top of her sneaker. Maybe I was boring her, but this was all moving too quickly, like a window slamming shut. "I should get to practice," she said. "I'm sorry if you're disappointed. You're a great guy."

"A great guy," I repeated. "Sounds like an insult." Yet I didn't feel insulted or disappointed. I felt as if I were on the verge of something exciting and wonderful.

"Trust me. It's a compliment," she said. "Are we good?"

"Yeah," I decided. "We're good."

For a few awkward seconds, we eyed each other. Finally, I offered a light hug, which she accepted. We kept our cheeks several inches apart.

* * *

DRIVING HOME, I RESOLVED NEVER TO listen to TLC or eat frozen yogurt again. And those clothes Elaine had picked out for me, I'd wear them in art class when I needed clothes that I wouldn't mind dirtying with charcoal and ink. I rubbed my fingers through my feathered hair until the feathering disappeared. Then I turned on 89X. Full blast.

They were playing "Jeremy" by those Pearl Jam fakers, trying to cash in on Nirvana's success with their heavy-handed and pretentious lyrics, and Eddie Vedder's theatrical one-note vocals were a mockery of Kurt's piercing moans. In their videos, the Pearl Jammers paraded for the cameras with their long hair falling in their faces, in brand new plaid shirts wrinkled to look worn, a complete parody of my idea of real grunge. And even though Kurt called them out in every interview he gave, they only got more popular.

Everything about Pearl Jam was cheap and false. So why, when I heard their song that afternoon, did I feel like crying for joy?

Exchange

JUSTIN DIDN'T ASK ME ANYMORE ABOUT Elaine or any other girl until the last day of school, when he wanted to know about my summer plans.

Staring at his black velvet Vans, I confessed, "We're hosting this French girl for two weeks, and then I'm going back with her to visit her family." Justin had just bought the Vans, and to sneak them past our dress code dean, he covered the labels with neat strips of black duct tape.

"Ari's got a Hot French Girl." Justin gave me a high-five, and the warm, not unpleasant sting of his fingers lingered on my palm. Was that the hand he jerked off with? "I'm expecting details," he warned before sauntering away for the summer.

My homework assignment for summer vacation. I'd impressed Justin, and to continue impressing him, I'd need a few racy French girl stories. But what would I have to do exactly? How racy would the stories need to be?

I hoped that the Hot French Girl would take charge of the situation. No such luck.

Decked out in a rumpled fluorescent green dress with white polka dots and puffed sleeves, her straw-colored hair tied back in a stiff French braid—so those braids really were French!—Juliette

Levy kept turning her head and frowning as if worried that she'd arrived at the wrong airport.

We waved from the other side of customs, where red, white, and blue bunting left over from July Fourth sagged along the terminal walls. "Juliette! Juliette!" I called out.

Some jerk yelled back, "Romeo!"

Mom had arranged the exchange via a friend who owned a gallery specializing in French art. Juliette's father, an antique dealer from Nice, claimed his daughter spoke "a little" English, a gross overstatement. Sadly, our French wasn't much better. Dad remembered a few words from high school while Mom had made a valiant attempt at Rosetta Stone but hadn't progressed past *"Comment t'appelles-tu?"* And despite my A's in two years of French, I learned it was far easier to fill in textbook exercises about the weather in Paris than to communicate with Juliette in the backseat of my dad's car.

After some effort, my parents and I worked out that Juliette's flight had been uneventful, that she wasn't hungry, and that she liked "the American music pop."

"What American bands do you like?" I asked. Juliette made a strange guttural noise. I asked again, and she made the same noise. It sounded like, "uuuhh-duuhhh."

Finally she scribbled on the back of one of Mom's ketubah business cards: "U2."

Mom laughed while Dad demanded to know who this U2 was; the name struck him as vaguely Satanic. I was disappointed. I'd expected a French girl to be more worldly and sophisticated. Couldn't she have liked the Jesus and Mary Chain or the Pixies?

I told Juliette in French, "But U2 is Irish."

Blinking away tears, Juliette picked at her carefully painted fingernails.

"Wait until she sees the bathroom," Dad said. "In Europe, hot and cold water come out of different faucets and you have to mix them in the sink."

"That's ancient history," Mom said. "Europe is more modern than we are. There's public transportation everywhere, and so organized. They have high-speed trains." To my mother's shame, the only public transit we had in Detroit was the sluggish SMART bus system that brought maids and other labor back and forth from the city.

As we drove up to the house, Mrs. Taborsky was pulling weeds on her lawn, brazen as an advertisement. It was summertime, which meant Mark would be out of school, had every right to come home for a supervised visit.

I shaded my face with my hand until we disappeared into our garage.

Dad took Juliette to the bathroom and turned on the faucet. "Two handles. One faucet. Hot, cold. See?" She smiled but seemed unsurprised. Disappointed, my father retreated to his den to ride his stationary bike before dinner while Mom and I showed Juliette our spare room. We'd bought a new set of sheets and pillowcases, and a basket of dried lavender and scented soaps from a French-themed chain store at the mall.

Juliette said, "Sank you," and shut the door.

I knocked on it an hour later. Juliette appeared, still in her green party dress, with white ankle socks. I invited her to see my bedroom, part of my seduction strategy. French girls, bedrooms—a natural combo.

"*Comme tu veux*," she shrugged. Whatever you want.

I'd covered my windows in sheer curtains that let in light but blocked the view. The walls were a collage of my current obsessions: the cover of *Sassy* with Courtney Love smooching Kurt, a ghostly photocopy of my hand, pictures of people smoking torn from old magazines, a poster for the movie *Singles*, glow-in-the-dark plastic stars, and several of my favorite life drawings, fixed with hairspray so they wouldn't smudge. Mom asked if I was sure I wanted to hang them up, where anyone could see.

"Don't you think they're good?" I said.

"Of course they're good," she said. "I just think—well, never mind."

Juliette sat primly on the edge of my zebra-striped beanbag while I played a mix tape that Justin had given me. Most of the words on the label had been crossed out in black marker. He promised to write up a playlist to go with it, but he never did.

Juliette didn't like the music, so I switched to Nirvana, which she'd never heard or heard of. I chose *Incesticide*, a compilation of the band's earlier music rushed out by DGC Records to cash in on the band's sudden success. I loved everything about *Incesticide*, the title, the random pile-up of songs, and the cover art, a painting by Kurt of a brain-damaged baby clutching its skeletal mother while stretching out its neck to sniff a poppy. Also, in the liner notes, Kurt had written:

> *"If any of you in any way hate homosexuals, people of a different color, or women, please do this one favor for us—leave us the fuck alone! Don't come to our shows and don't buy our records."*

I repeated those lines as if they were Bible verses. Kurt was on my side.

Juliette asked something in rapid-fire French that sounded like, "Do you like the Whitney, the Madonna, the Paula Abdul, the Janet Jackson?" I tried to explain to her what alternative meant. At first she seemed confused, but then out came another flood of French in her breathy accent. All I understood was "Boy George" and "Elton John."

I turned off the stereo. "Are you tired? Do you want to take a nap?" I put my hands under my right ear and mimed snoring noises.

"*Sank you,*" Juliette said and returned to her room.

CHERRIES

MARK USED TO TELL ME IN France, you couldn't pop the girls' cherries because the girls there all popped them themselves. I don't know how he knew all this since he'd never been out of the U.S., not even to Israel. He often got excited about French things: French kissing, dirty French movies, French-style underwear.

Shut up, shut up, I thought, but he wouldn't shut up. I could still hear his voice, that thin, angry, nasal bark. I didn't want to, but I saw him in my mind's eye, poking and prodding a cherry until he drew blood.

In Case of an Emergency

Mom and I tried to entertain Juliette with a few highlights of the Detroit suburbs: Twelve Oaks Mall, a waterpark, and my grandparents' dim apartment, decorated in bulky, shiny drapes and mahogany furniture. The heat was turned up, even in the humid hell of Michigan summers, because lately my grandmother was always cold. Mom worried about them as if they were her own parents, both buried in Philadelphia.

My grandparents were crazy about Juliette, particularly my grandmother. "Maybe you want one more cookie?" she asked between hoarse coughs. My grandparents, who'd emigrated from Russia before World War II, spoke English with an accent even thicker than Juliette's. "Ari, isn't she a nice girl? Give her one more cookie."

"Pass her the plate, Ari," Mom prodded me. "That's how you treat a lady."

I waved one of my grandmother's powdery Russian wedding cookies under Juliette's nose, but she shrugged.

"She doesn't eat," said Mom. Cookies weren't allowed on her diet, so she crumbled hers into dust on her gold-rimmed plate. My grandparents liked gold on everything: watches, faucet handles, picture frames, even gold paper plates. Mom tried to nudge them to more tasteful mustards, or burnt amber, but they stuck to their golds.

"Max was same at her age," my grandmother said. "We would say, Max, eat, but he only wanted American style. Hamburgers. French fries. Only American."

"Everything, he only wanted what was American," my grandfather chimed in while winding his watch, a knock-off Rolex studded with fake diamonds. He'd promised to leave it to me in his will.

"We wanted to teach Max Yiddish, but no, no, that's not American," my grandmother said. "He speaks Yiddish like this girl speaks English." She touched my chin. "*Redst du a bissele Yiddish?*"

I forced a smile, took greedy gulps of a glass of water—it was blazingly hot in that apartment—dabbed at the sweat on my face with the back of my wrist.

We got up to leave, and my grandfather, who was a noisy, sloppy kisser, said to Juliette, "Come here, lovely girl, I want to kiss you." She ducked past his lips before scurrying outside, so my grandfather gave me two kisses, one to give Juliette later. "I know something from French girls." He advised me to buy traveler's checks, and to leave my parents a phone number where I could be reached in case of an emergency.

Emergency? Did he believe Mark was capable of following me across the ocean? And how had *Zaide* found out about him? We'd never told my grandparents. My story would have made for a very unhappy ending to their American Dream fairy tale. Was this what they'd crossed the ocean for, to have a grandson like me?

But then I realized, to my shame, that when my grandfather said "emergency," of course he meant my grandmother, not me.

FOR YOUR LADYFRIEND

"ARE THE DOORS LOCKED?" MOM ASKED as we headed to Detroit down the Lodge Freeway, which ran below street grade after Eight Mile Road. I peered up at the homes perched above the highway, the smashed windows, the balconies stripped of their iron railings. Which exit led to Justin's house?

Desperate to show Juliette a good time, we drove past Tiger Stadium, (my dad's idea), then visited the Detroit Institute of Art (my mom's). I smirked at Rodin's *Thinker*, out on the front lawn, naked but hunched over as if to protect his privates. His hands were totally out of proportion. Ian would have had a hissy fit if Rodin had been his student at the Royal Oak Art Association.

Before lunch, we passed the Shelter, an ordinary building with a brown sign; maybe you had to go inside to experience the magic. Then we rode the People Mover, an elevated train to nowhere. Finally, we ate saganaki in Greektown, sitting outside under the spindly trees strung with Greek flags and Christmas lights. "Do you like this?" we kept asking poor Juliette, whose smiles looked increasingly strained.

While we carved up our flaming cheese, an elderly black man offered to sell me a cellophane-wrapped rose, "For your ladyfriend," as he put it. Mom bought one for me to give Juliette. "How humiliating," I said, handing the flower to Juliette, who grunted her thanks, then resumed cutting her oozing cheese into ever smaller pieces that never completed the journey from plate to tongue.

"Is this new attitude of yours a Kurt Cobain thing?" asked Mom, still pissed at me because I'd dyed my hair orange with Manic Panic to celebrate summer vacation. Unfortunately, I hadn't known to bleach my hair first, so the color only registered faintly, in direct sunlight. "I doubt Kurt Cobain would treat his girlfriend this way."

"Kurt doesn't have a girlfriend," I said. "He's married."

"I'm sure he didn't get that way by treating his fiancée like *dreck*."

After lunch, we visited Trappers' Alley, an old warehouse that had been converted to a shopping mall selling obscene greeting cards, trolls with fluorescent hair, and cheap T-shirts with messages like, "Detroit, Where the weak are killed and EATEN!" Juliette picked up a brochure titled "New Detroit," which turned out to be a relic from the last New Detroit, five years earlier. "Adorable," Mom said, peering at a fudge shop where black teenagers shaped puddles of oozing fudge on marble slabs and sang Motown songs. She then humiliated us by smiling and clapping along with the other suburban moms who were bending over their toddlers and pointing and saying, "Dancy, dancy, dancy!"

Would this nightmare never end?

"This is why we don't come to the city," Mom said later, after paying the garage attendant. "Parking costs a fortune, and you're not going to leave your car on the street."

* * *

AT HOME, JULIETTE LOCKED HERSELF IN the bathroom for an hour. She didn't appear much different coming out from when she'd gone in, except that her French braid looked more tightly wound. Also, the bathroom smelled strongly of sweet perfume.

Juliette's room was next to mine, and sometimes I put my ear to her bedroom door to listen to her sing her favorite pop songs to herself. She didn't know the words, so she'd hum until she got to the choruses, like "Hmm, hmm, hmm . . . *I love you!*" Or "Hmm, hmm, hmm . . . *my love, my love, my love* . . . hmm, hmm, hmm . . . *my love* . . . "

I felt bad for Juliette, who'd come here to see America, and instead we gave her Detroit. Now she was stuck here with a surly kid like me, who wanted to trick her into performing sexual favors so I could serve up a juicy tale for Justin in September. I wished I could explain myself to her. We could have made up some great stories.

I Adore France

To better communicate with Juliette, Dad enlisted the help of Dan Sklar, or as David and I called him, "the famous Dan Sklar," because Dad talked about him so much.

"Dan Sklar and I are best friends," my father would say. "We never see each other or call each other. It's the perfect friendship."

My brother and I had heard this particular routine so many times—about how wonderful it was that they never talked to each other, blah, blah, blah—that we'd cut my father off mid-stream or mock him openly by repeating his *spiel* word for word. David burped, farted, blew his nose. I rolled my eyes, groaned, begged him to stop. Nothing worked. When my father felt the urge to tell a story, it had to be told to the end.

As the famous Dan Sklar's dented station wagon inched up our driveway, I realized it had been so long since I'd seen him in person that I'd forgotten what he looked like. Dad instructed me to call him Mr. Sklar while Mr. Sklar invited me to call him Dan, but I could only think of him by his full name.

The famous Dan Sklar had a head like an inverted triangle that came to a point at his white goatee, appropriate, I thought, for a psychology professor at a local community college. He wore stylish frameless glasses that caught and played with the light, muting his thin-lidded blue eyes and making him look as if he were constantly laughing at us.

"I'd hardly call myself fluent," he said as we presented him with Juliette in our foyer, "but—" A few simple French phrases tumbled from his lips, ones I could have managed, but in an accent far less fluid and slippery-tongued than his.

Juliette answered in a high-pitched rush of French that made Dan Sklar laugh with pleasure. She too seemed to be enjoying herself, her face animated, her voice tinkling like a glass bell, her fingers flying as if she were doing the Spanish fan dance in the *Nutcracker* ballet.

How lonely she must have been. I resolved to be kinder to her in the future, more patient, more interested in what she was trying to say.

"What's she saying?" my mother demanded. "What does she want?"

"She likes you," Dan Sklar reassured us. "She likes everyone." I liked his crushed blue velvet jacket and rumpled pinstripe button-down shirt. Would I look good in an outfit like that instead of my black t-shirt and ripped jeans?

"All that to say she likes us?" my father asked, then turned to me. "Why are we paying all this money for you to go to Dalton?"

Why? I thought. You fucking know why. So I can be safe, that's why.

"I thought you got an A in French," Dad went on.

"She has a strong accent," I said, ashamed that I couldn't demonstrate my few skills in front of a worldly college professor. They continued speaking at dinner, or rather, Juliette spoke while the famous Dan Sklar made brief interjections whenever she took a break to breathe or eat a bite of Mom's manicotti. He handled his knife and fork in careful movements, unlike my dad, who cut up his food as if he were sawing wood and chewed with his mouth open. At the end of the meal, Dan Sklar lined up his utensils at an angle on his plate to indicate he'd finished, so I did the same.

"Doesn't she like Italian food?" said Mom, whose cooking was regularly described by her friends as "fine." Not "fine" as in just okay, but as in fine dining. "What else could we make her?"

The famous Dan Sklar informed us that Juliette liked everything, but what she really craved was a baguette sandwich with ham and cheese.

"We don't eat ham in this house," my mother said. "But I could take her somewhere. Where could we get a ham sandwich?"

"I thought she was Jewish," Dad said.

"You eat bacon," I pointed out.

"Yeah, but not ham," he said.

"I envy you," the famous Dan Sklar told me. "I adore France."

I adore France. Someday, I wanted to be someone who said things like "I adore France." What could Dan Sklar have in common with my father, who pushed his food on his plate with his thumb and believed you could fart in public if you said, "Excuse me" afterward? The famous Dan Sklar was a Democrat while my father referred to the not-so-new president as "Slick Willie." "He'll pander to any group for votes," Dad sneered. "That's what this gays in the military thing is about."

"I wouldn't mind serving in the military beside a homosexual," said Dan Sklar.

"Maybe in a desk job," Dad said. "But what about on the battlefield, with all that blood flying everywhere? Bad enough I'm now forced to wear gloves in my office in case of the HIV, which limits my hand skills. For a few people who won't wear condoms, I have to wear gloves and hurt the rest of my patients. What are they going to do in the military, make the soldiers wear rubber gloves while they're firing their machine guns?"

"Do you realize how ignorant you sound?" said the famous Dan Sklar.

"Still, you have to admit, that's what you were thinking," Dad said.

At least Juliette had the good fortune not to be able to understand what they were talking about. I wished Clinton had never started this debate, which had become an excuse for people to say the nastiest things about gays. On the news, politicians were visiting tightly packed bunk beds on ships, and open showers.

In other words: don't bend over if you drop the soap!

After dinner, we sat on the patio while my parents did the dishes. Juliette happily sipped a Coke while Dan Sklar stretched his legs and closed his eyes, either asleep or thinking great professorly thoughts. Beyond the pines at the end of our yard, puffs of smoke billowed up from a barbecue. A brittle fingernail of moon hung in the twilight sky.

Then the famous Dan Sklar opened his eyes. "I shouldn't have agreed to teach summer session. Only slackers take summer classes." I laughed, as if I got the joke. "My mouth feels tired from moving up and down all day. When I get home, all I want to do is not talk. I suppose that cost me a marriage."

I knew he lived in Royal Oak, near the Art Association, and the record stores and cafes on Main Street. It was like a real city there, buzzing with people walking on sidewalks, even late at night, a place you could call for help and someone would always hear. "What's it like living where you live?" I asked, but Dan Sklar spoke over me.

"How are you?" He leaned forward in his chair. "I hear you've had a rough time."

"Dad told you?" My voice cracked, and I cleared my throat. "I mean, I didn't realize." Juliette was sipping her pop, her smooth pale face the picture of bliss.

"He asked my advice," said the famous Dan Sklar. "Informally. I don't take on clients any longer. That chapter of my life is closed."

"I already saw a therapist," I said. "I'm over it now."

"Your family likes to be over things," he said, "rather than experience them."

Don't you see I'm different from my family? I thought.

Later, as we watched Dan Sklar drive off from our front porch, Dad said, "Some guys are like that." We were in full view of that other house across the street, like an awful unblinking eye, always observing, always waiting to catch me alone and unguarded.

"Like what?"

Was Mark visiting? I hadn't seen him arrive.

"Wearing flashy clothes, driving flashy cars," he said. "My papa, when he could still drive, always had a Cadillac. But when I had to go to college, no money." Dad held up his hands as if to pose for a statue of poverty. "I had to take out loans, get a job in a bar, serving rich kids making fools of themselves."

"Dad," I said, then cleared my throat. "Say something in Yiddish."

"What?"

"Say. Something. In Yiddish."

My request startled him. Then his face relaxed to its familiar, slightly ironic smile. "*Ich hob dich lib*," he said. I love you.

I couldn't recall Dad saying that he loved me in any language. Now, hearing those words, I didn't know if they were real or just another verbal strategy for him to win the particular conversational game we were playing.

Mom came outside with an envelope. "This belongs across the street," she said. "Mailman screwed up again. Honey, would you drop it off in their box?"

"Me?" I asked.

"Yeah, you," she said, holding out the envelope, a piece of

junk mail that no one would have missed had I thrown it down a storm drain.

"I can take it," Dad said.

"No, I asked Ari," she said. Why? Was she tough-loving me into shape? Or was it a punishment for the shame I'd brought this family, my loss of manhood.

There was no arguing with her when she was in this frame of mind, so I took the envelope and turned toward the street, head bowed, hands trembling. Mom and Dad were watching, which made me feel worse, knowing they felt obligated to watch over me, a baby taking his first steps, in danger of falling at any moment and skinning his tender knees. The sky was a funny shade of purple-blue, like a bruise. The lawn felt wet and slippery under my sneakers. I thought I smelled something burning.

Our neighborhood had been suffering from teenagers who enjoyed playing "mailbox baseball," so the Taborskys, like many others, had recently replaced their mailbox with a solid green plastic model, apparently not so tempting a target for baseball bats. As I fumbled with the little door to their box, I felt as if I were trespassing.

I imagined what Kurt Cobain would have done to this mailbox. In one of his interviews, he'd called rape one of the worst crimes on earth. "The problem with groups who deal with rape is that they try to educate women about how to defend themselves. What really needs to be done is teaching men not to rape. Go to the source and start there."

Yeah, I thought, start there. "Fuck you," I muttered, then kicked the post with my flimsy Converse sneaker, stubbing my toe. "Jesus," I said, massaging my foot.

Even that bastard's mailbox still had the power to hurt me.

For some reason, that made me laugh.

FLOWER SNIFFIN' KITTY PETTIN' BABY KISSIN' CORPORATE ROCK WHORES

OUR PLANE SLOWLY DESCENDED TOWARD THE airport in Nice, and I took a break from studying my guidebook to watch the pink sunlight reflected against the rippled blue-green surface of the Mediterranean at sunrise.

Juliette spotted her parents and burst into tears. After hugging each of them tightly, she ordered a ham baguette and bit into it with a moan of satisfaction.

As the Levys extended their greetings, I only half-listened, wondering what they knew, what special instructions Mom and Dad might have given to keep me out of harm's way. Or were my parents continuing to maintain our conspiracy of silence, trying to pretend it had never happened? Moving on. Progress!

Mr. Levy spoke effortless yet formal English, which turned out to be unnecessary; I opened my mouth to greet Juliette's mother and younger brothers, and a stream of French burbled forth. The two weeks I'd spent struggling to communicate with Juliette had paid off. My initial bout of nerves disappeared in the shock of my sudden fluency.

"*Bravo!*" Mr. Levy pumped my hand. "These are Juliette's brothers, Yves and Henri. *Yves et Henri, je vous presente à Ari.*"

I expected to shake their hands too, but they presented their cheeks for me to kiss. Yves was nine, with blond curls, wide blue eyes, and a sweet smile. Henri, twelve but almost thirteen, was dark and striking. He looked me up and down before rubbing his warm cheek against mine. I felt flattered. Then he pulled his sister's braid while she munched on her sandwich, and she almost choked.

"*Arrêt!*" Juliette screamed and stamped her foot.

Henri's eyes caught mine, and we both laughed. I let my over-sized backpack, stuffed with everything I'd brought from home, slide to the floor, and I took a deep breath of French air, which smelled of perfume from the duty free shop nearby.

Henri knitted his dark brows, then asked me in thickly accented English, "You like football?"

"No," I said, blushing.

"Not all boys like football, Henri!" his dad said sharply in French. "Ari, I'm sorry. Juliette told us that you are alternative, and we want you to be happy staying with us."

They knew what alternative was? Had there been a Lollapalooza in France?

And then, as if to answer my question, Henri pointed to my shirt. I was wearing my Nirvana T-shirt, the one that said, "Flower sniffin' Kitty pettin' baby kissin' corporate rock whores" on the back. The front had a smiley face with x's for eyes and a tongue dangling out of a wavy mouth.

"Cool," Henri said, one of the few English words he could speak with confidence.

Henri thought I was cool. I took a minute to enjoy that.

* * *

To get to the Levys' home, we drove up a steep, curvy highway that hugged the jagged Côte d'Azur, with the spectacularly blue sea falling away from us on one side and on the other, dried brown vineyards and fields of sunflowers with spiky petals rising up the hillsides. I felt bad for Juliette, having traded all this beauty for the boxy white strip malls and bland subdivisions of Michigan.

The Levys' fourth-floor flat was crammed with curlicued antiques, claw-foot sofas in floral print silk, and landscape paintings crusted with thick swabs of oil paint and framed in thick wood painted gold, probably things Mr. Levy couldn't sell in his gallery.

There were three bedrooms, one for the parents, one for the boys, and one for Juliette. I guessed I'd get the living room sofa, but because Juliette had had her own room in America, I had to have my own room in France. So Juliette landed on the sofa while I got her poofy pink bed, with its lacy comforter and plump mattress. Graciously, she didn't seem to resent me for this. Maybe she was so glad to be home, she didn't care where she slept. Plus, this way, she could stay up late watching awful French TV.

Mrs. Levy insisted on helping me unpack, opening and refolding my clothes, then placing them in Juliette's dresser, emptied in honor of my arrival. I grabbed my underwear before Mrs. Levy could get to it. She laughed and said, "Easy now. Didn't I have two boys already?" Returning to the folding, she added, "I never saw a boy who has so many black clothes. Are you in mourning?"

Yes, I wanted to say. You guessed my secret.

Mr. Levy stopped by to say that if I needed amusement, he had some French books translated into English. "Gide, Genet, poetry by Rimbaud. Writers you'd enjoy."

I didn't know these writers, but I thanked him.

"It's a very pink room," he said. "I hope you will not mind."

"It's fine," I said.

"We are glad you are an artist, not a macho American cowboy. We all love the arts here." Then, to my surprise, he added, "Juliette says she very much enjoyed America."

"I'm glad," I said, bewildered by this news. I resolved to be more pleasant to Juliette at breakfast.

"She particularly enjoyed meeting your grandparents. Both Mrs. Levy's and my parents died very young, from maladies they contracted during the war. In the camps."

Here, "the war" meant World War II, not Vietnam or even Iraq.

"I'm sorry," I said, still processing the idea that Juliette had enjoyed America.

"It's just the reality. Sleep well, my good boy."

He turned off the light and closed the door. The bed felt strange, starchy and empty. Outside, I heard the piercing cry of a bird I didn't recognize. Though I wasn't cold, I wrapped myself in a flannel shirt and thought of Justin, imagined him slapping me with a high five again and again.

Artists

Shortly after dawn, I woke up and for a second couldn't remember where I was. I slapped my fingers on the night table, searching for my alarm clock, which I'd left back home. Oh yeah, France, I thought.

I tiptoed on the cool tile floor to the windows, opened the shutters, and was hit full in the face by the brilliant sun of southern France, bold and honest, so unlike the feeble, greasy light in Detroit, always filtered through trees, like weak tea. My usual view of the Taborskys' house was replaced by cheerful window boxes of flowers across the street, signs in French saying "Snack Tabac!" or "Drogerie."

I let out a deep breath that had been stifled in my chest for a year, inhaled deep whiffs of air fragrant with motor scooter exhaust and cigarettes from the street.

The Levys ate breakfast on their terrace, where I experienced the first of several small miracles: coffee or hot chocolate served in bowls instead of cups, sliced baguettes, and various spreads, including butter, jam, and Nutella. Chocolate for breakfast? The adults went for butter, Juliette chose jam, and the two boys slathered their bread in the Nutella. Henri licked the chocolate off his knife in a way that struck me as obscene. His mother scolded him, saying it wasn't polite, but he did it again anyway and winked at me.

Another miracle: Mrs. Levy wore a sundress, and as she cleared the plates, I saw thick patches of black hair under her armpits.

We toured Marseille, which despite its lovely-sounding French name was an industrial port with few attractions, not so different from Detroit.

During our walk, we stood aside to make room for two dark-skinned men walking arm-in-arm. "Be careful of the Arabs," Mrs. Levy warned as I stared after them. "The Arabs here are like your blacks in U.S.A." She must have thought the dark skin was what I'd been staring at. Then she told me a French joke: What kind of exercise did Arabs like to do? Aerobics! Apparently this made a pun in French.

"I have no problem with black people," I said. "My friend is black."

"There is a nice exhibition in our art museum," Mr. Levy said, changing the subject. "Of American artist Keith Haring. A tragedy, such a talent died so young, from AIDS. Tell me, in America, is it still very common, this irrational fear of men like him?"

"You mean artists?" I said, and Mr. and Mrs. Levy burst out laughing.

"Yes, yes, artists," giggled Mr. Levy, wiping away tears. "That's very witty."

It was? Sometimes I felt I understood the Levys better when they spoke French.

But instead of visiting the museum, we rode a ferry to a former island prison that had figured in a classic Alexandre Dumas novel I hadn't read. Mr. Levy explained why Dumas was such a great writer in French, because of the "delicacy" of his style. I liked listening to Mr. Levy talk about literature as we walked along gleaming rock walls, with deep blue water lapping at the stones. "If you like," he said, "we can go to the beach. Maybe Saint-Tropez, where they made *La Cage aux Folles*."

"What's that?" I asked.

He seemed astonished. "But you don't know it? You must see this film. It's famous in the whole world. You would greatly appreciate the humor."

I bought a postcard for Justin, but right after I bought it, the idea of mailing it seemed stupid, even tactless. Here I was touring France while he worked at his dad's Christian summer camp, wiping snotty noses and cleaning up graham cracker crumbs.

As we waited for the ferry back to town, I asked where Henri was and Mr. Levy pointed to a crouched figure by the water.

"Is he hurt?" I asked.

"His mother scolded him for wearing black socks with his baskets and she preferred him to wear white." It took me a second to get that "baskets" were gym shoes. "He's sensitive. Leave him alone."

However, I knew what it was to sulk off in a corner and wait hopelessly to be found. So I joined Henri, sitting with his chin on his knee and tossing stones into the water. He clutched his dark socks in his left hand.

"Where I live, people think it's cool to wear black socks with baskets," I told him in French, though that was only true for the alternative kids I saw on television or on the streets of Royal Oak. He shrugged. "Do you want to talk?"

He shook his head.

"Are you sure?"

He shook his head again.

"Can I sit here with you?"

He didn't respond, so I sat on the ground with him, and as we gazed blankly at Marseille across the water, I knew what he was feeling, a deep well of sadness so familiar, I could call up the feeling whenever I wanted to, and when I didn't want to.

Yet here in France, I didn't feel sad. The water and sky were too beautiful. Detroit was too far away. All these strangers really were strangers, without any possible connection to Mark and all that. I was free here.

I peeked at Henri, who was tall for his age, almost as tall as I was. Had he started thinking about girls? Or boys?

"Henri!" Mr. Levy yelled, walking briskly toward us. "You're ruining Ari's vacation with your nonsense." He yanked his son up by his arm, and Henri burst into tears. "Stop it now!" Mr. Levy gave him a sharp slap.

Henri stopped crying, but flashed his father a look of seething hatred.

In an instant, Mr. Levy became a monster to me.

* * *

ALL AFTERNOON, I DREAMED OF HENRI and I saving each other from our unhappy homes. So that evening, during dinner on the terrace, when Henri rested his head on his father's shoulder, while Mr. Levy ruffled his hair, I watched with queasy curiosity. My father had never touched my hair. On holidays or birthdays, we shook hands.

"Ari, you don't eat the dinner," said Mrs. Levy. Her English was poor, but she made a great effort.

"I'm not used to such big portions," I said. I didn't like the salads, droopy julienned vegetables marinated in vinegar and mayonnaise, plus a thin, salty fish soup they made a great fuss about. Then, after dinner, a green salad. "In America, we eat salad before the main course," I explained.

"How odd," said Mrs. Levy.

"It's true," said Mr. Levy, still combing through his son's hair. "I have seen it during my trips to the States. They believe it stimulates the appetite." He asked me in English, "What do you like? We want to give you what you like."

I couldn't think, too engrossed in the spectacle of Mr. Levy's fingers in Henri's silky hair. Finally, I uttered the first dish that entered my head: "Fried chicken."

"Then tomorrow we will have fried chicken," Mr. Levy said.

After dinner, Juliette performed at the piano, a piece by Bach, her father's favorite composer. My mom liked him too, but Dad was still hooked on Springsteen. "*BORN* in the USA!" he'd sing along with his Walkman while riding his treadmill. David asked if he even knew what that song meant. "Why does music have to mean anything?" Dad asked. "It makes me move faster. That's the meaning for me."

Just to see his reaction, I once played him a rougher Nirvana song, "Territorial Pissings," and he bellowed, "Turn that off! It hurts my ears!" Later he told Mom, in a loud voice so I could hear, that I only pretended to like the song to drive him crazy.

"Didn't you do that to your parents when you were a teenager?" she said.

Juliette's fingers trotted nimbly across the piano keys, while her feet switched back and forth over the pedals. She pressed her eyes and lips together, and her nostrils flared. At one point, she leaned so far forward over the instrument it seemed as if she were trying to melt into it. When she finished, her whole body trembled.

Mr. and Mrs. Levy applauded adoringly. I wanted to congratulate Juliette, but Henri whispered to me, "*Viens*," so I followed him to his room. "Watch me now." He took out a handheld video game and we sat on his bed, knee to knee. "You try," he said, then giggled as my thumbs slapped vainly at the controls. He said I was "*très cool,*" which made me nervous. How soon before he realized that I was a loser who let guys like Justin cheat off my homework to win their friendship?

Yves came in. "Can I play?" he asked. "Let me play. It's my turn."

"What do you say?" Henri asked me.

"He can have a turn," I said.

"Okay. Whatever the guest says, that's what we do."

Even Justin had never been so kind. What if this was where I'd been meant to live, and all my life until now had been some horrible dream?

I played him "Smells Like Teen Spirit" on my Walkman, which Henri seemed to like, judging by the way he banged his head to the beat. Though he didn't get the words, he sang along in his own way: "Na-na-NA-na! Na-na-NA-na!"

"Let me hear," Yves pleaded. We ignored him.

"Why were you so mad at your father?" I asked.

"When? I love my father." Henri jumped off the bed and pranced to the windowsill, where he played an invisible piano. "Look at me! I'm Juliette. Aren't I beautiful?" he warbled. "Stop it, Henri. Be quiet, Yves. It's me, Juliette, the princess!"

The deal was clear. To be one of them, I'd join their alliance against their sister.

AT THE BEACH

THE NEXT DAY AS WE DROVE to the beach, Henri pulled Juliette's hair, calling her "Princess," or imitating her habit of saying "Même!" or "Exactly so!": "Me-he-he-me. I'm Juliette the goat. Me-he-he-me." Yves and I tittered, Juliette screamed, "Arrêt!", and Mr. Levy told Henri to knock it off.

We stopped in Cassis, which Mr. Levy said was the start of the French Riviera. The beach was all rocks and I had to pick my way carefully to the water. While the boys and I splashed in the sea, Juliette determinedly dog-paddled in place, keeping her face above water, her hair protected in a bathing cap. Her brothers, like most of the guys there, wore Speedos, while I wore a baggy bathing suit that dripped down past my knees.

Henri asked in a loud voice if I thought Juliette was *gros*, or fat. I confused the word with *grand*, meaning tall, and said yes.

Juliette let out a shriek, then dashed out of the water to tell her parents. I ran after her to explain, but I sounded ridiculous.

"Don't be so sensitive," said Mrs. Levy, patting her sobbing daughter on the back. "Boys like teasing girls. Didn't you know?" She winked at me.

"What did I do?" Juliette gasped between sobs. "Why do they hate me?"

"Sorry, Juliette," I said. "Honestly, it was a mistake," but her mother shook her head and put her finger to her lips.

"Shh, shh. No one hates you," said Mrs. Levy.

Later, I lay on my towel with my eyes closed, letting the sun bleach the poisons out of my skin while I listened to Nirvana on my Walkman. My body felt light, weightless. I could dissolve into the warm, salt-scented breeze of that beach.

Henri jolted me awake and pointed to the towel next to ours. A woman was undoing her bikini top, letting her breasts swing free. Alarmed, I looked at Mr. and Mrs. Levy, who didn't seem to mind. Then I remembered this was France.

For a while, Henri napped and I sneaked a few sketches of him in my little book, to stay in practice, that's what I told myself. I liked the hollow of his stomach beneath his breastplate, like a pink conch shell. His tiny ears. The smooth soles of his feet.

During the car ride home, I felt wrung out and cranky, unused to so much company for so long, and I wanted to be alone with my thoughts. Henri, who'd borrowed my Walkman, listened to "In Bloom" and tried to sing along to the chorus, which he didn't understand. He howled, "Hmm, sing a song, but he dodo vada deems."

"'He don't know what it means,'" I said. Kurt Cobain would have loved this.

"'He don't know what it means,'" Henri sang, but Mr. Levy corrected his grammar, explaining that in English, third person singular required "doesn't," not "don't."

I closed my eyes, hoping to sleep, but Henri flung his arms around my chest and squeezed. "You're my Ari!" he said in French.

I grabbed him back. "No, you're my Henri!"

"*Non!* You're my Ari!"

"Such children!" Juliette huffed from up front.

But this game didn't feel childish. Back and forth we went, squeezing each other harder as if our skins might merge, as if we might squeeze the last breath out of our lungs.

"Whose am I?" Yves asked plaintively.

Fried Chicken

For dinner, Mrs. Levy brought out a platter of chicken glistening with oil, all fried, but without breading. Were they always so literal in this country? To express my appreciation, I said, "Wow, here is the chicken!" Only instead of *poulet*, I said *poubelle*, or garbage.

The Levys laughed so hard they were crying, even Henri. I'd finally been found out. There'd be no more squeezing each other or ganging up on Juliette. Instead I'd become the family jester. So France was not paradise after all, just more of the same hell.

Before I went to sleep in Juliette's bedroom, Mr. Levy came in and asked if I could forgive his family for laughing at me. I said I'd forgotten about it. "Good boy," he said and sat at the edge of the bed. Then he told me about a friend of his, an art business colleague who'd died of AIDS. "He told me his regret for all the time he wasted in hiding, instead of being himself." He clapped my shoulder. "Don't repeat his mistake."

I sat up with a jolt. How had I been so dense? The book and movie recommendations, the Keith Haring show, now this story. Jesus, he thought "alternative" meant gay—he thought I was gay! Even more bizarrely, he didn't mind.

There were a couple of soft taps on the door. "Someone wants to see you," Mr. Levy said, smiling. It was Henri. Did he know too?

Henri stood by Juliette's dresser until his father left, then flopped down on the bed.

"You all don't like me anymore," I said, testing him.

"You're wrong," he said, tugging my ear. "We like you a lot." Then he kissed me good night, his lips chapped and wet on my face.

A Lovers Quarrel

I WANTED TO STAY HERE FOREVER.

I liked going to the supermarket, or as they called it here, a "hypermarket," where in the frozen section they sold profiteroles and escargot instead of TV dinners. I liked the trouble of converting the prices from francs into dollars. I liked watching Juliette's brothers making her scream by pressing a rough-skinned artichoke to the back of her neck. I liked Mr. Levy's movie recommendations. I liked the new cherry red shirt Mrs. Levy had bought me, a bright, happy color. "Now you're not in mourning," she said.

I liked the neutrality of the view out of my bedroom window.

I liked being alternative.

And best of all, I liked speaking French. Somehow, it made me feel taller, more confident. Foreign words seemed less weighty, less connected to my core, somehow cheaper and therefore easier to spend.

I wrote my grandparents a postcard saying I loved the Riviera. Then, feeling daring, I filled out the postcard I'd bought for Justin:

"France is amazing. But sometimes I miss home, and maybe you too. Don't take that the wrong way or anything."

***

I WROTE HIS ADDRESS, BUT DIDN'T send it.

Later, the boys and I went to the park to "play" and while Henri and Yves shot baskets, I sat on a bench and drew Henri, stretching for the basket, elongating his body into a thin rope. Yves asked me why I only sketched men.

"Don't ask such stupid questions," Henri said. "Don't you know he's an artist? Artists do whatever they want."

It was nice having an excuse to do whatever I wanted.

When we came back, my formerly dirty clothes, now wet and smelling of perfumey French detergent, hung from the clothesline over the terrace. Also, Justin's postcard was missing.

"The one with the picture of the Chateau D'If? I mailed it for you," Mrs. Levy said. "I found it on the floor, so I affixed the necessary stamp and put it on the box." She smiled generously, as if she expected me to thank her.

"*Merci*," I said, blushing. When Justin got that card, I'd be a dead man. I only hoped it might get lost in the mail.

I called my parents, who said I sounded glum.

"Just five more days," Mom said. "Make a list of everything you want to do in the time you have left and the time will fly."

"What's wrong?" Dad asked. "You and Juliette having a lovers' quarrel?"

Departure

As the date of my departure got closer, Juliette grew happier and chattier. My last evening, Mrs. Levy made another fried chicken dinner and Juliette gave me a pink perfume bottle as a gift for my mother.

I had an early flight the next morning, so after dinner, we headed straight to bed.

Henri paused at the threshold of my room. "Don't go," he whispered.

Even in the dark hallway, I could tell his eyes were wet.

"I don't want to go," I whispered back. "Come to Michigan with me."

And then he said the strangest thing. "Maybe if I was older."

NOTHING TO WORRY ABOUT

BACK HOME ON MAGGIE LANE, MOM laughed at my France stories and made real fried chicken while Dad invited me to watch
baseball with him on TV. "This house has been real quiet without
your Nirvana blasting all the time," he said, then added in a low
voice, "Your mother is a different person without you boys here.
Imagine how she'll be when you join your brother at U of M."

David came in from Ann Arbor and said I'd spent so long with
those frogs that my face had turned pale green.

When my pictures came back from the drugstore, we went to my
grandparents' apartment. It wasn't one of my grandmother's good
days, so we sat beside her bed and passed the snapshots around. Some
were taken at odd angles, or with half the scene cut off, my failed and
self-conscious attempts to create art, but I pretended I liked them.

"Aren't you glad you took French?" Mom said. "He almost
took Spanish."

"What would he do with Spanish?" Dad said. "Order a taco?"

I held a picture of me with my arm draped around Henri, who
was shorter than I'd remembered, more boylike. My smile was easy,
relaxed. My face was a handsome brown, and my eyes were bright
and clear. I didn't recognize myself.

"I have just one question," my grandmother said, pointing to me with a shaky finger. I tried not to cry in front of her. "This French girl, is she your girlfriend?"

"No," I said firmly. "We're just friends. I have no girlfriend."

"Ah, ah," my grandmother said, her voice dissolving into a coughing fit.

During the car ride home, Mom explained, "I should have told you to say yes. She's hoping to see you settled with a nice Jewish girl."

What my mother didn't say, but we all knew, was that my grandmother was dying. I'd disappointed everyone, her, Justin, my whole family, with my French summer.

"It's alright," Dad said, turning into our subdivision. "They know you're a good kid, so with you, there's nothing to worry about."

* * *

MOM HAD LEFT THE BLINDS OPEN in my room. As I went to close them, I saw Mark's room, with the shades fully open, and the lights blazing. I should have moved away. And then Mark himself appeared, a phone in his hand and he was talking a mile a minute, his lips moving so fast. Who was he talking to? What was he telling them about me?

Our eyes met. His face darkened and he bared his teeth, like a dog scowling at a stranger, preparing to lunge, and to bite.

I shrank against the wall, a brick wall that no BB gun could penetrate. I saw that awful expression on his face, those sharp white teeth. He'd seen me. He'd remembered I was still alive.

FIVE

WHEN ARI PULLS INTO THE PARKING lot for the game, he wonders about the appropriate time to text. Justin had directed him to send a text on Sunday. Sunday morning before leaving for the game? Sunday right when he got to the game? When he walked into the arena? He's out of practice at this. M should have been here to give advice. Though perhaps, given what's happened, Ari's better off without M's advice.

Ari's extra ticket is burning a hole in his pocket, next to the Pesek Zman candy. There's no point in trying to sell the ticket. The team is not very good. The arena will remain half-empty the entire game.

Finally Ari decides to send a text from the parking lot.

"Just arrived. Really cold today! Heading inside now."

There is no immediate response, not that he'd expected one. Maybe Justin is still making his way to the arena. Or schmoozing with important people who are good at numbers. Or looking after his sons—Ari read in an online profile that Justin has two sons now, just as Ari too might have had children had he been straight, or had he had any interest in partner-less parenthood.

I feel as nervous as a teenager, he thinks on his way to the arena. Maybe because I never got to be a teenager at the time. He presents his ticket for inspection at the entrance to the arena, and then a stranger hands him a red hat, with the University logo on the front and Justin's dating website's logo in the back. He accepts the hat. What for? What will he do with it? It would be too humiliating to put it on. Justin would think he's trying to kiss up to him or something. Well, it's his now anyway.

Maybe Justin never wanted to meet. His command to text him is just a dodge. Later he'll say, sorry, my phone died or offer some other excuse. Ari learned all about such polite methods of disengagement back when he was in grad school and actively sought out dates. He'd been on the receiving and giving end of such excuses. He remembered the last date he'd been on before meeting M. The evening had started off pleasantly enough. Ari managed to recommend the one type of wine he recognized from the menu, and his dinner companion, who had very nice blue eyes and those thin-wire framed glasses Ari liked, seemed to enjoy it too. Seemed impressed.

But somehow the man's ex came into the conversation. They'd broken off their seven-year relationship a few months earlier, and the division of the furniture had been particularly acrimonious. By the time the food arrived, Ari was trying to think of the gentlest story he could concoct for ending the night early. He managed to deflect dessert with "I'm on a diet." And when they left the restaurant together, before Ari could offer his excuse about papers to grade, his date said, "I guess I wasn't as ready to put myself out there as I thought. Were you totally bored?"

"Oh, no," said Ari. "I know how you must feel."

"Can I offer you a hug?"

"Of course."

It was a brief hug, the kind straight men might exchange.

"Bad timing, right?" said his date.

Why the hell is my timing always so off? Ari thought.

Perhaps the worst rejection he'd ever endured—until M, though technically what M had done was a betrayal, not necessarily a rejection—was when he'd brought a bouquet of daisies for a meeting with an unsuspecting fuck-buddy.

"Look, I get what you're trying to do," was the response. "But we don't have that kind of relationship. You just broke the rules unilaterally and I don't appreciate it." He ordered Ari out of his apartment.

Crestfallen, Ari said on his way out, "I didn't know there were rules."

Maybe, because he doesn't know the rules, that's why he's on his own, yet again. Maybe he was born in the wrong age, harboring his old-fashioned romantic ideals in a gay culture of online dating and fuck-buddies and men who take offense at bold romantic gestures like meeting his old high school crush at a basketball game.

ARI CLIMBS UP TO HIS SEAT, up an absurdly high set of stairs. The cheap seats. Tipoff isn't for a little while, so he goes back down the stairs to the bathroom, which has an old-fashioned metal trough for peeing. Ari is glad that he is not pee-shy so he can relieve himself immediately, rather than wait for a stall. The man peeing next to him simultaneously lets out a fart and a belch, either of which in centuries past would have been grounds to challenge him to a duel.

"Everything reminds you of the Middle Ages," M often complained.

"Of course," said Ari. "They're the foundation on which much of modern life is built. Why do you think I'm interested in the past? To better understand the present."

"But the past doesn't necessarily prefigure the present. If anything, studying the past makes the present seem less inevitable, shows us that if not for a few lucky accidents, things the way they are right now might be completely different. And isn't it when we attempt to repeat the past, to mis-apply the lessons of yesterday to today that we get into trouble? Like fighting Vietnam because of the wrong lessons from World War II?"

"I'll make you a deal. You let me teach you about poetry, and then you can teach me about history," said Ari.

He realizes he has become far too dependent on M for his social life. Ari liked to complain that M felt it was his duty to force Ari out of his comfortable home to air him out in public like an oft-used duvet cover. M teased him right back. "Quit playing the old curmudgeon, for once, would you?"

The good old days, Ari thinks now, washing his hands, though he hadn't realized how good they were at the time. How the hell is he going to vote when the committee wraps up its "investigation"? Already he can hear Aimee the art professor: "Soft on sexual harassment!"

But of course he knows how he'll vote. He has no choice. Guilty, guilty, guilty.

M really isn't such a bad guy deep down. Flawed, yes, but not bad. Perhaps helping him might actually serve the cause of justice. Though isn't that what they all say about all the perpetrators? Oh, you don't know him like I know him. Maybe that's what Mark's parents had told the cops all those years ago.

No, M and Mark, these are two different people. Right? I know M's true nature, and it's a good one at heart.

Or perhaps the truth is that the student who'd suffered M's grabby hands, he's the one who knows M's true nature, while Ari's the one who's been bamboozled all this time.

WHEN HE RETURNS TO HIS SEAT, the players are about to perform. Still no text from Justin. Oh, well, as long as I'm here, I might as well enjoy the spectacle. Ari is one of those rare academics in the humanities who isn't morally repulsed by the exploitation and even violence of college sports. Compared with the sports of the Middle Ages, when violence was not only a source of entertainment but also humor, the sports of today seem relatively courtly.

Courtly behavior on a basketball court. There should be some kind of good pun to be mined there, but Ari can't think of one. He's too nervous for comedy.

About midway through the first half, his phone buzzes in his pocket. His hand shakes as he looks at the text. But it's just a Campus Alert. A man has been spotted pleasuring himself outside the Sciences Building. Do not confront the suspect. Weirdly, Ari's first reaction is: Are they talking about me?

As soon as he puts the phone away, it buzzes again. His nephew is updating him with the score in another game. It buzzes once more. This time it's his parents extolling the weather in Florida. Doesn't he want to visit, to escape the cold? In fact, nothing could be colder than his parents' air-conditioned house in Florida, a land without history, in a newly built mansion in an invented neighborhood.

The phone buzzes again, and finally it's Justin.

"Can I meet you at halftime? Outside Section 25?"

It's Justin. These are his actual words. He asks, can I? Can he? As if it's a privilege? The phrasing, in the form of a request, sounds like a line of poetry, or another kind of line, an invisible digital line thinner than fishing wire connecting them across the expanse of this basketball arena, over all these warm bodies in hard seats.

His first instinct is to tap back, "Perfect!" but then he types: "Sounds good." He's very slow at texting, always hitting the wrong keys and accepting the oddest auto-corrections that he then has to delete. It's an unnatural effort.

According to the map of the arena on the back of his ticket, Section 25 is diametrically opposite of where he's sitting. With all the luxury suites, of course.

BURN

THE NEXT NIGHT, MARK WAS GONE. His curtains remained half-closed at all times, and his lights did not come on again for the rest of the summer. Occasionally I saw his mom, dad, or brother driving in or out of the garage, but never him.

Maybe it was the influence of listening to so much Nirvana that summer, back and forth between *Nevermind* and *Incesticide* while waiting for their follow-up album *In Utero* to come out, but now when I thought of Mark, I felt intensely, furiously angry. No more shame. Instead of refuge, I dreamed of vengeance. I wanted to fly out to that school in Canada, wherever it was, and tell everyone there what he'd done to me. Or hide somewhere, wait for him to walk by, and then hit him with a hammer, a rock, anything blunt and heavy. I wanted to spray-paint the smooth beige façade of the Taborskys' house with bright neon graffiti swastikas, so they'd think it was some neo-Nazi who'd done it. Destroy their baseball-bat-proof mailbox with a sledgehammer. Spread stinking manure all over the lawn, pour honey on the front steps to attract killer ants. Or best of all, douse the foundations in gasoline, then light a match and see that thing burn.

A Familiar Face

I READ IN THE PAPER ABOUT a gay movie called *The Living End* playing at a local arthouse. The ad featured two handsome men staring intently into each other's eyes. One of them was shirtless and held a gun.

The image haunted me, not just because the two actors were handsome and clearly and openly looking at each other with desire, but also because of that don't-fuck-with-me gun. I wanted to borrow their attitude for a while.

I drove by the marquee a few times, then turned into the parking lot and sat in my car, wondering who else might be inside. Finally I approached the box office, waiting behind a pair of Jewish grandmother types, who wanted "two seniors for the new Woody."

I said what I wanted, then watched the old man in the booth for a subtle, sudden backward jolt of the head, a slight uncomfortable rise in the shoulders, or that "I didn't realize you were one of those" tone of voice I dreaded. But the guy just rang up the sale.

The previews were ending as I slipped into the theater, which was fairly empty. I'd bought some chocolate, but for once I was too nervous to eat.

The cinematography was grainy, as if the action had been filmed through a nylon stocking. The plot meandered, then lurched suddenly into action. The dialogue dragged. And I didn't find the actors as attractive as advertised.

When the movie ended, I stayed in my seat, waiting for something—I wasn't sure what. Eventually, I got up to slowly make my way outside, but along the way I dawdled, searching the audience, hoping stupidly someone might talk to me. One man's face in particular caught my eye, the kind of conventional-handsome face that made you feel you'd seen him before: sharply cut nose and jaw, carefully sculpted hair with a part on the side, and bright eyes which were moist with tears. Maybe he was a local weatherman?

As the faint lights of the credits flickered on his cheeks, tears streamed steadily down to his chin, and then I finally realized why I recognized this guy. He was Hal Wentworth, our librarian at Dalton.

What was he doing here? Maybe he just liked alternative cinema?

I'd talked to Mr. Wentworth maybe ten times or so, to check out a book or ask for help locating an article for a history paper. Would he recognize me? Could I slink out of this darkness without his knowing?

The lights suddenly came up, and Mr. Wentworth's damp eyes met mine. "Oh!" he said, then wiped a tear from his left cheek. "Hi, Ari, right?"

"Yeah," I said. "Hi, Mr. Wentworth."

He sank slightly into his seat as I said his name aloud. The rest of the audience, entirely male, was filing out of the theater in silence.

I waited as Mr. Wentworth felt around and under the seats for his jacket and a Borders Bookstore shopping bag. What was he reading? He fitted a Boston Red Sox baseball hat snugly onto his well-shaped head, casting his face in shadow. He put on a pair of aviator sunglasses and then we headed together out of the theater.

Out on the sidewalk, my stomach went queasy as he talked about how warm this spring had been for Michigan. This winter had been a cold one. Not very cold, but cold.

He leaned in closer to me and pulled his jacket collar tight around his neck. "Please don't tell anyone you saw me here."

"Oh," I said. "Okay."

"I mean, there could be repercussions. I could lose my job."

Was that really true, or was he just trying to scare me into silence?

"I promise," I said, though all this time I'd been afraid that I was the one in trouble, that Mr. Wentworth would report me. But to whom and for what crime? The Dalton Handbook was silent about what movies you could or could not see off campus.

"Thanks, man." He coughed twice, then said he had to go. As his car peeled out of the parking lot, I felt strangely light-headed, like a kid who'd eaten too many cupcakes.

* * *

I DIDN'T WANT MR. WENTWORTH TO think I was stalking him, but I didn't want to lose this strange connection we had made. At last, I had met an actual gay person. So I spaced out my visits, stopping by every three days, counting them off in the calendar where I wrote down my homework assignments. Occasionally Mr. W. nodded from his wooden stool behind the counter, but that was it. Maybe he thought I liked him? I didn't. Wentworth was too square, too straight-nosed and clean-cheeked and khaki-clad for my taste. Still, I could see him attracting attention in some bar.

Was he the type who went to bars? Was that the kind of life I'd have someday?

How did a person go from someone presumed to be straight to a publicly acknowledged homosexual? Whenever you saw a gay person on a TV show or in a movie, they were, well, fully sprouted. But what about someone like me, who'd been out on a date with Elaine Rosen and had kissed her at the end of it? Someone who, thanks to years of listening to his dad's television blaring, knew the rules of baseball? Someone who was friendly with stoners and tennis players, and a handsome smart aleck like Justin Jackson?

Hay Fever

More and more, I was thinking seriously that I might tell my parents, and how I might tell them. Something like I loved them and I wanted to be honest. Or, this was not a phase, and could not be cured. This wasn't their fault or anyone's fault.

Maybe they'd cry, or say in a sorrowful voice that they'd known all along, or suggest I go back to therapy. Maybe they'd throw Mark in my face.

It was important to do it at just the right moment. Like after a nice belly-busting dinner in front of a cozy roaring fire, or over glasses of iced tea on your deck on quiet Sunday afternoon. In other words, anytime besides the one when I chose, after Dad and I had returned home late from a Tigers game—a spontaneous and surprisingly successful attempt at male bonding. The Tigers had won, I'd eaten six hot dogs, our section had been largely void of overly drunk fans, and my father and I had spent several hours in each other's company without a single argument.

We were standing in the kitchen, and Mom was pouring diet pop. "Is that enough ice?" she asked me. "I can get you more ice."

Her hands hovered over my glass as if I were still a child who couldn't get his own ice. But I was sixteen and a half years old. I shopped for my own clothes in men's sizes. I drew naked people. I hit tennis balls with strength and purpose. I was a real man with real feelings and needs.

How would Kurt have told them? He'd probably have grunted "I'm gay or whatever," and then stomped out of the house, knocking over a chair along the way.

I hated the cliché, "I've got something to tell you," so instead I said, "I've got to tell you something." As I uttered words "I'm gay," my glass slipped from my hand. I caught it before it could smash thanks to my new dexterity with my body, yet I wished I had let it drop, to hear it shatter like the glass under the groom's foot at a Jewish wedding.

Dad said nothing.

Mom asked, "Is this because of what happened with that jerk across the street?"

"It has nothing to do with that," I said.

"You're confused," she said. "You experienced a traumatic event."

"I'm not confused." I looked hopefully at Dad, who was staring at the floor in a daze. "I have some gay friends. They're nice people."

"Like a cult," Mom said, rubbing a streak on the counter. "Like Waco."

"They're not a cult."

"Do you realize this means a life with no children, if you can call that a life?" she asked. "And what if you catch the virus? That's a death sentence. One wrong move and you could die. That's what you want? That's the risk you want to take?"

I turned to my father, still mute. "Dad?" I said.

"I can't even believe we're talking about this," said Mom. She picked up her glass, then put it down.

"That's it, then?" I said. "That's what you think?"

Dad finally spoke up. "We don't think anything. Except, you know, we love you."

"Of course we love him," said my mom, but her voice quivered and her eyes looked wet. "That's not the issue."

"Then love me for who I am," I said.

"I can't talk about this anymore. Maybe later. Maybe tomorrow." She went to the fridge and took out her labeled plastic containers of leftovers, opening each one and sniffing the contents. Dad shrugged helplessly.

In my room, I buried my head in a pillow. I considered crying but no tears came. I wasn't sad really, or angry. My mind raced through plans. I'd need money. I'd get in my car and drive away somewhere, finally escape Maggie Lane, go to a place where I had no connections, and reinvent myself for good.

The next morning, the kitchen was empty. I microwaved a frozen croissant-wich, consumed two containers of yogurt, a banana, and an orange. I felt hungrier than usual.

Mom came in, still in her bathrobe, hair rumpled, eyes bleary. She grunted a hello. I asked where Dad was. "Already at work," she muttered and banged the coffeemaker. "I thought I set this last night." As she grabbed the bag of coffee grinds from the freezer, it spilled on the floor. "Shit!" she said.

"Need some help?" I asked, startled. Mom never cursed.

"No, no." She scooped the loose coffee with her hands. "You'll be late."

"Well, okay then." I walked a wide circle around her. At the door, I paused, and then blew her a kiss. I wasn't generally a kiss-blower, and I had not kissed my mother goodbye before school, well, since ever. She gave me a pained smile. I quickly got into my car and almost crashed into our mailbox while pulling out of the driveway.

Somehow I drove to school, where I must have answered questions in class, taken notes, eaten lunch, though by the end of the day, I had no memory of doing any of those things. After the final bell, I thought about getting on the highway to Chicago or Toledo, or California. Instead I headed home and parked at the edge of our driveway, in case I needed to make a quick getaway.

When I walked in, Mom called out, "He's home!" She rushed over to hug me tightly. I didn't understand what was happening.

Dad was there too—he'd left work early—and we all filed into the kitchen and sat down at the table. "We visited with your doctor today," Dad said. "He says hello."

My doctor? I thought. I'm not sick. Then I realized they meant Dr. Don.

And then Dad added: "He says there's nothing wrong with you or with being gay, and that what we need to do is to love and accept you, so that's what we're going to do."

I didn't know what to say except, "Really?"

"Do you want to see him?" Mom asked. "To make an appointment, to talk?"

"No," I said. "I don't need to see anyone."

"Of course he doesn't," said Dad. "There's nothing wrong with him."

Mom nodded, as if she agreed, but her eyes looked tired, and the corners of her mouth seemed worn. I'd always thought she'd be the one to have an easier time with this. She must have met some gay artists through her work, and I'd foolishly believed she might introduce me to one. You and I, we're the same, I wanted to tell her. You like art, I like art. You like boys, I like boys. Maybe that was our problem: we were the same.

"What about that girl you took to the Cotillion?" she asked.

"She's gay too," I explained, then watched her face go rigid.

"Is everyone gay?" Dad said. "I'm feeling left out."

So typical of Dad, to clown around at a time like this.

He went on to say they were glad I had spoken, that now they finally understood why I'd been so moody lately, and why I'd developed a taste for dark, loud music like Nirvana and black jeans. "You probably felt you couldn't talk to us," Dad said. "But you can always talk to us. We want you to know that."

"Just be careful," Mom said.

"I'm not going to get AIDS, alright?" I said. "I don't even know any gay people."

"No, not just that," Mom said. "Of course you need to, you know, protect yourself. But I'm also talking about in the world, who you are. People might want to hurt you. And you've already been hurt once. This kind of detail about who you are is very powerful. It can change how people see you, how they treat you." Then she came up with a brilliant idea. Someday Elaine and I could get married, share a house, and split it in half. "No one has to know what goes on in your bedroom," she said. "You could save on living expenses."

"That's not how it works," I said.

"Deanna, he's gay," my father said.

"I know," she said, dabbing her nose with a napkin. "Sorry, my nose always runs this time of year. It's all this hay fever."

HALF-LATIN, HALF-GREEK

MOM DIDN'T HAVE TO WORRY. I was keeping my mouth shut, at least at school. One more year, one more year, I kept telling myself. But then a year was a very long time. In the middle of discussing *Romeo and Juliet*, our AP World Lit teacher Mrs. Hart, a forty-year Dalton veteran, dropped her chalk, straightened her skirt, and marched out of the room. As if some cord inside her had snapped and she just couldn't do this anymore.

I knew how she felt.

After a week of subs, the school settled on her replacement: Hal Wentworth. Apparently, he'd taught English at some high school in New Hampshire.

These days, Wentworth was generally recognized as Dalton's most eligible bachelor. A snapshot of him at Cotillion, surrounded by pretty seniors, had appeared in the *Dalton Lion* with the caption, "Lucky guy!!!" During our last pep assembly, the captain of the girls' softball team threatened to use him as a secret weapon to distract their opponents. And the Friends of Dalton had auctioned off a date with dear Mr. W as a fundraiser. There were no male bidders.

To punish Wentworth for his hypocrisy, I listened for him to make mistakes in English class, like when he confused Tom and

Thomas Wolfe, or claimed that Hemingway and Gertrude Stein were lovers. And while reciting a list of mnemonic word definition strategies during an S.A.T. vocab review, he claimed that words beginning with "hetero" were Latin-derived, as in "heterosexual."

My arm shot up in the air like a salute, and before he could call on me, I gleefully pointed out that in fact the word was half-Latin and half-Greek.

"Thanks, Ari," Mr. Wentworth said, sounding more sad than thankful.

"Half-Latin, half-Greek," Justin said after class. "Where'd you get that from?"

"Hey, I'm a man of mystery," I said. "I don't give away my secrets."

As I opened my locker, Justin leaned against the wall and closed his eyes. I took advantage of the opportunity to study his nose, his stubbled chin, his left ear with the subtle incision where he inserted a small silver hoop after school hours. "I'm sick of this place," he moaned, then opened his eyes slightly and watched me through the slits.

"We all are. We're seniors," I said.

"I want to burn this uniform." He stretched his arms. The tails of his shirt lifted out of his pants, but he didn't tuck them back in, and I didn't dare do it for him. All this silence, and being so careful all the time. I felt like a fucking spy.

I dug into my locker. "Maybe I shouldn't keep bringing you these." I held out a chocolate bar from Israel. "Maybe you're sick of these too."

He grabbed the bar from my hand, then tore the wrapper off and took a big bite of chocolate. "You know I love them," he said, chewing with his mouth open. "Hey, did I ever tell you I got your postcard? From France."

"That was a joke," I said quickly. "You knew that, right?"

"I did?" he said.

"I didn't really mean that I missed you. I mean, obviously, I didn't."

"Why not?"

"Well, maybe I meant part of it. But not in a weird way."

"So which is it? You missed me or you didn't?"

What answer did he want? "I don't know anymore," I said, barely able to breathe.

Justin lightly punched my shoulder. "You let me know when you figure out what you're thinking, instead of trying to guess what I'm thinking."

In Utero

Nirvana's *In Utero* finally came out that fall and debuted at number one on *Billboard*. Then, despite glowing reviews and tuneful radio-ready singles like "Heart-Shaped Box" and "All Apologies," *In Utero* skidded down the charts, way outsold by the new Pearl Jam, which for me was a point in its favor. But for Justin, the album's lack of sales meant it was a dud. Apparently, to be an alternative band with street cred, you had to be rejected by the public before finding success, not after.

What Justin refused to accept, no matter how often I tried to explain it to him, was that *In Utero*'s lack of popularity was its point, if there could be said to be a point to a confusing and maybe confused grab-bag of seemingly melodic but actually fuck-you-sarcastic melodies, walls of total noise, and a few soft-spoken, pretty ballads. This was Nirvana's protest against the unexpected success of *Nevermind*. They were sifting through their unwanted fans, separating the followers jumping aboard the grunge bandwagon from the true believers, outcasts like me, who were on Kurt's side.

And yet, I wasn't totally sure what it meant to side with Kurt. What was he for, exactly? The lyrics on the new album were even harder to decipher than those on *Nevermind*. Was Kurt saying stay or go away? Was he asking to be tempted or tested? Steal or steel the light inside me? Speak or spit out the truth? I listened again and again, trying to find a way in. The crazy song titles were of little help: "Scentless Apprentice," "Very Ape," and "Frances Farmer Will Have Her Revenge on Seattle."

In his interviews, Kurt was his usual unhelpful self. "None of my poems are coherent at all," he said. "It's just a bunch of gibberish. I try to have relations to some of the lines, and there's a lot of double meanings, and in certain senses, they do relate to something, but it's always changing."

I was a lot like Kurt. I knew all about double meanings, deliberate incoherence.

A Talk

MR. WENTWORTH BREEZED INTO CLASS WEARING a tight-fitting pale pink dress shirt.

"Looking sharp, Mr. W.," whistled one of the girls. "Love the pink." And Mr. Wentworth, the fucking hypocrite, winked.

"You know what they say, pretty in pink," I blurted out. "Wear that shirt on a hot date and you'll definitely get laid." Kurt himself couldn't have been more insolent.

The room got very quiet. A couple of kids shifted uncomfortably in their chairs. Justin bit at his cuticles and avoided looking in my direction.

Why was it that when guys like Kurt made snippy remarks, people found them charming or funny, but when I did it, it was as if I'd wet my pants in public?

Mr. Wentworth stood there, almost a full minute, without speaking. "See me after class," he said finally, turning a deep shade of crimson. Then he picked up *The Sun Also Rises*, wrote "THEME" in a shaky hand on the chalkboard, and instructed us to list as many examples as we could.

For the rest of the period, I told myself Wentworth deserved what he got, for his shitty teaching, his good looks, and most of all for playing it straight. Maybe I could spread a rumor that before becoming a teacher, Mr. Wentworth had been a gigolo.

After class, Justin snickered, "Have fun with teach," and squeezed my shoulder.

I shucked off his hands, as if I hadn't dreamed of them massaging my back or teasing my hair. "How'd you end up in AP World Lit anyway?" I said. "Why aren't you with the dummies in Creative Expressions?"

"I'm a man of mystery."

"Oh, shut up."

In Justin's world, telling your friend to shut up was the equivalent of a love letter.

Mr. Wentworth instructed me to follow him to the English Department office. I protested that I'd be late to Physics, but he said he'd write me a note. Ms. Bloom, who'd taught me the classics of American Lit last year, was sitting there, and Mr. Wentworth asked if we could have the office to ourselves. "Of course!" she said with her usual good cheer and gathered her books. I cast her a pitiful smile, but she didn't save me.

Mr. Wentworth gestured to the chair near his desk, then tapped the door closed with his polished leather dress shoe. "So," he said, sitting down. "Why are we here?"

I cocked my head to one side, the way I'd seen Krist Novoselic do in the video to "Heart-Shaped Box." "Because you don't like me."

"Look, sit down, why don't you?"

It seemed we'd be here a while, so I sat.

"I appreciate your . . . discretion about our running into each other last spring."

Had he really just said "discretion"? How humiliating.

"Hey, how've you been doing?" he asked.

For a cheeseball, he had a nice voice: soft but a bit crumbly at the edges, with an earthy quality. So unlike mine, too anxious and shrill to be taken seriously.

"I'm fine," I said.

"Is there something you want to talk about, related to that, that movie?"

"You don't ever to want to talk about it," I said. "Now you want me to?"

He looked over my shoulder at the door. "As confusing as these things are for you, they're confusing to me too. And it doesn't help when people know you a certain way. It's like an actor who's been typecast in a certain role. You're expected to continue playing it, even if it's a role you've outgrown."

"How was your date?" I asked.

"Date?" he repeated.

"From the raffle. They auctioned you off in a raffle, remember?"

His face turned crimson. "It was nothing, just a silly . . . "

"It's not nothing!" I said, cutting him off. "People should be honest. Or at least, don't encourage all this Casanova talk."

"And how do you suggest I do that? You're what, seventeen?"

"Sixteen," I said. "Almost seventeen."

"Sixteen," he repeated, his voice rising, as if he'd gotten tired of my corrections. "And you think you know everything. But you don't. That's why you're in school, to learn. And that's what you're going to do in my class. I'm your teacher, and there . . . there has to be discipline. If that means you're going to tell the world you saw me at some movie, then, well, I don't care if I do lose my job. I can't just let this go."

He covered his face with his hands. For a second, I considered blackmailing him into kissing me. Not that I liked Wentworth, but I'd never been kissed, not even by Mark, and this could be my chance. It was the kind of trick Mark would have pulled.

"Of course I wouldn't do that," I said. "I'd never do that."

Mr. Wentworth let his hands drop to the desk. "Thank you, Ari."

Things had been so much easier a few minutes ago, when I'd simply hated him.

"I wish it were always like this," he went on. "Why can't we help each other?"

"Maybe," I said skeptically.

"Look, I still have to punish you. You know, for mouthing off in class. It would undermine my authority otherwise."

"Yeah, I get it," I said.

Mr. Wentworth patted my shoulder. "Ari, if I've done anything to make you angry, I'm sorry. You know that, right?"

I felt the heat of his fingers through my shirt. I thought, I am being touched a gay man. Why wasn't it as thrilling as I'd imagined? "I'm not angry," I said.

He gave me a long, sad look, then let me go.

My punishment, in addition to the talk, was a week in detention. My reward was that Justin circulated the story of my insolence with Mr. Wentworth, boosting my popularity to new highs.

Today's Your Holiday

I TRIED TO FORGET MY FEUD with Wentworth and focus on Portfolio Day, which was coming soon. Ms. Hunter had commandeered a school van to drive the few of us with art school aspirations to Ann Arbor. Students from all over Michigan would submit their work to representatives from art schools who'd tell us our chances of getting in.

My parents listened politely as I listed the schools that were participating. Later I overheard Mom asking Dad if he thought I'd ever get this art bug out of my system.

Ms. Hunter seemed more interested in what I'd be wearing than in what I'd be showing. "You want to look sharp, but not slick," she said, and also advised me to brush up on my communication skills. "You can be real smart, but you're too quiet. Sell yourself a bit. Don't be so afraid to open your mouth."

I'd almost forgotten about the Wentworth thing until the week before Portfolio Day, when Mr. W asked to see me again after class.

What now? Ever since my stint in detention, I'd stifled numerous cracks I could have made about Mr. Wentworth's pedagogical methods, fashion choices, intermittent heterosexual flirty remarks, in short the audacity of his existence in our lives. I thought he'd noticed and in return, had ever so gently corrected Justin for identifying Daniel Day-Lewis as the main character of *Last of the Mohicans*.

Mr. Wentworth sat on the edge of his desk, which was something teachers did to show they were like cool, man. I caught the scent of his aftershave, woodsy and a bit sweet. After asking how I was—slowly with a long serious look on his face—he explained that he'd been charged with managing the *Lion's Den*, our school paper, and that I should draw for it. "Like an action drawing of the tennis team," he said, pantomiming a forehand with one of his graceful arms. "Our school in New Hampshire won state for tennis, you know?"

"Not that," I said quickly. "Maybe something related to art, or movies." Then I blushed, remembering *The Living End*. He seemed embarrassed too, so I added, "I mean general release movies. For everyone."

Mr. Wentworth chewed on one of his pens, one of my dad's dental pet peeves. I wanted to tell him that he'd ruin his teeth that way, but I was done correcting my teachers.

"Tell you what," he said. "Talk to Nick Miller. He's our *Lion's Den* film critic. He can tell you what he has in the pipeline."

"I'll think about it," I said. "I have a lot to do. Portfolio Day's coming up."

"Do more than think. Say yes. We have fun. We have pizza." He ruffled my hair, as if we were a couple of quarterbacks fooling around in the Commons Room. "We want you on our team, big guy."

You don't have to flirt, I thought. I said I'd think about it.

I was still thinking about it as I entered the Dining Hall. Strange, that Wentworth of all people should become my confidant.

Justin was sitting at a table of guys and girls wearing black t-shirts under their dress shirts and black leather bracelets around their wrists. An empty chair sat beside his.

But then Nick Miller shuffled up to me, his wrinkled school tie knotted up to his throat. A pre-emptive strategy to ward off bullies intent on strangling him? "Ari!" he said, gawking at me through his oversized glasses, which magnified an unfortunate string of acne by his nose. "I hear we're sharing a beat for the *Lion's Den*."

Nick had been born in Brazil and lived there until he was twelve, when his mom divorced his dad, who worked in the foreign service. In part because of this background, he was known as something of an oddball. Also, freshman year, while trying out unsuccessfully for the football team, he'd dashed into the woods behind the goal-posts and returned without his helmet. The rumor was that he'd taken a shit in his helmet. Nick vehemently denied it, but where was the helmet?

As Justin drained the last of his chocolate milk, I said, "Nick, what do you want?"

"So my next piece is going to be a home video column, recommending the work of a great director. Like Vincente Minnelli or George Cukor. You know who they are?"

"Of course," I said, insulted by the question. "*Gigi. My Fair Lady.* But I prefer Merchant Ivory."

His eyes widened. "Hey, that's perfect! I love Merchant Ivory! And a new edition of *Maurice* just came out on home video, so that can be our peg."

He said the name so casually, didn't even lower his voice a jot. *Maurice.* Luckily most Dalton kids had no idea what *Maurice* was. They'd probably pronounce it "Mo-REES" instead of "Morris."

"I never saw it," I mumbled.

Nick lowered his voice. "We could rent it together sometime," he paused, "at my house. I have my own VCR."

"Maybe," I said. "Can I get back to you later?"

Justin turned to wave at someone who wasn't me.

"Later," Nick repeated as if English were his second language. "Okay. Call me tonight." He handed me a printed card with his number, name, and the caption "Occupation: Explorer."

As I stuffed the card into my pocket, Justin got up, deposited his dirty dishes and silverware in the bins by the door, and left. I slumped down at my usual table with the tennis team. One of them whistled and asked about my new boyfriend, Nick Miller.

"You're all jealous because the only action you get is with your right hand," I said. "Hey, watch me stuff this whole slice of pizza into my mouth."

That shut them up until after school, at tennis practice, when they teased me about Nick again. Though Nick was known for being a nerd, not a gay guy, the idea of us as a couple had caught their imagination. If we got married, who'd be the husband and who'd be the wife? Who'd do the cooking? Who'd bring home the bacon?

"Look at him serve," said Ryan. "He tosses the ball like a girl."

"Big talk for someone who's double-faulted a hundred times this season," I shot back. "At least I get it in the box."

"That's the only place he gets it in the box, on the court!" Ryan said, hooting.

I told them all to suck my dick and left early to hit the showers.

As usual, the boys' locker room at Dalton smelled deep and musky, like a barn. Breathing through my nose, I found an empty shower stall, turned on the water as hot as I could stand, and stood under the showerhead, letting the water rain down my neck, drip down my nose, and soak my skin. I still hated getting naked in public, but I forced myself to do it. I had every right to take a shower if I needed to.

While toweling off, I heard someone hiss my name.

Who'd followed me in here? I wrapped my towel tightly around my waist, then stuck my head out of the curtain. It was only Justin, dry, half-naked, barefoot. "Oh, hi," I said, stepping out of my stall and dripping on the floor. How much could he see through my damp towel? I allowed myself five seconds to look at whatever I could, the muscles of his torso, the dark, almost ashy-colored nipples, the fuzz of black hair on his chest and stomach. A tattoo on his upper arm said "Mighty Like a Rose." What did it mean?

Raising my head, I caught Justin looking at me too. What part of my body was he looking at? Then, weirdly, I wondered if I had lint stuck in my belly button.

Finally, he extended his right hand, almost touching my wrist. "Happy Simat Tora," he said.

"What?"

"Simat Tora? Today's your holiday."

He meant Simchat Torah. Did he want to celebrate it by inviting me into the shower with him? Then I felt a stubborn tingling in my groin, so I ran. "Yeah, thanks," I said over my bare shoulder.

* * *

WHILE YANKING MY STREET CLOTHES ON, I thought about that shower and Justin's heavy look, the drooping eyelids, the crinkled nose. His hand extended as if to take something from me. Was there any way . . . ?

No, impossible. His father was a minister in Detroit. He moved in a crowd of hipper-than-thou friends. He had no reason to risk all that for me.

An Outing to the Movies

THE NEXT DAY IN ENGLISH, I tried to avoid talking to Justin too much or looking at him, because every time I did I saw him again in that towel, the two of us by those showers. But then, on our way out of English class, Nick waved to me. Justin saw and asked what that was all about, so I explained that Nick and I were working on the movie section of the *Lion's Den* together.

"Oh, yeah?" said Justin. "That's cool. I like movies."

"Really? What movies do you like?"

"*Beverly Hills Cop II*. That's a good movie. And *History of the World Part I*."

"Wow," I said sadly. "How mainstream of you." Lately, I'd been listening carefully to the things and people he said he liked, hoping for any promising clue.

"Yeah, whatever." Then he said, "We should see a movie some time."

"A movie?"

"Yeah, you know, those things they show on screens in theaters."

"Thanks, asshole." Just us two, off campus? I didn't think we had that kind of friendship. "So which movie did you want to see?"

"That's why you go to the theater, to see what's playing. Then you pick."

"What if what's playing is no good?"

"They're all no good. It's just something to do." He stood closer to me, and I smelled the lunchmeat on his breath. "Enough talk. You want to or not?"

"Yeah," I said softly. "I want to."

"Then let's fucking do it."

"Now? I've got History in five minutes."

"And I've got bio or some such shit. Dude, we're seniors."

He opened his collar and loosened his Dalton tie, and I saw him again in a coarse white gym towel. But then, these days, every-thing—walking, talking, even breathing—prompted me to replay that scene of us by the showers in my mind. And each time, that towel slipped further down his hips and finally to the floor.

I said, "Okay."

We rode together in Justin's car, a battered Honda that he'd bought off his uncle. My dad always said that when he saw someone driving a Japanese car in Detroit of all places, it reminded him of all the laid-off factory workers now surviving on welfare.

Justin flung off his Dalton blazer and put on a black jean jacket with a rip down one sleeve. The passenger seat was littered with empty bottles of iced tea, a black leather-bound journal decorated in worn stickers, and a broken ice scraper. Like a modern Sir Walter Raleigh, he threw it all in the back to make room for me.

As we drove out of the school parking lot, I rolled down the win-dows, closed my eyes, and let the wind hit my face. The radio was playing "Groovy Train" by the Farm, insufficiently cool for Justin. He put in a mix tape of screechy bands I'd never heard of, with names like Big Jesus Trash Can and Killer Chihuahua. Even after a year of studying *Spin* and *The Metro Times* and imported copies of *NME* and *Select*, I couldn't keep up with the new, increasingly oddly named bands he kept discovering and name-checking with a worldly practiced air I'd never master.

"I can't wait for college," Justin said, pulling off his tie.

"I know." I tried to sound depressed, though I loved Dalton because he was in it.

"If you can make it to college," he said, "you're free, bro."

If they're all like you at college, I thought, I can't wait. But then the thought popped into my head, where was Mark going to school?

"I just finished my application to U of M," he said.

"I'm almost done with mine too," I confessed. Would Mark be going there? Half the kids I knew went to Michigan. If he was going there, who would warn me?

"Do you ever think you want something bigger. You know? More than the usual get married, buy a big house in some suburb."

"Drive a convertible," I added, thinking of Rabbi Taborsky's flashy car. "Buy ugly art to hang over your living room sofa."

"Yeah, that's a good one," he said, snorting.

"Promise that you and I won't turn out like that."

"We won't," he said. "We're going to do something with our lives. Like, we could move to Chicago." He pressed the accelerator. "We could go there right now. I could turn right now on Telegraph, hit I-94, and then just keep going west."

He changed lanes, and for a second, I thought he was serious. "And miss another enlightening discussion of world literature from Mr. Wentworth?" I said.

"Aren't you the perfect Dalton boy," he said, sounding disappointed.

"I'm not." I blushed, because I had no proof he was wrong.

We went to a multiplex on Nine Mile Road that my parents said was dangerous because the patrons were mostly black and some Jewish guy, the father of a kid I once went to camp with, once got shot there.

All the movies playing were awful, so I agreed to the least offensive option, an action flick with a tough-sounding two-word name like *Real Deal* or *Hard Fight*. I paid for Justin's tickets plus a soda and popcorn with my parents' credit card, which they gave me for gas money. Justin tried handing me a ten, but I insisted, "It's on me."

Two hours later, we staggered out of the theater feeling stupid, miserable, and cheated. The soles of our shoes were sticky from melted butter and spilled soda on the floor. Three of the four urinals in the bathroom were out of order. The popcorn tasted stale and the soda was flat, like colored water. Our stomachs hurt.

"For a guy who's so picky about music, you have crappy taste in movies," I said.

"Next time," Justin said, "you can pick the movie in advance."

"I told you so, moron." I slapped the scrubby top of his head in as straight-boyish a manner as possible, not lingering too long, hitting just hard enough to hurt a bit. He smirked back at me. I'd done well.

So there would be a next time.

NOT THE ONLY ONE

NICK MILLER LIVED IN A SMALL Tudor-style house in historic Huntington Woods, behind the elephant house at the Detroit Zoo. It was good we were watching *Maurice* at Nick's instead of at my house, where Mom would have huffed in the background while Dad would have made embarrassing remarks that were meant to be funny.

On my way to Nick's, I listened to *In Utero* and thought over which drawings to include in my portfolio. It was like choosing a track list for a mix tape. You wanted enough variation so it wasn't boring, but also some consistency, some kind of narrative that said who you were. So what was my narrative? All I had were drawings of the random women who happened to work as models at the Royal Oak Art Association.

The Millers had no garage, just a carport where Nick's mother parked her beat-up Toyota with the ragged "Visualize World Peace" sticker on the bumper. His mother, who'd tied up her frizzy red perm with a silk headband, offered me sugar-free Dutch-processed hot cocoa or natural ginger soda. I said I wasn't thirsty.

"Cool shirt," she said, referring to my baggy skater-boy smock. Though I didn't skateboard, I liked the look. "I wish Nick would branch out a bit, fashion-wise."

"Nick is very happy staying branched in," he said.

"I'll leave you two alone." On her way to the living room, she slapped Nick's butt. "Don't do anything I wouldn't do."

"Mother, I'm going to have to kill you."

Nick looked different out of his school clothes, but still odd. His jeans were stiff and the wrong brand, and his shoes and tube socks were blindingly white. "Sit wherever," he said. The only options were the bed or the floor, so I chose the floor. His TV was as enormous as a suitcase. After putting the tape into the VCR, he turned off the lights and sat on the floor next to me. I moved over to make room.

The movie was fairly slow until the scene when Hugh Grant rested his head on James Wilby's knee, and James Wilby ran his fingers through Hugh Grant's hair. The two men hugged, pressing their pale, manicured hands into each other's bodies until a noise came from the hall and Hugh Grant jumped to his feet, just as James Wilby's friends rushed into the room, demanding tea.

I wanted to see that scene again, but I lacked the words to ask. I glanced over at Nick, who seemed as engrossed as I was. He turned my way and then I realized that he hadn't invited me to watch this movie because he was a Merchant Ivory fan. In the dim light of the room, his acne didn't seem terrible. Even his glasses seemed thinner. He had lips. He had hands. He had what James Wilby and Hugh Grant had.

"Sorry," I said, "Could I turn up the volume a bit?"

"Sure." As Nick handed me the remote control, our fingers met, or, I let them meet. For a second anything seemed possible, until the hard nail of his thumb scratched the inside of my palm.

"Oh," I said, as if I'd touched something oily.

Nick stared at me, leaning on his elbow.

I dropped the remote on the floor and took back my hand.

He asked, "Did you think because I'm a nerd, I have no sex drive?"

Yes, but I couldn't say so. "I like you, but not that way."

"Sorry." Nick got up and turned on the overhead light. "I shouldn't have tried anything, only I get so tired of being the only one." He looked right at me. "Am I right?"

He stood between me and the door, watching me, waiting for my answer. I hadn't prepared one. I hadn't thought I'd need to. But before I could think up some dumb-ass excuse, he said, "It's okay," and sat down again. "I won't tell anyone."

I remembered what Elaine Rosen had told me, that if I told on her, she'd ruin my life. And I thought of poor Rory, though he didn't seem so badly off these days. It wasn't like everyone liked him, but they generally were used to him now, and let him alone.

"How did you know?" I asked gloomily.

"Ever heard of gay-dar? I mean, you never talk about girls."

"How would you know what I talk about?"

He grinned sheepishly. "Because I listen."

I wondered if he knew about Wentworth. "Who else in our school do you think . . . ?" I asked. "I mean, can I ask you about someone?" He nodded. "Justin Jackson?"

"That's an easy one. Straight." Nick squared his shoulders and spoke in a booming voice. "'Dude, what's up with the big game last night?'"

"That's just a stereotype," I said. "He's different. I know him."

"I prefer smart Jewish guys." He looked right at me.

I felt freakish, being admired. "They're all fixated on their mothers," I said, trying to make a joke. "Their noses are too big."

"I like them that way," he said, and his face had this kind of unsettled look.

"I don't."

"To each his own. We're not attracted to ourselves."

"What about teachers?" I said. "Do you think they'd fire someone for being gay?"

"My friend in public school has a gay teacher," he said. "But Dalton?"

"Maybe it'd be alright if the person kept it quiet."

"No way. You know how straight people are," he said. "They think gay guys are all sex-crazed pedophiles."

How clever Mark had been to say that I wanted it, to turn himself into the victim of his own aggression. And now my only defense, that I was straight, was gone. Nick had this new power over me, if he chose to use it.

"Maybe we should put the movie back on," he said.

"Yeah, whatever," I said as if I weren't eager to see it too.

He reached across my lap for the remote control and then paused, searching my eyes. And then I realized, I was the one with the power here. I was the one he wanted to please. No one could force me to do anything I didn't want to.

"I said yeah," I told him. "I'm ready to watch the movie."

His expression relaxed into its usual blankness. "Your wish is my command."

PERSONALITY

PORTFOLIO DAY WAS HELD ON A Sunday morning in the empty classrooms of the University of Michigan art school. While lugging my black vinyl folder between the wooden racks of drying canvases that lined the hallways, I inhaled smells of turpentine and wet clay and peeked at the other kids, most of them in black outfits and lugging their own black folders.

Was this what it would be like to become a real artist?

There were five of us from Dalton: a photography whiz senior who was sure to get into the school of her choice, three underclassman, for whom this was all a lark, and then me. We separated, then found each other between meetings to compare notes. Stuff like, the woman at RISD's an asshole, so don't even bother. CCS is only interested if you can draw a car. The guy from Michigan's nice.

The guy from Michigan was in fact "nice" to me, polite if not exactly excited. He complimented my "feel for the line," then paused over a drawing of a plumpish woman. "Witty," he said. When he got to the end of the portfolio, he smiled and told me, "I think there's something we can work with here." Then he gestured for the next person in line.

Hardly a ringing endorsement. But I didn't need one. Dad was going to talk to someone he knew at Michigan about me. I considered this an unfair advantage and I told him so. He said that I was qualified to get in on my own merits. This was just insurance.

Next, I stopped by two smaller schools I'd never heard of, ones whose tables had no lines, ones where I had no intention of going. Both the reps raved, and one of them, from somewhere in Pennsylvania, said she was sure she could offer me a scholarship. Maybe I didn't suck after all.

Taking a deep breath, I headed for the long line in front of the table at Parsons School of Design, which was so crowded, they had three evaluators. A girl ahead of me said, "Watch out for that guy in the middle. He's nasty." Of course he was the one I got, a thin man with a wisp of a mustache and wearing a colorful paisley shirt that belonged to a friendlier person. My newly minted gaydar buzzed wildly. I tried to radiate optimism, poise. Maybe I'd have a shot with him, out of gay solidarity.

Or maybe not. He flipped through my drawings the way a patient might skim through one of the old copies of *People Magazine* in my dad's waiting room. "Tits and ass," he sighed in a high-pitched voice. "This composition is cliché."

"That's a copy of a Degas," I said. Maybe I should have kept my mouth shut.

"Congratulations on copying Degas," he said in a snarky tone, then slid the portfolio across the table to me. "Anything else?" He fussed with a button on his shirt.

"Wait." I opened my backpack and pulled out my sketchbook. I'd debated about showing it. "You might like these."

You might like these, because they're images of men, not women.

He flipped more slowly through my pages and pages of Justin, Justin dozing off, Justin from the side, Justin draped over a school desk with a sleepy sullen look. "At least there's some feeling here," he said before tossing the book back at me. "Still, there's something pinched. Not enough personality."

"What does that mean?" I said, shoving the book roughly into my backpack. "I don't understand what you want from me."

He combed through his dark, smoothly brushed hair, his face void of any emotion. "What I'm saying is, I've looked at all this work of yours and I don't know who you are."

ALL AGES WELCOME

WHEN I'D ASKED JUSTIN IF HE wanted to go see another movie sometime, he looked at me funny and said, "Let me get back to you." But the day after Portfolio Day, just as I thought he'd forgotten all about the invitation, Justin told me to meet him in the school parking lot that Friday night. "And wear clothes you don't mind getting dirty."

"Why?" I asked suspiciously. "What kind of movie are we going to see?"

"Don't ask so many questions," he said.

So I showed up at the appointed time, wearing one of my painting shirts, splattered with streaks of vermillion and cerulean blue. Justin was a bit late, so I sat in my car and brooded some more about that nasty review I'd gotten from Parsons, as I'd been doing all week, even though Ms. Hunter told me to forget it.

All this work of yours, and I don't know who you are.

But there was a very good reason I couldn't show anyone who I was. Anyway, who cared who I was? Either I had talent or I didn't. Wasn't that all that mattered?

Justin pulled up in his beat-up Honda. He had on beat-up jeans and a thick, faded hoodie, worn and very soft, even more exciting.

Maybe he'd let me borrow it some time, to fold up and tuck under my ear at night like a pillow. We could trade clothes. So what would he want of mine?

"Ready?" he said as I got in beside him.

I shrugged. "I guess," I said. "I don't know what I should be ready for."

Justin shoved my arm. "What's up with you tonight? Why are you so gloomy?"

"I'm just hungry," I lied.

So we stopped for candy at a grocery down the road from school. "I love suburban supermarkets," Justin said, his fingers trailing over boxed sheet cakes, their smooth white planes of frosting dotted with pink and yellow roses. "Where I live, all the rolls and cakes are so old, you could use them for penicillin," he said. "The sausages are dried up like raisins. You can sink your thumb right through the tomatoes."

"You're exaggerating." I took advantage of the joke to poke his side.

"Not by much." He poked me back, just above my hip.

I took out my wallet to buy the candy, but Justin said, "You're always buying me stuff. Like I can't take care of myself."

"Fine," I said, depressed as I put my wallet away.

"A pack of Twizzlers for my boy here," Justin told the daydreaming girl with braces at the register, busy mouthing the words to a chirpy love song playing overhead.

Back at the car, Justin said, "I think you dropped something."

"Huh?"

"Check your seat, brain."

Sitting on the passenger seat were two waxy white rectangles of paper with a Ticketmaster logo on the top. Two concert tickets. "All Ages Welcome," I read aloud, and then paused. Two concert tickets. All Ages Welcome. To Nirvana.

Nirvana? "How did you get these?" I asked, pinching the tickets to make sure they were real. Yes, that's what was printed on those tickets, cradled in my trembling palm. I'd never attended a real concert before. When these tickets had gone on sale late last summer, they'd all been bought up before I could even figure out where to buy them.

"You don't want to go?"

To have Justin and Kurt in the same room, it seemed like too much.

"Yes," I said finally, emphatically. "Yes, yes, of course, I want to go. Justin, this is the nicest thing anyone's ever done for me."

"Good," he said with a gracious, relaxed smile, for once, with no trace of irony. "You deserve to have people do nice things for you."

* * *

THE CONCERT WAS ONLY TWENTY MINUTES away, at the State Fair Grounds Coliseum, just inside the city limits. The crowd streaming out of their cars was mostly white kids in beat-up jeans with shredded hems, plaid shirts and worn T-shirts thin as vellum paper, scrawled with the names of punk bands that even Justin didn't know.

He refused the money I offered him for the ticket. "Remember, I promised to give you something from Detroit? Anyway, the ticket was only twenty-five bucks. You probably spent more than that on candy from Israel all these years."

"You knew I bought it for you?" I said.

"I kind of figured it out," he said sheepishly. "You're not a very good liar."

"No," I laughed. "I guess not."

One of the warm-up bands was already playing when we walked into the hall—apparently that's what you wanted to do, miss the warm-up acts. Our tickets were "general admission" and Justin grabbed me by the elbow, trying to get us as close to the stage as we could, though not all the way where the mosh pit was. I admired how experienced he was at this.

The air in the room had a dense, grassy, sweaty smell and felt heavy and warm on my cheeks. I tried to check out the people standing near me, just in case there was someone in the crowd who might be the bullying type, ready for a fight, but it was impossible to get a fix on anyone, everyone kept moving around. As I stretched out my right arm to roll up my sleeve, I accidentally hit some guy in the back. I apologized twice, but he didn't seem to notice or care.

The band on stage screamed their lungs out and beat the crap out of their drums while we in the audience milled around in small circles of conversation and ignored them. I felt sorry for them up there, though I didn't care for their music. When they finished, Justin and I stood our ground as people filled in any empty spaces they could find. We were not talking, and maybe not minding that we weren't talking. Anyway, I couldn't think of words. I was too busy taking it all in: dyed, stringy hair damp with grease, pierced ears and noses and eyebrows and lips, thick, rough bodies pushing past us toward the black wall of speakers on stage, the anxious pre-concert chatter of the crowd around us, everyone only half-listening while keeping an eye up front for the slightest sign of movement, and thin clouds of smoke rising in wisps up toward the rafters, where a pair of unlucky pigeons were flying in sloppy frenzied circles, searching for an exit.

Two guys next to me were debating whether *In Utero* or *Nevermind* or *Bleach* was Nirvana's masterpiece when the lights all went out, and everyone screamed at once. I heard a harsh buzzing noise, followed by the squeal of a guitar, and then the lights came back on, spotlighting Dave Grohl behind the drums. The crowd pressed Justin and me forward, and a heavy boot kicked the back of my leg as Krist Novoselic bounced onto the stage, bopping up and down, tall, lanky, and awkward. Someone up there, maybe Krist, yelled "Dee-troit!" Finally Kurt himself appeared. He was maybe fifty feet away, or was it a mile? He'd planted himself at the microphone and hunched forward into it, almost reluctantly. Behind him loomed a large mannequin with its guts exposed.

Here they were, Nirvana, I thought. Nirvana is here.

He seemed smaller than on screens or magazine covers. His hair was red, orange, brown, and blond at once. His baggy clothes dripped off his narrow shoulders. A guitar dangled from around his neck, as he leaned forward to howl out the lyrics to "Drain You." His voice sounded thinner, more piercing than on the album, fragile to the point of breaking, especially on the high notes, and then occasionally, surprisingly melodic.

A fat guy with long blond Jesus hair and a beard was thrashing around in a circle, trying to get his own private mosh pit going. I was afraid to lose Justin, who was jumping up and down and screaming. I didn't know why. He said he didn't like Nirvana, said he was only here for my sake. A girl was hoisted up over our shoulders, and her boot hit the back of my neck. Another guy rammed into me and Justin pushed him back. The guy, instead of getting mad, howled "Yeah!" and Justin howled, "Yeah!" and then at me, "Come on, brain!" So I jumped too, carefully at first, and then higher, harder, until soon I was slamming my body around in a circle, flinging my fists in the air over and over.

And then they played "Rape Me."

Just before the release of *In Utero*, the single "Rape Me" caused a brief ripple of controversy when Wal-Mart refused to carry the entire album until the song was relabeled as "Waif Me" on the packaging. The mainstream media all demanded to know: Was Kurt for or against rape?

Go ahead and rape me, Kurt was singing, do your worst. Be a big man. You think you made me your victim, but I won't let you because I'm giving you permission to do it. I can take anything you've got, and survive.

Yes, yes, and yes, I wanted to scream. Maybe I was screaming.

Someone took off his shoe and threw it at Kurt's head. Kurt grabbed the shoe, looked at it for a second, then threw it back at the crowd and stomped off the stage. A few minutes later, circus music played on the sound system, and then the lights came up. The concert was over, but I could still hear the music, could still sense it in the buzzing in my ears, the smell of smoke on my clothes. I was happy.

Justin, covered in sweat, glowed beside me like some kind of angel.

See You in School

Back in the Dalton parking lot, we sat in Justin's car for a while. My skin was warm and tingling, and I kept wiping my forehead with my sleeve. My ears were still ringing. I wondered if Justin's were too.

I tried analyzing Justin with my underdeveloped gay-dar; he struck out on all counts. His hairstyle wasn't unusually fussy. He liked sports. He didn't care about fashion or female singers. Still, he'd bought me this ticket. It meant something.

"You're quiet again," he said. "Aren't I entertaining you?"

"It's nothing."

"Aw, fuck off, Ari. Just tell me what you're thinking."

I couldn't do that, so I told Justin about Portfolio Day, minus the part where I showed those pictures of him to the gay guy from Parsons.

"One asshole didn't like your work," he said. "Someone else will. You're good."

You're just saying that, I thought. You don't know. "It wasn't that he didn't like it. It was the way he didn't like it," I said.

"They just have to make up some bullshit. He probably wanted to get done with you so he could go get a doughnut or something."

That made me laugh, the idea of that Parsons rep, Mr. Quintessential New Yorker, in line at Dunkin Donuts. "He said he didn't know me."

"Yeah? Well, I know you."

"Do you?" Something in the air that night, or maybe the after-glow of the concert, made me feel like being frank all of a sudden. "Justin, why don't you have a girlfriend?"

He hunched his shoulders. "Do I need a reason? How about you, Mr. Don Juan?"

"I haven't met the right person, I guess."

"At our school? No wonder. Might as well wait until college."

"Yeah," I said. "I bet the girls will be all over you there."

He cocked his head. "So, Ari Silverman, what do you want to do now?"

"I don't know." My tongue suddenly swelled up in my mouth. "Go home?"

He smirked at me. "Yeah? Is that what you want to do?"

"No," I said in a low voice.

Justin stretched his legs and yawned as if preparing for a nap.

"Nick Miller's gay," I blurted out and instantly felt awful for spilling his secret.

Justin opened his eyes wide. "How do you know that?"

"He told me. You know what else he said? He says he knows, that he can tell, if someone else is gay too. Like a kind of sixth sense. Isn't that funny?"

But Justin wasn't laughing. "No one can tell that, just by looking at someone." He gripped the steering wheel tightly, his fingers making small rubbing noises against the vinyl. "I have no problem with the whole gay thing. It's bisexuality that really weirds me out. Like, make a choice one way or the other."

"Yeah," I said, but I wasn't really paying attention.

"So is that half-Latin, half-Greek?" he asked. I gave him a quizzical look. "Bisexuality? You know, the word?"

"Oh, oh. No, it's all Latin. If it were half-Greek, it would be 'disexuality.'"

"Die, sexuality! Die, die, die!" Justin said, giggling. Who was this guy?

I touched my forehead to the cold pane of the passenger window. "Anyway, it's not like a math equation," I said, shivering. "I mean, sexuality, it's not that simple."

"Why are you always so down on math?"

"We weren't talking about math, we were talking about sex."

"Were we?"

I rested my fingertips on his shoulder. He looked at my hand, then at me. "Yeah," I said. "I think we were."

Justin was staring at my face so intently I thought he might attack me.

"You want to do something?" he asked in a low voice, barely above a whisper.

"I—" I couldn't finish the sentence.

He reached out with his left hand, his fingers trembling. I thought he might grab my hand and force it down his pants, but instead his fingers landed so gently, tentatively on my nose, at the top, just between my eyes, as if to poke one out. His finger slid down the ridge of my nose and stopped at the tip. "Your nose is so cool."

"My Jewish nose?"

"Your handsome nose," he said. "Ari's handsome nose."

As his finger slid off, I grabbed it and touched it with my tongue.

With his free hand, Justin reached for the back of my head. I thought he wanted to kiss me, but he pushed me down, toward the crotch of his jeans. I felt betrayed. Was there some manual for straight guys? Find the nearest gay guy and he'll suck your dick. Close your eyes and pretend he's a girl.

My head hovered above where his penis pushed against the fabric of his pants. I ran my hands up and down his legs, his thighs, and when I touched his stomach, along the waistline of his jeans, he moaned softly.

This was really happening.

Because of Mark, I knew what Justin wanted and how to do it quickly, easily. This time will be different, I told myself. I'll draw lines in the sand that I won't cross. I'll touch it but he can't make me put my mouth on it. He's not strong enough to force me. If I have to get out of this car and walk home, I will.

He closed his eyes, flexed his hips, and unbuttoned his jeans.

But if I got out of that car, I'd be dead. He'd run me over to shut me up. He'd say it had been an accident, that he didn't see me walking in the dark.

I grabbed him through his underwear. "Can I kiss you?" I whispered.

"Yeah," he said, breathing roughly, his eyes squeezed shut. "Come up here." I reached into his waistband as I sat up and stretched toward his smooth cheek, my head crammed against his shoulder, my lips meeting his jaw, inches from his mouth, which gaped open as my hand moved back and forth. His hips dug into the seat. My other hand stroked the back of his neck and the woolly curls of dark hair behind his ear. His fingers flexed. His shoes pressed into the dirty floor pads of the car. I kissed his neck again and again and moved my hand until he sharply sucked in his breath.

His face crinkled as if he'd stepped on glass, and then he sighed deeply and opened his eyes. I let go and sat up. I wanted to say something meaningful, poetic.

"I got some napkins in the glove compartment," he said.

"Okay, thanks." They were Cinnabon napkins. I took one and offered him the rest. When he finished drying himself, he rolled down the window and tossed out the napkins, wrinkled white paper balls on dry black asphalt.

"I gotta get home," he said.

"You're mad," I said.

"What? Of course I'm not mad."

"You don't sound happy."

"I'm not. I mean, it's like, I don't know what I am, okay?"

I felt dizzy with shame. What if Mark found out? They'd let him out of religious school, rescind his conviction, put me on trial for perjury.

"Thanks for the concert," I said as I opened the passenger door.

"Yeah, sure."

"Just do me one favor. Please don't tell anyone what I said about Nick."

He shrugged. "See you in school." But he sounded ticked off.

Who I Really Am

THE NEXT DAY, JUSTIN SAUNTERED INTO English class a minute late, sat in his usual seat next to mine, and stared straight at the board. I tried to catch his eye until the bell rang, and Mr. Wentworth asked me to stay for a chat.

"Hey," I said as Justin shoved his books in his bag. He nodded, then darted off. I didn't get it. Now that he'd discovered he wasn't alone, didn't he want to talk some more? Or did he want to pretend that last night had been a lapse in reason, a case of temporary insanity caused by an art film and a night in the suburbs?

At least for now, the secret was safe. So why didn't I feel relieved?

Mr. Wentworth closed the door. I wondered if he knew what I'd done with Justin in his car, and that's what he wanted to discuss. Maybe he could teach me a few pointers, but then I doubted it. It was the kind of thing you kept private, for the same reason famous chefs never shared prize-winning recipes.

"We can't run this in the *Lion's Den*," Wentworth said, slapping my illustration for *Maurice* on his desk. I'd drawn the two men, one on the other's lap, in that armchair. "You keep trying to start something with me, and I'm telling you now, back off."

"I don't understand," I said. "What did I do?"

"Two men kissing, really?" He didn't need to explain any further. "What exactly have I done to make you hate me so much? Because I'm not a good role model? Well, alright, I'm not a model. I'm a human being, and believe it or not, I have feelings."

"Honestly, Mr. Wentworth, I'm not trying to get you in trouble. I haven't told anyone about you. I promise."

He narrowed his eyes at me.

"This isn't about you." I paused. "When people look at my work, I want them to know who I am. Who I really am."

Mr. Wentworth's shoulders relaxed. "I see." He picked up my column and inspected it again. "Look, we don't even have a gay-straight alliance at Dalton. You can't expect the school to allow us to run a sexual drawing of two men."

"Being gay isn't only about sex," I said. "It's about love. That's what this movie is about, love. I thought you weren't like the other teachers here."

I wondered where he lived, what TV shows he watched, what snacks he stashed in his pantry. Maybe he kicked off his dress shoes and put on fuzzy slippers. Maybe he'd been unpopular in high school. In another universe, we could have been friends.

"Look at it this way," he said. "I'm doing you a favor." He glanced over my shoulder at the door. "What do you think people would say about you if they saw this?"

My insides burned. "That I'm a talented artist. With vision."

Mr. Wentworth picked up a book at random from his desk, thumbed through the pages. "You're a senior. Hang on a bit longer. You'll see, in college, there'll be so many people to help you."

"Who's helping you?" I asked.

"No one," he said with a helpless smile. "I'm helping myself, whatever that's worth."

The upshot of all this was that I wasn't in trouble, but my drawing would not run in the paper. Nick would write a column about the films of George Cukor or Vincente Minnelli. I could draw something for that if I wanted to.

I didn't want to.

Afterward, I ran out to the parking lot to find Justin, but his little red Honda was gone. "You bitch!" I said to no one in particular.

* * *

I WAITED UNTIL NINE O'CLOCK TO call him at home. Or, rather, five minutes after nine so it wouldn't look like I'd planned it too carefully.

His father answered and confused me with Brandon as usual. Maybe all white people sounded alike to him? Then Justin came on the line. "Wait," said he said. I heard some noise in the background, and then what sounded like a door closing. "Brain," he said, "let's not make a huge deal of this."

"But it is a huge deal," I said. "I wanted it to happen. Not just the sexy part of it."

"Jesus, the way you talk sometimes."

"If you just want to forget it, it'll never happen again, I promise. It would be enough, I mean, I want . . . " I paused. "I want to be near you. I can't go back to the old way, all those secrets."

Justin said nothing.

"Was it a mistake, what happened?" I asked, my voice shaking.

"There you go again. Do you have to talk this way?"

"What way do you want me to talk?"

"I don't know."

"Should I hang up then?"

Justin paused. I pressed my ear to the phone, if only to hear him breathing, but there was nothing. "No," he said finally. "We can talk a bit more."

* * *

THE NEW *LION'S DEN* CAME OUT, so I stopped by Nick's locker to congratulate him on his Vincente Minnelli column. "They're so dumb, they think they're guarding the heterosexuality of our youth by exposing them to Judy Garland's husband," he said.

"Good one," I said.

"So you want to watch another movie some time?"

"Sure," I said. "Just don't drool over me too much."

"You don't have to say yes. I won't blow your straight cover."

"Maybe I want it blown," I said.

Nick gave me a skeptical look. "Brave words, my friend. You sure you know what you're asking for?"

The Joy of Being Selfish

JUSTIN TOLD ME TO MEET HIM outside of our English classroom after school, so when the final bell rang, I threw my coat and backpack over my shoulder and ran there—but no Justin. I waited five, ten, then fifteen minutes. Still no sign of him. Had he changed his mind? Then I peeked into the room.

He was sitting beside Mr. Wentworth, who'd kicked off his dress shoes and unbuttoned his shirt dangerously low. I was ready to barge in on them, until I noticed a sloppy looking half-eaten tuna sandwich languishing beside Mr. Wentworth's elbow. He was stooped over Justin's textbook, and his pen was poised in the air. Occasionally he made careful marks on a sheet of white paper like a child learning to form letters for the first time. Then Justin saw me and smiled. The universe righted itself.

Mr. Wentworth said, "You see? Is it clearer now?"

"Mm-hm," said Justin in a way that I recognized meant no, it wasn't clear and it might never be the way Mr. Wentworth was explaining it. It was all Greek to him. Or Latin. Or half-Latin, half-Greek.

Mr. Wentworth could flirt all he wanted. Justin was all mine. If I'd been a bigger person, someone as sensitive and sympathetic as Mr. Wentworth, perhaps I'd have invited him to celebrate my good fortune. But at that moment, I was too filled with joy being selfish.

SIX

WORRIED HE'LL BE LATE TO MEET Justin, Ari leaves just before halftime. He has to go down two sets of stairs, through a door, and then push his way through the crowds. He's rushing and trying to pretend like he's not rushing. On either side of him, vendors are selling nachos and beer and other junk, an imitation of a medieval marketplace, though without the foul smells of human waste, the guts of dead animals, the rivers of piss and beer and fetid streams choked with waste. Now where is Section 25? There's 24, so 25 should be nearby.

And then he sees Justin, standing there. Waiting. A head taller than the crowd. He must be several inches above six feet. Was he this tall in high school? Was it possible to keep growing after high school?

He's wearing a navy blue windbreaker of the thinnest, lightest material that clings nicely to the places where his shoulders end and his arms begin. He's as lanky as ever. He's . . . what? Well, he's Justin.

When Ari calls out Justin's name, it feels magical to say it, amazing that this name has the power to cause this tall handsome man to turn his way and break into a smile, a natural, relaxed smile that feels warm like a compliment, like sunlight.

Ari's ready to shake hands, clap arms, whatever's required, but Justin offers one of those man-hugs, neither too careful nor too pressing, firm enough to be real, a medium amount of pressure. Do you remember, Ari wonders, and then the hug is over before Ari realizes it's begun and Justin introduces the woman Ari hadn't noticed standing next to him, a woman more than a foot shorter than he is. "This is my wife Lisa."

In the days when they were still a couple, M suggested various things Ari could say to test out Justin's "flexibility." But neither he nor Ari had anticipated that Justin might bring his wife along. She has a long, delicate face and ironed brown hair. Her dark eyes are carefully outlined.

Ari has not the least bit of trouble accepting the idea that Justin might be married to a woman, might even be happy in such an arrangement. He'd always sensed that the things he and Justin used to do together—Jesus, how do you put such activities into language?—that they had a different meaning for Ari than they had for Justin. What he does wonder, though, is A) whether Justin recalls those experiences with anything like nostalgia or regret and B) does his wife know about them?

"Hi there, Lisa," Ari says in that effortlessly cordial tone his mother had taught him to use at any social engagement. "So nice to meet you."

"This guy saved my life in high school," says Justin, which hits Ari with a jolt. No, no, he thinks, it was the other way around. "So, how's it going, buddy?"

The "dude" of their teenage years has transformed into "buddy." In Ari's world, no one calls another person "buddy," but Justin must use this word quite often. Is that a higher echelon business way of speaking, a way for CEOs to pretend they're like the working classes, like Shakespeare's ahistorical Henry V carousing with Falstaff? Or is this "buddy" a vestige of Justin's working class roots?

Justin's voice sounds deeper now, and the Michigan accent has faded to a whisper. Now he doesn't sound like he's from anywhere, except maybe from "MBA school." How long has it been? They fell out of touch years ago, when Ari went to their state school and Justin attended a historically Black college not far away from where they now stand.

Justin mentions that he has three boys, one of whom is thirteen. Thirteen years old, almost the same age as Justin and Ari when they first met. How can that be?

"You got any kids?" Justin wants to know.

"No," Ari says, feeling the painful lack of them. "For so long, I thought because I was gay, it would be impossible, and then when things changed, well, they didn't change for me. You know?"

Justin nods as if he knows. It's the first time that Ari mentions the fact that he is gay, and Justin does not appear bothered. Why? Because he's accepting of gay people or because it's good for business? Or because it's not news at all.

If I'm gay, Ari thinks, what does that make Justin? He scans Lisa's face, which looks neutral, friendly. No, she doesn't know, Ari must believe that.

Ari and M used to argue about "outing." To M, it was fair game, but Ari has always made a distinction between men who have sex with other men and men who declare their attractions openly for the world to recognize. "Being gay is a privilege," Ari said. "If you don't claim that privilege openly, then you can have sex with as many men as you like, but you're still not gay."

"In an ideal world," M argued back. "So it's okay for men to have sex with men on the down low, then use the cover of being able to pass for straight to benefit from the privileges of heterosexuality? To advocate policies oppressing their gay brothers?"

Ari wonders, is Justin ever "on the down low"? Did he ever experiment again, after high school? He's the picture of a corporate executive, ready at any moment to pose for a magazine cover with a family. His family. He has a family now and Ari's not in it.

Ari takes out his new ball cap and displays it in front of his chest. Justin offers a round of mock applause, a strain of sarcasm Ari remembers from school. "You're doing well," Ari says.

"Can't complain," says Justin. "Love is a highly profitable commodity."

"Until it goes sour," says Ari.

"Even then," says Justin. "Doesn't work one way, you try again, right?"

There it is: that boundless American MBA confidence, coming from the same guy who used to sneer at Kurt Cobain for being a corporate sell-out. People change, Ari thinks. And then the weight of that cliché hits him with a wallop.

"Hey, how are you?" Justin asks. "You good? You're teaching at the University?"

"Yes, yes, I'm a Medievalist." The blank expression on Justin's face indicates that Ari might as well have confessed to being a Seventh-Day Adventist or even a Branch-Davidian. He wishes he were better at talking about what he does. His evident discomfort conveys a sense that his work is something shameful, that further questions are unwelcome, though in fact, he'd welcome the chance to talk more, to explain. Ari doesn't ask much about Justin's work either. He's never been able to shake this part of his upbringing, that it's not "classy" to talk about earned money in a social setting, a point of politesse most likely dating back to a time when earning rather than inheriting money was in itself shameful. Also, frankly Justin's success is the kind that doesn't interest Ari, though he admires it at a cold distance, the way he might view the work of pastry chefs who spin sugar into nests, or ballet dancers who crack their toes *en pointe*.

And yet, boring as it may be, Justin's success in business is impressive. His kids will not need scholarships to attend the schools of their choice. Ari's kids wouldn't have needed the scholarships either, not because of his salary but thanks to the money that naturally and effortlessly flowed through to him from his family.

"Do you ever get back to Michigan?" Ari asks. "To see your family?" He remembers Justin had that younger brother. Where is he now? Is he single?

"Sometimes for the holidays," says Justin. "But we go to Lisa's parents every other year. You have to split the time, you know."

No, Ari doesn't know. Well, he knows, intellectually, but he doesn't really know. M rarely talked to his parents, and never expressed any interest in Ari meeting them. In another time, when Ari and M would have shared a phone line, perhaps Ari would have picked up when M's parents called, and they might have spoken by accident. To be fair, Ari never pressed the issue. The fact that he and M's parents had never met was probably a relief to all concerned parties.

"I was glad you contacted me. I was thinking about you," says Justin.

You were? Ari thinks. Are you sure you should say so in front of your wife?

"I always wondered if you were happy," Justin explains. "You seemed like you weren't when we were in school, so I kind of hoped that now you would be."

"Indeed I am." And as Ari says it, he realizes it's true. In his own cockeyed way, he is happy, though maybe not as he would have defined that term in high school. Or maybe more precisely, he is learning to live his life as honestly as he knows how.

"That's good, then. I'm really glad."

Ari's still absorbing the beauty of this moment as the conversation moves on somehow, to the topic of moving. "We've moved four times because of his career. It's a lot," his wife is saying. What's her name again? Oh, yes, Lisa. She seems lovely, and maybe a bit wounded by having to move so often, though also understanding, good-natured about it. Ari feels genuinely bad for her. He too has moved many times, just not with children.

Ari mentions he lives in the Park.

"Our son went there to soccer camp last summer!" husband and wife both marvel.

"We sometimes go out there," says Justin, "without the kids, we go for dinner."

Ari's convinced now that Justin is not on the "down low." He's settled completely into his new life, the highlight of which is a night out without the kids.

Ari has nothing to say about going out for dinner in the Park. He finds the restaurants in his neighborhood mediocre, and anyway, he's not big on eating out alone. Justin and his wife exchange looks, and then they say they have to get back to their party. They're having forty people up there, in a corporate suite, with a corporate team.

"Well, you've got my number," says Justin. "Give me a ring. We'll grab a beer."

Another thing men do in Justin's world. They grab beers with buddies.

Ari wants very much to grab the beer, though he fears that if he did, it might ruin this moment they've just shared. It's really worked out. Or has it? Dear Justin, I have so much to say, but really it's not so very much, just that I used to like you, have always been grateful for knowing you, even with the way it all ended. My God, you're still beautiful. I love the light and the length of you. How your face shines in the lights.

They shake hands, and then what the hell, Ari goes in for another hug. It's strange now how this distance of twenty years makes their relationship feel more intimate. And then, as Justin and his wife are about to disappear, Ari says, "Oh, wait!"

Lisa appears startled. Maybe Justin has told her? But Justin's face seems a picture of calm. Maybe it's all that corporate training. How to handle any emergency. Pretend everything's normal. Or is that Ari's own coping strategy for emergencies?

"I brought you this. I just thought . . . " Ari reaches into his pocket, takes out the candy, opens his palm.

"Ari, wow," Justin says. He takes it. "That's very nice, thank you."

He sounds like a diplomat accepting a bouquet of flowers from some local little girl in a native costume, a bouquet that will be handed off to a senior aide when she's out of sight, and then probably plunked into the garbage.

"Yeah, well, I remember you used to like them," says Ari.

"Hey, you still listen to Nirvana?" Justin asks, fiddling with the candy bar.

"Not regularly," says Ari. "On the radio sometimes."

"You used to be so obsessed with them," says Justin. "Funny, what we used to be into. And what we're into now."

What do I say to that, Ari thinks. Music, he reminds himself. The subject of this conversation is music. "So what do you listen to now?" he asks.

"I can send you some stuff. Are you on Pandora?"

"Not yet," says Ari.

"Get on Pandora and I'll share my playlist with you."

The last thing Ari needs in his life: more technology. But that's where people live these days. That's where you have to go to keep up. "That would be very nice," Ari says finally. And who knows, maybe it would be. Who knows, maybe it will actually happen.

THE BUSINESS OF DESIRE

AFTER SCHOOL, I WANDERED THE HALLS, waiting for Justin to finish his work-study gig, assisting the coach of the girls' tennis team.

I was looking openly at guys, in a way I'd never before permitted myself to do, and not just at their bodies. After the final bell, we were allowed to molt out of our uniforms and into our street clothes, and I loved watching my male classmates' real selves emerge: T-shirts featuring their favorite bands or athletic teams, jeans in a dizzying variety of cuts, colors, and washes. And the sneakers! So many different types of sneakers. Plain Converse All-Americans doodled with ballpoint flourishes. Vans in multi-colored suede. Adidas in Samba black or Stan Smith green and white. Laceless British Knights that you slipped on like gloves. Everyone seemed so free, so happy and relaxed to be who they were. People I'd never spoken to since I started at Dalton were now greeting me as if we were old friends. It made me sad, actually, thinking how much I'd missed these past years by closing myself off, hiding behind shame.

When Justin was done, we'd meet at his car or mine and cruise the neighborhoods near Dalton, hunting for shady culs-de-sac or empty parking lots, anywhere to fool around in private with the stereo blaring and the heater breathing down our crooked elbows and bent necks as we contorted ourselves to fit in the tight spaces of our cars.

This business of desire had turned out to be complicated, and I feared I wasn't very good at it. I always winced or shrank away from his hands at the wrong moment. At first, I had a raft of justifications. His fingers were cold. I was ticklish. This was all new to me. But by now my excuses had passed their expiration date. "Am I hurting you?" Justin used to ask. Lately he sounded confused and annoyed. "You sure you like this?"

So I'd say, "Just hold me for a while," or "Let's just talk," and then my blood would rise, my face would flush, the justs would melt away, zippers and buttons would open, and when the fireworks were over, we'd reach sullenly into his glove compartment for stacks of paper napkins purloined from various fast food establishments. We'd clean off our hands and our skin without looking at each other.

So, yes, I liked what we were doing, but I also feared it, especially that inevitable loss of control, as much in me as in him. Because in my excitement, I might allow anything to happen. It was as if there was something weird about me that made guys want to be sexual, but not to talk, not to get to know who I was.

"Sometimes I think you're afraid of me," he'd say.

I'd thought that by being with Justin I would join a new crowd, kids who listened to Depeche Mode or rented David Lynch films from indie video stores. Girls who wore black lace tights. Guys who wore mismatched socks on purpose. One day, Justin promised, he'd take me to the underground places he'd told me stories about, introduce me to his off-campus friends, and then I'd understand what "alternative" really meant. One day. But for now, we—and whatever we were to each other—remained secret.

"Can't we go somewhere?" I asked him once. "Do something together?"

"You mean like a date?" he sneered.

"Well, yeah, why not?" I said.

"Uh, because we're two dudes," he said. "You want to get beat up? Killed?"

Still, every so often, he'd take me to A Room of Our Own, a collectively owned bookstore café in Oak Park, just outside the Detroit city line. We'd drink awful coffees without milk or sugar, prepared by a white barista who spoke like a black man and doodled designs for graffiti tags in a leather sketchbook, the kind I used to always carry with me. Watching him draw, I felt guilty. *I'll get back to work later,* I promised myself.

But I hadn't touched a pencil or brush in weeks, not since I'd gotten into art school at the University of Michigan—thanks, Dad!—and been summarily rejected by Parsons, Cooper Union, CCS, Art Center, RISD, Pratt.

All the big name art schools were in agreement: I had no talent.

A Room of Our Own specialized in new and used biographies of Che Guevara, guides to feminist pregnancy, collections of lesbian erotica, and an impressive collection of art books that I coveted but never bought. I didn't deserve them yet, at least not until I got back to work, but it felt so deliciously lazy doing nothing, basking in Justin's company, simply absorbing the fact that he was mine, finally mine!

What if those other schools were right and U of M had made a mistake by admitting me? What if my parents were right, and I wasn't talented or lucky enough to make it as artist? What would I do with my life?

"In high school, the kids used to call Kurt gay, just because he was different," I told Justin. "So he said, you know what, go ahead, call me gay. He used to spray-paint 'God is gay' all over his hometown."

"You really are a true believer," Justin giggled.

"That's why he kissed Krist Novoselic on *Saturday Night Live*. That's why he sings 'Everyone is Gay' on 'All Apologies.' He's using his fame to confront his mainstream fans with their homophobia."

Justin looked at me as if to say, "Are you kidding?" I'd come to recognize that look. "Let's talk about something else besides Kurt Cobain. I don't care about him."

"What do you care about?"

He patted the top of my head, as if I were his dog. "Oh, I don't know." He said it very quickly, in a way that made me dizzy.

We'd get lost in the narrow pathways between the shelves, stuffed with peeling paperbacks that smelled of wet paper. Scratchy records by Billie Holiday or The Ramones played on the aging stereo system, which was actually capable of dealing with 8-tracks. Posters scotch-taped to the walls urged us to take back the night or go vegan. After looking at books, we'd sit in the café, rocking back and forth in our stiff chairs with uneven legs. The floors were covered haphazardly with ragged squares of stained carpet, and the walls seemed to secrete a sticky brown wax-like substance we could never identify. We'd sip our bitter coffee, served in mismatched cups.

Later Justin and I stood outside next to the outdoor table of unwanted books, the ones going for a dollar or two each, and exchanged our usual hug, the manly, brotherly kind that we wouldn't give us away to strangers.

Before letting me go, Justin buzzed in my ear, "Did you think about," he shrugged, "you know?"

Justin was too cool to state plainly what he wanted: to rob me of my virginity. He didn't know another a thief had gotten there before him.

"I thought about it," I said.

I'd always suspected that this whole thing with Justin would one day get spoiled. It was only a question of how long I could put it off.

"I just want to be close to you," he breathed in my ear. "Really close."

I felt as if my insides had been shaken and then spilled out onto the cement.

What He Really Wanted

MOM DISLIKED MY NEW ALTERNATIVE LIFESTYLE—NOT just the gay part, but also the alternative part. What did I plan on studying in college when I wasn't drawing naked people? Who was feeding me all this nonsense about the evils of corporate America? Where had I learned to speak in such an affected, grumbling tone of voice? She pestered me about my music, my clothes, my sullen manners, the strange and inconsistent hours of my exits and entrances at home, where my wrinkled shirts and pants reeked bitterly of coffee. "You hate coffee," she said.

"Leave him alone," Dad said. "He's being a typical teenager." That pleased him, that I was a typical teenager.

"Have you ever seen him drink a cup of coffee in this house? But he comes in smelling like a can of Sanka."

"He's a good kid," said Dad.

After dinner, Dad stopped by my room and advised me to "lie low" for a while around my mother. I wanted to take his advice, but lately everything I said or did rubbed her wrong, maybe because of the decline of her art business, the O. J. Simpson trial, my coming out, or some toxic combination of all three.

"Thanks, Dad," I said. Sometimes I really thought we might become friends.

"I have something I wanted to give you." Dad dropped a brochure on safe sex on my bed, then picked it up and put it on my dresser, as if putting it on the bed gave me permission to act out the illustrations in the brochure. I opened the brochure and a pair of plastic-wrapped condoms, one with a yellow ring and the other green, fell out.

"Don't worry," I said. "There are all kinds of things guys can do together. Not everyone wants to do everything."

"Just in case," he said, but this look of peace settled on his face.

How could I take that away from him?

Still, when he left, I closed the door and read the brochure. It hardly seemed possible that this, this process could happen to me again. And with my consent. Even more impossible: that it might give the person getting it any kind of pleasure. It seemed too angry, too violent to do to someone you loved.

A few jagged shards of memory: Rhythmic stabs of pain. My face jammed into the wooden floor. A sour taste surging up my throat. A prayer to God to let it end. But it had never ended. Maybe it never would.

But this was what Justin wanted, and what Justin wanted, he must have.

I opened one of the wrapped condoms with my teeth as the brochure instructed, and inhaled its nauseating odor of ammonia. I leaned a chair against my door handle, and then to be safe, turned out the lights, got into bed, under the covers, and pulled down my pants. Yet when I tried to put on the condom, I kept thinking of that other time, and then of Justin. Was that what he really wanted? For me to hurt him that way? Did he even know how much it would hurt? Inevitably I went soft.

Finally, I threw the condom in the garbage.

What if Mom found it?

So I fished the thing out again, wadded it up tight in some tissues, and threw it away once more.

EXTRACURRICULARS

JUSTIN AND I WERE IN HIS car. I felt relieved because we'd just had one of our more successful encounters. I'd been studying his body, noting carefully where he liked to be tickled (the back of his neck), scratched (the happy trail of dark hairs below his navel), pressed (along his spine), and poked (the inside of his thighs, and then edging backwards and up, dangerously). He had a mole beside his left armpit and a scar along his collarbone where he'd cut himself on a broken swing set at a local park.

While Justin zipped up his pants, I said, "I thought your Dad wanted you to throw those away?" They were black with rips along the sides. He wore them with a black leather belt studded with squat metal spikes.

"I don't care what he wants."

"Do you think he suspects about us?"

"Are you serious?" he said. "I don't think they've even heard of what we do."

"Is that what you call it?" I said. "What we do? An extracurricular activity like tennis or archery?"

"I don't see you blabbing about us to your parents," he said.

"Only because of you. You're so afraid anyone might find out."

"Newsflash. Detroit's not Bloomfield." He pursed his lips and pinched his nose. "We're so proud of our homosexual son. We're making a ten-thousand dollar donation to the gay rights movement in his honor.'"

"Shut up." I hated when he called attention to the differences between us, even the imaginary ones. "No one talks like that in Bloomfield."

"No?" he said, nuzzling my ear. "I thought you guys talked like that all the time."

Rather than continue the argument, I buried my face in his chest and hoped we might stay that way, very still. My breath felt hot and short, and my eyelids grew heavy. But then Justin slid his hands up over my nipples and squeezed. I ground my teeth, waiting for him to stop. "Doesn't this feel good?" Justin whispered.

"Yeah," I gasped. It was a poor acting job, and he let go.

"You and your secrets." He pressed himself tightly against me, which I disliked, while nuzzling my ear, the way I did like. This was how you'd train a dog, feeding him chicken to bribe him to sit still. "You never want to do more."

His weight felt like a heavy, hairy blanket. "I never said it was a secret," I said through clenched teeth. Being with Justin used to feel liberating, as if I'd finally escaped Mark. But at moments like these, he and Mark seemed like the same person.

"Yeah, but you never give me a straight answer when I ask you." Justin rubbed his lips against my neck. "Sometimes I'm afraid to touch you. Don't you trust me?"

I wriggled out of his arms, then held his long face. "I don't want to ruin what we have."

"It wouldn't. Nothing could."

It continually surprised me, how someone like Justin who acted so jaded all the time could be so innocent about life, about all the ways your life could go so horrendously wrong. "There's something I have to tell you first," I said. "Then, if you still want to, you know, then we can. But not tonight."

"Of course." He squeezed my nose. "What'd you think? We were going to go at it here and now? You really are the goofiest."

"Is that a compliment?"

"You're fishing," he said.

"Maybe. Tell me you like me."

"I like you," he said, and the air rushed out of my lungs. He squeezed my hands with his warm, soft fingers. Looking right at him hurt too much, like staring at the sun.

"Yes, but why?" I asked.

"There you go, fishing again."

THE RETURN

MOM RENEWED HER ATTEMPTS TO CAJOLE me into going to
Jewish youth group events, a tour of the Ford Motor plant, a Buddy's
pizza party, a trip to Boblo Island. And she shifted from criticizing
to "teasing" me, about my dark clothes, and my new hairstyle, subtly
spiky in front. And then girls. "What about Kim Basinger?" she'd
say. "Really? You're not turned on by Kim Basinger? She could convert anyone."

I resented that word, "conversion," the same process by which a
non-Jew became kosher for marriage. It was as if by coming out, I'd
joined a different tribe and now she was desperate to get me back
into hers.

"Mom, I'm gay," I said.

"How could I forget? You keep reminding us," she said, a flash of
her old bitterness. Finally, as a gesture of peace, I agreed to go to a
Shabbat dinner my mother had seen listed in the *Jewish News*.

"You might meet a guy there," Dad said. "We don't expect you to
be a monk."

"You love to be an idiot, don't you?" Mom told him. "Kids his
age talk more about going around with each other than they
do anything."

Apparently she'd decided that I was only saying I was gay as part of my new alternative act. Somehow she'd heard about Kurt Cobain in high school telling people he was gay when he wasn't and the story had stuck with her. Maybe I was saying I was gay to be rebellious, a big talker, not a big doer. But it was just the opposite with me and Justin. We "went around" much but talked little. We went around and around and around.

* * *

I FELT OUT OF PLACE THE moment I entered the social hall of our synagogue. The other boys wore personalized yarmulkes, hand-knit or printed velvet, and pressed flat to their skulls like a natural outgrowth of their hair, while I'd just grabbed a wrinkled black nylon beanie from the bin by the door and placed it atop my head like a dunce cap. Instead of a tasteful tweed or wool sport coat, I wore a brown velvet smoking jacket that I'd bought for fifteen dollars at a vintage store. It clashed perfectly with my army green cargo pants and bright green Converse sneakers.

I grabbed the first open seat I found, at a table of unfamiliar Jews from distant suburbs who were comparison shopping teen trips to Israel. A few kids from my old school nodded at me from across the room, as if I carried a disease communicable by touching. One of them asked in a painfully slow voice, "So where are you going to school next fall?" as if she believed the answer involved special education. I planned to mimic her later, to make Justin laugh. He and I needed to laugh more.

After two girls lit the Shabbos candles, we sang the blessing for wine, then blessed, broke, and passed fat loaves of eggy challah to tear apart with our bare hands. The bread was rich, yellow, and pillowy compared to the white squares of pre-sliced sawdust they served us at Dalton. I figured it would probably be the highlight of our over-salted, dried-out kosher meal.

The Junior Rabbi, to whom such shit tasks as this dinner fell, announced: "To inspire us with a very meaningful D'var Torah, we call upon Mark Taborsky."

"Jesus H. Christ," complained the kid next to me. "When do we eat?"

My stomach folded in half. I spat the wisp of challah I'd been chewing into my napkin.

I must have misheard.

They hadn't really said "Mark Taborsky" but some other, similar name.

My chest felt tight and cold. My heart gave an extra squeeze.

After several agonizingly slow seconds, a tall, square-shouldered young man emerged from a shadowy corner. I immediately recognized his emphatic way of walking, the stark angle of his neck, the sharp cut of his nose.

No, I had not misheard.

As Mark took the mike, the crowd offered light, bored applause. How could I slip out of here unnoticed? I sank in my chair, shading my eyes with my hands, watching him through my fingers.

He'd grown a faint black beard, and he wore thick glasses with old-fashioned black rims. He used to lighten his hair with "Sun-In," but it was dark now, brushed smooth, and covered with a rumpled black velvet yarmulke. Like a real *yeshiva bocher.* Or maybe he was a real one now, thanks to the sentence his father had arranged: religious school rather than juvie hall. Rape thy neighbor, then atone by reading Torah.

I could run. Or hide under the table. Or trip a fire alarm and disappear in the ensuing chaos. Any of this might have been possible, but I couldn't move. My fingers swelled up as if they'd been bitten by a swarm of wasps. My legs felt encased in lead.

At the head of the room, Mark squinted at his notes, as if he'd accidentally picked up someone else's speech. "This week's *haftorah* is the Book of Hosea," he said in that same reedy voice I remembered from years ago, though now a little bit deeper in tone, and tinged with a Yiddish accent.

If I were drawing him, I'd use a steely black conte crayon to create the ridge of his nose. Then I'd let the blank page come through to show the glaring whites of his eyes.

Mark said that the prophet Hosea had complained to God, or as Mark called Him "Ha-Shem," that the people of Israel were unworthy of His favor because of their sins. "In response, Ha-Shem commanded Hosea to marry a harlot."

A harlot? Since when did Mark Taborsky, or anyone, use the word "harlot"?

I bent over my plate, hoping to shelter behind the flower centerpiece, thoughtfully filled with low-lying blooms to promote cross-table chatting. Think, think, I told myself. I used to plan what I'd say or do if I ran into Mark at the movies, the grocery store, and especially in a synagogue. But now it was happening, and my guard was down. I was trapped with no plan. The exit was somewhere far behind me, at the end of a long hallway with hard, slick floors where footsteps would echo like drumbeats. I'd have to sit through the speech, then wait for the noise of dinner conversation to muffle my escape.

Mark was finished speaking. He removed his glasses and stared at the crowd, at us. I bent over, pretending to tie my shoe. A woman wearing a pink snood called out, "Everybody, enjoy!" Several waiters in tuxedo uniforms brought out hot, over-salted chicken soup. By the time they reached our table, I'd left the room.

I was traveling down a dark, narrow corridor lined with memorial plaques in bronze, each with its own red electric bulb that got turned on once a year to mark the *yahrzeit*. My grandmother's name had been added recently—no time to search for it now. Though I moved as quickly as I could, it was not fast enough. I felt as if I were wading through a bowl that warm, viscous chicken soup they were eating in the next room.

My leather soles scuffed the black and white floor tiles. I was freezing in the overzealous air conditioning, despite my vintage velvet sport coat. I stuffed my hands into the side pockets, and in the left one, I found a library checkout card, stamped with years of due dates in multicolored ink.

Midway through the hall of dead names, I heard Mark's voice echoing behind me.

"Ari Silverman," he said. "It's me, Mark."

There was no point in running. Mark would catch me no matter where I went. It was like in dreams, when you lose control over your own legs. Even if I made it to that massive parking lot, he'd follow me, and out there with no witnesses for miles, anything might happen. At least here, if I cried for help, someone might come.

I stopped, turned to face him. And then Mark stood before me, as if he'd traversed the entire hallway in a single powerful leap.

His new beard gave his face a rough, sandpapery edge, though his expression seemed milder than I'd remembered. He'd grown several inches, looked thicker in the arms and legs, but so had I. The difference between us was not as dramatic as before.

"What do you want?" I asked.

"That's all?" He laughed. From nerves or conceit? "After all this time?"

He stood so close I could smell his breath, slightly sour, as if he hadn't eaten in a while. I took a step back, against the wall, my shoulders braced against dead people's names in bronze. The noises of dinner sounded strangely distant.

"I won't hurt you." Mark extended his hand, decorated by a blocky gold ring with a diamond in the center. A high school senior, still wearing his bar mitzvah ring. Was I supposed to kiss it? I stared at the tiny dark hairs growing near his knuckles.

"Listen," I squeaked, then cleared my throat, "I'm in a hurry."

Mark laughed again, folded his arms as he sized me up, from my wrinkled yarmulke to the tips of my Converse shoes. "You're a terrible actor. You're still afraid of me, though you act like you're not."

"Really, I'm in a hurry," I said.

"Do you usually go to this *shul* or somewhere else?"

A security guard popped his head into the hallway from around the corner. "Dinner's in there, boys." He was practically a kid himself, maybe a year older than we were. A diamond stud glittered against his dark ear.

"We know," Mark said, smiling and waving. The guard gave a mock salute, then resumed his rounds. I started to go after him, but Mark caught my sleeve. "Hey, I've changed. I've made a new relationship with Ha-Shem."

I flung off his touch. "That's great for you."

"You could at least try to believe me, when I say that I've changed."

"Fine, I believe you," I said. "But if you've changed once, you can change again."

The old anger flashed across his face: eyes hard and mean, nose flared, lips tightened. The yarmulke, the silly beard, the whole disguise collapsed. He had a dangerous curiosity, like a scientist unconstrained by ethics, one who'd have gladly sawed through a live human body without anesthesia or electrocuted a hapless animal, just to see what would happen. Perhaps the rabbis at his yeshiva had taught him about the existence of empathy, yet he didn't seem to have experienced that emotion himself.

"I'm sorry," Mark said. He held up his hands as if he'd forgotten to turn off the stove back home. "Things, you know, they went too far. That's all I wanted to say."

"And now you've said it. Let me go."

His eyes searched my body in a way I didn't like. I heard a blood-curdling shriek of laughter from dinner.

"So where did you find that sport coat?" he asked.

"Why, you want one?" I asked.

He made a grunt as if I'd said something absurd. "What's it supposed to represent anyway? This way you're dressing. You know, you look different."

"I'm the same inside. I still remember everything."

Mark opened his lips to speak, then paused. "I only ask that you consider what I said. We learn that Ha-Shem can forgive sins against Him, but if you've sinned against your fellow man, only he can grant you forgiveness."

"I have to go," I said in a small voice that I willed into speech. Then, to discourage him from following me, I added, "Someone's waiting for me."

"I don't blame you for what you did," said Mark. "I mean, yeah, you kind of wrecked my life a bit, but I get it. You were confused."

"How was I confused?"

"I mean, calling the cops. You thought . . . You know, the truth is, I wasn't really meaning to hurt you. And actually, in my own way," Mark stepped closer, as if to confess a secret, "in my own way, I thought I was helping you. I mean, when I met you, you were really repressed, really sheltered, you know?"

"Helping me?" That was a good one. I gave him my best wide-eyed, curly-lipped Kurt Cobain sneer. "You promised you'd go away now."

He held up his hands, as if to surrender. "Okay, okay."

"Good." I backed away slowly, fixing my eye on him until I reached the end of the corridor. He stayed where he was. And then, only when I rounded the corner, I ran.

* * *

DRIVING HOME, I MISSED A TURN that any other night I'd have found blindfolded, then went on driving, got lost, and didn't care to get found. Where was there to go?

Home would never be safe, no matter how many locks or alarms we installed on the doors and windows.

Where Justin lived? I couldn't visit my troubles on him.

David's apartment in Ann Arbor?

No, none of these. I couldn't hide any more. First because I was sick of it, and second because no matter where I went, Mark could always find me.

I'd always feared Mark wouldn't disappear from my life entirely, but I hadn't thought he'd re-appear like this, neatly dressed, a bit soft-spoken, an earnest yeshiva student, the perfect cover for a homicidal maniac.

I found Mom asleep on the living room couch with a copy of *Tess of the D'Urbervilles*, the latest selection for her book group. On TV, a blonde woman with a stark white face, smooth as a mask, described a shooting in Detroit in a sorrowful tone. No matter how late I came home, she'd wait for me, to make sure I got in okay. Did she do this for David too, or was this unique to me, because she thought I still needed protecting? I didn't want that to be the answer.

"How was dinner?" Mom asked, pulling her bathrobe closed around her neck.

"Harmless." I resolved to take Dad's advice and be nicer to her. As I kissed her cheek goodnight, I noticed a few wrinkles by her mouth. "No big deal."

When I got to my room, I undressed with the lights off and shut my blinds tight.

A Confession

M<small>Y</small> <small>PARENTS WERE DRIVING UP TO</small> hear David sing in some
a cappella group he'd joined, and they were staying in Ann
Arbor overnight.

"This came for you," Mom said before they left. She deposited
an envelope on my dresser, stationary belonging to Mark's
father's synagogue, but no stamp or postmark. I supposed it
was junk from some Jewish youth group, but inside was a note
from Mark:

"I really want to talk," it began.

Mark's handwriting looked stiff, childlike, even angry. I folded
and refolded the note until it was the size of a postage stamp, the
paper stubbornly resisting my attempts to fold it into oblivion.

"You sure you're okay alone?" my parents still asked me after all
these years. They didn't know that I'd made sure that I wouldn't be
alone. I'd invited Justin to stay.

"That's great," he said when I explained my parents would be
gone. "So, should I bring, uh, protection?"

"Yeah," I said sullenly. "Just in case you feel like, you know."

"Just in case?" he repeated. "Or don't you want me to come?"

"No, no. I want you to come." Did I? I'd said so.

As soon as my parents left, I locked all the doors, turned on the burglar alarm, but then I turned it off. What was the sense?

The bell rang. I checked the peephole to make sure it was Justin, and no one else. He looked handsome in a black jean jacket. I wanted to steal it, wrap it around shoulders, and close my eyes, waiting for his cocky self-assurance to seep into my muscles.

"My mom made lasagna," I said. Actually, I'd made it, but I lied because I worried he'd think my cooking him dinner was too feminine.

We ate on the mahogany dining room table, which had been custom built for the room and was too heavy to move. It was a quiet dinner. Justin wasn't much of a conversationalist in any event, and I was too preoccupied to fill in our usual gaps. I served the lasagna on my parents' best china plates. There was a story about them that I didn't feel like trying to remember that evening. I had my own story to keep straight. Occasionally I glanced at the windows, or listened for footsteps on the porch.

Justin cleaned his plate with the side of his fork and licked that too. At one point, he said, "This room's bigger than a museum."

After dinner, I turned on the gas fireplace. Justin studied an abstract painting in the living room, a splash of bold yellow, then asked, "Is that supposed to be a banana?" He wanted beer, but I said wine was more romantic. While we were rooting around in my parents' bar, Justin found the Manischewitz.

"That's not exactly wine," I explained. "We drink it on Jewish holidays."

"You mean if I'm not Jewish I can't have any?"

"No, of course not. Try some. You'll see, it's gross."

He took a swig. "This is good, like a grape popsicle. Usually I don't like wine."

"Have as much as you want."

So we poured two glasses of the kosher wine and sat on the carpet by the fireplace. I sprinkled a box of crystals over the flames. They were supposed to turn different colors, but we couldn't see anything. As Justin watched the fire, I watched its light flicker in his eyes, glittering as if he were about to cry.

I took his hand, examining it as if for the first time, all those lines crossing his palm like electrical wires. My forehead throbbed in the heat and the light of the gas fire.

I inhaled deeply. "I want to tell you something. Something important."

The fire snapped, and we both jumped. The sun had set, and the windows by the fireplace had gone black. A ruthless snoop could have watched us from outside, peeping through the large pine trees my parents had planted at the edge of our property as a screen. But no one was out there. We could have made love right by that fireplace.

"Not yet," I said, staying Justin's fingers, inching up the inside of my arm. "Remember, I have something to tell you."

"Later?" His body was inching forward, to engulf mine.

"No, I have to tell you now." I was so nervous, I wanted to vomit. I wished I'd skipped dinner.

He was hovering over me now. And then he let his head sink down, his cheek brushing the inside of my neck. He hadn't shaved that morning and his skin felt rough in a pleasant way. "Okay," he said, reaching over for his glass. "But hurry up, so we can get to the good part." He gulped the rest of his wine. "You got any more of this?"

I went to the bar, retrieved the whole bottle, handed it to him.

"Come forth and confess your sins, my child," he said, crossing himself before he refilled his glass. "In the name of Jesus Fucking Christ."

"Be serious," I said. "Because what I have to say is serious."

"Oh, yeah? What, you had sex with your teddy bear when you were a kid?"

"Just listen," I said.

* * *

I PLEADED WITH MARK FOR MERCY but he dragged me by my wrists across the floor. I tried to make myself as heavy as possible, but we were already in the kitchen. He opened all the drawers, digging through serving spoons, spice bottles, until he found a bread knife. He said he would slice off my balls as if I were a stray dog.

"No!" I screamed, backing against the oven. "Please."

"Shut up." He pulled on his crotch and pressed the knife closer to my nose.

"Please." I twisted back and forth, squirming away from the jagged blade.

Mark pressed me to the floor, ordered me to strip. "This one kid in Detroit," he said, "he was so weak, they cut off his dick. And no one ever got punished for it. In Detroit, you can do whatever you want, and no one ever does anything to you."

"But we're not in Detroit," I said.

Mark ignored me, unzipped my jeans and hiked them down along with my boxers. He pinched my penis so tightly that the pain prickled up to the base of my neck. He dragged me to the laundry room and fell on top of me, pressing me to the wood like a mattress to a frame, his fingers molding my soft shoulders and arms, the stiff hairs on his legs scratching mine.

At the blast of pain that followed, I screamed, but he covered my mouth and twisted my head around. "You want to die?" Then a second bloody thrust. I thought he'd made good on his threat to penetrate me with a knife, but it wasn't a knife. It was him. My cheek smashed to the hardwood floor, I bit my tongue as hard as I could. Don't scream.

Don't die. Why was no one here to protect me? My mind raced to blame my classmates and teachers, my family, God, everyone in the world except the one who was there, his body making frenzied slapping sounds. His fingers squeezed my cheeks in time to his throbbing hips. He grunted like a pig sniffing through mud for food.

* * *

AS I SPOKE, THE EXPRESSION ON Justin's face went blank, which I took as a hopeful sign. When I finished, the room fell silent except for the occasional snapping of the flames. I felt wrung out, impatient to hear his reaction, and a bit angry.

For a while, Justin sat there biting a bit of dead skin off his thumb. His eyes looked tired, very red. He took a sip of wine, then suddenly drained the rest. "You couldn't get drunk on this if you drank the whole bottle." He frowned. Because he didn't like my story or my wine? "This all happened, like, right here?"

"Yeah."

"Weird. That it happened in a place like this."

This wasn't how I'd expected the conversation to go. "What do you mean?"

"Like, this is supposed to be a safe neighborhood."

"Sometimes," I said, "I think I'd feel safer in your neighborhood."

"Don't ever say that." He sounded angry.

"Why not?" My stomach tightened, and I had to remind myself to breathe. "Don't I have a right to my feelings?"

"Yeah, sure. Whatever." Justin raised his glass to his lips, then remembered it was empty. "So I'm just trying to understand. Your thinking was, that after telling me this, we would go ahead with our romantic evening, like everything was the same?"

"Maybe," I said, but then, seeing his look of disgust, I added, "I mean, no, of course not. Or, I didn't think about it. I didn't think past telling you."

Justin gestured to the fire with his empty wine glass. "How do you turn this thing off?" He got up, pushed a switch on the wall, turning on the porch light. "You've got too many lights in this place. What do you rich people need all these damned lights for?"

I turned off the porch light and the fire, then sat next to him on the carpet. He was staring away from me, squeezing the toe of his shoe.

Wasn't I supposed to confess the truth? Wasn't that the right thing to do?

"Was it wrong to tell you?" I asked.

He raised his head. "Hey, this is some heavy shit you just laid on me."

"I know that," I said.

"I mean, did you think about the way you were going to tell me this?"

"Yeah, of course. Why? How else should I have said it?"

"I don't know. It's just that now you seem different, suddenly."

"Why does everyone keep telling me I'm different?"

"Everyone? Who else are you talking about?"

I felt a painful rush in my brain. "I don't know."

He stood, then paced the length of the room. "Why didn't you tell me before?"

I grabbed his arms to make him stand still. "Justin, it happened to me, not to you. Why should this bother you?"

He shook his head.

I buried my face in his chest. "Justin, I love you."

"You say you love me, but all this time, you've been hiding from me."

"I was afraid," I said, my voice muffled in his shirt.

"Afraid," he repeated in triumph, like a math teacher proving a theorem. I let go of him. "How can you love someone you're afraid of?"

"I don't know how. I just do." But he was slipping away from me.

"This is a funny wine." He rubbed his forehead and sat on a hard decorative chair that my mother had picked out to match the design scheme of the room. The few people who'd sat there never did it twice. "So what, you're afraid I would do what that guy did?"

"No, this had nothing to do with you."

"But you got me involved in it by bringing me here and telling me what he did to you here. In this house."

"Why does it matter where Mark," I didn't want to say the word, but I forced myself, "raped me?"

Justin winced. "Do you have to say his name?"

I kneeled in front of him, took both his unwilling hands and squeezed. "Do you see why I didn't want to tell you? I shouldn't have told you."

"Well, you're safe now. Isn't that why you told me about doing it with him? To get out of doing it with me."

"That wasn't why." My throat ached. It was hard to talk.

"How do I know you're not going to call the police on me after? Some black kid from Detroit broke into my house and raped me."

I wanted to punch him, hard, where it would hurt. "You're being an asshole."

He stood up from his uncomfortable chair and wiped his eyes. Because he was tired or crying? "Where's this Mark guy now? When's the last time you saw him?"

I told the truth. It was perhaps my most damning confession of the evening.

* * *

JUSTIN DIDN'T WANT TO DRIVE IN my suburb this late at night because he thought the cops would pull him over. Plus, his head ached from all the kosher wine. So I gave him my bed while I lay awake on the couch, using one of his shirts as a blanket.

My mind was so busy that I didn't think I'd manage to doze off, but I did, I don't know for how long, until I felt a hand on my arm. Still half-dreaming, I thought the hand belonged to Mark. "I changed my mind," Justin said. He wasn't wearing any pants.

"Oh," I said, still foggy on where I was, what was happening.

He climbed on the couch and kissed me feverishly. I kissed him back. My fingers searched for his hips and then crawled toward his soft groin. He yelped, as if in pain.

Come on, I kept thinking. We love each other. We can erase everything bad if we just get close enough. Justin kissed me again, squeezed my skin so hard I thought I might bruise, but nothing changed. Finally, disgusted, he threw himself off the couch. "What's wrong with me?" he complained.

"Maybe you need more time," I said, pulling up my sweatpants.

Justin shook his head. "I'm sorry for all that shit that happened to you. But this night is so weird." He rubbed my cheek a bit, then turned away from me.

I sat up. "Talk to me. Can't we just talk?"

His eyes were wet and then he closed them. "I have to go."

"Not like this."

"No, I'm going," he insisted.

I blinked a few times, and then he was gone. He drove away so fast his tires squealed on the pavement.

Relics

WAS THIS REALLY THE END? IT seemed impossible. If I'd known, maybe I'd have spent the last few months differently, taken things more slowly, savored them, committed them to memory. As it was, I'd saved a few relics from our relationship: movie ticket stubs, a candy wrapper with Hebrew writing, his awful, mysterious mix tapes. Also, he'd left his worn army duffel bag with his change of clothes in the foyer, which I hid in the trunk of my car. Maybe later we could arrange for a transfer in the neutral ground of Dalton.

I'd pressed Justin's carnation between the leaves of my English text because I'd read about a lover doing that in some story. I put the flower up to my face, brushing my cheeks with the scentless petals, then threw it in the trash. It would die anyway.

Not Exactly Wrong

In English class, Justin sat apart from me. Not on the other side of the room—too obvious—just a few desks away, as if he suddenly desired a change of scenery. Though we had no other excuse to run into each other, I knew how to find him because I'd memorized his schedule. (Why had he never bothered to learn mine?) After his advanced calculus class, I cornered Justin next to the bushes outside the Learning Center, connected to the main building by an outdoor walkway. We'd freeze out there in wintertime, get drenched during a rainstorm, but today the late spring sun fired up flowering dogwoods and forsythias like stained glass. A lover's lane.

"You left your bag at my house," I said. "What should I do with it?"

He led me away from the entrance, where kids marched in and out of the Learning Center. Justin and I had worked so hard for so long at giving people nothing to notice, but today I didn't care what they heard or saw.

"Bring it to school, I guess." His face seemed older, harder, that morning. His pant cuffs looked dirty, and the knot in his tie was too tight. I used to fix it for him.

"Nothing compromising in there?" I knew I sounded snotty. I hoped he felt hurt.

He just smirked, then shook his head.

"So how should I act around you in school? Do we just ignore each other?"

He squinted in the sunlight. "We're going to college soon, anyway. You'll be with kids who are more like you."

"You mean Jewish or white?" I lowered my voice. "Or gay?"

He shrugged. "All kinds of ways."

I wanted to slap him, not to hurt, but to wake him up. Justin, it's me here. It's me and you, and no one else is supposed to matter. "I thought you and I weren't like anyone else except each other," I said. "Was I wrong?"

"No, you weren't exactly wrong," he said, but he walked away.

Waiting

At home, I found an envelope from Mark's father's synagogue. I threw it away without opening it.

Later that week, I opened another envelope, containing my application for housing at the University of Michigan, which depressed me deeply. I'd dreamed of sharing a room with Justin. But Ann Arbor would be just like high school: Justin and I would pass each other in hallways between classes as if we were nothing.

Classes were now just a way to kill all those long hours between waking up and going to bed at night, when I hoped to see Justin in my dreams. But even there, he remained as stubbornly absent as he was in waking life.

I pulled out my old sketchbooks, but my clumsy pencils refused to move. Their points remained dull and lifeless no matter how often I sharpened them.

So I shut myself in my room and listened to "All Apologies" on repeat until I'd memorized every word of the song, could mimic every one of Kurt Cobain's vocal tics as I sang along, adding extra emphasis to the line, "Everyone is gay." I desperately wanted to apologize, but for what and to whom? I couldn't figure out what I'd done wrong, but it had to be something. Or else why would I be in this position?

Funny, in the song, Kurt hardly seemed sorry. He sounded more resentful at the fact of being expected to apologize at all, for the simple crime of being alive.

Who ever heard a ballad with such forceful drumbeats? Such ferocious guitars? And that croaky howl that at the end of the song faded into darkness, silence.

The New Voice

Mom said I'd been moping in my room so long, I was in danger of turning into a vampire. "I could help you with one of your ketubahs," I said.

"I don't think so," she said, laughing. "You'd hate it, trust me."

"No, I wouldn't," I said. "Show me how."

"Trust me," she said. She wasn't laughing anymore.

Instead she had my father drag me to the Jewish Center. I could work out while he played racquetball. Or I could play racquetball too. "It's a great game," he told me. "You can play it your whole life."

"No thanks," I said.

While he played, I sat on the brown vinyl couches in the locker room next to naked old Jewish men wearing towels around their necks, who let their shriveled dicks rest limp on the furniture. Together we listened to dating advice for housewives, investing advice for retirees, dieting advice for everyone. Nothing for me.

Feeling bored, sad, and bored with being sad, I wandered the halls, peeking into classrooms where kids dipped their hands in paint to daub rivers of Egyptian blood on construction paper, for Passover. Further on, boys and girls in braces practiced for their bar and bat mitzvahs. Someday, they'd flirt with each other in Jewish youth groups before heading to college to meet the men and women of their dreams, or at least someone who might consent to marry them and keep a semi-kosher kitchen (bringing in *treyf* was okay if you ate it on paper plates). They'd have a kid or two, and then return to the Jewish Center, dragging an unwilling child to art class to learn about the ten plagues by dipping their fingers in blood-colored paint.

Walking by the small auditorium, I stumbled upon an after-school Torah study group. The leader was Mark Taborsky. Of course it was. Four years of freedom, and now I was seeing him everywhere. I wanted to hurry on, but he noticed me and waved.

What the hell, I thought.

He'd shaved off his beard and his cheeks were pink, as if he'd spent the afternoon on the beach without putting on sunblock. He wore glasses with chunky black frames and cradled a black leather book against his white button-down shirt, part of the religious Jewish uniform, minus the little polo player riding a horse on his chest pocket.

Mark told the students to take a break while we walked to the wings of the stage. I kicked away a piece of chalk on the floor. "Here we are again," he said. His teeth gleamed a blinding, artificial white, which surprised me. Somehow I'd imagined Orthodox Judaism taking a dim view of cosmetic dentistry.

"You going to Michigan this fall?" I asked. I could already imagine it, Mark, Justin, and I all bumping into each other. Was it too late to apply elsewhere?

"No, I'm not going to college. I'm going to Israel. To learn."

"To learn what?" I said. "How to torture Palestinians?"

"You've become very cold. Not angry or sad, just cold. Pure ice."

"Why do you care what I am?"

"Have you thought about what I told you? Do you see now your role in all this?"

I shook my head. All the men in my life, asking me favors.

"If you want to have a happy life, you need to confront who you really are."

"You," I lowered my voice. "You were the one who assaulted me," I said. "You were the one who did it to me."

"Raging teenage hormones are a terrible thing," he said.

"You're blaming it on hormones?" I said.

"You should talk to your rabbi. Where do you go to *shul?*" he said.

"I don't, if I can help it."

Mark looked horrified. "Not anywhere?"

"Why should I?"

"Someone's been influencing you," he said. "This isn't your natural voice."

I was glad to hear it. "I like this new voice better," I said.

The kids were filtering back into the room. "I have to get back to class. But we should talk some more."

"Why? What do you want from me?"

He grinned. "To acknowledge the truth."

* * *

DEAN DEMUTH ANNOUNCED A SPECIAL ASSEMBLY in the gym for Dalton seniors on "college readiness." Justin climbed the bleachers with Brandon Jenkins and as he passed me, he said, "Hey," and I said "Hey," back. So he was hanging with jocks now?

Soon we'd hardly see each other. It hurt to see him, and it hurt not to see him.

"Maybe they want to teach us about sex," Nick whispered, but it turned out Demuth was warning us about political correctness. We'd had four years to develop good habits. Now, at college we'd face a lot of temptations—"So this *is* about sex," Nick whispered—like the temptation to change our opinions to fit in with the academic herd.

"In this day and age of so many "isms," stay true to yourselves," Demuth said. "Let logic and good common sense be your guide."

I stared at Justin until he caught my eye. He pointed to his heart, then at me, and resumed his whispering with Brandon.

What the hell did he mean? But as soon as the assembly was over, he and Brandon quickly made their escape.

"What's wrong with your buddy Justin?" Nick asked as we filed out. He knew that I was obsessed with him, though not that we'd been a couple. "He looks like Jimmy Stewart at the end of *Vertigo*. You didn't tell him, did you?"

"No," I said in a flat voice.

"Don't waste your time on straight guys," Nick advised. "We're almost in college. Be patient."

The News on MTV

Friday after school, I came home, expecting another lonely weekend, when my mother said I had a phone call. I heard Justin's voice and felt a twinge of hope. He's forgiven me now, I thought. We can work it out.

"Did you hear the news?" he said. "Turn on MTV."

Kurt Loder was reading off "the facts as we know them" in an emotionless rush. A gunshot wound to the head. A self-inflicted gunshot wound to the head. And a note. In a guest cottage—somehow that detail struck me.

Kurt Cobain, the poet of depression and despair, had killed himself. The cold logic of it confused me. How could someone who sang with such understanding about suicide actually go through with the deed?

"My God," I kept saying, which seemed so small.

"Sorry," said Justin. "I know you liked him."

This should have been a moment for us to come together. So why didn't we? Maybe, besides our mutual attraction, at root we'd had nothing in common. Maybe we'd have broken up even if I hadn't told him the truth.

The rest of the evening, I flipped the channels from the local and national news to CNN to MTV and back again. Phrases darted in and out, like "the John Lennon of the so-called Generation X" or "captured the conflicts of people in their twenties" or "grunge pioneer." Let the mythmaking begin, I thought.

I was sitting in the living room with the lights off, the television glowing on my face when Dad asked my opinion of "this Cobain fellow."

"There's nothing to say," I said. "He shot himself."

Did everything I loved have to be taken away from me?

Kurt Cobain is Dead

RABBI TABORSKY'S CONGREGATION WAS ONE OF the few that hadn't fled from the Oak Park-Southfield-Huntington Woods ring of suburbs during the last White Flight. The building was dusty with checkerboard linoleum tile floors and water-stained drop ceiling panels. The parking lot badly needed repaving.

Mark didn't seem surprised to see me stroll into his father's office. After serving me a Styrofoam cup of instant coffee, he pulled his father's worn leather chair out from behind the desk and rolled its squeaky wheels up to where I was sitting, on an electric blue vinyl couch that could never been fashionable. His dad was away somewhere, so Mark was leading the *mincha/ma'ariv* service, starting in a few minutes.

"I want you to listen to me. I want you to stop mailing me stuff," I said.

"Alright," he said.

"I want you to stop contacting me. I don't want to hear anymore about what you think, what you have to say. Kurt Cobain says rape is the worst crime on earth. You've committed the worst crime on earth."

"Kurt Cobain is dead," he said.

"And that probably makes you happy. You know, you're really sick."

"I'm trying to help you," he said. "Just as I'd help any Jew who was suffering."

"I'm not suffering," I said. "I had a boyfriend. At my school where I go now. Because yeah, I'm gay. So there. Are you shocked?"

"No, not very." He tapped my knee, and I jerked backwards.

"Don't touch me. Just because I'm gay doesn't mean I ever wanted it with you."

"I know," he said. "I know that."

"Oh," I said, surprised.

"You said 'had'?"

"What?"

"You said you had a boyfriend."

"It's over now."

"I see." He paused to consider this information. "This boy, was he Jewish?"

"No."

"Maybe that was the reason." He waited, as if the answer were so obvious I should have come up with it. "You and he were too different."

"Oh, and you were meant for me, right? I thought you were Mr. Religious now."

He inched closer in his seat. "You don't understand," he said.

"I shouldn't have come here." I held up the coffee like a shield. "I'm going. Don't ever bother me again, or—" Or what? I was going to say I'd shoot him, which was nonsense. "What do I do with this coffee?"

He put his hands around the cup, and touched my hands. "May I?" he asked.

His touch was warmer and softer than I'd expected, also softer than Justin's. Justin had this way of doing exactly whatever it was he was doing, but Mark was far more, was that the word? Subtle? No, more like insinuating, testing the waters. Dipping a finger here, a toe there to check the temperature of the water before diving all the way in.

"I thought you were religious," I said, eyeing his fingers touching mine.

He pried the coffee from my grasp. "Listen now, while I explain."

* * *

Mark was inviting me to pray with him.

"You'll feel better," he said. "I promise."

The small sanctuary was filled with grey-haired men bent over their yellow-edged books, rattling through the tissue-thin pages while muttering holy words just under their hot, garlicky breath, though they'd said the prayers so many times, they didn't even need the books. I thought I'd remember the prayers from my Hebrew school days, but the words had flown out of my brain, crowded out by Nirvana lyrics.

My attention wandered, and the old man next to me kept tapping my elbow to whisper what page number we were on. Still, I couldn't focus. For starters, Mark had shared another bit of news: at the ripe old age of seventeen, he'd gotten engaged. He was going to Israel to get married and devote himself to studying Torah.

All this time I'd wondered about Mark's fate, he'd barely thought of mine. He hadn't been bent on revenge after all. It was a very lonely feeling.

"Page 47," hissed the old man.

"Sorry," I whispered back.

The same Mark who'd pulled down his pants and mine with such greedy eagerness would now become a husband, a father, a holy man while I was an abomination. In one act, he'd bound me to him for life, yet now that his little experiment was complete and I'd served my purpose, he didn't want me, like dirty toilet paper.

"Page 50," said the old man. "Why did you come here, just to stand? Page 50."

Praying should have come more easily after all those years of morning services at Stern, mindlessly mouthing holy words in our school gym. However, I'd always been distracted, looking at other boys with a fascination that I now understood as longing.

The idea of God hadn't seemed rational to me for a long time now, just a giant fuzzy teddy bear to make people feel better about death, though these Jews who followed His word didn't seem any happier to me than anyone else. Anyway, what kind of god would have made up a story like mine?

Mark invited those in mourning to rise to recite the kaddish prayer for the dead. To stretch my legs, I stood too, and as the others launched into the prayer, I thought of my grandparents, and Justin even though he was alive. And Kurt.

That's when the weight of those awful ancient words seized my chest. I saw Kurt's white body drained of blood, turned cold, burned to ash, and then the ashes spread over some field, no one knew where. Or at least those who knew weren't saying.

Cremation was against Jewish law, as was suicide. No one who committed suicide could be buried within the walls of a Jewish cemetery. But there were always exceptions. Distinctions were always made between suicides of a "sound" and "unsound" mind, and who of a sound mind would ever want to kill himself?

Kurt's eyes were such an intensely delicate shade of blue. No amount of shrieking, spitting, guitar thrashing could ever hide those gentle, pretty eyes.

Afterward, several men shook my hand, congratulated me for coming. Two of them had daughters my age. Daughters with phone numbers.

"How was it?" Mark asked.

"Weird," I said.

"It will become normal to you," he said. "You just have to keep coming back." Then he turned to shaking hands around the room like a politician.

But I was never coming back. "Goodbye," I said. And I left. I don't know whether he heard me or not.

Commencement

Dalton usually held commencement ceremonies in our auditorium, but this year it was under renovation. So instead they'd booked a nearby hall: the sanctuary of my synagogue, which had recently begun renting out space for badly needed extra cash.

We marched down the aisles in alphabetical order, and I fell between two members of the Nerd Herd, both of whom would attend Ivies in the fall. Elaine Rosen, sitting a few seats down from mine, was heading west. Rory Fox was going to acting school in New York. Even Brandon Jenkins had gotten into college, on a soccer scholarship. He sat there snickering beside Justin during the valedictorian's speech.

It was weird seeing all these Christians, Muslims, and Hindus lining up for their Dalton diplomas on the same dais where I'd nervously chanted Torah verses for my bar mitzvah. Cameras flashed continuously, which during services, would have been strictly banned. The reading of each name was met with hearty applause, a sound I'd never heard in synagogue. You didn't clap during prayers.

Dean Demuth presided over the ceremony with a proud smile. Our class had held up the school's 100% average. 100% graduations. 100% college acceptances.

All the faculty were there, even Mr. Wentworth, posing for pictures with female Dalton graduates who clung to his shoulder. Ms. Hunter was running around, upset about something. Ms. Conrad, our drama teacher, handed out little cards with her headshot on them. Miss Laker distributed Hershey's kisses.

After the ceremony, I watched Justin take pictures with his family. He looked handsome in a conservative-looking sport coat I didn't recognize. I thought his dad might feel squeamish about being in a synagogue, but he was beaming in a bright ivory-colored suit next to his wife, who straightened Justin's tie, smoothed Justin's sister's hair, and dusted off her husband's shoulders. When she ran out of people to fix, she stood to the side of her family and covered her mouth. I didn't see Justin's younger brother, whose blood I was supposed to use to make matzo on Passover.

Nick and his mom stood with Mr. Wentworth. "We did it!" I said, hugging Nick.

"Was there ever any doubt?" said Wentworth with a wry smile.

Yes, there had been plenty of doubt, that I'd survive high school at all. "This school saved my life," I said, the back of my throat getting hoarse.

"Nah," he said. "You probably saved your own life."

We were supposed to be celebrating. We could dye our hair or strip naked in public. We could smoke and drink and blast ungodly music. We could fucking pledge our allegiance to Satan. We were free. So why did I feel so empty?

David, who'd soon start his internship in Washington, was wearing a summer sport coat, a purple checked shirt, and loafers without socks. He looked ready to go yachting. He'd cut his hair and talked about "effecting change from the inside."

"Where are Mom and Dad?" I asked.

"I lost them on the way out of the sanctuary," he said. "Where's your boyfriend?"

"Who?" I'd never told him a word about Justin.

"Don't worry," he said. "When you get up to Ann Arbor, we'll find someone for you. I know a few gay guys."

"I don't need your help," I said. "I had a boyfriend but it's off now."

"Yeah? Which one is he?"

"No way. You'll embarrass me."

"You're lying. You never had a boyfriend."

He knew how to get under my skin. I pointed to Justin.

"Stop it," he said. "You're into black guys?"

"I guess you think it's funny to refer to a person by the color of his skin."

"So why'd you split up?"

Just then, our parents found us in the mess of laughter and tears. Mom looked elegant in her best wool suit, the one she wore for High Holidays. She caught my face in her hands and studied it before kissing my cheek.

"I guess I made it out alive," I said, trying to sound funny.

Mom seemed caught off-guard. She opened her mouth to speak, then saw a former pair of clients whose kid was in my class. "I feel as if I did their ketubah a month ago. And now look, just look at how the time goes. I'll be right back, honey," she said, kissing me again before going off to say hello.

David disappeared too. Probably to confront Justin, just to add to the humiliation of the two of us being in the same room, unable to talk. But Justin's family was already heading out the door, and I didn't see my brother with them.

Dad pumped my hand. "I was about your age when I met your mom," he said. "I don't know why she gave me a chance." He wore the same outfit he'd bought for David's graduation, which annoyed me. Didn't my graduation warrant a new outfit?

"Why did she?" I said.

He looked up to his left. "Who remembers, at this point? Does it matter?"

"Of course it matters!" I said.

"Did I ever tell you about my roommate in college? Jerry Horn?" He had not.

"Nice Jewish guy. Cultured. His parents were well off." He scratched at his cheek. "So this guy, he never did get married. They called him a lifelong bachelor." He looked at me. "Like you, I guess."

"It's not impossible for two men to fall in love and stay together for a lifetime," I said. "Like for you and Mom."

"I really hope so."

I said I believed him. And you know what? I really did believe him.

* * *

THE GRADUATION PARTY WAS IN THE synagogue basement. The theme was "Up, Up, and Away": in other words, an easy excuse for a room full of balloons. On the sign-up sheet for DJ requests, someone wrote "Smells Like Teen Spirit—or is it too soon?" It was not. They played the song and everyone danced, including me, thrashing my head with such energy that I cleared a small circle around me.

We were given yearbooks to trade and sign, and suddenly I felt it was my duty to collect as many signatures in my book as possible, mostly from people with whom I'd barely exchanged two words in the past four years. Everyone kept asking me to draw something in their yearbooks. They seemed to think I was going to be the next Picasso, though I was already coming up against the limits of my own talent and considering doing something else art-related, like working in an art gallery or museum, or becoming an art therapist. But that night, I enjoyed the attention, and the drawing.

I searched everywhere while pretending not to, but I didn't see Justin.

We were supposed to stay there all night. I left after an hour, which was when I found Justin waiting in the parking lot in his car, now parked next to mine. It hadn't been there before. I would have noticed it.

I got in next to him. He'd changed out of his graduation regalia into a polo shirt, beige shorts with a braided belt, and topsiders. His bracelets and rings were gone, and his hair looked neat and trim, as if he were running for student council.

"I thought you'd want me to sign your yearbook," Justin said.

"What for?" I said. "That's all over now. Up, up, and away." Still, I handed mine over. He took it, scribbled something, then gave it back. I didn't look at what he wrote.

"I'm not going to Michigan," he said. "I decided to go to Howard, in D.C."

I pretended this news didn't concern me. "Tired of being surrounded by white people?" I said, which I meant to sound like a breezy joke.

"Something like that." He sounded serious. I was surprised. I guessed I hadn't known him as well as I'd thought.

"So then I really won't see you."

He winked. "Not unless you want to." He touched my thigh.

"What about Mark? It doesn't bother you now?"

"Ancient history." His hand was still on my thigh, squeezing.

"I don't know, Justin," I said. "I don't know anymore."

"Do you think, is there any way we could, not start over, exactly, but try again?"

The tender look in his eye made me hope. "Try what again exactly?" I asked. "What was it that we were doing that you want to try again beyond fooling around with each other? You know, I'm a person, not just a body. I have feelings, opinions. I like to talk about them. I want to do things. See movies, go to art museums, like other couples."

That's when I saw it, the cringe when I said the word "couple."

"What am I to you anyway?" I asked.

He dug his hands in his pockets. "Do I have to say it?"

"Yes, you do. Now that we're out of school, who are we hiding from?"

"It's so much easier for you, in the suburbs," said Justin. "It's fucking trendy."

"Bullshit," I said. "You're just scared."

"What do you know about it? How many times have you been to Detroit?"

"Okay, let's try it this way. Justin, I'm gay. How about you?"

He looked at his feet.

"No, I guess you're not. If you can't say you are."

Justin reached out, threaded his fingers through my fingers, squeezed my hand in the dark. "Why are these labels suddenly so important to you?"

I let go of his hand. "If you can't say it, then you shouldn't be it," I said.

"Oh, yeah? What about your hero Kurt?"

"Kurt Cobain?" I said. "What do you mean?"

"Why do you think he offed himself? Dude was gay."

"No," I said. "He was gay-friendly."

"No, he was gay-obsessed. He wanted what he couldn't have, not without ruining his reputation. So he disappeared. I guess he was a sell-out after all."

Sometimes Justin said random things to sound controversial, but tonight he seemed serious. I thought about what he was saying for a bit, then dropped it. At this point, what did it matter? Kurt was still gone either way.

"I don't know what he was," I said. "But I know what I am."

"We could still hang out sometimes this summer."

"Maybe." But I knew it wouldn't happen.

Justin seemed to hear what I was thinking. "Can I at least kiss you goodbye?"

I wanted to resent him, and I didn't want to. He'd trusted me with his darkest secret, and I had trusted him with mine, and wasn't trust the chief virtue of a generous heart? Yet despite all that, we never truly knew each other. Whose fault? Impossible to say. Now it seemed too late.

"Yeah, okay," I said.

He looked around first to make sure no one could see, and that's when I knew for sure this would be the last time. I was done with secrets. But I kissed him anyway, one last kiss. For a few seconds, I let myself experience the old thrill.

No Apologies

At home, instead of entering through the garage as usual, I pulled up the driveway and stepped onto the front porch. I stood there a long time, breathing in the scent of freshly cut Kentucky bluegrass lawns, listening to the symphony of night-time on Maggie Lane: the hum of air conditioning units, the sawing of insects scraping their legs together, the occasional soft purr of a car searching for home. All these sounds yoked together by chance combined into a kind of music, without meter or meaning. Just as a pattern began to emerge, some new noise would pop out of the darkness and break it.

Kurt Cobain, gay? Perhaps by some lucky, freakish twist of fate we could have been boyfriends. Could I have saved him? A stupid fantasy, but I hung onto it for a while. Anyway, I may not have been able to save Kurt, but Kurt perhaps had saved me.

Justin once told me that white people could feel safe anywhere. They could move into a new neighborhood, stand on their front porch, and throw open all their windows and feel safe. What made them think they could do that? "We feel like we have to put bars up and hide in the dark," he said. "Why? Is it that you all demand better?"

Yes, yes, that had been my trouble: I'd never demanded better.

I was humming a tune without realizing it. Nirvana again. "All Apologies." I hummed a few more bars. It was the kind of tune that once in your head, you couldn't quite get out, no matter how hard you tried. But what the hell did I have to apologize for?

SEVEN

THE NEXT MORNING ARI WAKES UP and feels strangely light-headed. He has Justin's number on his cell phone, and Justin's message there too, words that Justin has typed. Ari is in love with the world. Everything looks brighter, more beautiful. He feels lighter, happier. Like a young, unspoiled child. It makes no sense.

Justin was radiant, beautiful in a sleepy way. And he was there, waiting for him.

On Sunday mornings like this one, Ari and M used to sit on their front porch, and while Ari read a book, M would watch the older high school boys or the occasional college student walking or jogging by and say things like "Isn't he a tall drink of water!" or "I wouldn't mind seeing him in a gym locker room" or simply "Wouldn't you like to suck his fucking cock?"

Lately, Ari's been feeling implicated by association for listening to this kind of talk without comment. But now, if he's being completely truthful, he occasionally looked at the boys too. In fact, now, thinking of Justin, he's tempted to join in the raunchy talk. "I want to suck Justin's fucking cock," he tells his kitchen sink. It sounds weak, unconvincing, like the first few punches he'd thrown back when his dad had dragged him to karate class.

He makes some eggs and sits with the Sunday paper, but does not read as he eats. Is Justin thinking about this encounter today? Or has he already moved on to real life, his wife and the kids and his stock options? And what exactly are stock options?

And I, Ari wonders, what do I have? A few memories. And my book, and some articles, and tenure.

My inner life. Culture and art. And my feelings.

It's so quiet in the house. This is a quiet neighborhood. That's why the homes here go for such a pretty penny.

I could have said something yesterday, Ari thinks. I could have taken him aside, away from his very nice wife, and told him the truth about all those years ago. And that would have ruined it, voicing those feelings. At least now I have the very unlikely possibility that we might someday grab a beer, right?

Life's an inherently dangerous business, infinitely more dangerous than in the Middle Ages, in spirit if not in body. Just ask M. These days, it seems like the art of survival depends on keeping one's mouth muzzled. And if nothing else, at least I'm surviving.

Ari wanders over to the living room window, looks out at the weathered porch and the sad front yard, beaten down by a snowstorm that's already melted, patchy in places where desperate, starving squirrels have been digging for food. It's too rainy and cold to actually go out, so he just stands there looking.

He's decided now what he has to do to M, and maybe for M. M must go down for his mistake, a terrible mistake. Yes, it's true that in one sense, M is right. It is definitely a tough and futile business, this assigning of rules to something as ungovernable as the urge toward romance. And yes it's also true that in some ways, what we're doing now may seem as silly to the people of the future as the rules of courtly love seem to us now. Still, it's important to keep trying to figure out what is right and what is not, to keep asking ourselves:

Where do we draw the lines? For all his education, it's the one thing M still needs to learn.

The doorbell rings. Ari peeks through the curtains and sees a boy. His face is familiar. Ari's seen this kid around the neighborhood, clattering along on a skateboard, checking his phone, laughing in a group of other boys his age. The boy is wearing a black ski hat and has long stringy blond hair sticking out of it. Very Kurt Cobain, in fact. Are the styles of Ari's youth making a comeback?

Usually Ari would pretend he wasn't home, but today he opens the door.

The boy looks startled. His eyes land somewhere between Ari's chin and chest. This generation, Ari thinks, they're so used to staring at their phones, they don't know how to look you in the eye. "We have a box for you," says the kid.

"I'm sorry," says Ari. "A box, for me?"

"You're 465 Lockwood," the kid explains. "We're 465 Sussex, so they sometimes get the mail screwed up. My parents sent me over to bring this to you."

He hands the box over. It's printed with green leaves and smiling oranges dancing across the top. Ari's parents send him this box every year, when they go to Florida for the winter. A box of fresh oranges, or not so fresh by the time they get to him. They think it's something he'd like. Or maybe, as he discovered the one time he'd gone down to visit them, it's a cottage industry in Florida, just something that older people in Florida think they're supposed to do for their children. Part of the experience, like early bird dinner specials and shell collecting on the beach. But weirdly, even though he often ends up throwing away half the oranges, Ari looks forward to getting the box each year.

"Thank you," says Ari.

"No problem," says the kid. You'd think he'd want to leave at this point, but he just stands there, taking in the view. Does he expect a tip?

"So, what's your name?" Ari asks. "Since we are neighbors."

"Noah," he says.

"Nice to meet you, Noah. Tell me, do you know how Pandora works?"

He raises his eyebrows. "Uh, yeah, sure."

"Would you mind showing me, if you have a minute? I have my phone right here."

"Okay."

Ari steps out onto the porch. It feels too intimate to invite him inside. They sit on the porch swing, leaving a wide gap between them. The young man has it done in a minute. He hands Ari back the phone with a triumphant smirk.

"Thanks again," says Ari. "If I receive any of your packages, I'll be sure to bring them over. Want an orange for your trouble?"

"Naah, I don't like fruit," says Noah. "At least, not the fresh kind. You know, like oranges, all that peeling. It's annoying, you know?"

"Yes, I can see how that would be," says Ari. "Let me try out this Pandora while you're here, just to make sure it works. If I want to listen to something . . . "

"Here," says the kid and grabs the phone. "What do you want to listen to?"

Ari allows for a dramatic pause. "Oh, I don't know, maybe Nirvana." The kid grins. "I like that guy," he says.

They're a band, not a guy, Ari wants to say, but he doesn't push it.

"Here you go," Noah says. "Now they're on your playlist."

It's interesting that for all their faults, young people are so generous in sharing their technology. It doesn't seem so hard. Maybe, Ari thinks, I can download the app for Shut Up and Kiss Me. They must have a gay section. You see how addictive the new technology is? You've got to be so careful, or you'll be sucked right in. It's important to pick and choose, make these social media decisions carefully, about when you will and when you won't participate.

And yet it's becoming ever more clear to him that perhaps he's been just a bit too careful. Not just about social media, but also the social part of it.

My God, won't M laugh when Ari tells him about all this. Someday. When they can be friends. Ari's willing.

"Anyone can do it," Noah says, tapping Ari's phone for him a few more times, and then handing it over. "See how easy it is?"

"I do, thank you." Ari takes back his phone. "Amazing," he says. "It really is an amazing world we're living in."

Acknowledgements

THIS NOVEL WAS BORN OUT OF a chance conversation with Elizabeth Searle while bouncing around story ideas, so thank you, Elizabeth! Also, I owe a great debt to all those who read early versions of this book and shared valuable insights to improve it, including Cait Johnson (who gave me crucial encouragement to continue this project when it was just getting started), Maureen Brady, Bobbie Ford Bensur, Mark Derenzo, Avi Landes, Peter Levine, James Magruder David McConnell, Lesléa Newman, Carol Rosenfeld, Steven Salpeter, Suzanne Strempek Shea, and Mitchell S. Waters. I'd also like to acknowledge the entire Stonecoast MFA community for all their wisdom and warmth, as well as to all my writing students over the years, who've taught me at least as much as I've taught them. Thanks to Michele Karlsberg, Kenny McNett, and Brooke Warner, for help with publishing advice and other matters. Thank you for inspiration and spiritual guidance to Melanie Cashdan, Gordon Powell, Tom Rini, and Tara Brach. Thank you to my family, especially my loving husband Anthony Palatta. Peter, Kat, and the entire team at Three Rooms Press has been a joy to work with. I deeply appreciate their efforts on this book's behalf. Thanks also to the editors of the various magazines and anthologies who published excerpts from the novel in different forms. And a special thank you to Michelle Wildgen, Emma Komlos-Hrobsky, and Rob Spillman at *Tin House*, who gave me the chance to write an important piece called "Sweetness Mattered" that touches on some of the themes of this book. Fellowships from the American Academy in Rome and American Academy of Arts and Letters, Civitella Ranieri Foundation, Yaddo, and Djerassi allowed me time and space to develop my craft. Finally, I'd like to acknowledge the many activists with whom I've worked since 2016, whose persistence and dedication to bringing fairness and justice to our country inspired me to apply that same fortitude of spirit to my writing life.

ABOUT THE AUTHOR

AARON HAMBURGER IS THE AUTHOR OF the story collection *The View from Stalin's Head*, winner of the Rome Prize from the American Academy of Arts and Letters and the American Academy in Rome, and Violet Quill Award nominee. His second book, the novel *Faith for Beginners*, was a Lambda Literary Award nominee. His writing has appeared in *The The New York Times*, *The Washington Post*, *The Chicago Tribune*, *O, the Oprah Magazine*, *Details*, *The Village Voice*, *Tin House*, *Subtropics*, *Crazyhorse*, *Boulevard*, *Michigan Quarterly Review*, *Poets & Writers*, *Time Out*, *The Forward*, and more. He has been awarded fellowships from Yaddo, Djerassi, the Civitella Ranieri Foundation, and the Edward F. Albee Foundation, and earned first prize in the Dornstein Contest for Young Jewish Writers. He has taught creative writing at Columbia University, the George Washington University, New York University, Brooklyn College, and the Stonecoast MFA Program. He currently resides in Washington, D.C.

RECENT AND FORTHCOMING BOOKS FROM THREE ROOMS PRESS

FICTION

Meagan Brothers
Weird Girl and What's His Name

Ron Dakron
Hello Devilfish!

Michael T. Fournier
Hidden Wheel
Swing State

William Least Heat-Moon
Celestial Mechanics

Aimee Herman
Everything Grows

Eamon Loingsigh
Light of the Diddicoy
Exile on Bridge Street

John Marshall
The Greenfather

Aram Saroyan
Still Night in L.A.

Richard Vetere
The Writers Afterlife
Champagne and Cocaine

Julia Watts
Quiver

MEMOIR & BIOGRAPHY

Nassrine Azimi and
Michel Wasserman
Last Boat to Yokohama:
The Life and Legacy of
Beate Sirota Gordon

William S. Burroughs & Allen Ginsberg
Don't Hide the Madness:
William S. Burroughs in Conversation
with Allen Ginsberg
edited by Steven Taylor

James Carr
BAD: The Autobiography of
James Carr

Richard Katrovas
Raising Girls in Bohemia:
Meditations of an American Father; A
Memoir in Essays

Judith Malina
Full Moon Stages:
Personal Notes from
50 Years of The Living Theatre

Phil Marcade
Punk Avenue:
Inside the New York City
Underground, 1972-1982

Stephen Spotte
My Watery Self:
Memoirs of a Marine Scientist

PHOTOGRAPHY-MEMOIR

Mike Watt
On & Off Bass

SHORT STORY ANTHOLOGIES

SINGLE AUTHOR

The Alien Archives: Stories
by Robert Silverberg

First-Person Singularities: Stories
by Robert Silverberg
with an introduction by John Scalzi

Tales from the Eternal Café: Stories
by Janet Hamill, with an introduction
by Patti Smith

Time and Time Again:
Sixteen Trips in Time
by Robert Silverberg

MULTI-AUTHOR

Crime + Music: Twenty Stories
of Music-Themed Noir
edited by Jim Fusilli

Dark City Lights: New York Stories
edited by Lawrence Block

Florida Happens:
Bouchercon 2018 Anthology
edited by Greg Herren

Have a NYC I, II & III:
New York Short Stories;
edited by Peter Carlaftes
& Kat Georges

Songs of My Selfie:
An Anthology of Millennial Stories
edited by Constance Renfrow

The Obama Inheritance:
15 Stories of Conspiracy Noir
edited by Gary Phillips

This Way to the End Times:
Classic and New Stories of
the Apocalypse
edited by Robert Silverberg

MIXED MEDIA

John S. Paul
Sign Language: A Painter's Notebook
(photography, poetry and prose)

FILM & PLAYS

Israel Horovitz
My Old Lady: Complete Stage Play
and Screenplay with an Essay on
Adaptation

Peter Carlaftes
Triumph For Rent (3 Plays)
Teatrophy (3 More Plays)

Kat Georges
Three Somebodies: Plays about
Notorious Dissidents

DADA

Maintenant: A Journal of
Contemporary Dada Writing & Art
(Annual, since 2008)

HUMOR

Peter Carlaftes
A Year on Facebook

TRANSLATIONS

Thomas Bernhard
On Earth and in Hell
(poems of Thomas Bernhard
with English translations by
Peter Waugh)

Patrizia Gattaceca
Isula d'Anima / Soul Island
(poems by the author
in Corsican with English
translations)

César Vallejo | Gerard Malanga
Malanga Chasing Vallejo
(selected poems of César Vallejo
with English translations
and additional notes by
Gerard Malanga)

George Wallace
EOS: Abductor of Men
(selected poems in Greek & English)

POETRY COLLECTIONS

Hala Alyan
Atrium

Peter Carlaftes
DrunkYard Dog
I Fold with the Hand I Was Dealt

Thomas Fucaloro
It Starts from the Belly and Blooms

Inheriting Craziness is Like
a Soft Halo of Light

Kat Georges
Our Lady of the Hunger

Robert Gibbons
Close to the Tree

Israel Horovitz
Heaven and Other Poems

David Lawton
Sharp Blue Stream

Jane LeCroy
Signature Play

Philip Meersman
This is Belgian Chocolate

Jane Ormerod
Recreational Vehicles on Fire
Welcome to the Museum of Cattle

Lisa Panepinto
On This Borrowed Bike

George Wallace
Poppin' Johnny

Three Rooms Press | New York, NY | Current Catalog: www.threeroomspress.com
Three Rooms Press books are distributed by PGW/Ingram: www.pgw.com